W9-BSA-478

ALSO BY RON HANSEN

Fiction

She Loves Me Not

A Wild Surge of Guilty Passion

Exiles

Isn't It Romantic?

Hitler's Niece

Atticus

Mariette in Ecstasy

Nebraska

The Assassination of Jesse James by the Coward Robert Ford

Desperadoes

Essays

A Stay Against Confusion

For Children

The Shadowmaker

THE
KID

RON HANSEN

SCRIBNER
NEW YORK   LONDON   TORONTO   SYDNEY   NEW DELHI

Scribner
An Imprint of Simon & Schuster, Inc.
1230 Avenue of the Americas
New York, NY 10020

First Scribner hardcover edition October 2016

SCRIBNER and design are registered trademarks of The Gale Group, Inc., used under license by Simon & Schuster, Inc., the publisher of this work.

For information about special discounts for bulk purchases, please contact Simon & Schuster Special Sales at 1-866-506-1949 or business@simonandschuster.com.

The Simon & Schuster Speakers Bureau can bring authors to your live event. For more information or to book an event, contact the Simon & Schuster Speakers Bureau at 1-866-248-3049 or visit our website at www.simonspeakers.com.

Interior design by Jill Putorti

Manufactured in the United States of America

10 9 8 7 6 5 4 3 2 1

Library of Congress Cataloging-in-Publication Data
Names: Hansen, Ron, 1947– , author.
Title: The Kid : a novel / Ron Hansen.
Description: New York : Scribner, 2016.
Identifiers: LCCN 2016011975 | ISBN 9781501129759 (hardback) | ISBN 9781501133336 (ebook)
Subjects: LCSH: Billy, the Kid—Fiction. | Outlaws—Fiction. | BISAC: FICTION / Westerns. | FICTION / Historical. | FICTION / Biographical. | GSAFD: Biographical fiction. | Western stories.
Classification: LCC PS3558.A5133 K53 2016 | DDC 813/.54—dc23 LC record available at https://lccn.loc.gov/2016011975

ISBN 978-1-5011-2975-9
ISBN 978-1-5011-3333-6 (ebook)

Chapters 1, 2, and 3 of this novel first appeared in *Epoch*, and chapter 4 in *Narrative*.

for my sister Alice

Not that it matters, but most of what follows is true.

—WILLIAM GOLDMAN, *BUTCH CASSIDY AND THE SUNDANCE KID*

MAJOR CHARACTERS

BILLY'S FAMILY

Catherine Bonney McCarty Antrim (1829–1874) Emigrated to New York City from Ireland; gave birth to sons, Josie and William Henry; met Billy Antrim in Indiana, married him in Santa Fe. Died of tuberculosis when the Kid was fourteen.

William Henry Harrison Antrim (1842–1922) Married Catherine McCarty in 1873; stepfather to Billy and Josie. Laborer and prospector.

Joseph Edward "Josie" McCarty (1854–1930) Saw nothing of his younger brother after 1877. Died penniless in Denver.

William Henry McCarty (1859–1881) Also known as Henry Antrim, Kid Antrim, William H. Bonney, and Billy the Kid.

BILLY'S FRIENDS

Charles Bowdre (1848–1880) Raised in Mississippi but became a cowhand in New Mexico for John H. Tunstall. A Regulator from 1878. Common-law husband of Manuela Herrera.

Richard M. Brewer (1850–1878) Born in Vermont and raised in Wisconsin. A cowhand for John H. Tunstall and later a Regulator.

John Simpson Chisum (1824–1884) Wealthy cattle baron on rangeland along the Pecos River and a financial backer of John H. Tunstall.

Sallie Chisum (1859–1934) Uncle John's niece and sweetheart of the Kid.

Franklin Coe (1851–1931) A farmer at La Junta on the Rio Hondo. A Regulator.

George Washington Coe (1856–1941) An Iowa cousin of Franklin Coe. Farmed on the Rio Ruidoso and became a Regulator.

Thomas O. Folliard, Jr. (1858–1880) A red-haired Texan of Irish descent who became a Regulator and was the Kid's best friend.

Alexander Grzelachowski (1824–1896) Called Padre Polaco, a former Catholic priest educated in Poland and the owner of a restaurant and store in Puerto de Luna.

Alexander Anderson McSween (1843–1878) A Canadian who studied for the Presbyterian ministry, then left for law school at Washington University. Wound up in Lincoln in 1876 and worked first for L. G. Murphy, then for his rival, John H. Tunstall.

Susan Ellen Hummer McSween (1845–1931) Ran away from her home in Pennsylvania at the end of the Civil War and married Alexander McSween in 1873 in Atchison, Kansas.

Paulita Maxwell (1864–1929) Wealthy daughter of Lucien Maxwell, educated at St. Mary's Convent boarding school in Colorado. Sweetheart of the Kid.

John Middleton (1854–1882) Worked as a cowhand for Hunter & Evans, then joined L. G. Murphy & Co. before signing on with John H. Tunstall. A Regulator.

Josiah Gordon "Doc" Scurlock (1849–1929) Attended medical school in New Orleans before finding work in the Southwest. Married sixteen-year-old Antonia Herrera and joined Charlie Bowdre, his brother-in-law, as a cowhand on John Tunstall's ranch.

John Henry "Harry" Tunstall (1853–1878) Educated at London Polytechnic Institution, clerked in his father's firm in Canada before becoming a cattleman on the Rio Feliz and founding the J. H. Tunstall & Co. Merchandise Store in Lincoln, a rival of L. G. Murphy's the House.

L. G. MURPHY AND COMPANY

Frank Baker (1857–1878) A cultured man from a good family in Syracuse. Became an associate of Jimmy Dolan.

Joseph Hoy Blazer (1829–1898) Iowa dentist who bought a ranch and sawmill on the Tularosa River and gave the mill his name.

James Joseph Dolan (1848–1898) Born in County Galway, Ireland, emigrated to America as a boy, joined the Army, was discharged from Fort Stanton in 1869, and joined L. G. Murphy & Co.

Nathan A. M. Dudley (1825–1910) A lieutenant colonel in the 9th Cavalry Regiment, assumed command of Fort Stanton in April 1878.

Jesse Evans (1853–1882) A horse thief for John Chisum at the Jinglebob Ranch, became head of an outlaw gang called the Boys.

John Kinney (1847–1919) Originally from Massachusetts, achieved the rank of sergeant in the Army, then ran a cattle-rustling operation from his ranch in Las Cruces.

Jacob Basil Mathews (1847–1904) Raised in Tennessee, moved west as a miner, then a farmer, selling his ranch to John Tunstall to tend the House saloon and serve as a deputy sheriff.

William Scott "Buck" Morton (1856–1878) Well educated in Virginia before becoming a foreman on Jimmy Dolan's cow camp on the Rio Pecos.

Lawrence Gustave Murphy (1831–1878) An Irish immigrant who joined the Army in Buffalo in 1851, retired as the commandant of Fort Stanton, and founded the brewery and store that would become the House. Called the Lord of the Mountains.

CIVIL AUTHORITIES

William J. Brady (1829–1878) From County Cavan, Ireland, a former Army officer who was elected sheriff of Lincoln County. Employed by L. G. Murphy.

Warren Henry Bristol (1823–1890) Appointed associate justice of the New Mexico Supreme Court by President Grant in 1872.

Huston Ingraham Chapman (1847–1879) An engineer and lawyer who established a practice in Las Vegas, New Mexico, and had Susan McSween as a client.

Patrick Floyd Jarvis Garrett (1850–1908) Raised on a Louisiana plantation, became a buffalo hunter in Texas, then a cowhand and saloonkeeper in Fort Sumner before being elected sheriff of Lincoln County in 1879.

Ira E. Leonard (1832–1889) Became a lawyer in Wisconsin, then a judge in Missouri before establishing a legal practice in Las Vegas, New Mexico, in 1878.

Ameredith R. B. "Bob" Olinger (1850–1881) Born in Indiana, followed his brother Wallace to Seven Rivers and became a stock detective, then a deputy sheriff in Lincoln County.

William Logan Rynerson (1828–1893) Educated at Franklin College in Indiana. Appointed district attorney for the Third Judicial District in New Mexico in 1876.

Lewis Wallace (1827–1905) Author, lawyer, Union general during the Civil War, and governor of New Mexico from 1878 to 1881.

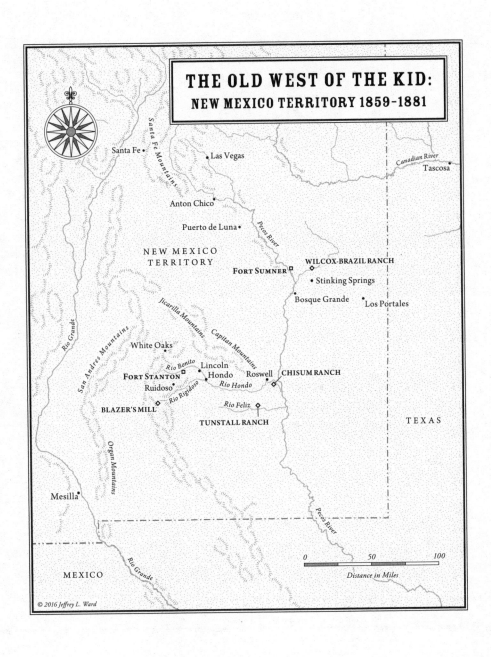

THE OLD WEST OF THE KID:
NEW MEXICO TERRITORY 1859–1881

Santa Fe Mountains

Santa Fe •

Las Vegas •

Canadian River

Tascosa

Anton Chico •

Puerto de Luna •

Pecos River

NEW MEXICO TERRITORY

FORT SUMNER ◻

◇ **WILCOX-BRAZIL RANCH**

• Stinking Springs

Bosque Grande •

• Los Portales

Jicarilla Mountains

Capitan Mountains

Rio Grande

San Andres Mountains

White Oaks •

Rio Bonito

Lincoln

FORT STANTON ◻ Hondo • Roswell • **CHISUM RANCH** ◇

Ruidoso •

Rio Hondo

Rio Rigidoso

BLAZER'S MILL •

Rio Feliz ◇

TUNSTALL RANCH

Organ Mountains

TEXAS

Mesilla •

Pecos River

0   50   100

Distance in Miles

MEXICO

Rio Grande

© 2016 Jeffrey L. Ward

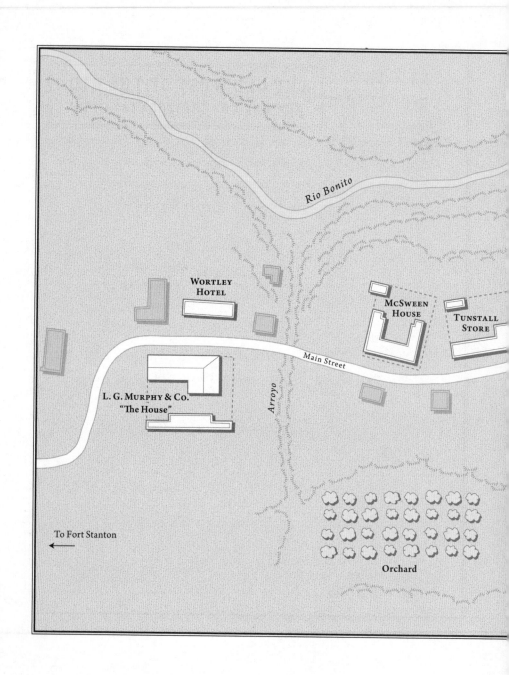

VILLAGE OF LINCOLN, NEW MEXICO TERRITORY

Adapted from *The Lincoln County War*, by Frederick Nolan

SITE OF DUDLEY'S CAMP,
JULY 19–20, 1878

TORREON

JAIL

ISAAC ELLIS
STORE

Main Street

JOSE MONTANO
STORE & HOUSE

JUAN PATRON
STORE

COURTHOUSE

Acequia

Cornfield

0   100   200

Distance in Yards

© 2016 Jeffrey L. Ward

PART ONE

BEAUTIFUL DREAMER

(NOVEMBER 1859–FEBRUARY 1878)

WIDOW MCCARTY

You'll want to know about his mother, she being crucial to the Kid's becomings.

She was born Catherine Bonney in 1829 in Londonderry, Ireland, a pretty Scotch-Irish girl with honey yellow hair and with a coy, happy, flirtatious personality that invoked courtliness and gentility in older men. She fled Ireland just to be free from her overbearing parents, sailing to America from Liverpool on the ship *Devonshire,* and earning fare for her passage and then some by serving as a lady-in-waiting for the child daughter of an earl. Catherine fell in with hard-bitten Irish in New York City's slum of Five Points, found menial work in a French laundry, and married an Irish dockworker named Michael McCarty, giving birth to Joseph Edward "Josie" McCarty on March 19, 1854, and William Henry McCarty on November 23, 1859.

She failed to get birth certificates for both boys, and so their ages would forever be fluid.

Soon after the start of the Civil War, Catherine's disenchanted husband discovered a high degree of patriotism in himself and joined the 69th Infantry New York State Volunteers, an Irish regiment. With the help of an Indianapolis cousin, Michael got permission to transfer to

Indiana's 5th Battery of Artillery Volunteers, and he served them without flair or distinction before dying of a gunshot wound in the Battle of Chickamauga in 1863.

So Widow McCarty took her sons to Indianapolis, where Michael McCarty's shirttail relatives were making do, and it was there in 1865 that she became cordial with William Henry Harrison Antrim, the American son of Irish parents who'd been for ninety days an infantry private with Indiana's 54th Regiment. His first three names were those of the ninth president of the United States, who died in office just before Antrim was born, but he grew up to be just an affable goof with a high forehead who pronounced the word *ain't* as "ainunt." A clerk and messenger for the Merchants Union Express Company, Antrim was twenty-three, or thirteen years Catherine's junior, but he was easygoing company and wasn't ugly, he adored his fine Cate when he wasn't drunk, and he got on with the boys, whom he demanded call him Uncle Billy. When Antrim became a lazing fixture on the chesterfield sofa in the house, it was determined that to avoid confusion Billy McCarty would henceforth be called Henry, his middle name. The Kid was not fond of it.

Catherine seemed not to have been overly fond of Antrim, either, because she left him with little more than a fare-thee-well, having heard fortunes were being made in the frontier cattle town of Wichita, Kansas. Mother and sons headed west, and in the summer of 1870, five years ahead of Wyatt Earp, she and Josie and Henry hauled their few belongings to a clapboard rental on Wichita's Main Street, where they occupied the second floor and she opened City Laundry on the first. She was dismayed when Billy Antrim slavishly followed the family like a tardy but loyal hound, and though she'd let him have his way with her on some overnighters when the boys were gone, she insisted on a semblance of ladylike propriety. So he filed for a homestead of farmland six miles northeast of town and got jobs as a bartender and carpenter just to stay in orbit around the spellbinding sun that was Widow McCarty.

When a petition to have Wichita become a municipality made its rounds, it was signed by 123 men of commerce and one sole woman: Mrs. Catherine McCarty. She was that alluring and revered. There was no public school in the region then, so their self-taught mother was the boys' only and quite excellent teacher. Because of his mental limitations, Josie ended up just a notch above illiterate, but in Wichita, Henry learnt to write a fair letter in a legible hand, seldom misspelled words, could swiftly handle arithmetic in his head, and became an avid reader of exciting tales from the Old Sleuth Library, the Police Gazette, and Beadle's Dime Novels. A favorite book was Edgar Allan Poe's *Tales of the Grotesque and Arabesque*, and he held fast in his head Poe's quotation "All that we see or seem is but a dream within a dream."

Seeing how nimble and graceful her son was, his mother taught him Irish jigs, English waltzes, and French quadrilles, and when he was in his late teens, Mexican sporting ladies would find themselves wanting him for his dancing alone. But at twelve he wasn't yet as tempting to the opposite sex as he would be; he was merely blue-eyed, flaxen-haired, and undersize, and even friends thought him rather pretty, his hands and feet too dainty. But he was chipper and quick and an ambidextrous marvel who stunned them by pitching rocks just as well with either hand, a trait that would pay off in gunplay later.

Wichita was wild enough then that huge herds of longhorn cattle were driven down the city streets to the Southwestern Railroad line, which connected to eastern cities; stinking, fly-swarmed hides of buffalo were laid out on the sidewalks for sale; and saloon owner Rowdy Joe Lowe and his wife, Rowdy Kate, sponsored public footraces in the Delano district that featured fully naked prostitutes running to their house of ill repute. Hearing of one announced race, Josie snuck Henry into the front of the hooting crowds of men for a look-see. Watching the gorgeous melons a-bobbling awakened a new excitement that Henry later innocently confessed to his mother. And soon after that she decided to leave Wichita.

But the wildness there had only a little to do with the move, for Widow McCarty's fortunes had turned sour when she took ill with night sweats, coughing, continual weariness, and loss of appetite. A Wichita doctor's diagnosis was that she'd caught the airborne lung sickness of consumption, for which there was no remedy beyond the help of the high, dry climates of the West. She shrank in weight and vivacity and finally decided to sell her dank, damp laundry and journey west to find a cure in the mile-high city of Denver.

Billy Antrim rented out his Wichita land and hand-built house and tagged along again, getting a job as a teamster with the American Express Company in Denver. Josie found the city so agreeable he would return there for good in his middle age, card dealing and horse gambling his sole professions, and dying in 1930 without ever telling a soul who his infamous kid brother was.

The McCarty family did not stay long in Colorado, for Catherine's kid sister Mary announced in a telegram that she'd married a Juan Salazar and was now residing in Lincoln County in the territory that was won in the Mexican-American War. And it just so happened that Billy Antrim's sister soon invited them to winter with her in the health-giving climate of Santa Fe.

And so to New Mexico the four of them went, and there, with a depth of pity and motherly courtesy for his caring, Catherine consented to marry William Henry Harrison Antrim on March 1, 1873, at the old adobe First Presbyterian Church, the Reverend David F. McFarland presiding. Henry and Josie, aged thirteen and eighteen, were witnesses and signed the marriage certificate. There was a small party for the Antrims in the Exchange Hotel, at which Henry treated them to the Scottish jig "Haste to the Wedding," singing in his choirboy tenor, "Come haste to the wedding ye friends and ye neighbors, the lovers their bliss can no longer delay. Forget all your sorrows, your cares, and your labors. And let every heart beat with rapture today."

Billy Antrim slumped in his chair as the wedding party applauded, because he was either in a champagne stupor or else plunged into a what-have-I-done depression.

There was no honeymoon, just a southward ride along the Rio Grande into Lincoln County, where Catherine's sister got the Antrim four lodging in a one-room piñon log cabin at the intersection of Main and Broadway in the mining community of the aptly named Silver City. Mexicans outnumbered the Anglos by four to one, so Spanish was the main civic parlance, and Henry, who could not not learn, became rather fluent in it just by mingling with the Salazars and his chums. Josie and the other Antrims did not.

Mr. Billy Antrim found a half-time job slaughtering and dressing cows and hanging the heavy sides of beef in the hot box of Knight's Butcher Shop. But he frittered away his wages on gambling and was ever more fascinated with scouring for precious metals in the hills of Georgetown, Piños Altos, and Chloride Flat. So Mrs. Catherine Antrim became the family's financial support, baking sweetcakes and pies that she'd sell across the street in front of I. N. Cohen's dry-goods store or to the kitchens of the Keystone and Star hotels. She also accepted desperate male room-and-boarders who'd just arrived in the West and agreed to sleep on straw mattresses on the floor of the boys' quarters, which were sectioned off from the main room with hanging wool Army blankets.

Coincidentally, one renter was an Eastern newspaperman named Ash Upson, who nine years later would become the ghostwriter of *The Authentic Life of Billy, the Kid, the Noted Desperado* by Pat F. Garrett. But thirteen-year-old Henry Antrim was then just a scrawny, jesting schoolkid who shared the room. It was the jaunty, radiant Catherine whom Upson fell for. Writing of her in 1882, Upson couldn't help but rhapsodize that she was "courteous, kindly," and with a "benevolent spirit."

"She was about medium height," he noted, "straight and graceful in form, with regular features, light blue eyes, and luxuriant golden hair. She was not a beauty, but what the world calls a fine-looking woman. She kept boarders in Silver City, and her charity and goodness of heart were proverbial. Many a hungry tenderfoot has had cause to bless the fortune that led him to her door. In all her deportment she exhibited the unmistakable characteristics of a lady—a lady by instinct and education."

Catherine was also loved by Henry's friends, whom she welcomed after school with raw milk fresh from the cow and with just-baked oatmeal cookies still so hot from the backyard oven that they bent in the hand. She'd take a rag to their faces like their mothers, but unlike them she was fond of jokes. Like "Paddy went to a pub"—she pronounced it "poob"—"and tole the bartender he'd been having himself a draft of whiskey each hour to ease his dyspepsia. A doctor overheared him and says, 'There's a better cure for you than that,' and Paddy tole him, 'Hush now. I don't wanna know it.'" Or "You boys recall the one about the petty thief getting sentenced by the judge? Judge says, 'Either five pounds or five days in jail,' and the scoondrel give it some thought and says, 'All right then, I'll take the five pound.'"

She laughed so heartily at her own jokes that the jolliness itself was a cause for their laughter.

And Henry was much like his mother. Ever smiling, witty, and genial when not riled by an injustice, he collected friends without effort and, because of his quick mind, became without campaign their leader, initiating pranks and risky competitions and being as overrambunctious as boys can be, so that an insulted local journalist called the lot of them the Village Arabs.

The Kid took after his mother physically, too, with fine, handsome features, tawny blond hair when freshly washed, dead leaf brown when not, and with ever twinkling, canny, mischievous eyes that were blue as Wedgwood and checkered with sunlight. Like his friends, he favored moccasins over shoes and wore his felt hat far back on his head. His aching teeth with their rabbit centrals had never seen a dentist, and he only cleaned them by eating apples. He would reach a full height of five feet seven and never weigh more than 130 pounds. A fourteen-year-old in 1874, he was much smaller.

And that amused Levi Miller, owner of a ramshackle shelter with the signage of THE VILLAGE BLACKSMITH. Earning ten cents an hour, the Kid, as he was called by Levi, worked the bellows, raked the stalls, walked in horses in need of shoeing, and took grief for his littleness, with Levi or the loiterers in the shop jerking him up off the ground and dandling him, flinging him in wide circles by wrist and ankle like he was a fine delight, and calling him a peewee, a pissant, a walking hat. Sometimes the Kid's mouth trembled and wet filled his eyes, exciting more ridicule from the miners there. Levi's wife warned her husband that he was "turning Henry mean," and the hot-tempered boy finally showed it one night by borrowing a shotgun and destroying the fire bellows with a coup de grâce of twelve-gauge holes, then blowing out the B in the sign so Levi became a LACKSMITH.

Silver City people heard the shotgun explosions, but there were so many each night in the hurrahs and quarrels outside the saloons that no one could pin the wreckage on the Kid. Levi suspected him, though, so Henry took a job at the City Meat Market.

Although there were refining operations that hung foul smoke over the city, Catherine's health got a little better now that she was far from the weather extremes of the Midwest and at an elevation of over six thousand feet, and for a time she was able to entertain onlookers with the highland fling at the dances held at McGrary's Hall. But the tuberculosis took over. She tried to no avail the sulfur baths at Mimbres Hot Springs some miles southeast of town and was finally conveyed home in a one-horse shay, lolling this way and that in a faint.

She stayed in bed for four ever more hacking months, being tended to by a friend, Mrs. Clara Truesdell, who'd been a registered nurse in Chicago but now owned a millinery shop, and whose son Chauncey was Henry's schoolmate. After a coughing jag that spotted her handkerchief with blood, Catherine fell back and said, "I'm so knackered, Clara. So utterly weak."

The nurse told her, "Well, that's to be expected with an affection of the lungs."

"Am I truly dying?"

"Alas, I believe so."

Catherine considered it, then squeezed Clara's hand gently while saying, "Oh, I do thank ye for not giving me false hope."

Realizing that her shiftless husband would be selfish and neglectful in raising the boys alone, Catherine asked the nurse to watch over them once she'd passed. Mrs. Truesdell consented.

"I'm leaving my sons in wild country," Catherine said. "Wild, wild, wild."

All that summer she would cough through the night as she struggled for the hidden treasure of breath. She told Henry, "Oh, my darling, I'm fading so very fast. I'm on a train there's no getting off."

Warned by Mrs. Truesdell of his mother's serious decline, Henry sent the telegram YOUR CATE WORSENING to Billy Antrim via his new job at the Metcalf Copper mine in Clifton, Arizona.

VERY SAD, was Antrim's insufficient reply.

Without his mother's pastry income, and with Josie unwilling to share his scant earnings from the Orleans Club, where he fetched and carried, Henry was forced to ignore the eighth commandment and conceived a scheme to steal the jewelry in the front window display of Matt Derbyshire's furniture store, inveigling another schoolmate to join him in the burglary. "We'll fence it in Old Mexico," Henry said, having read the gangster lingo in the Five Cent Wide Awake Library.

But on the night of the heist, his schoolmate weakened and confessed the plan to his father, saying he'd joined the Kid in plotting the crime because "Henry had me hypnotized."

Both boys were sternly chastised by the owner of the furniture store, but were then let go since nothing illegal had actually been done. Yet his bedridden mother heard gossip of it and got up as high as she could on her chair of pillows to wheeze for air as she scolded her favorite son, saying she had a mind to put him over her knee for a paddle and worrying that if he went on thieving he'd be hanged before he was twenty-one. Soon worn out with speaking, she shut her eyes and covered them with a forearm, and Henry guiltily listened as she wept.

Henry's lunkish, lubberly, hard-to-love older brother feared the hex of Illness, so he hung shy of his mother to silently observe the dying from afar like a vulture. But each evening Henry would feed and tend to Catherine, tenderly holding her hand or petting her damp-with-fever hair as he sang her to sleep with Scottish ballads like "Annie Laurie" or, because of her maiden name, "My Bonnie Lies over the Ocean." When she was near the end, Henry softly sang for her a final, old, mournful hymn: "I'm just a poor wayfaring stranger. I'm traveling through this world of woe. Yet there's no sickness, toil, nor danger in that bright land to which I go. I'm going there to see my father. I'm going there no more to roam. I'm just a-going over Jordan. I'm just a-going over home."

She died on Wednesday, September 16, 1874, at the age of forty-five.

Henry was fourteen.

2

THE HABIT OF LARCENY

The funeral service was on Thursday in the Antrim house, Clara Truesdell in attendance with her husband and joined by Lincoln County Coroner Harvey Whitehill and his wife. The sons were stoic; her husband, Billy Antrim, was, as ever, not present.

But Antrim had sent a telegram to arrange for the boys to reside in the home of Richard Knight, the butcher whose shop Antrim had once helped out in, and weeks later, when Antrim feared they'd exhausted the patience of the Knights, he shifted Henry to the former Star Hotel, which was now owned by the Truesdells, while Josie was sent into the home of Joe Dyer, the proprietor of the saloon called the Orleans Club, where he ran errands, served whiskey, swept up the peanut shells on the floor, and became addicted to the opium tar he would smoke through a dream stick in Chinatown.

The Kid's grief over Catherine's death first caused him to feel disoriented and in a trance, then fiery in his anger at Billy Antrim and, irrationally, the Silver City that had failed to heal her. There was a lot of *Why me?* in his ruminations. And it was his undoing that in his aloneness and loss he fell in with a wild and vice-laden crowd. Would have become an adored, happy, skylarking captain of all he surveyed had he not first linked up with miscreants like Sombrero Jack—so named because of the spangled Mexican hatwear he favored. Jack was ten years older, held a stonemasonry job, and just for company let a lonely fourteen-year-old orphan tag along like a tolerated little brother when Jack was pursuing thievery, an excess of whiskey, or the card games of monte and faro.

Was Jack who urged the Kid to leave his lodgings in the Star Hotel, where he was a waiter and dishwasher, and join him in Mrs. Brown's rooming house. And it was Jack who goaded him into stealing three pounds of fresh-churned butter from a buckboard, selling it to a grocer on Texas Street for fifty cents. Coroner Harvey Whitehill had just been given the job of sheriff, after the former officer of the law ran off with some of Lincoln County's funds. And the Kid was one of Whitehill's first arrests. But the new sheriff just smacked the boy's cringing head three, four times and wagged a finger as he lectured him, since he knew folks reacted hard to the loss of a mother.

Was Sombrero Jack, too, who one Saturday night smashed out a front window of the Chinese laundry owned by the Celestials Charley Sun and Sam Chung, Jack crawling through moon-glinting shards of glass in order to scavenge two Ruger Old Army cap-and-ball pistols, a stack of wool blankets, and the fineries floating and puffing on the backyard clotheslines in the soft October breeze. Skedaddling out of town and hiding his loot in Crawford's Mill, Sombrero Jack later realized it was doing him no good there, so he retrieved it and returned to Mrs. Brown's, telling the Kid he'd go halves with him if the worshipful boy would sell it.

A few days after that their landlady espied Henry Antrim, as he was still called, in an English gentleman's shirt with a stiff, winged collar and in frock trousers so overlong he'd folded the cuffs up high as his calves.

Mrs. Brown said, "You got yourself some fancy clothes of a sudden!"

With no hesitation other than forcing a smile, he answered, "My uncle died and left em to me in his will."

"Oh yes, passing on and passing the remnants along; that's what we all bound to do," she responded.

But she doubted him enough to investigate a steamer trunk in his closet when he was gone and found a soap-scented bundle of lady things and a Livingston suit he couldn't afford, so she hustled out to the sheriff's office to rain overdue judgment down upon Henry.

Sheriff Whitehill felt the late Mrs. Antrim would approve of him scaring her son into gallantry by locking him up in the county jail on the charge of larceny. Whitehill's children, however, were friends of Henry, sharing a pretty Englishwoman's classes in the one-room public school, and those seven children raised their voices against their father in high dudgeon that evening, and even the sheriff's wife wanted him to at least escort the fourteen-year-old to their house for a nice breakfast in the morning.

Sombrero Jack, by then, had heard of the Kid's arrest and skinned his way out of town and out of this narrative, but he would find Jesus and finally reform his life and wind up a justice of the peace in Colorado.

According to a jailer, the circuit court would meet in session in Silver City the third week of November, six weeks hence, so, forlorn with fear of a final conviction, the Kid conceived a plan to extricate himself from his dilemma. Working on the sheriff's instinct for leniency, Henry conned him into a free half hour of exercise each morning in the corridor outside his cell, and then when a jailer for once wasn't watching, the Kid ducked down into the fireplace and, skinny as he was, clawed and scraped and laddered his way up the narrow chimney flue until he could fall out onto the roof and then hurtfully to the ground.

A gardener with a hoe saw the Kid's soot-blackened hands and face and asked, "You playing in a minstrel show?"

"You won't tell on me, will you?"

"Oh, I'll tell. The fix you're in don't mean nothing to me."

Hearing of the escape and getting on his knees to peer up the tight fit of the chimney, Sheriff Whitehill was impressed, telling the jailer, "Henry has an ingenuity with which I have heretofore not been acquainted."

"You could tell he's a hard case," the jailer said. "He's got them dancing eyes."

Meanwhile Henry hightailed it to the kitchen of Clara Truesdell's hotel. She got him cleaned up and harbored him in the pantry for a spell, then put the orphan and his box lunch on a dusty, jouncing stagecoach through hostile Apache territory to Chloride Flat in the Arizona Territory, where his stepfather was.

The Kid formulated some high hopes for his meeting with Antrim, whom he had not seen for half a year, but then he found the former Hoosier fruitlessly panning for gold upstream on a trickling creek that ran into the San Francisco River.

Billy Antrim knelt back on his haunches as he stared up at Henry, who detected a distinct lack of welcome. "Weren't you farmed out?"

The Kid lied, "I was lonesome for you."

"Oh, me too. I been pining." Antrim looked around for a horse. "How'd you get out here?"

"Walked. Took me an hour. You get anything?"

"Tracings this week. Hauled in a nugget a month ago. Where's Josie?"

"Running errands at the Orleans Club."

"Well, he'll never amount to much anyways." Antrim stood. "Copper mine won't be hiring none more if that's what you're thinking."

"I'm just footloose and fancy-free."

Antrim squinted his distrust. "I got just the one upstairs room and no provisions, but I guess you can stay overnight."

Antrim's upstairs room was over the Two Galoots Saloon, where he seemed customary. A couple of soiled doves in their next-to-nothings were acting flirtatious, but Antrim wouldn't acknowledge them, only excusing himself by saying, "I have needs like everbody." He ordered two shot glasses and a full bottle of Old Overholt Straight Rye Whiskey and filled the jiggers for himself and Henry, but the boy was preoccupied by a large hanging picture of a naked female slave in a harem. Antrim noticed and said, "They tell me that's an odalisque. Don't ask me how to spell it."

"She's pretty," Henry said.

"Ainunt no *she*. It's a *picture*." Antrim lifted his shot glass. "Down the hatch," he said and swilled the whiskey.

Henry found the consequence of imitating his stepfather unpleasant. Coughing, he said, "Harsh as hellfire and never-ending, all the way down."

"You get used to it." Antrim poured himself another shot glass and tilted his head back for it. "Ah," he said; then, "This Old Overholt whiskey was Abraham Lincoln's favorite. That ought to tell you something."

"And Abraham Lincoln's dead, isn't he?"

"But not from the whiskey. A bullet. Lead poisoning."

"Are you going to stay here for a spell?"

"Oh, me, I'll prolly get restless I expect."

"Want me here?"

Antrim frowned into his whiskey, then drank it. "Not really," he said.

Silence took up residence for a while. Antrim doffed his dirty felt hat. He wasn't clean and he'd lost still more hair and the sun had wrinkled his face so that he looked far older than his thirty-two.

The Kid flashed him the insincerest of smiles. "You haven't asked about the funeral."

"Whose?" he asked, then said, "Oh."

"Entire city turned out," the Kid lied. "There was an uplifting sermon and stirring hymns about the attributes of paradise, but folks kept pestering me about 'Where's Cate's husband?' Told em you were too stricken with grief, that you thought you might could kill yourself over it."

"Oh, that would surely gladden you, wouldn't it, Henry?"

"Was just what came out at the time."

Antrim ordered them both porterhouse steaks and russet potatoes, wetting each chew with more whiskey. Which began to have an effect on him. He became fractious. "So what's the real reason you're here?" he finally asked. He pushed a jigger of truth serum toward the boy, and the Kid pushed it back.

"Wore out my welcome in Silver City."

Antrim was as skeptical as an examiner. Were he wearing bifocals he'd have been watching the Kid through the bottom half-moons. "Why's that, Henry?"

"I was selling used clothes."

Antrim scowled. "Lot of people do that."

"But they locked *me* in jail for it."

With outrage, his stepfather said, "Ainunt fair at all!"

Henry agreed. "Exactly my thinking. So I escaped."

Billy Antrim leaned over the jury box formed by his crossed forearms and told his stepson, "Don't try to lie to a liar, liar! I believe the jail part. What about the clothes?"

"Stolen," Henry confessed.

"Stolen!" Antrim fell back in his chair as though flummoxed. "Suspected as much from your scoundrel airs. Even knew it from your childhood. You was wrong, wrong, wrong from the very inception." He got another shot glass of whiskey.

"Had enough?" the Kid finally asked.

Antrim finished it and said, "I'll stop when I'm just beyond plenty."

"I was here to forgive and forget how you ran out on your wife."

His stepfather sneered. "Well, you can go to Hell with your forgiveness, Henry. Don't want it and haven't earned it."

"I'm tired," the Kid said. "Been a long day."

Antrim hung his head as though himself seeking rest. "I have a judgment to render, which is if a thief is the sort of boy you've become, you got to get out. I got a hard-won reputation here."

Henry thought he was kidding and laughed.

"You heard me! Get!"

The Kid stood up and saw Billy Antrim was incapable of standing. "I'll just clear out my things," he said.

Wearily, Antrim waved him off.

Upstairs, the Kid rooted around until he found two dollars and change and a loaded Colt 1849 Pocket revolver, and just for spite he stole some fresh clothes. Then he rumbled downstairs and out of the Two Galoots Saloon with nary an *adíos* for his stepfather. They'd never see each other again.

In 1922 at the age of eighty, William Henry Harrison Antrim would die in Adelaida, California, in the home of his niece. At his funeral service he was remembered as a pious and highly regarded gentleman.

3

STOLEN HORSES

Hardly ever did hold a job for any length of time. There was some cowboying for the Kid at the Sierra Bonita Rancho, located in the Sonoran Desert east of Tucson and six miles southwest of Camp Grant. Hitched a ride to it on a freight wagon. The foreman liked the fifteen-year-old who called himself Kid Antrim, but he was the skinniest pickaninny he'd ever laid eyes on, and when he saw what a misfit the Kid was alongside his hardy and violent Mexican vaqueros, he shifted him to helping the chuck wagon cook. The job was snidely called the Little Mary and after a host of insults to his manliness, the Kid let himself be let go.

The Kid had taught himself to cook in the final months of Catherine's life, when she couldn't do for herself, so in April 1876 he hired on in the kitchen of the four-roomed Hotel de Luna, just down the road from the Army post named for Ulysses S. Grant.

Wasn't long before he left the Hotel de Luna's oven heat for a summer job as a hay reaper that paid just as poorly but at least was outdoors, and he liked looking beyond the yellowing hayfields to the far and wide flatlands of pinkish scrabble greened here and there with creosote bush, buckhorn cholla, prickly pear, and desert tea. Off in the distance were orange foothills as jagged as dragon tails but blued in their heights by the shade of foaming anvil clouds that looked tall as forever. And he found himself thinking, *I'm happy in Arizona. I could stay here.*

And then he fell under the unfortunate influence of a Scottish former 6th Cavalry trumpeter named John Mackie, who rented the sleeping room next to him in the Hotel de Luna. Mackie was twenty-seven and had enlisted during the Civil War when he was just fourteen, but he'd never lost his Fife dialect and was still so hard to understand that some folks just shook their heads when he talked. The Kid, however, could decipher it, and John found him clever and amusing company on his sprees.

The Kid had felt fatherless since his vague early memories of New York City, and he forever found himself generating fierce loyalties for confident older men who paid him the least bit of attention. And that, for now, was a Scotsman whose current stint was horse thievery.

Strolling at eventide from the Hotel de Luna and heading down the lone street to the saloons, Mackie introduced the Kid to his nightly pursuits as if they were not only just but proper. "Sorry, laddie," the Scotsman said, "but them loons what's dinna tie up their mounts good, nae watch o'er em, are a-*beggin* for me to reive em. It's the Code ay the West."

"Seems to me the Code of the West means you have the right to hold your ground. The right to defend yourself."

"'Tis indeed! And also if ye hae a strong want for what belongs to wheelthy others, it's in yer rights to make free with it."

"And they hang you."

"But I chore from *soldjers*! Ye think they owns the animals? Naw. Airmy property. So ye and I would joost be takin from them who's back east in Washington City. Why they ginna hang me, like? They woon't even *know*."

Walking up between them was Windy Cahill, an Irish former Army private in Camp Grant and now the owner of the local farrier's shop. Windy was a wide, muscular, gorbellied hooligan much heavier than the Kid, and he had a history of finding humor in rankling the teenager with shoves and slaps and throw-downs. And now just for fun he intentionally collided with him, knocking Henry into a stumble that Windy thought was a hoot. "Oops," he said. "Blundered you akilter."

"What is it with blacksmiths?" the Kid grumbled as he found his pace again.

Windy turned to Mackie. "Hello, John."

"Ahwrite," Mackie said.

The farrier leaned toward him and hushed his voice. "I need two saddles and blankets for Old Man Clanton's ranch."

"What kine? Nae Mexican, I hope?"

"Nah. The thirty-dollar kind."

Mackie nodded. "See ye eifter."

Windy told him he'd be in George Atkins's cantina for just a nip and strode ahead so he wouldn't be associated with them. Mackie and the Kid headed onward to the east side of Grant Creek and George McKittrick's bagnio, called by Mackie a "big-no" and called by soldiers the Hog Ranch. The front was a saloon and dance hall filled with havoc and music, but upstairs and also behind in a long adobe bunkhouse were rooms for cavorting, each small as a sty.

Mackie eased up to a buxom madam in a frilled, ankle-length white apron and softly spoke with her. She pointed upstairs, and he headed there, stopping after four steps to turn to the Kid. "Ye comin?" he asked, for the Scot earned a fee for whichever newcomer he lured into harlotry.

The sixteen-year-old followed him up, his stomach queasy with his daring.

The upstairs hallway was lined with parlor chairs on which shy cowhands and soldiers were sitting primly, like schoolboys soon to be punished.

"Ye feel no weel?" Mackie asked the Kid. "White as a ghoost ye are."

"The blood's all gone from my face to my nether region."

The madam huffed up the stairs to the hallway with a brass school bell, which she rang so close to the Kid that he ducked.

Six Cyprians soon crowded into the hallway and smiled at the men and lifted their long draperies thigh-high to show their hosiery and wares. Selections were made and the couples went off. In his shyness, the Kid instead stayed seated. A leftover Anglo who was less than pretty walked over to him. She waited for him to look up or speak, but he was finding intrigue in the hallway's Axminster rug. She said, "You're quiet as a shadow."

Without raising his eyes he said, "I'm unacquainted with the process."

"You have two dollars in your pocket?"

"No."

She sighed. "One?"

"Just that."

"Hand it to me."

After he'd done that, she tugged him up to standing and took his forearm to guide him sideways into a narrow room with a hodgepodge of furniture. She smoothed a fresh towel on the patchwork quilt of the bed and hiked up her dress as she laid herself down and widened her legs. She wore no underwear, just knee-high white stockings.

The Kid was overwhelmed with his seeing. "You're so beautiful!"

"No I'm not. But you are." She glanced at his bulging. "You can't stick it in me," she said. "I'll get pregnant."

"What then?"

"Stick it between my thighs. They tell me it feels kind of the same."

The Kid unbuttoned his jeans, excitedly got on top of her, and found purchase as she clenched him. "This is amazing!"

Like a yawn, she said, "I'm so glad."

"Could I touch your bosom?"

She nodded.

Henry used his left hand and felt a softness that was the size of an orange. Hurrying more, he asked, "What's your name?"

She turned her head away as he shoved faster. "Mildred."

"This is so nice of you. Letting me do this."

She was surprised but found he was serious. She giggled in spite of his chafing, then heard him groaning. She noticed the wet. "Are you finished?"

With embarrassment he said, "Afraid so."

She felt between her legs. "My goodness, you were so pent up!"

"Yes, ma'am."

"Was it good?"

He got up and adjusted himself. "Don't have much to compare it to."

She was using the towel. "So I'm your first?"

"Yes."

"Well, that makes me feel real special," she said, but he construed that was untrue.

The singing piano man at the upright Steinway downstairs completed "The Vacant Chair," waited for applause that did not happen, and pursued a sketchy new tune that he wished to be "The Lost Lady Found."

Mackie was leaning back against the bar, grinning at the Kid's face. "Ye get yer pipes cleaned?"

"Yep. Had me a time of it."

"We hae a job of work to do now, laddie."

Which was just untying the reins on two brown, fifteen-hand US Army horses from the hitching post in front of McKittrick's and riding them to Francis P. Cahill's farrier shop. Windy was waiting there, and he smiled as he watched them uncinch both black McClellan cavalry saddles. The blacksmith folded the saddle blankets and handed each man a limp ten-dollar bill with a grim Daniel Webster on the left front and a vignette of Pocahontas on the right.

The Kid asked, "How much will the caboodle get you?"

"Oh, prolly fifty dollars." He winked. "You're wholesale, I'm retail."

Without stirrups, the Kid and John Mackie stood up on a plank of the farrier's fence to jump onto the horses, and they rode them bareback to a hiding place up Aravaipa Creek. "Ye'll be needin ye ain horse, Kid. We'll get one of these swapped out for ye."

"I favor roan-colored."

"Ach, roan it is."

Walking back to their rooms in the Hotel de Luna, Mackie told the Kid horse stealing seemed to suit him, that they could continue it on a regular basis.

The Kid smiled. "And whoring?"

"With regularity."

Success in thieving fetched the Kid his first horse, but he failed to name it, having none of the affection for the loyal animals that caused old hands to conjure poetry about Mackerel, Rusty, or Dan. A horse was just a ride to him, and he went through half a hundred in the next few years. Of greater importance to him was his purchase of a fine tooled, right-handed holster with a new 1873 Colt single-action Army revolver snug inside it, a Winchester Model 1873 rifle, which accepted the same .44-40 caliber cartridge as the six-shooter, and quite an assortment of fancy clothes—owning such being another one of the vices he was becoming accustomed to.

But he had his reverses, too. Such as when he stole a sergeant's horse from the tie-up at Milton McDowell's store in November 1876. The sergeant and four privates tracked the horse into Pinal County and overtook the Kid near the Stonewall Jackson mine, seemingly on his way to McMillen's Camp, where his stepfather now labored and perhaps had a hankering for a 6th Cavalry mount. The Kid never got there, but he had such a way about him that the five soldiers let him go once they had collected the gelding. Still, to get home Kid Antrim would have had to walk a hundred miles in wild country filled with hostiles. Instead he went to the tiny village that called itself by the highfalutin name of Globe City, and there in its only saloon he was accidentally reunited with John Mackie.

Went on stealing Army horses, this time at Cottonwood Springs from soldiers posted to Camp Thomas on the Gila River. Hearing that an arrest warrant for horse theft had been filed against "Henry Antrim, alias Kid," he and the Scot sought exoneration by giving up five stolen horses to the surprised quartermaster at the camp.

Incorrectly presuming legalities were now squared away, in February 1877 the horse thieves returned to Camp Grant and soon were served warrants for their arrest at their eggs-and-bacon breakfast in the Hotel de Luna, the officer of the court being Miles Wood, the hotel's Canadian owner and the recently elected justice of the peace. The horse thieves were promptly locked up in the Camp Grant guardhouse, and none other than Windy Cahill was called in to rivet iron shackles and chains around their ankles.

In his dejection Mackie sank down to a hard sit on the dirt floor, but Kid Antrim clanked around in his shackles and chains, looking at the hasps and locks on the one door, the knit of the stone and mortar foundation, and the upright, overlapping planks that formed the twelve-foot-high walls. Seeing there was about a foot of space for ventilation between the ledge of the walls and the roof overhang, the Kid noted, "I hear the regimental band is playing in the officers' quarters tonight."

"So?" Mackie said.

Still looking up, the Kid smiled. "I love music."

At eight o'clock the Army band commenced their concert with the Civil War song "When Johnny Comes Marching Home," then "The Little Old Log Cabin in the Lane" and "Silver Threads Among the Gold."

Kid Antrim was standing on Mackie's shoulders. "That song was my mother's favorite," he said.

With suffering Mackie said, "Joost reach the sill, will ye?"

The Kid got both hands on it and scraped his boots against the planks to get higher, finally achieving enough leverage with both elbows to heave his right leg up and over. Then it was just a matter of hanging on the outside and falling five feet to the ground as the band played "Beautiful Dreamer" and a female contralto sang the lyrics:

Beautiful dreamer, wake unto me,
Starlight and dewdrops are waiting for thee.
Sounds of the rude world, heard in the day,
Lulled by the moonlight have all passed away!

Cumbered by his shackles, the Kid found it slow going out of the fort, but as he'd predicted, the soldiers on duty were caught up in the music and failed to look in his direction. In fact, Kid Antrim was in the back room of George Atkins's cantina, having a bartender use a crowbar to pry off Windy Cahill's rivets, before the sergeant of the guard reported the escapee to Major Compton as he was dancing with his wife.

The Kid did not find a way to free John Mackie, but the Scot was let go when an Army adjutant determined there was insufficient evidence to convict him of horse stealing. Mackie even ended up reenlisting at Fort Walla Walla in Washington and did not retire from the Army until fifteen years later. And it was not until 1920 in Milwaukee, Wisconsin, that John Mackie died peacefully at the age of seventy-two.

- 4 -

THE KILLER

Henry Antrim got hired again as a hay reaper, this time for an Army contractor named Sorghum Smith, whose ranch was near Camp Thomas. The Kid's horse and tack and guns and such had been confiscated in his arrest. Easy enough, for *him*, to steal another horse, but he felt he needed weaponry and finally had to request an advance on his wages from Sorghum Smith. The rancher offered him ten dollars, but Henry said he needed forty. The Kid had a talent for wooing folks into obliging him, and it worked again on Smith, so that the boy came back from the post trader's store with a six-shooter, a holster, and a fifty-cent box of cartridges.

And then in August of 1877, orphaned by his worthless stepfather, his mother nearly three years gone, his luck took a turn for the worse. Homesick for his friends in the saloons outside Camp Grant, he thought he could sneak back, have himself a time, and get out of the settlement again before Sixth Army officials found out he was there.

The Kid wasn't yet eighteen but even looked shy of fourteen, being just five and a half feet tall and no more than a hundred fifteen pounds. Ever smiling. And now he was prinked up and citified, in a Sunday-go-to-meeting suit and foulard necktie, with laced black shoes instead of boots and with his felt hat cocked off his head like a pretty child about to be photographed.

Strolling into George Atkins's Bonita Cantina, he saw some young-ish ladies of the evening who were familiars, and he spoke a little with them in Spanish, letting one touch the six-gun stuffed in the front of his trousers as he confided a joke that made the girl giggle.

Kid Antrim, as they knew him, was hunting a card game and found an empty chair at a poker table, its only disadvantage being that Windy Cahill was there. As the Kid took a seat, the stout, thirty-two-year-old farrier was holding forth as was his habit, full of false information and lies. The subject now was Cahill's free congress with a virgin from Tucson whose ignorance of manly things desperately excited her curiosity. To hear Windy tell it, as a Sixth Army cavalry private he was quite the paramour, and she was so pleased with the overwhelming pleasure of him that she turned to full-time prostitution.

The Kid seemed confused as he anted. "You mean she lived through it?"

Windy eyed him.

"I figured the story would end with you crushing her flat."

"Are you saying I'm fat, Kid?"

"Oh no. You're not overweight, Windy. You're just underheight."

There was general laughter, and that riled the smithy. Cards were dealt as he thought out an insult. The Kid folded his nothing hand, and Windy finally offered, "I guess you get to know lots about whores hanging out at the Hog Ranch like you do."

"I *have* received a fine education."

Windy pretended he was only joshing, grinning as he ruffled Henry's hair, which Windy knew he hated. The Kid shrugged away from it. Windy said, "Hell, we're pals, right? We let bygones be bygones."

The dealer said, "Your bet, Windy."

Cahill scrutinized his cards and tossed in a nickel on his pair of fours. The cowpoke next to him raised to a quarter, and Cahill folded out of turn so he could face Henry with a policeman's concern as he solemnly asked, "Would you mind if I asked you about your philandering?"

It was a new word to him. "Philandering?"

Seeming to think the Kid had the same arrangement with the Hog Ranch that John Mackie did, Windy asked with gravity, "Was it your momma who taught you how to pimp?"

Henry took a second to interpret the meaning, and then he stood up in his fury. "You son of a bitch! Don't you say nothing about my mother!"

Windy hauled off and hit the Kid so hard in the stomach that he lost all his air in one of those will-I-ever-breathe-again *oofs* and fell to his knees. And that was not all. Windy jabbed his stovepipe boot against the Kid's left shoulder, forcing him over onto the floor, and then he got up and lifted the Kid like he weighed no more than a gunnysack of sugar and slammed him down hard.

Like a child, Henry yelled, "Quit it!"

"But I'm just beginning to have fun!" the smithy said, and he wrestled the Kid up on his feet only to fiercely throw him down again. And then he squatted on him, his tonnage bucking up and down on Henry's chest and denying the Kid inhalation. Windy slapped the Kid's cheek and said, "You doll yourself up like some country jake . . . you waltz in here all brazen." Windy slapped his other cheek. "Horse thieves oughta be in the hoosegow or strung up with a noose."

The Kid caught enough breath to say, "Get off me, you sloppy bag of guts!"

Cantina drunks were hooting and urging him on as Cahill found mean enjoyment in smacking the Kid's hotheaded face left and right, reddening it scarlet.

Henry yelled, "Stop it! You're hurting me!" like he was ten.

"I *want* to hurt you! That's why I got you down," Cahill said. But he seemed unaware that the Kid's right hand was loose and squirming beneath Windy's heavy hocks to find his hidden .44.

"You know what? Maybe I'll bite off your nose so you won't be so perty." And Windy was flattening on the Kid, with his head sinking low and his teeth looking hungry for a meal of the Kid's face, when the gun struggled its way to Windy's belly and there was a loud *bang!* and the odor of singed shirt.

Windy said no more than "Oh" and fell onto his back, both hands holding his bleeding side. "I'm gut-shot," he told the cantina.

"Well, he's a goner then," a farmer said to no one in particular. "Either he'll bleed out or venoms will rot his insides."

Waving gun smoke away, another man said, "Seen it happen. Ugly way to die."

Windy's face was squinched up in his agony as Henry scooted out from under him and got up on his shoes. Looking around, he saw no one felt called to do anything about him. "It was self-defense," he explained. "It's the Code of the West. He gave me no selection."

Everybody was staring at him and noticing the still-hot gun in his hand.

The Kid then ran outside into a rain torrent and found a racehorse named Cashaw tied up next to his own, and stole the fleet Cashaw to get his gatherings in the tent of Sorghum Smith's hay camp. The racehorse was soon run out with the getting there, so the Kid set it free to trot back to its owner, then stole another horse in Sorghum's corral and headed east through high desert and monsoons, swapping used-up horses for fresh ones all the way to the New Mexico Territory. The practice was called hedge hopping.

Francis P. Cahill died in the extreme pain of internal hemorrhaging and sepsis the next morning, August 18, 1877, being survived by one sister in Cambridge, Massachusetts, and another in San Francisco.

An inquest was soon held at the Hotel de Luna, and the six members of the jury ruled, "The shooting was criminal and unjustifiable, and Henry Antrim, alias Kid, is guilty thereof."

Kid Antrim was already certain he was wanted for murder and changed his Christian names to their originals: William Henry. And for his alias he chose his mother's maiden name of Bonney. William H. Bonney was a for-the-time-being thing, yet it would hold fast in people's memories in places he'd never been.

- 5 -

THE BOYS

Hiding out in Apache Tejo, south of Silver City, the Kid affected moccasins, buckskin trousers, a long-sleeved white guayabera shirt, and a floppy sombrero. Even Mexicans at first thought him Mexican until they noticed his *ojos azules*. Rustling stray calves from herds along the Rio Grande became his nightly livelihood, and in the afternoons he practiced for hours on end to become a pistolero, quick-drawing and twirling his Samuel Colt, shooting it from whichever hand until the gun barrel and cylinder were hot enough to burn his skin. Even showed off for his compadres by spurring his stolen horse into a gallop and tipping over from his saddle to fire from underneath the horse's flank and whang fruit cans into flight. His friends hooted and yelled and whistled their flabbergasted praise.

Word came to the Kid that Richard Knight, the proprietor of the meat market in Silver City, had won the contract for a stagecoach depot on his livestock ranch near the Burro Mountains, about twenty miles southeast of their former hometown. And because of a smallpox epidemic in the city, Josie Antrim had taken employment there as a horse tender.

Wanting to visit his older kinfolk, the fugitive from justice rode over to the depot with two Indian friendlies and, being judged Mexican, was at first scowled at through a dining room window by Mrs. Sara McKnight. She then recognized the Kid and jerked her head left, nosing him to the horse stables. The friendlies walked their horses to the water tank and drank of it themselves.

Josie was currying a Clydesdale in a stall with what's called a dandy brush when he happened to glance over the animal's croup and was surprised by his little brother. He let the brush drop to the straw and hurried around the Clydesdale saying, "Oh, oh, oh, Henry!"

The Kid told him, "It's Billy again."

Josie embraced him hard and rocked him from side to side. "Billy, is it? Well, I always did have higher hopes for the name."

"You can let me go now."

Josie stood back in the sunshine. He wore chaps and a John B. Stetson Boss of the Plains hat like he was from boot heels to topknot a Texas jackeroo. "How'd you know where I was at to find me?"

"The Antrim name's become famous."

"We got the report of your Arizona escapade. Even Mrs. McKnight, she guessed the feller had it comin. Things bein as they are, we was all worried sick to death that you'd soon be kickin air from a cottonwood tree."

"I been hanging fire in Apache Tejo over by the hot springs."

"Well, that's sensible. Them Mesicans won't give nairn to a posse." Josie seldom smiled because of the ruin of his teeth, but one smile finally drifted in as he said, "I'm so glad to see you!"

"Look at my stallion."

Josie tilted to value it. "Sakes alive! That's some proud horseflesh."

"Stole it from some Italian doctor. Roberto Olmetti. Even came with a doctor kit. You need anything stitched or amputated?"

"Not presently, knock on wood."

The Clydesdale nickered and swished his tail.

With bravado, the seventeen-year-old said, "And now I have to hit the outlaw trail."

"Oh, I expect."

Recalling a scene of sentiment from one of Dawley's Ten Penny Novels, the Kid said, "I'm going to the far horizon. We may not see each other for a spell."

Josie shrugged. "I guess this is where Momma would chide us that you reapeth what you sow."

"Really? She ever really say that?"

"She might would've," Josie said. "Bless her heart."

"She once did quotation me from some poet. 'He who fights and runs away may live to fight another day.'"

"Words to lock in your head," Josie said.

The Kid took a lunge into his taller brother for a final hug and kissed his whiskered cheek. "I'll miss you, you old scalawag!"

"You tryin to make me cry?"

"I'm just offering my fare-thee-well. Say goodbye to the McKnights for me." And then the Kid got on his fine stallion and trotted off with the friendlies.

His older brother returned to his currying, then halted for a little and dried his eyes with the heels of his hands.

Billy never saw him again.

Joseph McCarty Antrim would be footloose for much of his life, heading to Arizona to join his stepfather—they still didn't get on—then to Trinidad, Colorado; and Albuquerque, where he found an accord with Sheriff Pat Garrett; back to Silver City, where he halted a lynching; and to Tombstone, where he was a houseman at a faro gambling table and was fined for drunkenly knocking out a hotel porter. When faro and monte fell out of fashion, he took up Omaha hi-lo and five-card stud. He was dealing in a Denver casino when he died friendless and penniless at the age of seventy-six. Without a wife there was no one to claim his body, so it was donated to Colorado Medical School for dissection by doctors-to-be.

Soon Billy's weaponry skills were found out, and by September of 1877 he was hiring on with a gang of banditti that called themselves the Boys. The gang was organized and run by a former cavalry sergeant and stock thief named John Kinney, who was politically connected and whose ranch and slaughterhouse were on the Rio Grande just north of Mesilla. Rustled cattle were dressed out by his nonconformists and the sides of beef were fenced on the cheap to those who did not ask questions.

The captain of the crew of thirty or so desperadoes was Jesse Evans, whose former hazardous occupation was stealing horses from the Mescalero Apaches for John Chisum, the cattle baron. Evans was an orange-haired and freckled half Cherokee, six years older than the Kid and near his size, and he'd found in himself an inclination to kill for the gaudy thrill of it. Even the more murderous of the Boys were ofttimes standoffish and fearful because of Jesse's fickleness of temper and freedom with his gun, but the Kid was so happy to be adventuring in league with other daredevils that he rode in tandem with Evans and even jested with and about him in a humor that Evans for some reason tolerated. Such as, when Evans tried to sing, the Kid told him, "Jesse, you sure can carry a tune. The sore part is you try to unload it." And Evans was so pleased by the Kid's proverb "Don't let your yearnings get ahead of your earnings" that he rode back to each horseman with him to repeat it as if it was his own invention.

Their far-and-wide acquisitions included whichever livestock they hankered for, mules from the Mescalero reservation, equestrian assets from the L. F. Pass coal mine east of Silver City, a pair of Appaloosas from a ranch near the San Agustin Pass, and some mustangs from

Cooke's Canyon, where "Henry Antrim" was identified from afar by a Silver City resident and his name was published in the *Silver City and Grant County Herald* as being one in "a party of thieves." Eventually the Boys even tried to rob a stagecoach belonging to the Butterfield Overland Mail, found nothing of worth, and in an uncommon mood Jesse Evans forced the driver to partake of their Cyrus Noble whiskey.

The gang included some Indians and Mexicans, so Old West etiquette was outraged as they barged into taverns and ordered a feast and got roostered up on Old Orchard, and then moseyed out without paying the significant bill, Evans calling over his shoulder, "Chalk it up on our tab."

A posse of six went after them once, ran into a hornet's nest of gunfire, and retreated. The Boys exchanged bullets with George Williams at his ranch in Warm Springs but, unaccustomed to a volley of fightback, left without unnecessary delay. In their bravura, Evans sent a letter written by Billy to the *Mesilla Independent* newspaper stating five resolutions agreed to by the Boys, the final one being "Resolved: That the public is our oyster, and that having the power, we claim the right to appropriate any property we take a fancy to, and that we should exercise the right regardless of consequences."

The gang had stolen horses and mules owned by the partnership of a lawyer in Lincoln named Alexander A. McSween, an Englishman named John Henry Tunstall, and Tunstall's foreman, Dick Brewer, whose 680-acre ranch on the Ruidoso River was where the three men pastured their animals. Also missing were over two hundred head of Tunstall's cattle. Brewer estimated the value of their losses at $1,700.

Richard M. Brewer was a handsome and noble man born in St. Albans, Vermont, in 1850, but raised on farms in Wisconsin, where he became renowned for his strength and, in those littler times, was called a giant. At the age of nineteen, he ran off for the West after a soul-destroying quarrel with his fiancée, during which Matilda Jane told Dick she'd decided to become instead the wife of his cousin. Ever after, in the holiness of his love for Matilda, he fancied himself an unsullied Arthurian knight like Lancelot, hardworking, resolute, courageous, and chaste, and his friendship with John Tunstall originated in their joint determination to remain forever bachelors.

Somehow happening upon the village of Lincoln in 1870, Brewer took a job with the mercantile establishment of L. G. Murphy & Company, which later loaned him, at ten percent annual interest, the $2,600 he needed to purchase the Ruidoso ranch near Glencoe that Lawrence Gustave Murphy claimed he owned but for which he finally was found to have no actual title. Still, Brewer was forced to continue payments to avoid foreclosure, so he was in a cantankerous mood over the West's general lawlessness even before the cattle and remuda were stolen, and after that subtraction he became relentless in his angry pursuit of the Evans gang, racking out on the scout for them with an intensity that was playing out his horses.

Within the week he found the Boys on a San Agustin ranch that had a handsome porticoed house on the hillside and on the flats a windmill and corrals crowded with his, McSween's, and Tunstall's horses. The cattle seemed to have already been sold. With no lack of fortitude, Brewer walked up to the house and encountered Jesse Evans and his minions loitering on the porch. His hugeness may have stunned them, because he wasn't immediately shot. And then he had the grit to demand the return of his and his partners' horses.

Still sitting in his rocking chair, Evans smiled. "Well now, I don't think we can do that after all the trouble we went to to get em."

It eventuated that Brewer would have nothing of it.

Impressed by his gumption, Evans offered him just his own horses back.

Brewer looked down on the collection and saw John Henry Tunstall's favorites, a matched pair of dappled, pearl gray ponies that pulled his surreyed buggy. He told Evans he needed the Englishman's horses, too.

"Well, I guess you'll get nothing at all, then," Evans said.

Ire and menace smoldered in the faces of the Evans gang as Brewer regarded them, and he judged it healthier to leave without his stock.

The Kid later walked out of the house interior with just socks on and peeling an apple as he viewed a horseman riding off. "Who was that?"

Soon and very soon he was going to meet the man.

In mid-October Billy left the Boys at the south fork of the Tularosa River, and they headed down to Hugh Beckwith's ranch, where a half mile off from the adobe farmhouse the Boys overnighted in an abandoned dirt and straw hut that the Mexicans call a *choza*.

The news of the sheltering outlaws was taken to Dick Brewer by a Beckwith girl who was plainly smitten with the bachelor Adonis, and he thence went to Sheriff William Brady in Lincoln and urged him to get a vigilance committee together. The sheriff's reluctance shocked him, but Brady finally relented and even made Brewer foreman of a hastily assembled grand jury. And then Brewer and his force of legalized authorities galloped south after the banditti with the sheriff riding trail.

Sheriff Bill Brady was an Irishman from County Cavan, born in 1829, the son of a potato farmer. When he was twenty-one he enlisted for a five-year hitch with the US Army and left a sergeant, then reenlisted for another five before joining a New Mexico volunteer infantry, achieving the rank of major and adjutant to the commanding officer before he was mustered out and married a Mexican widow with whom he would have nine children. With no job but as an entered apprentice with the Masonic Grand Lodge, he went to his old Army pal and fellow Mason Lawrence Gustave Murphy and was given employment at his we-got-everything store that was being called just the House, and then Murphy connived to have him elected sheriff. Which meant the sheriff was also in cahoots with the Boys, who did L. G. Murphy's bidding.

It was a tangled web.

Semicircling the *choza* and the Boys just before sunup, the Brewer-Brady posse waited for the stirrings of life and finally saw Jesse Evans cracking his neck as he walked out of the hut, full tilt with dual holstered pistols and the chest of his flannel shirt x-ed with two cartridge belts.

The citizens had the decency to let him relieve himself and shake as steam rose up from the blue grama grass, then the foreman stood from his hiding and yelled, "Hands up, Jesse!"

Hot-blooded as he was, Jesse answered with both six-shooters, firing three shots that were just enough imperfect that Brewer heard the sizzle as the bullets zipped by his head. The posse did not stay reticent but retorted with similarly inaccurate shots as Evans crouched back under the Mexican blanket hanging in the hut's doorway. A hand would reach a gun out through the one window and go off and be withdrawn, then a rifle would angle out and only manage to crack a branch off a hackberry tree, or the door blanket would be touched aside by a nickel barrel and there'd be a *bang!* then a *zing* as a rock jumped in the air. And the posse themselves would reply with shots at the *choza,* exploding fists of dried mud from the walls and whapping the blanket into a toss. The wild riot of the gunfire was all so random, unaimed, and without consequence that each side seemed to grow tired of the melee and there was silence for a minute.

Sheriff Brady was lying in weeds, his gun silent, but he got up on his elbows to yell out, "Evans! You and your boys surrender in the immediate and you won't be lynched!"

Brewer was astonished by the lenience and gave the sheriff a look that he ignored.

They could hear the outlaws deliberating. The scarcity of food and water seemed an issue of importance. And then a hand lifted the door blanket aside a little and shook a handkerchief that was once white.

The sheriff called, "Okay. Walk on out slow with your hands on your heads."

Out came Evans and three other owl hoots. William H. Bonney was not among them. Their guns were collected and their hands tied behind them once they were saddled, and the citizens took the reins of their horses to trot them to Hugh Beckwith's hacienda for coffee and a feed since it would be a long ride to the new Lincoln County jail.

Which jail was just a dark, deep dungeon dug out of the earth and walled with hewn timber. There were no windows, just a cellar door and ceiling covered with a half foot of dirt and over that an adobe hut for the jailers to get out of the weather. Entrance to and exit from the cells was available only by a ladder that the jailers lifted out once the Boys were hunkered down there. And there was a threat of flooding with any thunderstorm. But soon the shackled four were playing cards like this was a sunny picnic and happily calling up to the six posted guards for a quart of Oh-be-joyful.

The intent was to have them on trial when the next court was convened, in December, but they would not stay kept for even a month.

About the time the gang was locked up in Lincoln, a horseless Kid staggered into the village of Seven Rivers and found his way to a flat-roofed adobe grocery store founded by Heiskell Jones.

He was close to fainting when he asked the bib-bearded, Amish-looking owner, "You have any job of work for me to handle?"

Jones glanced up at a dirty, ill-off, scrawny boy, his face peach-fuzzed and mesquite-scratched, his sagging and scuffed Wellington boots seeming to ache him, but a gun bulging under his wool coat and a Winchester rifle at parade rest. "How old are you, son?"

"Eighteen in November."

Heiskell looked outside. "Where's your ride?"

"Apaches stole it from me in the Guadalupe Mountains."

"And you walked all this ways?"

"Afraid so."

"Well, I don't have nothin to pay you." The Kid caved some, and Heiskell closely considered him. "You hungry?"

Heiskell's wife, Barbara, was called Ma'am Jones by all and sundry because of her gentle, maternal, nursing nature. She worried over the Kid that afternoon and evening, first seating him in a big fireside chair, feeding him salted steak and eggs and a tin cup of warm goat's milk, then yanking off his boots to find his poor feet were sockless and bleeding.

"You walked a long ways," Ma'am said.

"Yes I did."

"I'll heat you a bath so you can get the stink off. Hang your clothes on the chair for the laundry."

Watching Ma'am walk to the kitchen, he said, "You remind me a lot of my mother."

She turned and smiled. "You mean she's delightful, lovely, and very nearly perfect?"

"Yes, Ma'am. She *was*."

"Oh," she said. "I'm so sorry for your loss."

He said, "They say I'll get used to it." And he found himself adding, "I hope not."

Kid Bonney, as he was calling himself, stayed with the Jones family for three weeks, handling chores around the house, sleeping in a feather bed with some of the nine Jones boys, hunting deer and wild turkey for their dinners, and generally being so jolly, helpful, and courteous that the family later would not permit any nastiness spoken about him.

The Kid was closest to Johnny, who was his age and just as interested in gunslinging. They'd rustle heifers and swap them for cartridges, then invent games of skill at marksmanship that the Kid generally won. There was a trigonometry he'd learnt that let him forget about holding steady and aiming, instead freeing his mind to find intersections wherever his gun and the target were and then fire on instinct. He could even hold his rifle on his hip, watch Johnny toss a penny, and flip the coin with a gunshot. Johnny gushed to his brothers, "Kid's not just good; he's a wizard."

The Kid and Johnny hunted mountain lions with the cousins George and Franklin Coe, hardworking ranchers in their twenties, with stock farms on the Rio Hondo near La Junta and farther upstream at Dowlin's Mill. Franklin later remembered the Kid as "very handy in camp, a good cook and good-natured and jolly." He said Billy spent all his free time cleaning his guns and that he "could take two six-shooters, loaded and cocked, one in each hand and twirl one in one direction and the other in the other direction at the same time. And I've seen him ride his horse on a run and kill snow birds, four out of five shots."

Word got to John Kinney that the Kid was lodging with the Jones family, and because he needed his fearlessness and flair with guns, the gang leader sent about twenty of his hirelings over with a saddled horse and ordered Kid Bonney to rejoin the Boys. And that was it. Worried that he'd overstayed his welcome, the Kid gave Ma'am a kiss goodbye, told Johnny he'd stay in touch, and rode off with a gang hieing northward to the Rio Bonito and the fenced village of Lincoln, the county seat.

With more than twenty million acres of real estate, Lincoln County was one-fourth of New Mexico, as large as the state of Maine and two-thirds the size of England, but there were five times as many cattle as people and the village of Lincoln was just a jumble of sixty structures alongside a dirt main street that was forty yards wide. The Boys rode down it in the wee nighttime hour of three. It was November 17 and sleeting.

At the village's west end, where the Fort Stanton Road became Main Street, and just across from the Wortley Hotel, there was a big, two-story mercantile establishment with signage as L. G. Murphy & Co. Eastward there were houses and saloons no bigger than parlors and the still-under-construction J. H. Tunstall merchandise business, and beyond that was the Torreón, a three-story rock tower formerly used to ford off Apache Indian attacks. And east of that was the jail where Jesse and his amigos were holed up in the pit.

Half of the Boys stayed on horses facing every direction while the other half, including the Kid, hitched theirs to a rail and walked right into an unlocked jail shack. The jailer was snoring in a Victorian smoker's chair until the Kid shocked him by pressing a cold gun barrel to the jailer's forehead, warning, "Try me and you'll have a sleep you won't wake up from."

He was trying out a hoodlum persona.

The jailer looked up at the Kid and then to the others. "This job ain't nothin but puny wages for me," he said. "You fellers go on and do what you have to do."

Crew members with gunnysacks that were heavy with rocks

smashed the cellar door again and again until the boards splintered and gave way. Village residents must have wakened from the noise but wisely pretended to be deaf to it.

"Well, it's about damn time," Evans called up.

A man the Kid didn't yet know slid the ladder down. "Mr. Kinney wanted y'all to stew for a bit for givin up so easy that time there at Beckwith's."

"We was powerful thirsty is all" was a jailed man's excuse.

Jesse Evans was first up and free from encumbrance because of his fierce use of a garden file ever since dinner, but he was followed by three still in shackles that were soon chiseled off. The Kid stuffed a handkerchief into the jailer's mouth and tied it in with a bandanna as another character roped the jailer's hands and feet to the chair legs.

And then they vamoosed.

6

THE HIRELING

Who knows why, but the Kid took ownership of Tunstall's favorite dapple-gray buggy team and was found out and locked up in the same hoosegow he'd released Evans and his misfits from. But no one came for *him*, which contaminated his trust in their camaraderie. When he soon grew tired of his fetid dungeon, he asked a jailer to send for the offended party, and the Englishman, whose J. H. Tunstall & Co. ware-room was now open and vying with L. G. Murphy & Co., walked over to what Tunstall would spell as the "gaol."

Even in the November cold, the Kid was enjoying his hour of out-door exercise, a jailer watching for any funny business with a rifle slack in the crook of one arm. When he saw the victim of his horse thievery approaching, the Kid adopted a forlorn expression.

The Englishman was an inch under six feet tall, slender, twenty-four, and seemed genteel in his cashmere overcoat and swank suit of Harris tweed. His jawline was fringed with a quarter-inch scruff of whiskers, his mustache was hardly there at all, and wings of longish brown hair fanned out from under a slouch hat of ivory wool. Elegance and good grooming met in him. He wore no gun. "So you are the rascal who *purloined* my horses," John Henry Tunstall said in a lilting, patrician accent.

The Kid swerved his estimation of him off toward a Rio Bonito that was swollen with rainwater and loudly brawling eastward to the Pecos. "Embarrassed to say so," he said, "but I'm the culprit all right."

"I'm afraid my nose is a bit out of joint," the Englishman said. "All this stealing has cost me like the mischief, and scoundrels like you have chaffed me to the fullest extent of my patience. I have a mind to scold you in terms too true to be palatable."

Owing to his having had an English schoolmistress in Silver City, the Kid felt he understood, and he foresaw how politicking could help. "I deserve whatever you hand out in regard to admonishment," he said. "I done wrong and judge myself kindly in need of correction."

Surprise and happy ignorance gave the Englishman a flush. "What an extraordinary admission from a rustler! I never heard the like from Jesse Evans and his serviles."

The Kid hung his head some. "Well, I'm different from that ilk."

Still rheumatic, headachy, and faint from drinking alkali water on his new ranch on the Rio Feliz, Tunstall took a seat on the board sidewalk and gloved off the space beside him. "Please sit and we'll parley."

With a glance, Kid Bonney begged permission of the jailer and he nodded. The Kid sat.

"You're different from the rest how?" Tunstall asked.

"I feel like I was never given the scope to do other than. I'm an orphan since fourteen and I been making my own hard way with few means available to me. And there's so much thieving in the territories it just came to seem natural as a way to make do."

"And you fell in with bad company?"

"Afraid so, sir. And each mistake kept on breeding others."

"Are you a gunslinger?"

Tunstall seemed to be hoping for a yes, so the Kid said, "I'll admit I have been a shootist on occasion. I'm not a flagrant criminal, though. Each time my hand has been forced."

Seconds passed. Tunstall seemed to be examining him. "Are you given to strong drink?"

"Whiskey? I haven't never acquired a taste for it."

"And if you don't mind my prying: *señoritas*?"

The Kid shied from answering that and inquired as to why he was being so closely questioned.

"I have a need," Tunstall said. He was blind in his dullish, hazel-brown right eye, but his left was sympathetic and he sat snug enough that the Kid could smell a breath pepperminted with the Altoids that he ordered from Callard & Bowser in England. "It can be dull, venal work. You may feel like a hireling at times. But I daresay the tedium may be punctuated by sudden moments of danger. John Chisum pays his cattle protectors four dollars a day, or so it's rumored, but I can afford just one dollar per diem, plus room and board. Would you settle for that?"

"I got nothing but these old clothes and some high ambitions. Seems like wealth to me."

"Your name's Billy?"

"Yep. William H. Bonney, sir."

"How old are you?"

"Eighteen this November twenty-third."

"Are you Protestant?"

"Probably."

"Yes, but are your origins in the north of Ireland? Are your fore-fathers Anglicized and of the Orange Order?"

Because it seemed to matter so to him, the Kid nodded.

"Excuse me if I inquire again: In a pinch you'd be handy with a pistol?"

"Have had multiple trials and I passed em all."

"And have you a firm purpose of amendment?"

"Absolutely."

Smiling as he clapped a hand on the Kid's knee, Tunstall said, "Well, William H. Bonney, you're hired. Let us rise and go about changing your prospects."

The horse-stealing charges against the Kid were withdrawn by John Henry Tunstall through his lawyer, Alexander A. McSween, and Tunstall linked his arm inside the Kid's as he strolled him into the new J. H. Tunstall & Co. General Merchandise store, which was wide as eleven spaced porch posts and smelled of fresh pinewood flooring and the cedar fire in a hissing cast-iron stove. Employees were emptying boxes or working the till and coffee grinder, and the floor was crammed with crates and barrels and shelves overstocked with just-arrived groceries, dry goods, hardware, tools, guns, and even an apothecary of patent medicines and elixirs. Tunstall claimed with a grand gesture that his store offered more luxuries and necessities than did the so-called House kitty-corner from them, and he said he hoped to undercut that scoundrel Murphy until he captured even his Army contracts for groceries and meat. And he would be adding a bank, too, with the cattle baron John Chisum as its president and financial source. With some grandiosity he said, "I intend to get half of every dollar that is made in Lincoln County by anyone. And I will *deal* with those who oppose me. I do not suffer fools gladly."

Then, as gifts for the Kid's forthcoming birthday, the owner went about happily equipping charming Billy with batwing chaps, a holster and six-shooter, a Winchester rifle, .44-40 cartridges, whatever food he fancied, and, "not stinting anything," outfitted him with the rigging of a Colorado saddle with doghouse stirrups and took the Kid to the corral behind the store and let him select a fine white Army horse that Tunstall said he'd purchased for twenty-five dollars from the post trader at Fort Stanton. "And I would not take seventy-five for her now."

The Kid was overwhelmed with glee. Wanted to stop grinning but couldn't. He told Tunstall, "Went through a dozen Christmases with no gifts at all, and you just made up for all a child's wanting in one afternoon."

Tunstall bowed humbly to the Kid as he acknowledged, "Gratitude is the sign of a noble soul."

The Kid then rode beside Tunstall's buggy and the dapple-gray team he'd stolen earlier as they traveled south thirty miles to the JHT Ranch of 3,840 acres in the Rio Feliz valley, and while they traveled John Henry Tunstall revealed himself.

Hinting at inherited wealth, he said he grew up in the fashionable London borough of Hampstead, where his father, "the Governor," was "a financial success in the merchandise and shipping business." Tunstall had three sisters, whom he adored, and he'd attended the Royal Polytechnic Institution with the intention of becoming an accountant in his father's multiple firms. Since his father was also a John, all his friends and associates called him Harry, "And you may, too." He said he was fluent in French and adequate in German and was pleased to hear that Billy spoke Spanish "to help us find common ground with the locals." After graduation from the Polytechnic, Tunstall took a gentleman's grand tour of Europe, then boarded the Cunard liner *Calabria* for America and finally arrived by railway in Victoria, British Columbia. There he worked for three years in his father's mercantile firm of Turner, Beeton & Tunstall, but he left for California with the goal of investing some of his father's fortune in sheep and a fleece- and wool-making business. Hearing in Santa Barbara of the practically free, semiarid land in the New Mexico Territory, he instead went east and found himself in Santa Fe in 1876. There in Herlow's Hotel he met a Scottish Canadian, "a very shrewd fellow and a lawyer by profession, Alexander A. McSween," who persuaded the Englishman to go into stock raising in Lincoln. Tunstall hired as his foreman the "wonderful physical and moral specimen" of Richard M. Brewer, and because Tunstall was a foreigner, McSween and Brewer had to file the papers for him to acquire the Rio Feliz ranch on which he hoped to graze ten thousand cattle. "With overhead and losses you can't accumulate real wealth with less." Working for him as well were Robert Adolph Widenmann, who grew up over a hardware store in Ann Arbor, Michigan, but attended an excellent high school in Stuttgart, Germany; and Frederick Tecumseh Waite, a handsome half Chickasaw Indian who'd graduated from Mound City Commercial College in St. Louis. "So you'll be fraternizing with educated men."

"I like learning things, sir," said Kid Bonney. And he amended that: "Harry."

Tunstall admired him for a moment. "I could see that. The flames of intelligence gleam in your eyes."

The Kid was imagining an English manse or at least a handsome Mexican hacienda, but John Henry Tunstall's home in the high desert foothills east of the Sacramento Mountains was just a fourteen-by-fourteen hovel of a cabin constructed with adobe blocks and piñon logs. But Tunstall was delighted at seeing his property again and, as if they were objects of beauty, called Billy's attention to a heavy anvil and sledgehammer outside in the weather and a spade and a scoop shovel atilt against a lone mesquite. "I have tools!" he exclaimed. "I have forsaken the fancy drawing rooms and am *downstairs*, dining with staff!"

Hearing his voice, an English bulldog happily ran over a hill to his owner and wiggled and shrimped around in delight as Harry knelt to greet his Punch with high-pitched baby talk. Worry about the Englishman's sanity caused the Kid to examine the manic zeal in his face.

Tunstall interpreted his concern. "Don't be distressed, Billy. It shan't always be such a humble abode. I fully expect betimes a stately house with rooms upon rooms and pretty maidens to do our bidding."

White-bearded Gottfried Gauss, an ex-clergyman from Württemberg, Germany, and for thirteen years an Army hospital steward, worked as the ranchers' chuck wagon cook and that night served them grilled pork chops with a green chilli glaze as Harry talked passionately about the fortunes to be made. Without a table or chairs, they sat on the cold earthen floor, and Harry hunched over his food as he confided, "John Chisum was given a contract to supply eleven hundred steers for the soldiers at Fort Stanton. The Army agreed to pay him thirty-five dollars a head for the full-grown livestock, but Chisum only paid eighteen dollars a head in Trickham, Texas! The cattle drive took two weeks so there were considerable expenses, but the scalawag still netted over eighteen thousand dollars!"

"A lot of money," the Kid said.

Tunstall agreed and took that as encouragement to say more, going on and on about his wild ambitions until it was twelve, his "witching hour."

The Kid slept in the hovel only one night and then was relieved to be sent farther north to the winter-dead grasslands fed by the Rio Ruidoso. There the jigger boss, or second in command, was Charlie Bowdre, a twenty-nine-year-old from Mississippi who'd gone flat broke on a cheese factory in Arizona before finding work with L. G. Murphy's House as a gunman with Jesse Evans and the Boys. But in 1876 Bowdre had taken the teenage Manuela Herrera as his wifely servant and become domesticated, signing on to fork a saddle for the gentleman from London instead of being, as he put it, "ever on the skeedaddle and in a state of frantic."

The Kid recalled a lithograph of the author Edgar Allan Poe that he'd seen in Wichita. Charlie Bowdre, he thought, took a likeness to Poe with his sad, dour, seen-too-much eyes and his trying to balance his ever-gaining baldness with a walrus mustache and a wealth of dark brown hair behind his ears.

When the Kid rode up and introduced himself, Bowdre scowled, and in the snail's pace of Southern speech he asked, "William H. Bonney. Is that a consumed name?"

"Consumed?"

"Was you born with it or just take it on by your ownself?"

"Sort of."

Bowdre nodded. "Well, your secret's safe with me." His flat-topped hat was rakishly cocked rightward on his head like the straw boater of a city boulevardier, but he otherwise looked like a far older man who'd been in the hot or cold outdoors for too long. He spurred his gray ahead to swerve a maverick far from an arroyo, and the Kid trotted his white horse to catch up.

Bowdre asked him, "You ever buckaroo aforehand?"

"In Arizona."

"Which ranch?"

"The Sierra Bonita."

Bowdre took his measure. "With the vaqueros? You look too littlish for that."

"Well, mostly I helped around the chuck wagon."

Bowdre smiled. "Oh, you was the *hoodlum*!"

"They called it by another name."

"Was it the Little Mary?"

The Kid said nothing.

And Bowdre said, "Mr. Tunstall, he don't tolerate disrespect amongst our ownen."

The Kid was sent eastward as a flank rider, his sole job to bunch the cattle in their move-along and scare them with shrill whistles if they strayed wider. Though Bowdre was a hundred yards off, his voice carried, and the Kid could hear him sing, "It rained all night the day I left, the weather it was dry. The sun so hot I froze to death. Susanna, don't you cry."

At sundown Widenmann and three other hands in the nighthawk shift rode up to assume the overseeing, and with no more work for the weekend, Bowdre said Friday was his night to howl, and asked if the Kid had a place "to lay your wary head." Billy hadn't thought far enough into the future for that, a common problem with him, so Bowdre invited him to join him and his wife in his flat-roofed, two-room adobe house on the Rio Ruidoso. He'd purchased it from Lincoln's L. G. Murphy for fifteen hundred dollars, but with just three years to pay off the mortgage, foreclosure was inevitable, so Charlie and the woman he called his wife were just camping there and expecting to head for the horizon soon like most vagrant cowboys. Bowdre called it "searching for the elephant."

Manuela Herrera was a glamorous, exotic, high-spirited girl the Kid's age who seemed ill-suited to be heavily bundled up and frying tortillas in a skillet over a crackling fire in their front yard. The Kid hopped down from his horse and introduced himself in the formal Spanish way, kissing the sides of her cheeks as he said, "*Buenas tardes. Me llamo Guillermo Bonney.*" Good evening. I call myself William Bonney.

She blushed as she said, "*Con mucho gusto, Señor Bonney.*" With much pleasure, Mr. Bonney.

"*El gusto es mío.*" The pleasure is mine. The Kid felt sure she'd batted those gorgeous brown eyes.

Charlie Bowdre was watching them with jealousy. "You speak Mexican *excelente*, Kid. I'm unpressed."

"Well, I just get by, really."

"I ain't got the stick-with-it for learnin'."

Cold was nipping at whatever was exposed outside as Josiah Gordon Scurlock strolled over from the adobe house a little farther on with a girl of no more than sixteen. Scurlock was co-owner of Bowdre's ranch and the wrangler who handled the half a hundred horses needed on Tunstall's ranch, the cowhands often running through at least two per shift. The girl turned out to be his wife, Antonia Herrera, the younger sister of Manuela.

Doc Scurlock was twenty-eight, as blond as the Kid and an inch taller. He'd studied medicine in New Orleans and in the twentieth century would become a schoolteacher, but earlier in Louisiana he'd argued over a faro game and ended up killing his accuser with his gun, so he quit his physiology studies and fled to Arizona, where he partnered with Bowdre in a failed enterprise of making cheese. Wandering into the village of Lincoln, the pair found work as cattle rustlers for L. G. Murphy before preferring the more legitimate employment of the Englishman.

The five went inside to get out of the stiff wind and cold, and the Herrera sisters served hot-peppered steak fajitas. Just for conversation the Kid asked Scurlock, "Are you a doctor still?"

"Of horses," he admitted.

"Why'd you give up being a physician?"

Scurlock answered, "I guess I don't much like hospitals. I associate them with sick people."

He offered little else, but for the first time Doc smiled, revealing the quarter-size hole in his shattered front teeth that a gunshot took out in his struggle with the Louisiana gambler. The hole of the exit wound behind his throat had healed up like a button.

The Herrera girls were glancing shyly at Billy and giggling with each other as Bowdre and Scurlock talked about horse breeding. The Kid heard the sisters calling him Billito, and then Scurlock heard them saying the Kid was "*muy guapo*," very handsome, and he said, "They seem to like the cut of your jib, Kid."

It seemed more accusation than compliment.

The Kid hung his head a little.

Bowdre spoke so slowly it was like each word was his unique invention. "He's a ladies' man," he said. "I could tell that from the first instance."

"Innocence, flair, and helplessness conjoined," Scurlock said.

To change the subject or give an excuse for the girls' overfondness, the Kid said, "This being November twenty-third, it's my eighteenth birthday."

"*Qué dijo?*" Antonia asked. What'd he say?

Scurlock told his wife, "*Que hoy tiene dieciocho años.*" He has today eighteen years.

Manuela told Charlie, "*Entonces necesitamos una fiesta.*" Then we need a party.

And so Scurlock went off for his fiddle and Bowdre got his squeeze-box and changed into a fresh white shirt and red brocaded vest and the gold-striped trousers that he tucked into his boots. Scurlock and he weren't dancers, so they played the music and filled their whiskey glasses between songs and drunkenly watched as Manuela and Antonia taught the Kid an old Spanish dance, clicking castanets and clapping their palms and flouncing their skirts in a kind of disdainful, fierce, taunting quarrel whose final goal was seduction.

Scurlock fell asleep around ten, so his wife took him home, but Bowdre just kept tilting his whiskey bottle into his mouth until his hand no longer worked and he fell into a stunned insensibility, finally closing his eyes and snoring.

His wife said she was too excited by the company to sleep, so she stayed up and told Billito about the region. She said the Anglos called them Mexicans, but the people called themselves Spanish, for many still considered themselves citizens of the Imperial Spanish Viceroyalty of the sixteenth century, and even spoke in the formal, older ways of the explorer Coronado or like the characters created by Miguel de Cervantes. Had Billito read *Don Quixote de la Mancha*?

He hadn't yet but he'd get right to it.

She smiled and said in English, "But you can still call us Mexicans. All the Anglos do." She flushed a little as she added, "You berry nice to talk with. All days it is only my sister."

"Well, you got Charlie now," the Kid said.

Manuela looked across at the whiskeyed, snoring jigger boss. "Oh, heem," she said. "For heem I am only his servant. We no even married." She seemed to be sorting out thoughts, and then she turned to the Kid. "I have for you a . . . *regalo de cumpleaños?*"

"Birthday present."

"Jes." She then unbuttoned the bodice of her dark woolen dress to expose the full breasts of a girl of eighteen.

Smiling, he said, "*Precioso!*" Beautiful!

She whispered, "You may touch, too."

The Kid glanced at Charlie.

"He don care."

The Kid held them in his hands for half a minute, taking uneasy pleasure in it as he wondered what he would be doing next. He withdrew his hands. "They're exceptional."

She smiled shyly as she buttoned up her dress. "*Entonces, te gustó tu regalo?*" So, did you like your present?

"Oh yes," he said. "I'm very, very grateful." Yet he stood, hiding his erection, and went for his overcoat and hat.

Manuela was surprised and disappointed. "*No te vas a quedar?*" You're not staying?

"It's the wanting you," he said. "I don't have the discipline to handle it. And my only claim to virtue is my loyalty to my friends."

The Kid ended up sharing Dick Brewer's hundred-foot-long adobe ranch house and, with weaponry close at hand, cowboyed the cattle herd with Brewer and the mostly silent Chickasaw, Fred Waite. Waite and the Kid fantasized about owning a ranch together on the Rio Peñasco, but neither was good at husbandry so they were just spinning wool. Waite asked him once, "What do you really want, Kid? *Wanting* comes first, then the getting."

The Kid gave it so much thought Waite wondered if he'd heard. And then the Kid said, "To belong. To be liked. To be famous. To be feared."

Wordless, Waite just nodded.

The hands hunted snow geese for a Boxing Day dinner with John Tunstall, who sought to preserve his English customs even in the "Wild West." Watching from afar, Harry saw Waite and Widenmann fire into an overhead flock with shotguns and fail to bring anything down while the Kid lifted revolvers in his right and left hands and nailed geese with one shot from each gun. The felled birds flumped to the ground near the Englishman, and as Harry ran to get them he yelled, "How absolutely marvelous, Kid! That's really so cracking well done!"

George Coe was visiting that December 26 and later recalled that as the Kid painted butter over a crackling cooked goose the Englishman confided, "Billy's the finest young chap I've ever met. Each day he's a new and welcome revelation. I suspect there's nothing he won't do to please me, and in requital I shall yet make a proper gentleman of him."

Before dinner the Englishman heaved in a heavy box and handed out to each of his gunslingers there the mutually advantageous gift of fifty rounds of .44-40 cartridges. "I do hope you shan't need to use them in anger," Harry said, and then he entertained them by singing the British anthem "God Save the Queen," giving emphasis to the stanza:

> *O Lord our God arise,*
> *Scatter her enemies,*
> *And make them fall.*
> *Confound their politics.*
> *Frustrate their knavish tricks.*
> *On Thee our hopes we fix.*
> *God save us all.*

Evenings in January were spent by the hearth fire with the cowhands slouching in chairs or on the floor as they read books on loan from Alex McSween's hundred-volume home library. Because of the author's surname, Dick chose Reverend Ebenezer Brewer's popular *Dictionary of Phrase and Fable*. And Billy became absorbed in *Oliver Twist*, seeing his impoverished childhood self in the orphan Oliver, recognizing in his own Wichita and Silver City experiences many bullying oafs like Bill Sikes and juvenile pickpockets like the Artful Dodger. And he found himself pining for a sweet and nurturing Miss Rose Maylie, who so reminded him of his mother.

The Kid asked Dick, "Have you read *Oliver Twist*?"

Brewer turned a page of the Brewer book. "Yes."

"Me too," said Waite.

The Kid was not yet fully acquainted with the locale, so he asked, "Who's the Fagin of Lincoln County?"

Without looking up, they both replied, "Major Murphy."

7

THE RIVALS

Lawrence Gustave Murphy was born in County Wexford, Ireland, in 1831, or so he said. Hoping to be ordained a Catholic priest, he graduated from St. Patrick's College at Maynooth. But then he was expelled from the seminary for some infraction, and in disgust or shame he fled the potato famine by emigrating to Buffalo, New York. Enlisting at twenty-one in the US Army's 5th Infantry and serving in Texas, Murphy rose to the rank of hard-bitten sergeant before he was commissioned a first lieutenant in the New Mexico Volunteers in 1861. Became Kit Carson's regimental adjutant and quartermaster. When the Confederate Army retreated from the Southwest, the Volunteers found field exercise in slaughtering the ever-vexing Navajos and Apaches. All the killing gave Murphy a certain outlook.

Thin, five feet nine, mustached and goateed, with ever-squinting green eyes and a leonine head of Irish red hair, Murphy could be suave and gregarious in good company, but a childhood in the Great Famine and a hard, violent life in the Army had given him the fierce, canny, adamant disposition of a hungry dog. He made it to the rank of captain at Fort Sumner, then was a brevet major and commanding officer at Fort Stanton before mustering out in 1866 to form L. G. Murphy &

Co. with another former officer, Lieutenant Colonel Emil Fritz, who handled the finances loaned to them by a wealthy entrepreneur. At first they operated a civilian brewery, saloon, and store for provisions at Fort Stanton, but a fracas with an Army captain got them evicted from government property and they shifted their operation nine miles northeast to the village of Lincoln.

Emil Fritz, the cofounder of the House, was not yet forty-two but sick unto death with heart and kidney diseases. An osteopath falsified the German's medical exam so he could sign up for a ten-thousand-dollar policy from the Merchants Life Assurance Co. of New York in order to give his sister in America a nest egg. Emil named Alexander McSween the executor of his estate and then voyaged back to Stuttgart for an *auf Wiedersehen* with his family. In June 1874 he finally passed away. Would have left a gaping hole in the establishment were it not for James Joseph Dolan stepping up like he was Murphy's favored son and the store was his entitlement.

Jimmy, as he was called, was born in County Galway, Ireland in 1848, the son of a tallow chandler. Came over as a boy and attended a Christian Brothers grammar school while inhabiting the Five Points slum of New York City, but he got fed up with education and took a full-time job at twelve in a lingerie store. Enlisted as a drummer boy with the New York Zouaves in 1863, reenlisted to massacre Indians in Kansas, mustered out of the Army at Fort Stanton in 1869, and hired on as a clerk with Fritz and Murphy, having soldiered for the officers and seen they were kindred spirits. A few years later, when the L. G. Murphy & Co. provisions store and brewery was at the fringe of Fort Stanton and the village of Lincoln was still called San Placito, the fiery Dolan had been prosecuted for murder but was acquitted for Wild West reasons.

Oh, but he was a hotheaded pipsqueak, just a weedy five feet two, and as sourly pretty as a petulant damsel with his wavy, brown, ambrosial locks and ever-pouting disposition. Still, L. G. Murphy was so fond of him that most mistook them as doting father and son, and there was unseemly gossip about them sharing a bed.

In the fall of 1874 Murphy held the grand opening of the House and permitted himself to be captured by a wet-plate collodion camera for a formal carte de visite, with a glowering, wool-suited Dolan standing beside his seated boss, a hand affectionately atop Murphy's right shoulder as the brevet major, probate judge, and wealthy entrepreneur seemed to gaze off at his fabulous future.

The House was the third largest privately owned building in all of the New Mexico Territory and the first with a pitched roof. Within was a jammed store, a saloon, post office, savings and loan, a second-floor Masonic hall, and a lavish, high-ceilinged residence tidied by the housekeeper, Mrs. Lloyd. All of it made possible by overcharging for necessaries, practicing usury through their bank, selling deeds to properties the company didn't own and then foreclosing, and by finagling to win lucrative government contracts to be the sole suppliers of meat, produce, hay, charcoal, sugar, whiskey, and other commodities—much of it acquired illegally—to the region's Indian reservations and Army posts.

And some tricky accounting was afoot, with L. G. Murphy & Co. getting paid by the federal government for fictitious sales of hundreds of cattle from L. G.'s thirty-thousand-acre Carrizozo Springs ranch, for which of course he had no clear title. With Sheriff William J. Brady his employee and the highest government authority in Lincoln County, there was little Murphy did that was judged illegal by civic authorities.

Yet, in spite of all that financial heft and those seemingly favorable circumstances, by 1877 the overextended House had fallen on hard times and Lawrence Gustave Murphy and his partners were scrounging for money. Alexander McSween knew far too much about the operations of the House, so when he demanded payment of his immense legal bills, Murphy could do nothing more than transfer ownership to him of six acres on the plaza and his former adobe house next to the Wortley Hotel for "$1.00 and other good and sufficient considerations." Soon after that Murphy found out he had ravaging intestinal cancer, for which he claimed his doctor recommended he drink as much whiskey as he could handle to dull the pain. Warned that he had less than a year of his crooked life left, worn down with illness and misfortune, and in a perpetual state of inebriation, Murphy was convinced to withdraw from running the House, deeding it over to Jimmy Dolan, whom he also designated heir of his estate. The firm became Jas. J. Dolan & Co., and under that scheming management could have achieved prosperity again but for the undercutting competition of J. H. Tunstall & Co. General Merchandise.

Kid Bonney heard much of that from Waite and Brewer at nights and on the jouncing ride up to Lincoln from the Ruidoso ranch along the Ham Mills trail. Hitching his horse in front of Tunstall's store, he looked kitty-corner to the wide, handsome, two-storied House, with its second-floor veranda, which in the future would have dual wings of stair steps. And below in the shade of the veranda was L. G. Murphy aslant in a ladder-back chair, a quart of hooch cozied by his gloved hands and his overcoat collar up in defense against the cold air. Seeing something that troubled him, Murphy hurtfully stood up and tottered to the House's entrance, jarring open the front door to shout inside.

The Kid heard a man say, "They have a hankering for my hide," and he turned to see Alexander A. McSween walking eastward from his home next door to the Tunstall store, where he leased his law office. Waite, Brewer, and the Kid followed him inside.

McSween was a haughty, defiant Canadian in his thirties with a horseshoe mustache, a ribbony bow tie, and a Prince Albert suit underneath an Inverness topcoat. Educated for the Presbyterian ministry, Alex left it to enroll in law school at Washington University in St. Louis, staying with that program for just the first year of the usual two before hanging out his shingle in Eureka, Kansas. In 1873 he married Susan Hummer, and because of his financial malfeasance—but lying that it was due to his asthma—the couple fled to anything-goes New Mexico Territory and found out by chance there was no attorney in all of Lincoln County. At once it seemed to him there was a lucrative vacuum he could fill.

At first McSween lawyered and collected debts for L. G. Murphy, but he changed partners to waltz with an Englishman flush with his father's money and with the financial backing of John Chisum, and he seemed to feel no compunction about conveying to John H. Tunstall the confidential information of his former clients. As the House was hovering near bankruptcy because of its financial reverses and owings on construction loans, J. J. Dolan sought revenge against a traitor by convincing Emil Fritz's sister to swear out a warrant accusing Alex McSween of embezzlement of Emil's insurance money. Which was true, for McSween's piety did not overcome his chicanery, and he had deposited into his own St. Louis bank account the Emil Fritz settlement he'd gotten from the Merchants Life Assurance Co., permitting him to dress his wife in high fashion and furnish his house splendidly. Emil Fritz's sister never received a cent. In a further annoyance, L. G. Murphy sued Emil's estate and its executor, McSween, for $76,000 he claimed was owed him, but that action was dismissed by the probate court on January 10.

With a hefty overhead and fewer sales after Tunstall undercut their store prices and offered farmers credit, the House was going under, so on January 12, 1878, in a false gesture of friendship to the owners, the Santa Fe attorney and racketeer Thomas B. Catron accepted a mortgage on the House, its merchandise and past-due accounts, as well as the horses, cattle, hayfields, and forty acres of real estate associated with it.

On January 18, with a faith in the justice system that was without foundation, John H. Tunstall foolishly wrote a letter to the editor of the *Mesilla Valley Independent* indignantly charging Sheriff Brady and Jimmy Dolan with embezzling fifteen hundred dollars in taxes paid by Alexander McSween and meant for the commonwealth.

So it was that the Englishman John H. Tunstall and the Canadian Alexander A. McSween became the villains the Irish merchants in Lincoln could blame for everything that had gone sour.

And now the Kid stirred sugar into his hot coffee as he watched through a plate-glass window that warped them Jimmy Dolan and L. G. Murphy crossing Lincoln's only street to the Tunstall store, Murphy flinging a hand grandly and hollering sentences that were consumed by a hungry wind, and Jimmy crutching his staggering boss, a Winchester rifle cradled in his left arm.

McSween was watching, too. He took off his caped Inverness topcoat and then his citified top hat. His kinky brown hair was stacked as high as a chocolate cake. "Escort Jimmy into my office," he said and headed to the back of the store with his hat on the garment folded over his right arm. The Kid noticed that he carried no gun, a nonesuch in that era.

Dolan and Murphy let in the weather, then loudly shut the door. Cold eddied off their greatcoats.

Without emotion, Dick Brewer flatly said, "Well, this is awkward."

Dolan flew his glare around the store, despising whatever he lit on. "Where's Alex?"

"Yonder," Waite said and shot his right thumb backward over his shoulder. "But just you."

"Sure fine," Dolan said and marched to the lawyer's office, his Wellingtons clobbering the hardwood floor.

"And the Englishman not here either?" Murphy asked. His Irish accent made it "Anglish" and "I-ther."

"At the Jinglebob Ranch with John Chisum," said Waite.

"Well, more's the pity," L.G. said, falling back onto a Chippendale side chair by the stove and clomping the heels of his boots out wide. His head lolled until he fixed on the Kid, and he asked in his Irish accent, "Who might ye be, then?"

"William H. Bonney. They call me Kid."

"Workin for Tunstall?"

"Yep."

"And your age is all of what, fourteen?"

"Eighteen."

"Boot ye ain't even shavin yet!" Murphy grinned at Waite, who did not grin back. "The lad looks sweet as Baby Jesus in velvet pants!"

"Old enough to do damage," Waite said.

Murphy measured the Kid and frowned. "How'd a handsome fella like you fall in with this unholy bunch?"

The Kid smiled. "'To dig I am not able, to beg I am ashamed.'"

With a harrumph Murphy said, "Quotin scripture to me, he is." He took a bottle of Double Anchor whiskey from his overcoat pocket, screwed out the cork with his side teeth, and took a swallow.

Even passersby on the street could hear McSween shouting with exasperation that the Merchants Life Assurance Co. was in receivership and with his travel to New York to argue the case the residue of the Emil Fritz estate wouldn't even cover his fees.

"Aye right!" Jimmy yelled. "Away on that!"

"Look at the paperwork if you disbelieve me," said McSween.

Murphy ignored the office wrangling as he recited the placarded prices he saw. "Sellin a poond a butter for fifty cent. Doozen eggs, fifty cent. Even beef on the hoof, eight cent the poond. Headin for doom the Brit is at them prices." He fiercely gazed at Waite and Brewer. "We han't sold nary a thing in six weeks," he said, then his face changed and he hurriedly sought out the spittoon by his chair to vomit orangely into it.

The onlookers grimaced and fended the odor from their noses, but the Kid joked by asking the store, "Who else besides me is feeling hungry?"

Wiping his mouth on his overcoat sleeve, Murphy swished with whiskey, bulging his cheeks, and he swallowed as his gaze again lit on the Kid. "So, you're the joker in the deck."

"And I hear you're Lord of the Mountain."

"Ye heared right." And then he smiled as he limericked, "I have conquered the aging disease, that has brought lesser sorts to their knees. I'm a strapping old man and I've proved that I can blow out candles with only one wheeze."

"Could I jot that down for a hundert years from now?" asked the Kid.

Murphy just stared for a while. "So, ye a hired hand or hired gun?"

"Whatever needs doing."

He lifted his Double Anchor in salute and said, "Good on ye, sham."

Still haranguing his rival on future litigation, Dolan threatened, "We have friends in high places, you know."

And they overheard McSween saying, "You'll recall I have *encountered* the partisan Judge Bristol and our miscreant district attorney."

The famous sot in the front room sighed and called to the office, "Oh, go on with the talk, you!" And to the others he said, "Talk don't cost nothin but air, a scrape of the hind leg, and a jupe of the head. Riches is in the *doing*." And then he craned his neck to see the door. "Where's Brady finally?"

"Up to no good, prob'ly," Dick Brewer said.

Murphy smiled. "Well, that's the point, int it?"

And just then the sheriff barged in. He was a wide man with little slanted-down-at-the-corners green eyes, close to Murphy in age with a like Irish heritage, and the father of eight half Mexicans with one more on the way. His full, toast-brown mustache curtained his mouth, and there was a dapper paintbrush of beard affixed to the center of his chin. A tin badge of office was pinned to his navy blue overcoat lapel.

Murphy smiled. "How's the big size of ye, Bill?"

"Bang on, L.G.," said Brady. Seeming to look among the glaring faces for someone to properly address, he gave up and lifted a page overhead, the formal handwriting on it in the loopy Spencerian style. Crying out unnecessarily, he proclaimed, "I have a writ of attachment signed by Judge Warren Bristol on this store in its full entirety, exacted by the sister of Emil Fritz, deceased, and pursuant to a civil action against Alexander A. McSween, Esquire, the Englishman being in league with him."

Hearing his name called out, McSween emerged from his office and frowned in disdain. "Oh, this has gone far enough."

Jimmy Dolan instructed the sheriff, "And you'll inventory Alex's house next?"

"Uh-huh," Brady said.

"And Tunstall's livestock?"

"Oh, I expect."

Alexander McSween told the sheriff, "I have established no partnership with Mr. Tunstall. I merely lease an office from him. Any seizure of his property is plainly unwarranted."

The sheriff said, "You're in cahoots, Alex. You testified as such in Judge Bristol's court."

"I said no such thing!"

"Well, it got written down."

Two sheriff's deputies galumphed into the store and lodged themselves by the front door and cashier's till with shotguns at parade rest. "What stinks in here?" one asked.

With a loony wave, L. G. Murphy identified himself as the odor's source.

McSween was still recalling the hearing. "Are you altering testimony now? Is there no end to your prevarications?"

The onlookers worried over the word. Their educations failed them.

"You Irish . . . ," the Canadian said.

His hands inching up his slung Winchester, Jimmy Dolan said, "Be wide there, Alex, or I'll claim ye."

With contempt, McSween faced him. "You all *reek* of corruption."

Little Jimmy juggled the decision on whether to shoot the lawyer as he looked to the sheriff for instruction, but Sheriff Brady was in hushed discussion with Deputy George Hindman, whose face was ravaged into ugliness by the chew of a crazed black bear.

The Kid and Waite gently went to their guns, but just rested their palms on the grips when Brewer shook his head against any violence.

And then John H. Tunstall walked in, a flurry of falling snow in his wake.

"We thought you was at the Jinglebob!" Murphy said gaily.

"Alas, I found out John Chisum is still jailed in Las Vegas." He took off his felt hat and swatted flakes off it as he scanned all the faces. "We seem to be rather populated here."

The sheriff said, "I have a writ of attachment against your inventory signed by Judge Warren Bristol."

The Englishman was unsurprised. "Oh, what a nuisance!"

"And a fret, too, Mr. Tunstall," said Dolan, his hands so tightening on his rifle that his knuckles whitened. "Would ye like to forget the legalities and settle our differences here and now?"

The Kid's hand gripped his Colt's pistol butt and he readied for a gunfight as he sought a go-ahead from Brewer, then Waite, but they were ignoring the Kid's urgency. Just last May, Jimmy Dolan had killed a Mexican stable hand for the House, claiming Hiraldo Jaramillo had gone after him with a knife, but Waite and Brewer knew Dolan's fiery excitements often cooled with delay.

The Englishman may have known that, too, for he held up his hands and sought to pacify the twenty-nine-year-old by saying, "I'm not a combative man, Mr. Dolan. I don't earn my income that way. Besides, I have ridden over two hundred miles for naught. I have much energy to recruit."

L. G. Murphy was leaning forward like a theatergoer held in suspense and prepared to be entertained by whatever the outcome.

"So, you're a coward then," said Dolan.

"Have it your way."

"A quare fella."

"I shan't draw a gun, no matter the insults."

And then Dick Brewer interfered by calmly walking between the two, saying, "We'll just get our supplies and go."

"Won't be no sales today!" Jimmy Dolan cried out, but he lowered his Winchester. "We need to do an audit. Right, Sheriff?"

"Required by the writ of attachment," Brady said.

"There's nothing to be gained, hanging out here," Waite said and headed outside, his spurs jangling. The Kid and Tunstall and finally Brewer followed.

Murphy lifted his quart of Double Anchor and called out in farewell, "Leprechauns, castles, good luck, and laughter! Lullabies, dreams, and love ever after!"

And Dolan ran to the front door to shout after them, "I'll get ye yet, Englishman! And take heed of this: When ye write the *Independent* again, say I'm with the Boys!"

The Kid's hand went to his gun as he turned to face Jimmy Dolan, but Tunstall halted him and calmly said, "It's just a kerfuffle, Billy. We'll sort things out."

- 8 -

AFFRAY ON THE HAM MILLS TRAIL

Walking through the McSween residence with their house servant, a former slave who'd taken the name George Washington, Sheriff Brady noted things like "one parlor organ," "a lot of sheet music," "one wash bowl & pitcher," "one sewing machine." In Alex's office he'd counted "550 law books." Washington was outraged as he watched the sheriff hold up and inspect Mrs. Susan McSween's intimate things in a chiffonier's drawer, and he reported the violation to his employer. In retaliation, Alexander McSween wrote a letter on February 11 to Carl Schurz, the secretary of the interior, accusing the new Jas. J. Dolan & Co. and the federal agent to the Mescalero Apaches of conniving to furnish unhealthy stolen cattle and flour of foul mashed wheat and corn to the Indians of the reservation. "I suggest that you send a Detective here who will ferret this matter," wrote McSween. "A thorough search will disclose fearful villainy on the part of all concerned."

In a postscript he nominated "Robt. A. Widenmann of this place" to be the next Indian agent, not just because Widenmann was a friend of himself and John Tunstall but because Widenmann's father was an immigrant from Württemberg, Germany, just as Carl Schurz had been. He harbored the hope that they maybe knew each other.

Jimmy Dolan was the postmaster of Lincoln village, so Alex McSween took his letter nine miles southwest to Fort Stanton for mailing.

Meanwhile, Colonel William L. Rynerson, the presiding attorney for the Third Judicial District, was writing Jimmy Dolan, "It must be made too hot for Tunstall and his friends, the hotter the better, shake that outfit up till it shells out and squares up and then shake it out of Lincoln. Get the people with you, have good men about to aid Sheriff Brady, and be assured I will aid you all I can."

The next week was filled with threats and caterwauling and whose-was-which jockeying over horses and cattle, but the upshot was that gun portholes were drilled in John Tunstall's Los Feliz shack, the front patio and entrance were fortified like a stockade with heaps of sand-filled gunnysacks, and Gottfried Gauss, a Santa Claus of an old chuck wagon cook, took up habitation inside to oversee the cattle and property. And on the cold morning of February 18, 1878, with the instruction that Tunstall would "countenance no violence," a cavalcade left the Los Feliz ranch for the Lincoln plaza with six horses and two mules released from attachment by Sheriff Brady and which Tunstall intended to corral behind his merchandise store.

Fred Waite handled a buckboard to stock up on groceries in the village, and when the shortcut along the hilly Ham Mills trail got too rutted for apt-to-crack wooden spokes, Waite veered off toward the flatlands of the Wagon trail. Continuing on with Tunstall on horseback were just Dick Brewer, Robert Widenmann, William H. Bonney, and John Middleton, a heavyset horse thief of twenty-four who was wanted for killing a man in Texas.

Kid Bonney trotted a gray and spotted Appaloosa horse that was on loan to him and got up alongside Tunstall and his handsome but blind bay thoroughbred, Colonel. Looking to Billy, the Englishman said, "A splendid equine, wouldn't you agree?"

"Without question," Billy said.

"I have taught Colonel to high-step when the road gets choppy so his fetlocks aren't injured. And he'll prepare for changes of grade, up or down, just with my cautioning. Without any urging, he can walk twenty-five miles in five hours and a half. And he comes when I call him and follows me around as if he could see."

"Wish envy was a more honorable emotion."

Tunstall smiled. "I do hope I get to know you better, Kid Bonney. You have a certain *élan*, a *je ne sais quoi* that I find delightful."

"Well, I recognize that last word. Thank you."

Watching his forward cowhands rock in their saddles, Tunstall fondly said, "I feel the same way about Dick Brewer and Rob Widenmann. Rob takes as much care of me when I'm ill as if I were a fainting dowager. I get impatient with his coddling and once fetched my bulldog to snarl him away, but for generosity, courage, and the general manly virtues, Rob is truly a cracking good fellow."

"Wasn't aware you were sick," the Kid said.

"Oh, it's just rheumatism and too little sleep. Actually, I'm *still* very much below par, but I imagine I shall find my pins again by the time the buffalo grass greens up. In the meantime I have so many plans. Shall I tell you?"

His face gleamed with such childish exultation and fanciful sparkle that it felt a little like flirting. "Sure, Harry. Tell," the Kid said.

"Well, betwixt you and me, there is a ranch adjoining mine that I want very badly. It could be got for only six hundred pounds and I believe I could reap over three hundred per annum. I am more convinced every day that land here is as fine an investment as one of my father's merchant ships."

"Like to get myself some cattle property one day. Fred Waite and I have a notion to partner on a ranch soon's we get some cash."

"Oh do it, Kid. Put down roots. I'll help you."

"I'd appreciate it."

His employer's stare then went to the horizon as he ruminated in silence. The Kid could hear the shrill cowboy whistles far ahead as Widenmann and Brewer collected the troop of delinquent horses and mules whenever they threatened to wander. The frozen fescue grass crackled under the hooves of the Kid's horse. His Colorado saddle and doghouse stirrups creaked whenever he shifted his weight. Off in the distance there were galleons of shock-white cumulus clouds gathering in the wide sky's cerulean harbor, and their azure shadows floated over the flatlands. Billy surprised himself by saying, "I love it here. I'll never leave."

And Harry smiled. "Nor shall I."

Even at fifty-five, the white-bearded German, Gottfried Gauss, seemed too old and fat and harmless to harass, which is why John Tunstall had him stay behind at his hovel of a ranch house. And Gauss was squatting to tend a Dutch oven on a hissing fire outside when he heard the far-off racket of thirty horses and riders galloping toward the Los Feliz and stood with his hands on his aproned hips. Although he was so nearsighted that he often failed to make out faces less than five yards away, the cook recognized some of the gang called the Boys, but there were so many others with whom he wasn't familiar, their horses panting, neighing, shaking their manes, and bumping as the jammed intruders sought and lost ground with each other. And then Jimmy Dolan rode up and loomed over the cook from his fourteen-hand pinto, his face scarlet with windburn and fury. "We're a posse duly authorized by Sheriff Brady," he said. "Where's your boss?"

"A-vay," Gauss said and flung a hand northward. "Lincoln."

"He just left?"

"A-vile ago."

"Who all's with him in the beyont?"

"His hired hands."

"I needs a number."

Gauss counted no more than one right hand of fingers and said, "Five."

Jimmy told Jesse Evans, "We don't all need to go, then." And so he called out names: Jesse Evans, Frank Baker, and Tom Hill of the Boys. Deputy George Hindman of Lincoln. And Andrew "Buckshot" Roberts, Robert Beckwith, John Wallace Olinger, and William S. "Buck" Morton of the just plain ornery.

Gottfried Gauss would later testify that he heard Buck Morton cry out, "Hurry up, boys. My knife is sharp and I feel like a scalping." And then Dolan and his handpicked men vigorously raced toward the Ham Mills trail while those now with nothing to do shoed and curried their horses or partook of the old cook's food.

Around five o'clock and still ten miles from Lincoln, Widenmann rode back to Tunstall and said, "Vee haf seen a flock of wild turkeys. Would you like a goot dinner?"

"Capital idea," Harry said. And he told Rob to go off on the hunt, he'd mind the horses.

The Kid was two hundred yards behind, riding drag with John Middleton, who was claiming there was a twelve-hundred-dollar reward for his hide in Texas. And Billy said, "Well, if you die, and I hope you never do, I'll try to collect it."

"At least I'd be good for somethin'," the horse thief said.

Off to the Kid's right and far ahead, Brewer and Widenmann were in a kind of steeplechase over sagebrush and rills and runnels, hollering and laughing as they fired their pistols at wild turkeys that hopped aside or ran in a zigzagging way or flew in an ungainly flapping of wings that seemed to be without practice. And then the Kid heard galloping and spun in his saddle to see nine riders racing like floodwater over a hillcrest, firearms in their hands and lifting and holding on him. He saw spurts of smoke from the guns before he heard the gun reports, and then there was a sizzle as one bullet flew past his head.

Widenmann and Brewer were still lost in their childish joy in the canyon, hurrahing and circling as the wild turkeys succeeded in evading their horse-jolted and horse-waggled aims in the scrub oak and chaparral. The Kid spurred his gray to warn them and looked over his shoulder to see that a trio of pursuers were in a sprint right behind him, though their mounts seemed to be hard-used and tiring, a pinto whose owner was Jimmy Dolan being one of them. The Kid cried out to his friends and frantically waved both arms. Brewer noticed and frowned at the ruckus, then wheeled his horse around and fired his gun before ducking behind his horse's head when a fresh volley answered him. Widenmann hurried for a hillside that was jagged with tombstones of rock, and Brewer and the Kid did, too, jumping down from their steeds and hiding, then raising to shoot at the villains who'd grandly called themselves a posse.

The Kid called to Brewer, "Is that Buck Morton?"

Brewer shouted over the gun noise, "And Jesse Evans, I think."

The Kid said to himself, "We used to be friends."

John Middleton had seen that John Tunstall was far enough ahead to not recognize what was going on, so he sprinted his horse forward with half the posse in flagging pursuit and now getting out of pistol range, their horses were so done in. Middleton sang out, "Mr. Tunstall! Hey! Look here!"

Tunstall turned in his saddle. "What, John?"

"For God's sake, follow me!"

Tunstall seemed not to get why his hired hands were fleeing. "What, John?" he called again. And then he appeared to recognize Jesse Evans running hard at him, guns no longer firing, and since they'd joked and shared a flask of whiskey when Jesse was in the Lincoln jail, Tunstall must have thought Evans was delivering a helpful message, for instead of galloping away he swerved Colonel around and loped toward the three men, a free hand raised up in hello or do-not-be-afraid.

The trio halted and instructed each other as Tunstall trotted forward with a friendly smile for Evans and some familiar faces, including the frowning one of Tom Hill.

His heart racing, the Kid stood up from the cold protection of a doghouse of stone, seeing the separated gang of Jimmy Dolan, George Hindman, and others skirt their horses around and away from Harry's cowering ranch hands and head toward a trio some hundred yards off that seemed to be formally waiting for the genial Englishman. His horse Colonel nearly touched the nose of the horse of Buck Morton as greetings seemed to be exchanged. There followed a stillness, as if a secret judicial deliberation was going on, as if they were waiting for a verdict. And then the Kid watched in horror as Morton just calmly lifted his pistol and shot Harry in his chest. The force of it slammed him into a fall from his horse, and he was as quiet on the earth as a heap of coats.

Wanting to answer but realizing their guns would just spit up dirt at that range, Widenmann, Brewer, and the Kid could do nothing but hate as Tom Hill jumped down and, because his own gun was shelled out, took the Colt Peacemaker from the Englishman's holster and, for officious assurance, executed John H. Tunstall with a shot through his head.

Jimmy Dolan seemed to say something and Tom Hill turned to listen. Then he looked at Tunstall's solemn, unseeing bay horse, and Hill shot it in the head, too. Colonel fell on his front knees and then on his flank, fully dead. And in an insult they found hilarious, Evans and Hill laid Tunstall's body out and tucked his saddle blanket around him as if he were sleeping, his head bleeding onto the pillow of his folded overcoat. Likewise, Jimmy Dolan had the hoot of squashing Tunstall's felt fedora under the head of his favorite horse. And then the nine rode off.

John Middleton yelled out, "Boys, they have killed Harry!"

And I just watched, Billy thought.

- PART TWO -

THE
REGULATORS
(FEBRUARY 1878–JULY 1879)

9

"WORKING UP A GOOD HATE"

Sheriff William Brady wisely stayed on his dear-bought eighty-acre farm four miles east of Lincoln for all of February 18, playing with a few of his eight children when they were freed from the schoolroom run by Susan Gates. In the cold of twilight he wandered through his fruitless orchard and ghostly dry vineyard in his old blue Army officer's overcoat. Watching the sun flare red as blood against the scraps of cirrus cloud in the west, he wondered if the deed had been done. And then he went inside for dinner.

On Tuesday morning the ex-major rode his Arabian sorrel horse into Lincoln and heard that forty outraged villagers had congregated in Alexander McSween's house on the yesternight, offering Tunstall's hired men and the McSweens their sympathy over the loss of their friend and demanding some kind of judicial retribution. Worried about a reprisal, Sheriff Brady used his old connections at Fort Stanton to get a detachment of soldiers to ride into Lincoln with the object of preserving the peace.

John H. Tunstall's corpse was hauled the ten miles to the village in an oxcart and was examined in a postmortem by the post surgeon, Major Daniel Appel, who was assisted by Dr. Taylor Ealy, a Presbyterian medical missionary who'd just arrived in Lincoln at Alexander McSween's invitation. They found that one bullet fractured the right clavicle and tore through the victim's artery, which would have caused him to bleed to death within minutes; but there was another bullet that exploded just above the orbit of the left eye, fracturing the skull at entrance and exit.

In his diary that night, Taylor Ealy noted, "This is truly a frontier town—warlike. Soldiers and citizens armed. Great danger of being shot."

At a coroner's inquest into the death of John Henry Tunstall, employees and eyewitnesses Robert Widenmann, Richard Brewer, John Middleton, and William H. Bonney testified to the facts as they knew them with the result of a verdict of homicide against the so-called deputies Jesse Evans, William Morton, Frank Baker, Thomas Hill, George Hindman, and James J. Dolan. Recognizing that the sheriff would do nothing affecting his own posse, on Wednesday Lincoln's justice of the peace issued warrants that were to be delivered to the indicted by the village constable, Atanacio Martínez, and his newly sworn deputies, Fred Waite and Kid Bonney.

With Winchester rifles crooked in their left arms, the trio took their warrants to the House and found idling with whiskeyed coffee inside the store William Brady, Lawrence G. Murphy, and Jimmy Dolan—Irish who'd gotten out of their country during the Great Potato Famine but still felt the pangs of not-enoughness.

"We don't serve youse kind," Dolan warned.

And Waite said, "The fact is we're not interested in buyin what you're sellin."

"Aw, sure look it," Major Murphy said. It was an Irish expression that could mean anything. Seeing the wrath in the faces of Waite and the Kid, Murphy drunkenly fell his way toward the storeroom door and hurriedly spoke inside, and immediately there was commotion as a lieutenant and six gloomy soldiers with weaponry joined the Irishmen. "Ready" was the lieutenant's warning command, and the soldiers let their index fingers find the triggers.

Constable Martínez was cowed by the intimation of force, but Waite said, "We have warrants for the arrest of *you*, Jimmy, and for other members of the posse that the so-called sheriff here sent out to execute John Tunstall."

Little Jimmy Dolan glowered. "It was self-defense."

"The inquest said otherwise."

Sheriff Brady stood up. "Let me look at those warrants."

Lincoln's constable handed them over, and Brady scoured them one at a time, his lips moving as he read. And then he smirked and tore the papers in half. "All these names belong to a legally constituted posse of the finest citizens procurable."

Seeing the Kid inching up his Winchester, the Army lieutenant yelled, "Aim!" and six carbines were suddenly shouldered and leveled on the constable and his two deputies.

Martínez shrank down a little, but Waite just flatly stared at the guns as if indifferent to their shenanigans.

Sheriff Brady asked if the Kid's was a Winchester '73, heard nothing, and with a drill sergeant's experience of handling tyros he loomed over Billy and demanded, "Hand me that rifle, you son of a bitch." And when the Kid didn't do that at once, Brady wrenched it away and admired the Winchester's blued-steel breechblock and oiled walnut stock before socking the Kid's jaw with its butt plate.

The Kid yelled, "Ow!" and held his jaw. He could taste blood, and his face was blotched red with fury over the injury and with the shame of a helplessness he hadn't felt since adolescence.

The sheriff confiscated the rifle Harry had given the Kid for his birthday and announced to Waite and Martínez, "It's *you* three that are under arrest!"

Jimmy laughed and said, "Oh, ain't it grand!"

"Tis indeed," L. G. Murphy said. "Good on ye, Bill. And good riddance, laddies."

Waite seemed unsurprised, but Martínez protested, "*Pero por qué?*"

The sheriff answered, "Well, for disturbing the peace. And impersonating an officer of the law. And things I haven't thought of yet."

Eventually the lieutenant got the three arrestees in a tight formation with his Fort Stanton detachment around them, humiliatingly marching them to the jail like they were oafish new recruits.

Atanacio Martínez was let out of *la cárcel* before nightfall, but Waite and the Kid were held in the cold, fetid underground dungeon, and they were still there when the funeral for John Henry "Harry" Tunstall took place on Friday and he was buried in the horse corral behind his looted store.

The Kid said, "You and me, we could take over Harry's ranch and run his cattle for him."

Waite said, "You're no rancher, Kid. Hell, you don't even garden."

"So what am I s'posed to do?"

"Well, you're an able gunman."

Mrs. Susan McSween's foot-pumped reed organ had been carried into the corral, and the Kid could faintly hear the village congregation singing the hymns "Jesu, Lover of My Soul" and "My Faith Looks Up to Thee."

Handsome Fred Waite leaned against an earthen wall with his flat-brimmed hat tilted far back on his head. His black mustache was wide as a comb. Hearing the hymns, he stared across the darkened room to where the Kid was listening, too, as he squatted down, his arms hugging his knees.

Waite asked, "You know about the lawyers Thomas Catron and Stephen Elkins? Of the Santa Fe Ring?"

"A smidge."

"They were friends and classmates at the University of Missouri. But Smooth Steve served with the Union Army and Tomcat with the Confederacy. Enemies. Yet they're partners in their Santa Fe law firm now, letting bygones be bygones. Water under the bridge. And that's how it's gonna be with us. Civil war, with friends and neighbors against friends and neighbors. Afterwards it may be different, but for now it's unto death that we're parted. Lincoln County is a house divided."

The Kid was rocking back and forth on his boots, saying nothing.

Waite asked, "What's hamstering in your head, Kid?"

"Working up a good hate."

Within thirty hours Waite and the Kid were released from jail, in a rage over the injustices of the legal system, the factious stance of the Army, and the refusal of Sheriff Brady to go after murderers still very plainly at large.

Seeing their side of things, Lincoln's justice of the peace made twenty-eight-year-old Dick Brewer, whose record was clean, an official constable, and all of John H. Tunstall's former employees joined him as deputies when he formed a vigilante group he called the Regulators. Their stated purpose was to restore law and order in the enormous county, but each Regulator had his own fealty and resentments, his own scheme to make a dollar, his own childhood education in the uses of violence, and a wild craving for vengeance.

The Kid went to the grocery and tavern of Juan Patrón in Lincoln and took pleasure in telling the tequila drinkers there in Spanish that he was Brewer's deputy now and finally on the right side of the law and he intended to stay there. Could maybe run for sheriff next election.

The first arrests of the Regulators came on March 6, when Brewer, Middleton, Bowdre, Scurlock, and Kid Bonney found Frank Baker and William "Buck" Morton watering their horses on the far side of the Rio

Peñasco. Baker was raised in an educated and cultured family in Syracuse, New York, but took a wrong turning, joined the Boys, and found sick pleasure in several homicides even before he signed on with Sheriff Brady's posse to hunt down John Tunstall. Twenty-one-year-old Buck Morton grew up on a tobacco plantation in Virginia, clerked in a hotel in Denver, slit the throat of his gold-mining partner in Arizona, and was a sixty-dollar-a-month foreman on Jimmy Dolan's cattle ranch on Black River when he joined the sheriff's posse and shot Tunstall in cold blood. They both still rode with the Boys at times and were hightailing it to Texas when their means of locomotion got thirsty.

Wide-eyed at seeing the Regulators, the culprits fired at the five from a crouch, and in a wild panic hopped on their horses and spurred them southward. The Regulators crashed their own horses across a pretty fly-fishing river and gave chase through open but jagged country, the pursued in a hot gallop and twisting in their jolting saddles to shoot backward, hitting nothing but earth and sky, then having to frantically reload on the run. The Regulators sent a fusillade of gunfire at them, too, but the leaps and lunges of their horses also jostled their aims into ever-miss. Yet their five animals were fresher and Morton's and Baker's were hard-used and playing out, heaving for air and lathering up and stumbling with weakness until one just halted in a head-shaking statement of *I shall go no farther* and then the other horse joined him in sharing their exhaustion.

There was nothing for the murderers to do but jump down and hide in some tall, crackling tules in cold marsh water. Reeds nodded whenever they shifted position and guns could find their sloshing noise even when they couldn't be seen.

"Fish in a farrow," Bowdre said.

The Kid corrected him: "Barrel."

Constable Brewer shouted, "We could set fire to these weeds and burn you out! So surrender and we won't harm you!"

The Regulators could hear the hissing of whispered discussion and then, "Okay, we give up. Don't shoot."

One fell in the high reeds, making a commotion, and his partner criticized him, and then both sodden men showed themselves with their hands held high overhead but seeming skeptical about their futures.

Brewer said, "We'd rather have shot you both and had it done with, but as it is I guess you're under arrest."

Wet Buck Morton said, "We never did anything wrong. It was all justifiable."

And the Kid told Brewer, "Let's kill em now."

"We can't. We caught em."

The Kid protested, "We take them back to Sheriff Brady or Judge Bristol, and they'll just set them loose."

Brewer ignored him and got off his horse to take their guns and tie their hands behind their backs. And then the seven of them rode to John Chisum's fine hacienda on his South Spring River ranch, head-quarters of the Jinglebob Land & Livestock Company.

Cottonwood trees shaded a quarter-mile avenue from the main road to the residence. Eight hundred acres of alfalfa provided forage for Chisum's cattle. Orchards of apple, pear, peach, and plum trees had been imported from Arkansas. The hacienda was hedged with roses he got in Texas, and even the bobwhite quail and scarlet tanagers were foreign birds hauled all the way from Tennessee. In a region of rolling grasslands and a far-off emptiness, the Kid thought of the South Spring River ranch as a gorgeous, watered oasis, and he was so full of need and aspiration that he told Doc Scurlock, "I'll own this someday."

Doc flatly said, "Sure you will, Kid."

Sallie Chisum, the old man's niece, walked onto the front veranda in a high-collared teal dress to greet them. She said she was alone there with the Mexican cook and a Navajo servant and it was nice to have men around. She was a half year older than Billy and pretty and blond and welcoming enough that she at once made any men she encountered lovesick and overeager. Even the prisoners Baker and Morton, whom she'd note in her diary were "nice looking chaps with unmistakable marks of culture," forgot the jail they were headed for and gave her a spark, as was said then. Billy Bonney she thought of as an affable, funny, and very occasional friend but nothing more, so he was vying for Sallie while the sole object of her own flirtatious attentions, the strong, august, and dashing Dick Brewer—she alone called him Richard—avoided the contest for Sallie but still seemed to be winning it.

She relished having the crowded surround of seven sentimental, admiring men at the candlelit dinner table, Baker and Morton joining the Regulators for porterhouse steaks and roasted red potatoes but without utensils and with their gun hands tied to the stiles of their chairs so that they were forced to gnash the meat off the bone like dogs.

Still, Buck Morton fought for Sallie's notice against John Middleton and Billy Bonney. Sweet glances and winking, tee-heeing, and tickling only soured the meal for the married men Scurlock and Bowdre, and Doc chose to darken the mood by reciting to the accused, "Gather ye rosebuds while ye may, old time is still a-flying; and this same flower that smiles today tomorrow will be dying."

"Heck, that could be a poem," Middleton said.

And Scurlock said, "Is."

The Kid sneered at their captives and drew a finger from ear to ear in a cut-throat warning.

Buck Morton could not hide his horror over Scurlock's threat and the Kid's gesture, and after hurrying his dinner he requested stationery to write a letter to his cousin, an attorney in Richmond, Virginia, lying about his innocence and noting: "Constable Brewer himself said he was sorry we gave up as he had not wished to take us alive. I presently am not at all afraid of their killing me, but if they should do so I wish that the matter should be investigated and the parties dealt with according to law. If you do not hear from me in four days after receipt of this I would like you to make inquiries about the affair."

Sallie stamped the envelope, and Brewer promised they'd stop at the post office in Roswell on their way to Lincoln. Then the Kid heard knocking at the front door, opened it, and was grieved to see William McCloskey there. He was a scoundrel when drinking and a wheedler when not, and he'd fashioned a shoddy career of hiring on at Jinglebob roundups and branding times and otherwise handling janitorial work for the likes of Jimmy Dolan. "Saw the lights from the trail," McCloskey said. "Sallie here?"

"Yes."

"Wondered if the Chisums would let me stable Old Paint and rest my weary bones."

With dismay Sallie allowed it, and soon McCloskey was hunkering in the dining room with Brewer and hot coffee, flattering him and trafficking in gossip as he sought to join the Regulators, whom he'd heard were getting handsomely paid.

Sallie allowed the murderers to stay under guard in her frilly pink bedroom that night, chosen by Brewer because it lacked windows. And when she saw the Regulators had laid out their bedrolls on the floor of the dining room and parlor, Sallie said she was too excited by the company to sleep, seeming to hope that Brewer would invite her on a moonlight stroll. Instead it was the Kid who escorted Sallie outside into the darkness, where she said with fresh wonderment, "There are so many thousands and thousands of stars here. Ever so much more than in Texas. They're like a spill of sugar."

"Supposed to snow," Billy said, and then chided himself, *Weather, when she was being romantic.*

Uncle John Chisum grazed upward of eighty thousand cattle on rangeland that extended north one hundred miles, but only fifty or so were close enough to see beyond the fences, all watching Sallie with their sad and beautiful faces as she showed Billy the starry W of the constellation Cassiopeia.

Words were lost for the Kid. He tried to fetch a joke now and then but was so tardy in doing so that she just looked at him quizzically with no idea of his references. She stood still, hugging her overcoat, and just stared silently into the night, as though waiting for a train. *She wants me to kiss her*, he thought, but he hesitated and failed to touch her and finally Sallie said, "Brrr. That cold old wind cuts right through you, doesn't it?"

"The hawk is talking," he said.

She squinched her face at the boy oddity beside her.

"Old expression," he said. "Because a hawk's beak is sharp. Like a cold wind." Each further explanation made him feel stupider.

She considered him for a while and then she quoted, " 'We are such stuff as dreams are made on, and our little life is rounded with a sleep.' "

"So you're going to bed now?"

"That's what I was implying, yes."

Billy just watched Sallie walk back to the house alone, thinking, *Could've said you love her, Kid.*

An hour before sunup he tramped through fresh-fallen snow with his tack and petted the left side of a fourteen-hand roan called Tabasco that Alex McSween had loaned to him. He swatted the black saddle pad to free it a little of reddish hair and flew it up over the horse's withers, then hooked the stirrups over the horn and flipped up the cinch before hefting the saddle onto the horse's back.

Dick Brewer was drinking coffee from a tin cup as he humped his own tack to his stallion. "Up and at em early, Kid."

"I figure I'll sleep when I'm dead." He inserted and inserted again the leather latigo through the D ring at the end of the cinch and then necktied it.

Brewer put his tin cup on a fence post, and steam twisted from it. Catching up with his saddling, he said, "McCloskey tells me Jimmy Dolan already heard we caught Buck and Frank. Some pards of theirs saw the chase. Jimmy'll have lookouts posted east of Lincoln, so I figure we'll go north and around the Capitán Mountains and ride in from the west at night."

Sallie called from the front porch, "Richard? Shall I refresh your coffee?"

"I'm fine!"

"I'd like some," the Kid called back, but she was heading inside again. In his frustration he yanked Tabasco's flank billet too taut, then apologized to the horse as he loosened it.

Brewer stared over his saddle at the Kid. "McCloskey also heard Mr. Chisum is going to pay each Regulator five dollars a day."

A stolen calf fetched five dollars then. Rooms rented for that by the month. "Seem likely?"

"Well, this isn't a job, it's an obligation."

The Regulators were genial as they ate breakfast in the dining room, but the criminals seemed to be fasting. Frank Baker theatrically presented Sallie with a fine gold Waltham pocket watch, a horsehair bridle he'd plaited himself, and a farewell letter to be mailed to his sweetheart. William Scott Morton spoke only to insist that he wanted a fair trial.

Soon the Regulators and the accused, with their hands tied in front of them, were riding through the main gate. Wondering if Sallie was watching from the front porch, the Kid turned in his creaking saddle, and she was. He waved his sombrero in a haymaker goodbye, and she smiled and waved back.

Some time later William McCloskey asked him, "Why are you grinning?"

The Kid ignored him, jabbed Tabasco with his boot heels, and trotted forward to ride point ahead of his friends.

Roswell was just four miles north of the Chisum ranch. An Omaha gambler had invested in the arid emptiness by constructing a two-story hotel and an identical general store, giving the village the first name of his father. The next-to-nothing population would not increase much until a few years later when a farmer found an underground aquifer and water ceased being scarce.

Ash Upson was the government postmaster inside the general store, and he would have remembered Billy from his rooming with the Antrims in Silver City, so the Kid stayed outside and incognito, but he gazed though the front window glass as his friends happily purchased things with the income they now expected from John Chisum.

At the till, Morton confided to Upson, "I have a bad feeling, Ash. I'm afraid they're gonna lynch me."

"Well," said Upson. "That would be unfortunate."

McCloskey was a friend of theirs and swore, "Any harm comes to you two, it means they must've kilt me first."

Charlie Bowdre brought outside for himself and Billy dill pickles still dripping from the barrel, and after Buck Morton's letter to Richmond, Virginia, had been registered and mailed, Dick Brewer pushed him out of the general store.

McCloskey asked their boss, "Is there time for me to visit the hotel whore?"

Brewer looked at him like he was something the cat dragged in, and they all saddled up.

Could be that some skulking Apaches saw them; but otherwise no one spied the party until a Mexican shepherd with a flock of merinos viewed them from a hillside as they turned in to Agua Negra Canyon.

Night began to lower its curtain with the party strung out for two hundred yards fore to aft, the Kid and Brewer riding drag far behind the straggled Bowdre, Middleton, and Scurlock and overlooking the central three of McCloskey, Morton, and Baker. The trio were old gambling buddies yacking about electric dice and marked decks of cards you could buy for two dollars when Morton suddenly jerked McCloskey's six-shooter from its scabbard with his tied hands. And when McCloskey shied from the outreached barrel, Morton shot him under his jaw and upward. Alive one second, dead the next, McCloskey fell from his horse like furniture off a wagon.

Both the former captives then thundered off, ducking low and heading for a fort of high rocks, with Morton holding the only gun and crazily firing at the men who gave chase. The Kid counted five more shots, so the gun was used up as the still-tired horses of Sheriff Brady's possemen wore out and the avenging hunters caught up. And then it was nothing more than an execution as the Kid finally got his way and with John Middleton thoroughly killed the fleeing Frank Baker with five shots in the back as the other Regulators finished William S. Morton with nine.

It was a collective thing, but only Kid Bonney got accused of the murders.

Dick Brewer rode alone into Lincoln that night, slow-walking his exhausted horse toward the House, where the upstairs veranda was filled with loud, jolly suited men in rocking chairs and overcoats, tipping back square glasses of whiskey and smoking green cigars. Sheriff Brady was one, and his deputy George Hindman; Lawrence Gustave Murphy, of course; then a few citified strangers and, lo and behold, Governor Samuel Beach Axtell.

Axtell was an Ohio attorney who'd failed at gold mining on the

American River in California but succeeded in being elected a congressman in San Francisco. A Democrat then, he changed his affiliation to curry the favor of the Republican president, Ulysses S. Grant, and was given the post of Governor of the New Mexico Territory in 1875. Axtell was secretly in the thrall of Thomas Catron's Santa Fe Ring, and a federal agent would later claim he was more inept, corrupt, fraudulent, and scheming than any governor in the history of the United States. In fact, Interior Secretary Carl Schurz would soon investigate his administration and within months would have him dismissed from his office.

Sheriff Brady stood and called out, "Where's your crew, Dick?"

"Oh, here and there."

"And how about your prisoners?"

"We lost em."

The sheriff looked to his deputy, saying, "Go tell Jimmy," and George Hindman hurried in his halting way toward the east side of town. His left thigh had lost a good deal of muscle to the teeth of the mauling black bear, so he was forced to sling his leg forward like a wooden pedestal.

L. G. Murphy called, "Wait on, Dick!" Smiling hugely and resting a hand on the governor's shoulder, he yelled, "And who would our guest of honor be? The governor, do ye think?"

Dick Brewer just tipped his hat to Axtell and rode on, and the drunken Murphy yelled again, "He's intervening in our current situation!"

Axtell asked him, "Who is he?"

Murphy said, "Fella used to tend for me. I hold the mortgage on his ranch."

Axtell shouted loudly, just as he must have done earlier in a village assembly. "I seek only to assist Lincoln's finer citizens in upholding our laws and keeping the peace!"

But Brewer's back was shut to him by then. And by the time the Regulator got to Juan Patrón's tavern, he could see Jimmy Dolan and a slew of rifled men grumpily slouching down Main Street, having been denied their ambush.

Juan Batista Wilson, the justice of the peace, was just where he frequently was, standing at the east end of an ornate bar freighted in from Albuquerque, a jar of tequila in his hands. Seeing Brewer, he filled a shot glass for him from the jar and tilted and weaved in his drunkenness as Brewer reported on the capture of Morton and Baker. At the end of the recital of the events, Wilson told him the governor had just issued a proclamation that booted the justice from his office, voided all the legal writs and processes issued by him, and specified that District Attorney Rynerson and Sheriff Brady and his deputies were the only officers empowered to enforce civil law.

"Meaning what?"

Ex-Justice Wilson offered him an ironic smile. "Means you ain't a constable now and never wast. Had you self no deputies never. Warrants? They's worthless. Axtell even called em 'disreputable.' And how I figure it is you and your Regulators are outlaws. Oh, and also, guilty of murder."

With their freedom in jeopardy, Alexander McSween and Dick Brewer fled Lincoln that night to hide out at Chisum's ranch, where Susan McSween was to rejoin her husband after a few weeks shopping in St. Louis. At the South Springs ranch, Alex and Dick would hear that another two of Tunstall's assailants were done for, Tom Hill having shot and failed to kill a Cherokee sheep drover who fired back with an old Henry rifle that finished him. Jesse Evans was Hill's accomplice and was shot as he took flight, the Henry's bullet shattering his left elbow and yanking him in a fall off his horse.

Evans was soon arrested and taken to the post hospital at Fort Stanton for surgery, and then was locked in the post stockade to await his trial.

Of the Regulators, Doc Scurlock and Charlie Bowdre went to their women and scratch-ankle ranch on the Ruidoso while John Middleton and Billy Bonney sequestered in San Patricio, a village a few miles south of Lincoln on the Rio Hondo. The Kid was a first-rate card counter, so he made a nifty income by placing bets at faro only when the dealer got toward the end of the deck, when predicting the fall of cards got easier. Seeing the Kid was winning far too often, but not intuiting why, the saloonkeeper finally denied Billy access to the games, and he and Middleton just loitered on the sidewalks, target-practiced in the hills, and used up the nights of March courting pretty *novias* at the Mexican dances that were called *bailes*.

The Kid was particularly fond of a girl of fifteen named Carlota, and she seemed shyly responsive, flickering a smile at his jokes and courtesies. His gallantry was overseen by a judicious aunt who was the *dueña*, which can mean overseer, and Tía Hortensia seemed to hope for the match, praising Billito in Spanish for his fluency in their language, his Old World manners, and his gentlemanly respect for the old, the *viejos*, while Carlota talked of his flashing blue eyes, his sweetness, his smartness, his frequent smile.

On the night of March 31, Hortensia stood far behind her niece under the awning of a mercantile store, looking away when the Kid kissed Carlota. A hard rain was falling and the streets were flooding and the cool, clean air smelled like Armour's laundry soap. Carlota held the Kid's kiss for as long as he wanted, wrapping her shawled arms around his neck as his chest crushed against the cushion of her still-small breasts. She let her mouth be insistent, nibbling, and smearing, a vagabond in its wandering over his face with lips softer than the petal of a rose.

The Kid withdrew a little and asked Carlota, "*Qué estás haciendo?*" What are you doing?

She smiled. "*Te estoy enseñando a besar.*" Teaching you to kiss.

"Oh. *Muchas gracias.*" They resumed, and the Kid's hands were traveling toward Carlota's sweet rump when he felt a soft tap on his shoulder and fearfully turned to find not the *dueña* but San Patricio's constable José Chávez y Chávez and John Middleton with a giggling Mexican girl playfully twisting his black handlebar mustache.

José had lost his grandfather's farm to the Santa Fe Ring and sought to join the Regulators to extract some justice. So he told the Kid in Spanish that he'd heard Judge Warren Bristol and the semi-annual meeting of the district court were due in Lincoln on April 1, and Sheriff Brady intended to arrest Alexander McSween yet again on his announced return to Lincoln from the Chisum hacienda, urge the grand jury's prosecution of the Regulators for the homicides of Baker and Morton, and convince Judge Bristol and the jury that the sheriff's posse was legally constituted and acted in self-defense in the February killing of John Henry Tunstall.

Middleton waited for the rattle of Spanish to end in order to make his own contribution. "And then I'll wager he's gonna hunt us each down and kill us dead, just to get rid of the contrary evidence."

The Kid was fuming as he added to the list of outrages, "The sheriff stole my Winchester rifle."

Sheriff Brady took his breakfast of steak and eggs at the Wortley Hotel on April 1 and slogged across a sloppy street to the House, the Kid's Winchester slung over his forearm. Rain had turned to sleet in the cold of morning, but with the sun it would just be more of the wet.

The frail and ailing old lion Lawrence G. Murphy was alone and leaning over his elbows behind the bar, his thoughts flying and his first quart of Double Anchor rye whiskey being caressed by his hands. The sheriff barging in made him bolt upright in surprise. "Jaysis, ye put the heart crossway in me, Bill!"

"Sorry. Was there mail?" The House was also the post office.

"Oy, yes! And from hisself, Judge Bristol." L.G. staggered a little as he got an official letter from a warren of mail slots and handed it to the sheriff.

Brady slit it open just to see that it was the signed warrant for Alexander McSween, then shoved it in his overcoat pocket.

"You'll have a dram with me, Major Brady?"

"Oh, don't be troubling yourself."

"Ah, go way outta that, of course ye will." L.G. poured an inch of the rye into a square tumbler and slid it to him. "Cheers," he said as he lifted and finished his own glass, adding, "I always drink with my gun hand, to show my friendly intentions."

The sheriff's deputy George Hindman limped in with another mustached deputy, Jacob B. Mathews, who was also the House's bartender, the clerk at semiannual meetings of the circuit court, and a participant in the thirty-man posse that had hunted down John Henry Tunstall.

"Where's Jimmy?" Hindman asked.

"Out in the beyont," Murphy said. "Havin a whale of a time."

The sheriff swallowed what was left of his whiskey and carefully set the tumbler down. He asked his deputies, "Are we ready for the routine?"

They seemed to be.

He told Murphy, "We have a prisoner to release from jail, and then we'll camp out on McSween's porch. We're told he's heading in from Roswell."

"Hope it's any use," L.G. said and refilled his tumbler with whiskey.

J. B. Mathews later remembered that it was about half nine of the morning.

Sheriff Brady's men went ahead of him, for he was slow and over-weight and far older than his forty-eight years because of the too-muchness of drink.

Ike Stockton's wife, Ellen, was stamping mud from her shoes in front of the McSween house, and the sheriff chatted with her as he caught his breath. "It's a quare cold morning, isn't it?"

"Tis. But will you still be planting on your farm yet?" she asked.

"Ike is."

"Would otherwise with the earth so loose, but my walking plow got banjaxed."

"Ike might could fix it for ya," she said.

"I have tools meself," he said and tipped his hat before heading onto the wooden porch of the Tunstall store, stooping and peering through its windows to see the pretty schoolteacher reading to children from a book.

Hindman called back, "Shall we wait for you, Bill?"

Sheriff Brady stepped off the porch, yelling, "I'll be right there!" Then for some reason he glanced down the alley beside the store to a high gate of upright planks hiding a view into Tunstall's corral. And suddenly the gate swung open and a gang of men stood up and raised their rifles or pistols and fired. Shots hit his gut and wrist and spun him into a fall on the street. Sitting there in a daze, he said, "Oh Lord," and as if recognizing he was late for the train, he struggled to get up, only to be hit with another volley of gunfire, which hammered his left side and back and tore off a chunk of his skull.

Deputy Jacob Mathews ran into Lola Sisneros's house, and Deputy George Hindman was floundering for the Torreón when he was shot in the back just below his gun belt and fell face forward into the puddled street. Rolling over, he held his innards inside the exit wound and gasped with pain. Soon he was calling for water.

Dick Brewer wasn't among them, but William H. Bonney, John

Middleton, Fred Waite, Rob Widenmann, and José Chávez y Chávez were seen walking to the street and standing over the very dead sheriff.

The Kid resisted kicking him but said, "Ooh, that feels good!"

"Don't it?" said Middleton.

Billy hid the jitter of excitement in his hands and grinned with achievement. "We got *even!*" José took the credit for killing the Irishman, and the Kid said, "We *all* did," as he retrieved his confiscated Winchester.

Seeing their slackened wariness, Deputy Mathews fired on them from the Sisneros house, his bullet whapping through Rob Widenmann's trouser leg and scorching his skin before squarely ripping into the Kid's left thigh. Even as he fell, the Kid fired back at Mathews, splintering a doorjamb and sending him into hiding. Then Fred Waite helped Billy up, and he hobbled back to their horses in the corral as the others retreated with them, their guns blazing at nothing much, a stray bullet skewering Juan Batista Wilson's buttocks as he hoed his onion patch on a hillside.

John Middleton frowned at the Kid's leg and said, "You're bleedin."

The Kid gave him a no-kidding look.

The lull was a minute old. Soon other guns would be gotten and there would be a fray in which they were outnumbered. Some Regulators got on their horses as Fred Waite deliberated. "You can't ride like that," he finally told the Kid.

And so Waite and Middleton carried the Kid into the eastern backroom of the Tunstall store, where Harry's bachelor quarters had been. Taylor Ealy, the doctor of medicine whom Alex McSween had hired as a pastor of a still-unbuilt church, was now housed there with his wife, two small children, and Susan Gates, the teenage schoolteacher Dr. Ealy had recruited from Pennsylvania. The Ealy parents were elsewhere, and Susan Gates had been reading aloud *Alice's Adventures in Wonderland* to the children until she heard the guns. Now she rushed to the Kid, for she'd developed a crush on the good-looking, good-natured rogue.

Waite got a hammer, said, "They'll be scouring for him," and efficiently clawed up two wide floorboards.

Hugging his Winchester, the Kid groaned with hurt as he squeezed between the floor joists but offered a false and uneasy smile of good-bye to the schoolteacher, whose hands went to her cheeks in horror as Waite hammered the floorboards over him like the lid of a coffin.

And then Waite and the three other Regulators were galloping out to the east and toward San Patricio, John Middleton halting near the eastern courthouse, the Convento, to fire back at the crowds running to rescue Sheriff Brady and the dying deputy. They scattered.

Deputy Mathews watched the four exit the town and noticed Kid Bonney wasn't with them. Rushing to the Tunstall corral with a few men, he confirmed that the Kid's horse was still hitched there.

In the tight, stifling darkness, the Kid heard the back door crash open as J. B. Mathews shouted, "Where is he?"

"Where's who?" Susan Gates said. The quiet children must have been scared and clinging to her skirt.

Deputy Mathews ignored the schoolmarm, and the Kid heard a lot of boots overhead as the searchers undertook conjectures and interrogatories. He held his breath until in frustration and bewilderment they finally exited and there was silence. Then he heard the children being hustled to the front of the store to join their mother. Susan Gates seemed to be crouching close to him as she said, "Dr. Ealy is here now. He'll get you out."

The floorboards were lifted up again, and the Kid inhaled like he'd been underwater that whole time.

"Let me look at that leg," Ealy said, and the Kid sat on a yellow Empire couch to have his trousers unbuttoned and yanked down to his knees. Susan Gates shyly looked away. "Kerosene," the doctor said, and the schoolteacher carried over a crockery jug of it. The doctor dunked his handkerchief into the coal oil and told the Kid, "I have to hurt you."

Billy nodded.

Dr. Ealy used a pencil to poke the wet handkerchief into the wound of the quadriceps muscle until a quarter inch of the blood-soaked cloth exited the other side. The Kid seized the couch cushions with the agony of it, which only increased when the doctor tugged the handkerchief completely through the injury.

The Kid sighed in the aftermath and said to the ashen Susan Gates, "That was excruciating. I don't recommend it."

"We have to worry about infection," Ealy told him. "The hole won't kill you, but sepsis will." With a sewing needle and thread, he stitched the wound shut at entrance and exit, and the bleeding was stanched.

The Kid asked Susan Gates, "Was I wincing?" and she nodded. His left leg wrapped in a yard of gauze bandage, the Kid hoisted up his trousers and stood. "I have to go," he said and limped outside.

He took a moment to stand over John H. Tunstall's grave near the granary and pray a rest-in-peace and say aloud like an oath, "We're gonna get the rest of em, too." He managed to get onto his horse by boarding it on the right side, and he was the final Regulator to get away. He thought this would be his last visit to Lincoln, and so at the eastern extreme of town he forced himself to painfully stand on his saddle like this was a Wild West show, and he offered those lingerers who knew him a theatrical bow and a roundhouse wave of his sombrero to say goodbye forever.

But Lincoln would see him again.

10

VENDETTA

With Dick Brewer as their captain, the Regulators were on the scout again as soon as April 2. Rumor had it that some of those who'd connived to kill John Henry Tunstall had found shelter for their cowardice on the Mescalero Apache Indian Reservation southwest of Lincoln. Still holding as sacred his "disreputable" warrants for arrest, Brewer collected his allies Charlie Bowdre, Fred Waite, Doc Scurlock, John Middleton, the cousins George and Franklin Coe, and William H. Bonney himself, his gunshot wound resenting each jounce of the saddle. Trotting his horse down the Tularosa Creek, the Kid stayed alongside Brewer like a sidekick, his orphan's longing for a father or highly regarded older brother causing him to revere a hale, valiant twenty-eight-year-old he thought of as royalty.

Brewer spoke of the April Fools' Day assassination just once, solemnly telling the Kid, "I just want it to be known that I would not have advised nor consented to that dastardly act." And then the pair rode in silence for an hour.

On the Tularosa was an eentsy settlement containing a sawmill, a store, some adobe outbuildings, a hotel, and the office of the Mescalero Apache Indian agent. It was named Blazer's Mill after its owner, Dr. Joseph Hoy Blazer, an Iowa dentist and widower who'd tired of the villainous smell of mouths full of decay and chose instead hard labor on the frontier.

It just so happened that Andrew L. "Buckshot" Roberts was in Blazer's Mill and stewing because the mail was late. Off and on Roberts worked for the House, and he was part of the larger sheriff's posse that had sought to chase down John Tunstall, and he was so fearful of being indicted for the crime that he sold his farm on the Rio Ruidoso in March, and on April 3 he rode to the Indian agency's post office, hoping to collect the purchaser's check before seeking anonymity elsewhere. Around eleven in the morning Dr. Blazer saw Roberts waiting in the hotel and warned him he had better hotfoot it because an Apache had told him he'd seen a gang of men sleeping under the juniper fir trees on Apache Summit. The dentist wondered if they mightn't be Regulators.

Roberts gave Blazer a Colorado address where his letter could be forwarded and hurried up into the evergreens, but from a height he saw the mailman's buckboard rolling toward the mill town, and he forced his mule into a sliding, worried jog down the steepness.

The Regulators had arrived while he was gone, but Roberts failed to notice their horses in the corral. Middleton was posted outside the hotel and watched a little man he didn't know hitch his mule, hang his Colt Peacemaker and holster on his saddle horn, and clomp into the post office, a Winchester rifle aslant on his forearm. When Middleton overheard A. L. Roberts give his name to the postmaster, he recognized it as familiar and hurried to tell the Regulators, who were lunching on plates of tamales, frijoles, and mole poblano.

Hearing the offender's name, Brewer immediately stood with concern and announced, "We have a warrant for Roberts."

"I guessed that," Middleton said.

Even an aching old man's rise was impossible for the injured Kid, and when his right hand instinctively reached for his gun, he found air, the landlady having forbidden weapons indoors.

The gregarious Franklin Coe stood, too, and said, "My farm's alongside Buckshot's. Let me talk to him peaceably like a neighbor and get him to surrender."

Brewer permitted it and just pushed his food around with his fork for a while, often turning to hear snatches of Franklin Coe's affable persuasion and Roberts's hot refusals.

George Coe leaned from his bench to listen and commented, "That feller ain't tall but he sure is feisty."

They heard Franklin Coe saying, "You give up and nobody will hurt you," and Roberts saying, "That's what your gang told Morton and Baker."

Coe said more and Roberts said, "No, no, no," and in the dining room Charlie Bowdre grew impatient, clambering up from his bench and hustling outside to grab his pistol, with George Coe, John Middleton, and Doc Scurlock right behind him.

Brewer frowned at the exodus and called, "Oh, go ahead and let him argue, fellas." But the gang followed Bowdre, as did the Kid, who overcame his pain, grinned, and said, "I'd hate to miss this little frolic."

Brewer counseled, "You best just watch, Hop-along."

And then, before the Kid could limp to his friends outside, he heard Bowdre yell, "Roberts, throw up your hands!"

Roberts tilted around Franklin Coe to see Charlie and flatly said, "I don't believe I will," lifting his Winchester up and firing it from his hip just as Bowdre shot his pistol. Franklin Coe saw dust fly off the front and back of Roberts's jacket as he was drilled through his upper intestines. Simultaneously, the Winchester found Bowdre's cowboy belt buckle, the force of the blow knocking him off his boots as the bullet ricocheted into George Coe's gun hand. Blood jetted from his instantly subtracted trigger finger. Roberts still was standing and got off a Winchester shot that caught John Middleton in his chest, just missing the heart, then another shot that blasted into Scurlock's still-holstered pistol and deflected in a fiery scrape down his thigh, and a final shot that caught the Kid in his right sleeve, scarring him with a hot stripe of blood so that he backed up into the hotel, deaf from the noise of so much loud gunfire and watching the gray haze of gun smoke float over three downed Regulators.

Holding his gut, Roberts scuttled downhill to Dr. Blazer's adobe house, far away from his holstered Peacemaker. His Winchester was now empty, but in the house he found an old single-shot infantry model Springfield carbine hanging on hooks over the bed. The front of the house was open country with the Scranton Road and then just sand and scraggle and the creek, so he felt he could fort himself there at the house entrance. With considerable pain and with blood puddling wherever he stopped, he pulled a chain-spring mattress off a four-poster bed, slid it over to the front doorway, and lifted it, propping the Springfield atop the mattress edge to shake out cartridges from a box and push one into the carbine's loading gate.

Dick Brewer took care to see that the Kid was fine, ordered him to pull the injured men inside the hotel, then had to endure the government agent begging him to get his Regulators to just leave and end the donnybrook. Brewer looked at the agent with dismay and decided, "You, sir, are a blithering idiot." He twice glanced down the hill to where Roberts was hidden and told the agent, "I'll have that hombre out if I have to burn the house down." And then he ran out to the footbridge over Tularosa Creek and ducked his way to the sawmill without Roberts firing a shot.

At the south end of the sawmill, Dick Brewer squatted behind some raw pine timber and peeked over to see Roberts hiding beside the framework of the doorway, a carbine laid across a chest-high striped mattress, ninety yards away. Brewer fired but just hit the wooden frame. It fanned out like so many pencils. After waiting a little behind the timber, he lifted up to fire again, but Roberts had seen where the first shot came from and was aimed, his .45 caliber carbine bullet striking off pine before hitting Dick Brewer in his blue left eye and detonating his handsome head.

Buckshot Roberts fell to his seat after killing Dick Brewer, "feeling very ill," he later said, and he lost so much strength he was effortlessly arrested by the Kid and carried unconscious into a parlor in the hotel, where he howled with pain through the night, dying before noon on April 4, the check for his farm sale uncashed. Coughing blood from his damaged lung, fat John Middleton was hauled down to Tularosa Creek to lie in the cold water and drink it until he almost drowned, and George Coe held a cold washrag around his injury through the night, marveling aloud to those who'd listen that the phantom pain made him feel his missing finger was still there and being squeezed in a vise, its nail repeatedly hammered.

A stagecoach ambulance was sent for Middleton and Coe, and Regulator shovels dug side-by-side graves for Andrew L. Roberts and Richard M. Brewer.

Sallie Chisum shrieked in agony when she heard that Richard was killed. The Kid wondered in self-pity if it was his lot in life that anyone he loved or revered would soon be taken from him. And Alex McSween wrote a valedictory letter to the *Cimarron News & Press* calling Brewer "physically faultless; generous to a fault; a giant in friendship; possessing an irreproachable character and unsullied honor; kind, amiable, and gentle in disposition, he was a young man of kingly nature without vices of any kind. Sweet and pleasant be your slumbers, Dick. Ever green and fresh be your memory."

*　　*　　*

The Regulators had been misinformed. Warren Bristol, the cranky associate justice of the supreme court of New Mexico, would convene a grand jury in Lincoln not on April 1, but a week later, on the eighth, and the ten jurors completed their consultations a full ten days later, with none other than Dr. Joseph Hoy Blazer presiding as foreman. Reading the jury's conclusions, he began with the murder of John Henry Tunstall, "which for brutality and malice is without parallel and without a shadow of justification." Jesse Evans, J. B. Mathews, and James J. Dolan were among those indicted for the crime. Excluded because of their recent deaths were Frank Baker, William Scott Morton, and Andrew L. Roberts. Dr. Blazer continued, "We equally condemn the most brutal murder of our late Sheriff William Brady, and his deputy, George Hindman. We find responsible John Middleton, Fred Waite, and William H. Bonney." Seeming to believe they were not the same person, Dr. Blazer wrongly named Henry Antrim, alias Kid, as the killer of Roberts, even though he had not fired his gun. Also indicted for that were Charles Bowdre, John Middleton, Doc Scurlock, and the Coe cousins.

And finally, Dr. Blazer got to the claim that was the initial cause of the killings and counterkillings. "Your Honor charged us to investigate the case of Alexander A. McSween, Esquire, him being charged with the embezzlement of ten thousand dollars belonging to the estate of Emil Fritz, deceased. This we did, but are unable to find any evidence that would justify that accusation. We fully exonerate him and regret that a spirit of persecution has been shown in this matter."

But Alexander A. McSween would not forgive and forget the far worse crimes that followed the accusation. With a note saying it was "Authorized by John Partridge Tunstall of London, England," McSween placed an advertisement in various newspapers offering a five-thousand-dollar reward—a lifetime's income for many then—

"for the apprehension and conviction of the murderers of the English gentleman's son." Saying the "actual murderers are about twenty in number," McSween maintained he would "pay a proportionate sum for the apprehension and conviction of any of them."

The Regulators would seem to have been due some of the five thousand, but no transaction was ever made, possibly because the John H. Tunstall estate owed McSween more than six thousand dollars for the cattle, horses, and farms that were purchased to fulfill Harry's grandiose plans.

Jailed as an accessory to murder, Jimmy Dolan was freed after L. G. Murphy furnished his bail. The Murphy & Company store had been reorganized as Jas. J. Dolan & Co., which McSween condemned as the loathsome "Irish firm." But then even the House ceased doing business as Jimmy took the "extremely indisposed" Major Lawrence Gustave Murphy to Santa Fe for medical treatment at St. Vincent's Hospital and Asylum. There, according to Franklin Coe, "The Sisters of Charity would not let him have whiskey and that cut his living off. He died in a short time and everybody rejoiced over it." His obituary noted that the former officer and store owner, who was just forty-seven, was buried by the Masonic and Odd Fellows fraternities in their cemetery "in the presence of a large concourse of citizens"—all affiliates of the Santa Fe Ring.

The Regulators healed up in San Patricio or on their Rio Ruidoso farms, and aside from a few skirmishes there was relative calm for some time. Governor Axtell took credit for it, having signed a proclamation on May 28, 1878, that appointed as sheriff of Lincoln County George W. "Dad" Peppin, who misspelled his last name to disguise his French heritage and was called "Dolan's affidavit man" because of his willingness to lie for Jimmy under oath. The governor also commanded "all men to disarm and return to their homes and their usual pursuits," and he concluded, "I urge all good citizens to submit to the law, remembering that violence begets violence, and that they who take up the sword shall perish by the sword."

And yet a gang of some twenty roughnecks calling themselves the Rio Grande Posse rode north to Lincoln from Seven Rivers and just hung around the Wortley Hotel and the House's still-open post office for a week, ever on the lookout for Alexander McSween. Rustler and former Army sergeant John Kinney, who founded the Boys, was boss of this outfit, too. William Logan Rynerson, the freakishly tall district attorney who'd studied law with Governor Axtell, had sent Kinney there to help out Jimmy Dolan, who'd gotten Kinney sworn in as a deputy sheriff and promised him five hundred dollars for the assassination of McSween. Were the Rio Grande Posse themselves responsible for the killing, they'd get to divvy up Tunstall's cattle.

Informers got word to the Regulators and the McSweens, who retreated far away from Lincoln, the lawyer and his wife staying in a campaign tent pitched next to a sinkhole at Bottomless Lake east of Roswell. Wearied of waiting, the roughnecks finally took their treachery south.

With the commencement of the torrential rains in late June, John Chisum offered the Regulators the haven of his South Spring hacienda, with its many rooms and fine furnishings, its fragrant orchard and garden, and the pretty, saucy, and alluring Sallie Chisum. The Kid overdressed in his fanciest, trying to cut a swell, as was said then, and Ash Upson later related that Kid Antrim let himself be recognized in the Roswell general store just so he could buy Sallie a box of Cadbury chocolates. Whether the girl was aware the Kid was romancing her isn't certain.

On July 10, Sheriff Peppin, Jimmy Dolan and his ilk, and Deputy Sheriff John Kinney and his mercenaries were in San Patricio shaking down shopkeepers for information about the Tunstall faction, whom they denounced as "Modocs" after the famously rebellious Indian tribe.

Hearing details of it, Alex McSween left his hiding place for the South Spring ranch in order to write a report of the crimes and malfeasance for *The Cimarron News & Press*. And for those Regulators in the house who could not read, Alex stood in the dining room to proclaim his account aloud.

"Headed by Axtell's sheriff and J. J. Dolan," he announced, "the Rio Grande Posse killed and stole horses in San Patricio. They broke windows and doors, smashed boxes of fineries and robbed them of their contents, and from an old widow who was living alone they stole four hundred thirty-eight dollars! They tore the roof off the Dow Brothers Store, threw the dry goods out onto the street, and took for themselves whatever they wanted. With women they used the vilest language when not committing more unspeakable offenses. Citizens working in the fields were fired upon but made good their escape up the river. Kinney said in town that he was employed by the Governor and that he and his men would have to be paid three dollars fifty cents a day by the County, and that the sooner the people helped him arrest the Regulators, the sooner their County would be relieved of his expense. Dolan endorsed the speech."

After finishing his article, Alex McSween fell into a dining room chair as if flabbergasted by the indignities and injustice.

Sallie Chisum heard it all and seemed both faintish and excited by the upheaval, and she turned to the Regulators with wet, gleaming eyes as she theatrically inquired, "What say ye?"

All were silent until the Kid said with vehemence, "We need to end this!"

11

"THE FIRE BECAME PROMISCUOUS"

On Sunday, July 14, Sheriff Dad Peppin, Deputy Sheriff John Kinney, and the majority of his Rio Grande Posse were scouring the hills for their enemies, so they missed seeing Alex McSween's partisans and the Regulators defiantly trotting into Lincoln from the east, now more than sixty in number, their shined ordnance on display, their spurs jingling, their horses nodding as if on parade, each of the Regulators hurrahing and shouting ridicule.

Seeking to control access to the town, Charlie Bowdre, Doc Scurlock, a wheezing John Middleton, and a half dozen others holed up in the easternmost store owned by Isaac Ellis, while George Coe and two others peeled off to domicile in the granary behind the Tunstall store.

About twenty Mexicans, including Martin Chaves, the Regulators' leader pro tem, took over the Montaño house, just across from the castle keep of the Torreón, where five deputy sheriffs were on watch up top but chose to avoid their annihilation by sinking out of view and sharing their quart of Old Joel scamper juice.

Entering through the gate of the picket fence surrounding his property, Alex McSween saw Jimmy Dolan, who was on crutches because he broke a leg jumping from his horse when drunk. Watching McSween glumly from the front of the Wortley Hotel next door, Dolan seemed to be trying to slaughter him with his stare.

Alex shouted, "We have been out in the hills long enough. I have now returned and your ruffians shall not drive me away so long as I live."

Dolan said, "Duly noted."

The Kid took his and Alex's horses to the fenced stable and corral behind the house, and he stole a flecked brown egg from the straw nest in a hot chicken coop where a lot of hens were roosting. Cracking the egg and eating it raw, he looked to see McSween's two black servants, Sebrian Bates and George Washington, watching, but instead of scolding him for his thievery they silently waved him inside through the west wing's unroofed kitchen.

It was a fairly new, twelve-room, U-shaped house with an interior patio separating the wings. It had formerly belonged to L. G. Murphy but was no longer essential to him after he'd constructed his huge House, so he'd deeded it to McSween in exchange for his steep legal fees. The east wing contained the rooms of Alex's law partner, David Shield, and Shield's wife, Elizabeth, Susan McSween's older sister, as well as their three children, although David Shield was dealing with the legislature in Santa Fe. Alex and Susan, who were childless, occupied the west wing, and it was there that twelve in the McSween faction, half of them Mexican, including Billy's cousin Yginio Salazar, were to hunker down for the civil war they foresaw. Slatted shutters were fastened over windows, sandbags were piled in front of the exterior doors, and high walls of adobe bricks were stacked on the sills to fill in all the street-facing plate-glass windows.

The Kid laid his California bedroll down in a sitting room with stacked chairs, a violet Biedermeier sofa, a Singer sewing machine, a Viennese "Regulator" clock, and a bookcase containing *Little Women*, *The Hoosier Schoolmaster*, *Farm Ballads*, and *Marjorie Daw*. With Billy in the sitting room was Harvey Morris, a forty-year-old Kansan who'd ventured farther west in the hope of curing his galloping consumption and was now reading law in order to join the McSween & Shield partnership. With Billy, too, was Thomas O. Folliard, Jr., a red-haired Texan of Irish ancestry, six feet tall, twenty years old, and sixty pounds heavier than the Kid but otherwise similar enough to him in facial features that in an age of few photographs they were frequently mistaken for each other. There was a legend that Tom had just magically shown up in San Patricio, like a rebel angel fallen to earth, without a horse or gun or penny on him, and he told the Kid he wanted to hire on with the Regulators, that "I'm a motherless child and I'm so broke I can't even pay attention."

The Kid took to him instantly and said, "Well, I grew up with nothing and I still got most of it. Welcome to our fraternity."

The Kid handed on his artistry with guns, stole a horse for Tom, and made the recruit a warrior, and it was said that Tom Folliard idolized Billy like a canine, and if there were señoritas who still wanted to dance, Tom would stand outside the *salón de baile* and hold the Kid's horse without noticing if the dancing went on for fifteen more minutes or a few hours.

And now Mrs. Susan Ellen Hummer McSween walked into the sitting room with a tray of glasses and a pitcher of sweet tea. Seeing her regal entrance, Tom and Billy jumped up like schoolboys, swiping off their sombreros to introduce themselves.

She glared at the Kid. "You were one of those hotheads who assassinated Sheriff Brady."

He shied from her scorn and looked at the hooked rug on the floor. "Yes'm."

"Well, you just made matters worse. We had the town on our side up till then. And now we're embattled." She turned from him and strode out.

She was a haughty, handsome woman of thirty-two whose grandparents had been German royalty, or so she said, and even though she was Church of the Brethren, she lied that she'd been raised in a Catholic convent. Even when she married, she gave her maiden name as Homer instead of Hummer, as if she were hiding something, and rather than confess that she and Alex had fled to New Mexico because of their Kansas debts and his fiduciary misconduct, she said they'd sought the climate for his health. She dressed in elegance, clapped her hands when she wanted a servant, and wore an Antilles perfume called Flaming Hibiscus. When he felt a foreboding about his fate in late February, Dick Brewer had made her executrix of his estate. All the Regulators were just as in awe of Mrs. McSween. But William H. Bonney was loathsome to Susan, who later wrote, "I never liked the Kid, and didn't approve of his career. He was too much like Jimmy Dolan and did not think it amounted to much to take another's life."

Sheriff Dad Peppin and the Rio Grande Posse got back to Lincoln on Sunday night and aimed gunshots at the house across the street just because. Regulators in the house and stores fired back, but nobody on either side was much afoot and only a dray horse was accidentally killed. Like a bad penny, Jesse Evans showed up, freed on bail by Judge Bristol until he could stand trial for the murder of John Henry Tunstall. Also joining Dad Peppin were many of the others in the posse Sheriff Brady had sent to chase down the Englishman.

Some guns went off on July 15 but in a lazy kind of way, like an old cuss in a rocking chair spitting sunflower seeds. Because of overcrowding, Susan McSween sent away the servants Sebrian Bates and George Washington, and that Monday night she entertained her houseguests on the parlor organ with "Dear Old Pals," "Early in de Mornin'," and "Time Was When Love and I Were Well Acquainted." Tom Folliard hunched beside her on the bench and she taught him to play "Chopsticks," laughing with gaiety and saying, "Isn't that fun? It was composed in England by a girl just your age."

With some jealousy over Susan's attentions, the Kid later noted that Tom had gotten a haircut.

"Yes, I did."

"You do it yourself? With a bowl and scissors?"

"No, a barber fella helped me."

"Oh, Tom," the Kid said. "He was no help at all."

Folliard went to find a mirror as the Kid stayed up late with Alex McSween, who sipped from a snifter of brandy as he ruminated on their situation. "These are the ruthless devils we're dealing with. The lackeys and foot soldiers of Thomas B. Catron. He became an expert in property law and saw his iniquitous opportunity while looking into the old Spanish and Mexican land grants, held by families for generations. With his former law partner Stephen Elkins, a member of Congress, and himself the United States Attorney for New Mexico, Catron could rule that those land grants were fraudulently platted and were without a clear conveyance of title. Whereby he could steal thirty-four magnificent properties for himself, three million acres! *Connecticut* is only slightly bigger. And the Mexicans lost their farms, their homes, their ancestry. That is why so many of them have affiliated themselves with us. We are redressing a grave injustice in a West where judgments of legality go to the highest bidder or at the insistence of a gun."

The Kid nodded and said in a headstrong way, "We belong to the grievance committee."

"Well put."

The Kid asked, "Would you like me to find a six-shooter for you?"

The former candidate for the ministry seemed to find his misunderstanding repellent. "I cannot conceive of a circumstance in which I would intentionally harm another human being."

Jimmy Dolan, a former corporal there, rode southwest to Fort Stanton on Tuesday morning to lobby Lieutenant Colonel Dudley, the post commander, for his intervention in the "uprising." At an inquiry later both would lie under oath saying the conversation never occurred.

But that Tuesday evening, some Regulators on McSween's flat roof shot at "a colored man" riding in from the west on the Fort Stanton Road. Although he only fell from his horse in dodging the gunfire, he was a federal, a courier with the segregated 9th Cavalry Regiment, on his way to give a message conveying the post commander's promise of assistance to the sheriff.

Lieutenant Colonel Dudley thought the failed shooting was "an infamous outrage." Calling for an investigation of the incident, on Wednesday he sent three officers, including the post surgeon, Major Daniel M. Appel, who'd conducted the postmortem on John Henry Tunstall and doctored the gunshot injuries of Jesse Evans, John Middleton, and George Coe. Major Appel would report that "everything is closed in Lincoln, every home shut up, no one is in the street. In the east end of town there is a faction of men and in the foothills to the south there is another and these worthies are keeping up a persistent and continuous exchange of gunfire."

Also on that Wednesday, Doc Scurlock's bored father-in-law, Fernando Herrera, accepted the challenge to try to nail one of the Boys on the southern hill that was called Chichi because it resembled a woman's breast. Even with a Sharps rifle, it was an impossible distance. The Iowan "Lallycooler" Crawford was no more than an iota up there in the scraggle near the hill's nipple, but Herrera managed to shatter Crawford's spine, paralyzing him with what Herrera's congratulating chums called "among the great examples of marksmanship." And when the Army surgeon and his soldier aides floundered up the steep hillside to rescue the fatally injured Crawford, Regulators stupidly shot at them, too. Major Appel reported, "We thought the shots came from the Montaño house, judging from the loud whistling of bullets within a few feet of us."

In June 1878, Congress had forbidden the use of the military in a civil affair unless it seemed an insurrection. The post commander now felt that was the case. Lieutenant Colonel Nathan A. M. Dudley was a monocled, fifty-three-year-old bachelor and alcoholic with a gray whisk broom of a mustache and a Prussian officer's fierce and fixed ideas. Earlier he'd been court-martialed for disobedience, conduct unbecoming, and drunkenness on duty, but received only a verdict of forfeiture in pay and a short suspension due to the skillful lawyering of Thomas B. Catron. So Dudley was yet another who was beholden to the Santa Fe Ring and inclined to benefit a friend when he read the note from Jimmy Dolan (but signed by the illiterate Sheriff Peppin) stating:

> *If it is within your power to loan me one of your howitzers, you would confer a great favor on the majority of the people of this County, who are being persecuted by a lawless mob.*

Ever consistent in his bad judgment, Lieutenant Colonel Dudley, four officers, and a caravan of the 9th Cavalry Colored Regiment entered Lincoln around noon on Friday, July 19, with horse teams pulling a Gatling gun served by a feed of two thousand rounds, as well as a field howitzer cannon that fired a twelve-pound shell. Establishing his camp in midtown and frankly heralding whose side he was on, Lieutenant Colonel Dudley ordered the howitzer trained on the José Montaño store and house where the Mexican Regulators who'd shot at the post surgeon were on a cautious watch. And then he smoked a cigar in relaxation on a folding canvas chair as Dolan's men jockeyed for position in hiding places around McSween's house, including the horse stables of his backyard.

Seeing the cannon aimed at them and anticipating their obliteration, the Mexican Regulators waited only a few minutes before they scurried from the Montaño house to Isaac Ellis's store in the east. But the artillery officer merely redirected the howitzer. Soon both groups of McSween men were hurrying out to their horses and racking off for the foothills across the Rio Bonito. The Gatling gun traced each of them in their retreat, a sergeant saying "Pow pow pow" as he pretended to mow them down, his lieutenant having wisely denied him permission to shoot.

Alex McSween found relaxation only in work, so that Friday he wrote a carefree note to Postmaster Ash Upson in Roswell, requesting he send postage stamps and promising to help with establishing a school; then he sent a check to *Scribner's Monthly*, renewing his subscription.

Seeing his calm, John Middleton imitated Alex by writing a jaunty letter to his former employer, saying, "We have taken the town." After listing the killed and wounded on both sides, he noted, "Everything is fair in war. Seen Jim Reese the other morning walking down the street. Cried because he is on the wrong side but he cain't get out of it. All of them have taken an oath to stand by each other unto death, so I guess we will kill a lot of them afore they skedaddle."

The Kid took a ladder up to the roof and crept from the west wing to the east to scan the area, seeing in the north the majestic limestone castle of El Capitán looming over the greenery that moated it, and just beyond McSween's backyard was the gurgling, crystal-clear Rio Bonito. To the south the sheriff's men and a hundred soldiers freely walked about with guns at the ready, as if just waiting for an officer's instruction to overwhelm the Regulators. Hearing a man yell, "Hey, Billy!" he looked to the House and saw his old friend Johnny Jones waving and grinning on the veranda.

The Kid smiled as he called back, "Dang, Johnny! You siding with the devil?"

"Whoever's got the mostest cash!"

"Well, if you get the chance you'll make sure to miss me, won't ya?"

Johnny shrugged. "Reckon I'll have others to shoot at."

The Kid laddered back down and went to the sitting room. Alex McSween was standing with his Holy Bible and reading Psalm 86 aloud to Yginio Salazar and Vincente Romero, who were lolling on the floor. " 'Bow down thine ear, O LORD, hear me: for I am poor and needy. Preserve my soul; for I am holy: O thou my God, save thy servant that trusteth in thee. Be merciful unto me, O LORD: for I cry unto thee daily. Rejoice the soul of thy servant: for unto thee, O LORD, do I lift up my soul.'"

Cued by Alex McSween's fear and trembling, the Kid stood over the parlor organ to write a farewell letter on the upper-board. He was halfway through when Susan McSween noticed him hunched over his handwriting.

She asked, "Even in such jeopardy, you're writing a letter?" With the effrontery of the privileged, she looked over his shoulder. "To Miss Sallie Chisum! Well, she is a *darling* girl." She lifted the letter and frowned as she read it, even sighing. She tore the letter up as she said, "Oh, Billy, this will not *do* at all. Here, let me help you."

On July 20, just the next day, Miss Sallie Chisum received a hand-written letter from the Kid but dictated by Susan McSween:

My darling Sallie,

The indications are very strong that we shall have a battle soon, and I feel impelled to jot down a few lines that may fall under your eyes when I shall be no more. I have no misgivings about the cause in which I am joined. We are dauntless. Yet I fear you do not yet recognize that you have filled my heart with longing and my love for you is deathless. Oh Sallie, the memories of the blissful moments I have spent with you overwhelm me, and I feel most gratified to God and to you that I have enjoyed such cordial regard in your uncle's home. It is my intent to return to you unharmed but if I do not, please know, my dear Sallie, that I will whisper your name with my last dying breath.

Yours truly,
Billy

*　　*　　*

Within the hour on July 19, Deputy Bob Olinger, a lout and bully who'd joined up with the Rio Grande Posse, hunched across Main Street to crowbar the shutters off McSween's front windows. His accomplice smashed the plate glass and toppled the heaped adobe bricks on the sills. Olinger shouted inside, "I have warrants for you and others in the house. Will you surrender?"

Alexander McSween called, "We have warrants for *you!*"

Olinger was at a loss and could only inquire, "Where are they?"

The Kid yelled from inside, "Our warrants are in our guns, you cocksucking sons-of-bitches!"

His foul language caused Alex McSween to give him a disapproving glance.

Meanwhile John Kinney and some of his Boys were hauling lumber to the east side of McSween's house, the only property the Regulators still firmly held. Inside they were hot and stinking and without water. Alex went to the east wing and heard lumber being stacked and Kinney calling for kerosene.

McSween hastily wrote a note in pencil, and his ten-year-old niece, Minnie Shield, walked it to the commanding officer in the folding chair. Lieutenant Colonel Dudley read:

Would you have the kindness to let me know why soldiers surround my house? Before blowing up my property I would like to know the reason.

Nathan Dudley replied that he sought no correspondence with Alexander McSween and, deliberately misreading the lawyer's syntax, he stated in his note,

If you desire to blow up your own house, the commanding officer does not object.

Kinney's fire on the east wing of the house wouldn't catch or was doused, but Andrew J. Boyle, formerly a rowdy British soldier in Scotland and now a Seven Rivers rancher, flung lit dried wood soaked in kerosene into the outdoor kitchen of the west wing. Some firewood was stacked there, and dish towels and aprons, and flames soon crawled over the adobe walls as though ravenous for paint.

The Kid was the first to smell the acrid smoke, and he ran down the hallway with a Shaker broom, intending to swat out the flames, but he found a conflagration. And when he gave extinguishing the fire a go, he was shot at from the stables.

When he got to Alex McSween, he reported what was happening, and Tom Folliard, overhearing, said, "Don't worry. All is not lost."

McSween asked in exasperation, "If all is not lost, where the hell *is* it?"

The fire's fierce appetite shifted southward to the McSween quarters, and with temperatures nearing a thousand degrees, the hallway wallpaper curled, then blackened, then chafed into flying ash. The adobe bricks burned like charcoal. The houseguests backed up from room to room to avoid the heat and lung-racking smoke, and were soon crowded into the front parlor, their clothing drenched in sweat, handkerchiefs and dish towels held over their noses and mouths to inefficiently filter out the fouled air.

Harvey Morris looked out at forty soldiers and civilians waiting by the front fence and its south gate, and told no one in particular, "We're in a damned-if-you-do, damned-if-you-don't situation."

Alexander McSween said with despair, "I have no idea what to do," and fell onto a sofa, his head in his hands as though doomed. "I seem to have mislaid my mind."

His wife sat on the bench of her parlor organ and seemed to be itemizing all the expensive possessions they'd lose soon. Wood smoke grayly filled the room like a dense fog. Walls were hot as radiators.

Little Jimmy Dolan now tilted forward on his crutches to drunkenly watch indigo clouds of smoke roil up from the house next door to the Wortley Hotel. His room's plate-glass window so scalded his out-reached hand that he withdrew to the hallway to continue his staring.

Erratically choosing action, then inaction, Lieutenant Colonel Dudley was eating dinner from a mess kit and worrying that no women and children were exiting the incinerating house. He'd intended to explain to higher-ups his presence in Lincoln with a previously com-posed memorandum that he was going there "to protect women and children; and we shall not take sides." Charred bodies would not do. So he was relieved at nightfall to see five enlisted men hitch a wagon and go into the Tunstall store to get the Ealy belongings and to escort out of town Dr. Taylor and Mrs. Ruth Ealy, their two small children, and the schoolteacher Susan Gates.

Seeing the Ealys getting into an Army wagon and heading for Fort Stanton, Susan McSween ran next door waving a white handkerchief over her head and accosted a captain who was rolling a cigarette while lean-ing lazily against a post of the mercantile store. "We have three horrified children in that house," she cried. "I beseech you to give them protection."

The captain turned to Dudley, and he nodded. Hostilities ceased as Susan McSween, Elizabeth Shield, and the coughing Shield children walked out of the house and got into a navy blue Army ambulance. Once they were gone, a hail of bullets recommenced going every whichway, though actual human targets were lacking.

The captain looked at his master sergeant, a veteran of Chickam-auga and Marietta as well as the Indian wars. He asked, "What's your estimate of the gunfire? How many rounds have been shot?"

"Just today?"

"Yes."

The master sergeant seemed lost in arithmetic, then answered, "About two thousand."

Watching the dragon of fire grow wings, the captain told his master sergeant, "If the poor devils still in that hellhole get away, they're entitled to their freedom."

In the house, the Kid said, "We can't just stay here and fry." With handkerchiefs to their faces, they all turned at the sudden liveliness. "I'm thinking a few of us might could sneak out the kitchen for the east gate. We'll draw fire and distract the shooters enough that you can get out the river gate and slide down to the Rio Bonito."

The crack and collapse of an overhead joist fostered their agreement.

Harvey Morris, José Chávez y Chávez, and of course Tom Folliard joined the Kid in hanging out by the east wing's kitchen. The Kid took the loan of a gun for his left hand to twin with his right and was, as usual, smiling. "Okay, how do we get outta this?" he asked. When they frowned, he said, "Quick, fast, and in a hurry." And he took the lead in crouching outside into a night illumined by the bonfire of the once stately home before he raced to the east gate.

John Kinney's men and a few infantry and cavalry soldiers noticed and fired at his party, felling Harvey Morris before he'd gone three yards. But the Kid was shrewd and sudden at whatever he did. Gun sights would find and then lose him. Certain kills ended up cracking pickets and chopping dirt. With his Regulators running past him, the Kid fired with both hands like a trick shot artist, finally holding his aim on the face of his former employer, John Kinney, and in a rare miss shooting off only a wing of his mustache. The Kid then jumped the picket fence and took a hunkered run for the tamarisks alongside the Rio Bonito, followed by those who'd joined him.

They escaped homicide but others did not. Waiting by the north gate on the east side of the backyard were the Seven Rivers ranchers and possemen Robert Beckwith, Ma'am Jones's son Johnny, and Andy Boyle. Jones and Beckwith hated each other because of a cattle dispute, but they had been ordered by Kinney to position themselves near McSween's chicken coop. They saw McSween run out of his house with some Mexicans around nine p.m., but with the barrage of gunfire from the sheriff's men, they hustled back inside.

Andy Boyle later recalled, "Then the fire became promiscuous. And that was the time the big killing was made."

Robert Beckwith shouted, "I am a deputy sheriff and I have got a warrant for your arrest!"

A half minute passed in a lull as Alex McSween considered his dilemma, and then he called out, "Will you take us as prisoners?"

"I have come for that precise purpose!"

McSween then stated, "I shall surrender!"

Beckwith walked cautiously toward McSween's voice and found him crouching near the east kitchen against an exterior wall. Alex was without a gun, but when Deputy Beckwith held out a hand to help him stand, McSween so hated the loss of his possessions and his livelihood that he changed his mind, yelling, "I'll *never* surrender!"

An infantry soldier mistaught by the Indian wars took that as an invitation, and in friendly fire killed Robert Beckwith with a head shot.

Johnny Jones just considered the soldier with curiosity, like he'd been calculatingly rude, then he looked back at the scene. Hundreds of bullets chattered at Alexander McSween's crew, with the Canadian stuttering forward in his dying walk, hit four times from waist to neck until a shot located his skull and he fell dead, his three flourishing years in Lincoln ended by gunfire from every whichway. Vincente Romero and Francisco Zamora were next to die, and then the youth Yginio Salazar was hit with gunshots to his shoulder and back.

All was still except for a few far-off gunshots that popped like fiesta firecrackers. John Kinney and his Rio Grande Posse delicately walked into the yard to stand over the bodies and watch for breathing.

Oozing blood and playing possum, Salazar felt his ribs kicked testingly by Andy Boyle and heard Kinney say, "Don't waste a shot on that greaser, he's dead as a herring." Even as scavengers looted the Tunstall store and the victors celebrated with whiskey, Salazar waited.

The officers and men from Fort Stanton joined in the anarchy for a while but, once filled with rations and drink, were ordered into their tents and slept without nightmares of having done nothing to halt the bloodshed, help the wounded, or even bury the many dead, whose bodies stayed overnight where they'd fallen.

An hour before dawn, when only a few infantry guards were not sleeping, Yginio Salazar finally risked his hesitant, bloodletting crawl for help, squirming forward on his belly for more than a mile to reach the home of Miguel Otero. Much later Miguel would recall that Yginio told him in Spanish, "Even in our great danger, the Kid was the coolest man I ever saw."

Lieutenant Colonel Dudley took pride in waking before five, and he was fully dressed and inhaling the fresh morning air when he strolled to the incinerated house at sunrise, seeing only embers and ashes and a few kites of smoke. Robert Beckwith had been carried away by other deputies, but Harvey Morris, Alexander McSween, Vincente Romero, and Francisco Zamora were just where they'd fallen eight hours earlier. Some hungry chickens were pecking at their faces. In a gesture he thought of as gallant, the post commander found a patchwork quilt that had been looted from the Tunstall store and slung it over Alexander A. McSween's corpse, scattering hens, then he headed for a hot coffee.

- 12 -

ADRIFT

Excited, jittery, and still electrified by the threat of death, the Kid snuck back into Lincoln that night and stole cavalry horses for himself and Tom Folliard. Then they splashed north across the Rio Bonito to the foothills where Regulators in hiding whistled to them. They congregated on a mesa, and each squatted with his soft horse's head next to his own, reins in hand just in case there were soldier pursuers. A few partook of some kitchen rye. His heart still hectic with the could-haves of the murderous night, the Kid even smoked one of Fred Waite's machine-made cigarettes just to see if it would calm his jangling nerves.

Doc Scurlock read his Elgin pocket watch in the moonlight and announced, "Almost three in the morning. I was about to siwash."

Tom Folliard asked, "What's that mean?"

"Sleep. Old Indian term."

Charlie Bowdre told Billy, "Real sorry we had to absquatulate earlier."

Tom Folliard began to ask, "What's ab—"

"Decamp," Doc Scurlock said. "Hurry off. Leave abruptly."

"It's just a word," said Bowdre and returned to Billy. "We was sore tormented that they had that howitzer square on us so we hightailed it, but we sorta made you boys the escapegoats."

125

"Well, at least a few of us got through it."

Because he thought it needed saying, George Coe added, "And the rest dint."

Heads hung for a while. And then there was some desultory conversation about their footing from here on out.

Each recognized that the Lincoln County War was essentially over and they were on the losing side. A seemingly petty grocery store rivalry had conjoined some cattlemen's resentment of John Chisum's financial success and caused not only civil unrest and a number of murders but the closing of both vying stores that were at the origin of the struggle. And now the Regulators with other options were choosing to head elsewhere: the Mexican farmers to San Patricio and its outlying *placitas* and the Coe cousins perhaps traipsing north to farm in Colorado. Fred Waite wondered about a return to his father's prosperity in the Indian Territories; and Doc Scurlock and Charlie Bowdre thought they might could rejoin the sisters waiting for them on the Rio Ruidoso in order to get their gatherings and hire on as wranglers on the Jinglebob.

It would be remembered as "a war pow-wow." Franklin Coe noticed the Kid's silence and asked, "You got plans?"

The Kid stubbed out the Pearl of the Orient cigarette after inhaling again, coughing, and disliking it. "It's odd," he said, "but with the gun battle and risks and all, this is the most complete I've ever felt. So I guess it's not all over with me. I'm gonna steal myself a living until I feel revenged."

Eighteen years old, rootless, and jobless, Billy Bonney fell into a drifting life of catch as catch can, with horse thievery his main occupation. But first he went to visit Carlota in San Patricio just a few hours later on July 20, finding her heating tortillas in a skillet in the family hacienda with her overweight mother, Sofia, and Aunt Hortensia. Carlota shrieked with astonishment and joy when she saw him at the front door, calling him "*Chivato*," the Mexican-Spanish for Kid, and running to hug him as she kissed him over and over again.

"*Así da gusto verte*," he said. So good to see you.

She said she'd heard about the killings in Lincoln; she hadn't heard if he'd been among the dead.

"*Estoy vivito*," he said. I'm very alive.

Her mother and aunt welcomed "Bee-ly" into their casa like a prodigal son but were not beyond urging some morning ablutions upon him, for he'd been a few days without benefit of so much as a cat lick. Returning from the yard pump, his tawny hair still wet, he found a feast of huevos rancheros and cinnamon churros. Carlota was as close as a coat sleeve to him as she said, "*Mi madre te llama Ojos Brillantes*." My mother calls you Bright Eyes. "*Ella piensa que eres muy guapo*." She thinks you're very handsome.

"*Me veo feo*," he said. I'm feeling ugly. "*No he dormido*." I haven't slept.

Sofia heavily fell into a chair at the dinner table just across from the Kid and watched him like his famished eating was merry entertainment. After he'd cleaned his plate she asked, "*Ya terminaste?*" Are you finished?

"*Todo muy rico*," he said. Everything was excellent.

She folded her arms in front of her shelf of a chest as if in the midst of a quarrelsome transaction. "*Tenemos que hablar*," she said. We need to talk. In Spanish, Carlota's mother noted that the girl was fifteen now and therefore free to marry. She herself had married at fifteen, Tía Hortensia at fourteen. Carlota, she knew, pined for El Chivato; she no longer wanted to be just his *novia*, sweetheart, or even his *querida*, his lover. She wanted to be his *desposada*, bride.

Carlota softly whispered in the Kid's ear, "*Déjame embarazada*." Make me pregnant. "*Quiero un Billito*." I want a little Billy.

Carlota's mother overheard but just shrugged as she shifted to the main problem, telling Billy in Spanish that she thought of him as generous, heroic, a man of justice, the enemy of their enemies. She was glad when she heard the Kid was avenging the Spanish people even if he was not fully aware of it. She said in the English he didn't know she knew, "We sees you one of us."

"*Pero?*" he asked. But?

Well, he was *encantador y atractivo*, enchanting and attractive. Little wonder that Carlota was in love with him.

Carlota squeezed her arm inside his and tilted her sweet head on his shoulder.

But he would not be a good husband or father, Sofia told him.

Carlota cried in shock, "*Mama, no!*"

Sofia had heard he was wanted for murder in Arizona and New Mexico, so she realized Billy could never rest. Endlessly on the run and forever hounded, even in Mexico if he went there. She'd experienced American justice for the have-nots. Soon his name would be famous and rewards for him would be posted. Would he live a few years longer? Yes, perhaps. But gunmen end up in coffins so quickly. And she did not raise her child to become a widow at fifteen, eighteen, twenty.

"*Lo comprendo,*" the Kid said. I understand.

There was more, of course, Carlota crying in a childish, passionate tantrum and all three females yelling loudly and stomping and throwing their hands around. All during the dither the Kid found himself thinking how tired of wild emotion he was, how very much older than pretty Carlota he felt, and how piffling and unimportant the caterwauling seemed after all he'd been through, the dying he'd seen, the kill shots he'd avoided. So he got up from the table, hatted himself with his sombrero, and quietly exited the casa like his feet were on hot coals.

When she noticed he was gone, Carlota screamed "Bee-ly!" but she must have been restrained from running to him. And as he got onto his stolen cavalry horse, all that the Kid could think was *Another person subtracted.*

On the first day of August, Dr. Joseph Hoy Blazer got into an altercation with Morice J. Bernstein, the twenty-two-year-old bookkeeper for the Mescalero Apache Indian Agency headquarters at Blazer's Mill. The Iowa dentist accused the Englishman as well as the Indian agent there, an Army major, of funneling food and commodities intended for the Apaches to Jimmy Dolan for reselling. Which was probably true. Hidden in Bernstein's ledgers, Blazer argued, were faint penciled notes on the secret transactions. In high dudgeon, the feisty bookkeeper claimed he'd done no such thing and called Joseph Blazer a bloody liar.

Witnesses saw Blazer furiously stare at Bernstein before flatly announcing, "No one can call me a liar and stay alive."

On August 5, for old times' sake, a final collection of Regulators rode to Blazer's Mill to visit the grave of Dick Brewer. The Kid felt overheated, and he was joined by some parched Anglo friends as he veered off to dismount alongside a shaded mountain stream. He and Waite and the Coes knelt to dunk their faces in the water and drink, just as their horses did. And there they heard the gunfire of a disturbance among some off-the-reservation Apaches and Mexican Regulators, among them Atanacio Martínez, the former Lincoln constable. The Apaches thought the Regulators were there for some more horse stealing. Which was not yet true.

"Morris" Bernstein and the Indian agent were allotting salted meat rations to some Apache women when the bookkeeper also heard the gunfire and left his government office to ride out and calm things.

Seeing his opportunity, Dr. Blazer went from the mill to his house to get the Springfield carbine that Andrew Roberts had used to kill Dick Brewer, and he cantered his horse until he was just behind the bookkeeper. The Apaches and the Mexicans were already straggling away from each other and were shocked when they saw Blazer lift the carbine and fire it just inside Bernstein's left shoulder blade, where he knew the heart was. Bernstein fell dead into the tall blond cheatgrass. Blazer got off his horse and the Apaches and Mexicans got onto theirs, scattering elsewhere. Anglo trouble, not theirs.

Inventing in his head a gun battle with the Englishman as the luck-less victim, Blazer used Bernstein's pistol to kill him three more times, then changed the tale into an Apache robbery, collecting all the book-keeper's worldly goods, even turning his pockets out. Then he went back to the hotel, claiming he'd been running the Belsaw in the mill. Was that gunfire he'd heard?

The Kid's horse had scared with the gun noise and scrambled away, so he had to hop up behind George Coe and latch on to his waist as they loped toward a final three oddly successive gunshots. But they happened into the peeved and shot-at Apaches, who took off after them, rifles raised. Coe spun his horse around, and he and the Kid went to fleeing, hanging off to the side of the horse like trick riders do in Wild West shows to avoid more than fifty zipping bullets until the Apaches got bored with the chase and rode elsewhere, whooping and caterwauling in victory.

And then there was nothing for the Regulators to do but steal all the Indian agency's horses and mules in what they reckoned was fair trade for the disquietude they'd put up with.

Because it was a federal problem involving the military, Lieutenant Colonel Dudley ordered a thorough investigation, and an Army cap-tain interviewed all those staying at Blazer's Mill, each with a vested interest in agreeing to the owner's fiction. The investigator suspected anti-Jewish prejudice was behind the homicide, but only noted in his report that "Dr. Blazer neither expressed surprise nor regret at the murder of Mr. Bernstein, nor sympathy for his friends. He also insinuated to me that Mr. Bernstein frequently tampered with his letters."

Weighing all the evidence, there was only one thing Lieutenant Colonel Dudley could think to do: indict "the McSween band of outlaws" and "Antrim, known as Kid" for the cold-blooded murder.

Cavalrymen were sent over hill and dale in pursuit of him and were told one night he was holed up in the *jacal* of a Mexican sheepherder and his wife. In spite of their hammering continually on the flimsy door and hollering for access, it took some minutes for the nightgowned wife to let the cavalry in, excusing her tardiness with the claim of deep sleep. Some friction matches were lit. The *jacal* was just one earthen-floored room with some kitchenware, a few pieces of parlor furniture, and a high bed that the couple huddled together on, their stocking feet dangling. There was nothing more to see. "We been duped," a corporal said, and the hunting party left in a huff.

Hearing the hooves of the horses grow faint, the husband and wife scooted down and hauled the upper mattress that did not belong there off the hiding Kid.

With laughter he admitted, "I just about suffocated." And then he was too excited to sleep so he entertained them by singing in his Irish tenor "Beautiful Dreamer," "Aura Lee," and "Turkey in the Straw."

In frustration Lieutenant Colonel Dudley recalled his hapless cavalry to the fort.

Jimmy Dolan and his crew rustled a hundred John H. Tunstall cattle that were still being held for probate, so in a tag-you're-it, the Kid and his crew stole the Jimmy Dolan horses corralled on the ranch owned by kin of the deceased Emil Fritz. Included among the stock was an Arabian sorrel that was branded BB, being the horse that Sheriff Bill Brady rode into Lincoln on the day he was assassinated. The Kid took that sorrel as his own, saying the brand stood for Billy Bonney.

On the Kid's initiative, they took the herd to John Chisum's vast Jinglebob Ranch on the Pecos River, Billy presuming Chisum's hundreds of cowboys would be continually in need of fresh animals, and also hoping Sallie Chisum would still be there. She was. She hugged the Kid with delight and kissed his cheek and called him Willy, Sallie's proprietary name-changing being his first clue as to her new hankering. She looked over his shoulder at Waite, Folliard, Middleton, and the Coe cousins, still mounted and smirking or squirming over the public display of affection. She called, "We only have room enough for Willy here. But you all can find cots in the bunkhouse."

There were vulgarities and catcalls from his friends as they urged the stolen horses into a fenced corral.

Sallie linked her forearm inside his to guide the Kid down a wide hallway air-conditioned by a middle ditch of flowing water that was called an *acequia*. Crossing an interior footbridge, she told him he needed to heel his boots off because Uncle John hated filth on his fine Wilton carpets. She told him he could have Uncle's room as his lair. She'd have the maid heat water for his bath. Were those his only clothes? Well then, she'd find him some nice things in Uncle's closet. And as he was beginning to get undressed, she paused at his bedroom door to say, "Ever since you sent me that lovely letter from Lincoln, during the outrage, I have been thinking of you with such felicity and fondness."

Shying a little, he confessed that Susan McSween had helped him with it.

"Really?" she said. "Forsooth? But the sentiments were yours?"

He smiled. "Verily."

She evaluated him like a worried schoolteacher. "You're so adult now, so brazen, so something-or-other. I feel like I'm meeting you for the first time."

"I'll take real pleasure in getting acquainted."

She flirtatiously smiled, then turned away with "Ta ta."

The Kid took a bath in the kitchen with Sallie's teenage brothers, Walter and William, hunching forward on chairs near his scrubbing-up and questioning him about his storied role in the Lincoln gun battle. Walter offered to use a scullery brush on him but was denied, and William wrapped him in a voluptuous towel as the Mexican and Navajo cooks smiled at his nakedness and Billy scurried to his room. There Sallie had laid out John Chisum's scavenged "morning wear" of laced-up drawers, knee stockings, an overlarge black frock coat, gray trousers and a silver waistcoat, a white shirt with pleated front and a stiff white collar, and a cravat he chose not to wear to avoid the comments of the five comedians who'd be joining them for dinner.

The loyal friends Billy called Ironclads took off their guns, hats, and boots as instructed, but the noise was not softened as their footfalls shook the silverware and chair legs shrieked with their seatings. Each was as spruced as possible, his hair still wet, and even the Coe cousins' hillbilly beards had been scissored and combed. Sallie was the lone woman at the feast and reveled in the Regulators' smitten attentiveness, quietly queenly as she encouraged topics of conversation or ordered food to be passed counterclockwise, affectedly demurring when she was flattered, and often letting a hidden hand rest on the Kid's thigh. Quoting her uncle, she'd said, "Eat till you get tired, boys."

"Oh my yes," Tom Folliard said. "It's my intention to get stuffed like a turkey."

Fred Waite announced, "Well, I don't know where to start first, it all looks so edible."

"You lead the way and we'll precede," Charlie Bowdre offered.

"Proceed," Doc Scurlock corrected.

"Wasn't no one dint unnerstand him," George Coe maintained.

Doc noted in his Louisiana drawl, "But I have a jealous regard for the Queen's English."

Billy asked, "Would you like some pot roast, John?"

And Middleton said, "Is it good to eat or will it just do?" And then he said, "Just kidding, Miss Chisum."

Charlie Bowdre asked Doc, "Taters?"

And Doc said, "Lord no. I'm still gnashing this corn."

Charlie asked their hostess, "We savin the cobs for the privy?"

Sallie primly said no.

Franklin Coe asked the Kid, "Could you give me just a smidgen of that gravy for this biscuit?"

Billy passed the tureen as Sallie's hand got ever more personal with him. He was so distracted he did not feel at liberty to speak, nor could he stand without the ridicule of his friends over his evident excitement.

Sallie invited the men to discuss the secretary of the interior's overdue suspension of Governor Axtell and the gossip that President Hayes would replace him with Indiana's adjutant general, Lew Wallace.

There were no takers except for Charlie Bowdre, who scoffed, "They's all so crooked they could hide behind a corkscrew."

"Look at me just putting these victuals away," Tom Folliard said. "I cain't seem to quit."

George Coe asked, "Would there be pie comin, Miss Chisum?"

She nodded. "There's pie."

"And here I'm about to explode," a hefty John Middleton said.

Charlie Bowdre frowned at Walter and William Chisum. "You boys is awful silenced," he said.

Sallie lifted her hand from the Kid's lap as she answered, "According to their uncle, children should be seen but not heard."

The taller teenage boy groused, "We're not children." But he hung his head low.

Sallie dabbed her mouth with a linen napkin and said in a regal way, "I have attained a sufficiency. I do hope you all have enjoyed your dinner."

The Regulators lavished praise on it.

The Navajo cook carried in two hot apple pies with latticed crusts, and Franklin Coe asked, "How'd you get them pie crusts to do like that?"

The Navajo just smiled since English was not available to her when she was tired.

Sallie rose up, thanked the cook in rudimentary Athabaskan, and softly touched the Kid's hair, saying, "Willy, will you join me on the veranda?"

Tom Folliard leered as he hooted, "Hoo hoo, Kid!"

She sat next to him in the sloped leather Mexican chairs that were called *butacas*. She seemed about to comment on the flashing riot of stars overhead but instead inquired if the Kid had read William Shakespeare's *Twelfth Night*.

"Of course not," he said. Weeks ago, he thought, he would have self-consciously lied that he had.

She said, "There's a line sung to a girl: 'Journeys end in lovers' meeting.' Which I feel has happened here. With us. And then: 'What is love? Tis not hereafter. *Present* mirth hath present laughter. What's to come is still unsure. In delay there lies no plenty, then come kiss me, Sweet-and-twenty. Youth's a stuff will not endure.'"

"You're the Sweet-and-twenty?"

"Aren't you the clever one?"

"And I agree with that last part about youth. Ain't everlasting."

She hesitated as if second-guessing what she'd say next. She finally got out, "We're free spirits, we two. Anarchists, even. I'm fairly sure I'd be an outlaw if I were male, and what I'm about to propose is rather illicit."

The Kid confessed, "I'd tell you I like where this is heading, but I'm afraid I'd spook you off your conclusion."

She did not smile as she said, "No. You shan't." She looked off at nothing at all. "I have to go back to Denton, Texas, soon, and I have decided you should be the one to relieve me of my virginity."

"Hell yes, Sallie! I feature you in my favorite dreams."

She seemed far more straitlaced as she inquired, "Are you in possession of a so-called French letter?"

"Weeks ago I got a tin of Merry Widow sheaths at the *farmacia* just in case. Charlie calls them cum-dumbs."

The Regulators were then loudly trooping out of the hacienda, with Charlie offering all those in the bunkhouse some of his flask of tonsil paint.

Doc Scurlock asked Sallie, "When's your uncle get back?"

"Tomorrow."

"We'd sort of like to hire on with his outfit."

"Like I say: tomorrow." And when she and the Kid were alone again, she kissed him in a soft, nibbling, playful, pliant way. She said, "I feel like I should thank the girl who taught you how to kiss. You're far above average."

"You, too. You got my head reeling."

She whispered close to his ear, "I'll go to my room and make preparations. Wait ten minutes and just silently enter."

He took off Uncle John's fine clothing and with nothing at all on tiptoed to a door that swung open with just a tap of his finger. Sallie had kept a lacemaker's lamp lit so he could see her luxuriantly naked on a wealth of pillows like that fleshy female in the harem painting he'd seen years ago at the Two Galoots Saloon. Billy Antrim had called it an odalisque, but said "don't ask me to spell it." Sallie's face seemed concerned, as if she were evaluating the Kid's evaluation. She'd shaken her blond hair loose and let it fall. Even the hair of the crotch her thighs tightly clenched was blond. Sallie's breasts were so often confined in high-necked and corseted gowns that the Kid was surprised at how ample they were, but now flattening sideways over her ribs, the pink nipples as wide as dollar coins.

The Kid was so hard he ached.

She said, "You look nice, Willy. Bring yourself over to me." Because there were no windows, there was no moonlight, so she merely turned down the lamp wick as he walked over to her. "I haven't touched one before," she said as she did so with some childish medical curiosity before furtively licking the head and shaft and then closing her soft mouth around it while nodding.

"You're pretty good at that for a virgin," he said.

"I *read*." She returned to him and continued voraciously as he slid onto the narrow bed. She quit and said, "You're getting too excited."

"Shall I pleasure you instead?"

She smiled. "Are you *quoting*? Have you been reading, too?"

"Yes'm. *The Lustful Turk*."

"And you've been with whores?"

"But not lately."

"So you have no real experience in pleasuring a lady." She lay back and said, "I'll teach you."

They reveled until she'd attained a chaos of sufficiency. Catching her breath and with her eyes still shut, she heard him snap open a tin, and then he knelt over Sallie and seemed to be holding and steering himself.

"And now what are you doing?" she asked.

"Silently entering," he said.

*　　　*　　　*

The Cattle King of the Pecos returned from some legal wrangling in the east around noon. The Kid had already shifted his belongings to the bunkhouse and soon was sitting bootless, hatless, and gunless with Doc Scurlock and Charlie Bowdre in the hallway outside the office of the Jinglebob Land & Livestock Company. Sallie brought them lemonades during their hot wait and flushed when the Kid declared with fervor, "Really enjoyed our night, Miss Chisum."

Scurlock slyly asked him, "Oh, and why is that?"

She was going to fabricate a lie but decided instead to hurry from them when John Simpson Chisum, whom all and sundry called Uncle, walked out of his office and fixed a tired gaze on the three Regulators. Because his father was an Englishman, he'd found common ground in his partnership with John Tunstall and the Scotch-Canadian McSween despite having grown up in Texas. And now he looked on their former employees as mere unfortunate remnants. Uncle John had just celebrated his fifty-fourth birthday in St. Louis, but he seemed far older, with a cane he leaned on, a goiter in his throat, overlarge ears, and a waxed mustache with ends curled up like the horns of an Angus bull.

"You fellows here for a job of work?" Doc and Charlie allowed that's what they were hoping for, and Chisum said, "Well I'm not hiring. The cattle you see here are just for my repasts. Rounded up the rest and sent them to Texas. Sold em to the Hunter and Evans company."

"Begging your pardon," Doc said, "but who *is* hiring?"

"You could head up to Fort Sumner and try Pete Maxwell. He runs through cowpokes about as soon as I do a can of Folgers coffee." Uncle John penciled a note for them to give to the cattleman up north, and, like hirelings, they made a slinking, grinning, bowing exit. The Kid was embarrassed for them. Uncle John scowled at the Kid. "What about you, Billy?"

"You see those horses in the bunkhouse corral?"

"Hadn't noticed." Chisum went to his office window and looked out. "Stolen?"

"Yes sir. We got them from Jimmy Dolan."

Chisum turned. "I have troubles enough, son. You'll have to get them out of here."

"And do what with them?"

"Sell em in Texas. There's an itty-bitty town on the Canadian River. Tascosa. Cattle drives head right through it, and their horses are always ending up scoured or lame."

The cattle baron sat down in a creaking office chair as if their meeting was ended. The Kid hesitated before saying, "You owe me five hundred dollars."

Uncle John was writing in a ledger and did not look up. "How's that?"

"Bill McCloskey said you'd agreed to pay us five dollars per day for hunting down Harry's killers. And I read in some newspaper that you'd hired gunfighters like me at five hundred dollars a head."

Chisum tried to kill the Kid with his stare. "You were misinformed," he evenly said.

With a childish stridence he regretted, the Kid argued, "We put in the time. We risked our lives. We ought to get paid for it."

Uncle John tilted to slide out a side drawer of his ambassadorial desk, saying, "You make a lot of sense, Billy. Let me get out my petty cash." And then he lifted from the drawer his Colt .45 and cocked it. "You'll need to be leaving now, Kid."

"But we're only asking for what's right."

"Tell you what. You can steal my cattle when you're hungry."

"You're just giving us permission because you know we'll do it anyway."

Chisum smirked. "You're bright, Billy. Nothing gets past you."

*   *   *

And so it was that just John Middleton, the fawning Tom Folliard, and the Kid headed to the Texas Panhandle with the stolen herd while the Coes forsook horse thievery for a fresh start at farming in Colorado; Frederick Tecumseh Waite rejoined his roots in the Indian Territories, became a tax collector, served in the Chickasaw legislature, and never again fired a gun in anger; and Josiah Gordon Scurlock and Charlie Bowdre tucked their cohabiting sisters, furniture, and belongings into cells in the Indian hospital at the Fort Sumner that the Army had abandoned.

The Kid never again saw Sallie Chisum. She dutifully listed in her red journal Willy's mailed gifts of "a beaded Indian tobacco pouch" and "2 candi hearts," but then she seemed to fancy other men more and in 1880 married another Willy, a German immigrant who hired on as a bookkeeper for the Jinglebob company. When Uncle John died in 1884 from gruesome surgery on his jaw, Sallie shared in an inheritance of $500,000. She sent her sons overseas for schooling in Germany and became estranged from them. She divorced Willy in 1895 and married the man who gave his name to Stegman, New Mexico, becoming the town's first postmistress. She divorced that husband, too, and then remained alone as she ran a successful cattle company and died rich, aged seventy-six, in 1934.

In the few shabbily made adobes in Tascosa and the fifty or so campaign tents, some of them brothels, the Kid sold the stolen horses to cattlemen hawing their longhorns to Abilene for the railroads and eastern markets. Then he just hung around for some weeks, gambling on games of monte played on Army blankets, happily flinging señoritas at the Mexican *bailes*, even pitching with both left hand and right at a game of baseball "nines" before he was ejected for loudly doubting the umpire's impartiality.

An Irish fan dancer originally from Baton Rouge—called Frenchie because of her fluency in the language—became one of the Kid's familiars in Tascosa. Wild and dazzling, she made a fortune as an adventuress in the sideline of prostitution, and she later remembered Billy as "the best-natured kid and had the most pleasant smile I most ever saw in a young man."

Another friend there was a handsome, happy mail carrier five years older than the Kid whose name was Henry Franklin Hoyt. A former student at the University of Minnesota and the Rush Medical College in Chicago, but not yet an MD, he'd adventured west and found his way to Uncle John Chisum's ranch in 1877. Like the Kid, he was urged by Chisum to go to Tascosa for the opportunities, and he'd intended to become a general-practice physician for the injured and ill until he found there wasn't adequate funding from all the pass-throughs. Although they met in the Howard & McMasters General Store and Saloon, Henry and Billy shared a dislike of intoxicants; both were festive, carefree, inquisitive, and rambunctious; and the Kid's late-night conversations with Hoyt felt like an education in science he'd lost out on. When Henry Hoyt decided to wander farther northwest to the green meadows of Las Vegas, New Mexico—the Wool Capital and boomtown that was the western railhead of the Atchison, Topeka & Santa Fe—the Kid gifted him with Sheriff Brady's sorrel racehorse with the brand of BB, even inventing a bill of sale signed by William H. Bonney so Hoyt's good reputation would not be sullied. In fair exchange, Hoyt gave the Kid a little gold lady's watch he'd won at five-card poker and the Kid saved it as a Christmas gift for some damsel yet unmet.

In *A Frontier Doctor*, written forty-two years later, Henry Hoyt remembered: "Billy Bonney was eighteen years old, a handsome youth with a smooth face, wavy hair, an athletic and symmetrical figure, and clear blue eyes that could look one through and through. Unless angry, he always seemed to have a pleasant expression with a ready smile. His head was well-shaped, his features regular, his nose aquiline, his most noticeable characteristic being a slight protrusion of his two front upper teeth. He spoke Spanish like a native and although only a beardless boy was nevertheless a natural leader of men."

Just before leaving, Hoyt offered some final advice to the Kid, telling him that while he was still free and fairly solvent he should run off to Mexico or South America and forget about the outlawry, for the Kid was smart, self-assured, easy to like, and efficient; he'd be a success at whatever he chose to do.

Hoyt was not the first nor last to suggest a getaway, but the Kid hung on to the familiar.

Soon after Henry Hoyt left, so did John Middleton, who petted his handlebar mustache as he complained, "Everything is already stoled out of the country." He took a job again with the Hunter, Evans & Company firm and its cattle drive north, earning three hundred dollars that he used to finance a grocery store in Sun City, Kansas, and failing in the business. His marriage to a fifteen-year-old girl also failed, and he was cowboying again when he died of smallpox in 1882.

Word got to the Kid in November 1878 that Thomas B. Catron of the Santa Fe Ring, who was finally under criminal investigation, had formally resigned as United States Attorney for New Mexico; that Lawrence G. Murphy had died in October—his ranch in Carrizozo would much later be purchased by the actress Mae West—and that Rob Widenmann had journeyed from London to Las Vegas, New Mexico, with a gift of one hundred pounds sterling (about five hundred American dollars) from John Partridge Tunstall to Susan McSween. She wrote

Harry's father, "I am truely grateful as I was so very much in kneed," but then requested five hundred dollars more. She'd also hired a Las Vegas civil engineer and choleric lawyer named Huston Ingraham Chapman to sue Lieutenant Colonel Nathan A. M. Dudley for arson and "the murder of my dear husband."

President Rutherford B. Hayes had named Lewis Wallace, the fifty-one-year-old Indiana lawyer and former Union Army general, to become the reforming successor to hapless Governor Axtell in New Mexico, and soon after getting to Santa Fe, His Excellency announced "that the disorders lately prevalent in Lincoln County have been happily brought to an end." He noted that now those

> *peaceably disposed may go to and from the County without hindrance or molestation.*
>
> *And that the people of Lincoln County may be helped more speedily to the management of their civil affairs, and to induce them to lay aside forever the divisions and feuds which, by national notoriety, have been so prejudicial to their locality, the undersigned, by virtue of the authority in him vested, further proclaims a general pardon for misdemeanors and offenses committed against the laws of the Territory in connection with the aforesaid disorders, between the first day of February, 1878, and the date of this proclamation.*

The governor also pardoned officers of the United States Army stationed in Lincoln County, affronting Colonel Dudley, who construed the pardon as a slander against "the gallant officers of my command for offenses we know not of, and of which we feel ourselves guiltless."

The governor denied a pardon for any person "under indictment for crimes and misdemeanors, nor shall this operate the release of any party undergoing pains and penalties" for his wrongdoing.

The Kid read the statement over and over again, yet he so fully believed in his innocence that he seems not to have recognized that he was one of those unpardonable criminals, for he was under indictment for murder. And because he did not see it, he thought it was a favorable time to return to the New Mexico he thought of as his home. The Mesilla *News* foresaw that result, noting that "peace was dawning in Lincoln County when Governor Wallace extended a pardon to absent thieves, cutthroats, and murderers and virtually invited them to come back and make a fresh start in their occupations."

- 13 -

THE PARLEY

Lucien Bonaparte Maxwell left Illinois at seventeen to become a fur trapper in Nebraska, headed farther west as a scout alongside Kit Carson, and providentially married Ana Maria de la Luz Beaubien, whose heritage was of the French and Spanish aristocracy. With an inheritance from his father-in-law of 1,714,765 acres of rangeland in the New Mexico Territory and southern Colorado, Lucien developed a cattle operation that rivaled John Chisum's; founded three merchandise stores, a major gristmill, the Azteca Mine, and the First National Bank of Santa Fe; and in Cimarron constructed a glorious hacienda full of European wines, silver dishware, a redundancy of servants, and so many houseguests that there were two dining rooms. And then, as if he foresaw he would die of kidney failure four years later, in 1871 he sold off properties, gave up his rangeland to an English syndicate for $1,350,000—less than a dollar an acre—and moved his wife and six children two hundred miles south along the Goodnight-Loving cattle trail to Fort Sumner.

A forty-square-mile government Indian reservation on the Rio Pecos had been constructed there for 8,500 Navajo and 500 Mescalero Apache prisoners. Washington politicians hoped for civilizing instruc-

145

tion in farming and Christianity, but the project was a tragedy, offering only malnourishment, poisonous water, and, at an elevation of four thousand feet, overexposure to the fierce cold of winter. In frustration and defeat, the federal government finally released the Indians a few years after the Civil War, and the Army that had overseen and serviced the reservation abandoned the neighboring Fort Sumner, selling its many buildings to Lucien Maxwell for just five thousand dollars. Maxwell forsook his grand hacienda in Cimarron and converted the officers' quarters into a handsome twenty-room, two-story adobe house for his wife, Doña Luz; his only son, Pedro; and his five daughters, Emilia, Maria, Sofia, Paulita, and Odila. Twenty Mexican families followed him to the fort, establishing apartments in buildings such as the company barracks, the stables, the quartermaster store, the commissary, and the Indian hospital.

And that's where the Kid, now age nineteen, sought out Scurlock and Bowdre in December 1878, trotting his horse southwest from the Staked Plains of Texas along the Portales–Stinking Springs Road and entering the fort near the parade grounds where Pete Maxwell's sheep were gardening the wintry grama grass. The Kid saw Beaver Smith's saloon to his right and the great barn of a dance hall to his left, then rode the wide avenue between the Maxwell house and the former enlisted men's barracks to an orchard at the north end and Bob Hargrove's saloon. A hundred yards east were the old Indian corrals and then the former Indian hospital, where Doc Scurlock, Charlie Bowdre, and the sisters Herrera were housed.

Doc and Charlie had been hired as wranglers on Pete Maxwell's horse-overrun ranch and told Billy they'd found Fort Sumner congenial, with good hunting on the treeless plains, a peach orchard on the property, weekly frolics and dances, and fame among the Mexicans for the Regulators' stance against the House and the Santa Fe Ring in the Lincoln County War.

The Kid was mystified. "But we *lost*."

"We won their hearts and minds," said Doc.

"So we're fixin to settle right chere," Charlie said. "With the outly-ings we got near three hunderd peoples so our women got company now, and speakin for Manuela, she's sore put out with me forever wan-derin hither and john."

The Herrera sisters nodded their agreement.

The Kid smiled and said, "Wow, if times get any better you'll have to hire me to help you enjoy em."

"Well, we're tired of falling on stony ground," said Doc.

With a tad too much interest, Manuela inquired, "And what are jour plan?"

"It is my firm intention to put the dastardly gunplay behind me."

Doc frowned and asked, "You get that out of some damn dime novel?"

The Kid winked. "*Whip Penn and the Scoundrels of Whiskey Flats.*"

With no job or responsibilities, the Kid frittered away his time practic-ing his shooting, knocking a tin can into a twirl down the road, trim-ming the skeletal branches off trees, inventing situations and reeling around to slap leather and nail the evildoer, or galloping a horse and tilting off until he could snatch his rifle from the ground.

And he gambled at faro at Beaver Smith's or Bob Hargrove's saloon, generally favoring placing his bets on the lacquered face cards on the green felt and mentally counting and recalling what had already been dealt from the shoe so he could predict what would next fall. Like all gamblers, he said he won more than he lost, but in his case it was true.

His first Saturday in Fort Sumner there was a *baile*, a dance, with Doc and Charlie adding a fiddle and guitar to the trumpets and vio-lins of a six-piece band. It wasn't only songs from Old Mexico like "*El*

Tecolotito" but a mix of tunes such as "Rose of Killarney" and "I'll Take You Home Again, Kathleen." Doc invited the Kid onstage to sing the 7th Infantry's regimental march, "The Girl I Left Behind Me," and the Kid grinned widely with the lyrics as he sang,

> *Such lonely thoughts my heart*
> *Do fill since parting with my Sallie.*
> *I seek for one as fair and gay*
> *But find none to remind me.*
> *How sweet the hours I passed away*
> *With the girl I left behind me.*

Women were so scarce that Pete Maxwell's hundred cowhands and sheepherders took numbers and waited to be yelled for, were forced to dance with the oldest ladies first, and then again stirred in the hall with that form of despair that is patience.

The high stepping included a four-couple square dance called a *cuadrilla,* a side-by-side waltz called a *varsoviana* that was accompanied by the song "Put Your Little Foot Right There," and the excitement and shrieks of the schottische, a slow polka in Europe but faster in America, with wild pivots and twirls.

With an attractive señora named Celsa Gutiérrez, the Kid flirted with a *jarabe tapatío,* otherwise known as a hat dance, while her liquor-addled husband dully watched from an old Victorian office chair. Then she yanked the Kid over to happily introduce him to Saval, who seemed interested only in swallowing more mescal.

Celsa was very pretty, with a pouting, pillowy mouth, copper-colored eyes, and hair more brunette than black. She told the Kid in Spanish that she and Saval had found housing in the old quartermaster store. Would he like to sleep there? They had room. The Kid said he'd give it prayerful consideration. She asked his age and confessed she was three years older. She said her maiden name was also Gutiérrez, that she and Saval were cousins. Even though her husband was within earshot, she confessed she was not in love with Saval, the marriage had been arranged, and she'd fought the family over it until she'd finally just grown tired of Saval's ridiculous begging. Hearing that, her husband gave the Kid that woebegone, baleful look that no one wants to see, and the Kid excused himself to sit again with Manuela and Charlie, who was slumped in a chair with a fifth of Old Grand-Dad, his fiddle biding its time on his knee.

"Seen you talking to Celsa," he said. "Don't blame you a-tall. She's got them kitchen eyes."

"Kitchen eyes?"

Charlie smiled. "Saying, 'Come and get it.'"

Soon it was Celsa who came to the Kid in her husband's overcoat and insisted in English, "For favor, you take Celsa home." The Kid asked about Saval, and she said, "Like alway, he too *borracho*." Drunk.

She hugged herself and leaned into the Kid as they walked to the old quartermaster store and the apartment next to Beaver Smith's saloon. Celsa lit a hurricane lamp, and the Kid was startled to see that a tiny, dark-haired boy, maybe a toddler of three, was sleeping on a couch. Celsa let Saval's overcoat fall to the floor in a heap as the child whimpered and rubbed the sleep from his eyes. She petted his hair and in Spanish said she missed him, and then she carried him over to an Azteca armchair. His face nuzzled into the front of her dress as he whined, "*Leche*." Milk. She then unbuttoned her dress and lifted out a round left breast with a violet areola and nipple, which the toddler hungrily sucked on.

Celsa smiled as she saw Billy flushing in an interested stare. She asked in English, "You like?"

"Oh my yes. I'm very thirsty."

She laughed. "I mean Candido. You like heem?"

"Oh, the tyke. Of course."

In a flirting way she said, "Tell Candido he is beautiful and that you love him."

And Billy said, "You're beautiful and I love you."

The Kid stayed for the next few weeks with Doc, Charlie, and their women in the Indian hospital. And it was there that one of Maxwell's vaqueros handed him an envelope addressed to "Wm. H. 'Kid' Bonney." Inside was a formal invitation from "The Maxwells" requesting the pleasure of the Kid's presence at a six o'clock Christmas dinner. Seemed they'd heard of his exploits.

His friends jeered to hide their envy and joked about the faux pas he'd commit. "They's richer than clabbered cream!" Charlie said. "They's etiquette. Whereas you eat your food like a bachelor, right from the fryin pan!"

Doc counseled, "The Maxwells are highfalutin. You'd best spiff up in your fancy duds."

So the Kid opened the trunk of his finer things that Doc had hauled to Fort Sumner and he dressed in a white collared shirt and wide, planetary tie, a formal suit coat of blue velvet, gray slacks with cuffs he jerked down over his shined Wellington boots to make them look like shoes, and a charcoal gray derby hat cocked rakishly on hair dressed with Rowlands' macassar oil.

The Kid felt like a fish out of water as he walked through the gate of the white picket fence and onto the wide porch that shaded the first floor on three sides of the house. Chatter and laughter eddied through the front door, and he wanted to flee, but he rapped the brass knocker and soon a rail-thin man six and a half feet tall was there in a footman's formal livery. "William Bonney," the Kid said.

"Uh-huh," said the footman. Walking down the hallway, he said, "In the parlor."

The Kid saw on his left an ornate bedroom that seemed all leather and sienna brown, and across from it was a far more feminine bedroom, in which everything from the sculpted headboard to the chiffonier to the frilly pillows was white. And then there was the lilac wallpaper of a parlor overfurnished with Victorian love seats and armchairs and ten elegantly dressed people holding flutes of champagne. A stocky man who seemed about thirty was in a Prince of Wales tailcoat and was losing his hair but for an upswept central tuft. Seeing past his interlocutor, he noticed the Kid and with excitement announced, "There he is, our wild card, Billy Bonney!"

The guests turned to the Kid, and his hand was shaken by Pedro Menard Maxwell, who said, "Call me Pete," and tugged him through introductions to Ana Maria de la Luz Beaubien Maxwell, his fifty-year-old mother, his sister Emilia and her husband, Manuel Abreu, who oversaw the sheep operation, and Emilia's little sister Odila. Captain Alexander Chase of the Army was in his formal dress blues with full regalia and tilted down to introduce his sitting wife, Virginia, who seemed afraid of Billy and slanted into the officer's hip like a child seeking an apron. Also shy was Sofia Maxwell, now married to a disdainful Telesfor Jaramillo, who lifted his nose at the Kid and whose slicked, oiled, ebony hair shone in the candlelight. And lastly their "wild card" made the acquaintance of the fourteen-year-old, Paulita, a gorgeous girl half French and one-quarter each Spanish and Irish. She had freshly shampooed raven black hair piled in a fashionable pompadour and the deep-roasted, coffee brown eyes that Mexicans called *cafés*. Candlelight glittered in them. "So pleased to meet you, Mr. Bonney," she said. Her cheeks dimpled cutely when she smiled.

"We all are!" Pete Maxwell exclaimed and faked a shiver of horror as he said, "The fiend who revels in bloodshed! The child suckled on vice!"

"Pedro!" his mother said.

"Oh, he knows I'm joshing him. It's all direct from those idiotic newspaper stories."

The Kid tried the knife of a smile and then was nudged, finding Saval also in a footman's livery and holding out a flute of champagne. "No thank you," the Kid said.

"*No quiere nada?*" You want nothing?

"Water."

Saval sighed and headed to the kitchen.

Paulita seemed aflutter and was warily smiling at the Kid. He returned the flattery.

The very tall and dour footman announced that dinner was served, and they all crossed into a grand dining room of Sheraton furniture, an ironed lace tablecloth, and dishware and cutlery of pure silver along with chalices of fourteen-carat gold for the wine, the great wealth of it gleaming under a huge French chandelier.

Don Manuel Abreu whispered, "Remove your pistol."

"I'm not carrying."

Don Manuel gave him a tickled look like he'd just made a pretty good joke, *Ho ho.* And then it was he who gave the holiday toast, "*Feliz Navidad!*"

A Navajo cook named Deluvina delivered a lamb shank, a large turkey, and a goose on silver platters, and Pete nodded to the tall liveryman as he said, "We have Pat to thank for the fowl. Went hunting for me this morning." He asked his mother to "return thanks," and when she'd blessed the food and cooks in Spanish, he called out, "Like Lucien would say, 'Y'all be careful now or you're gonna fleshen up.'"

Saval the footman poured water into the Kid's chalice with a hint of rebuke, and furtive conversations about some of the clan Billy couldn't have met flittered in shorthand among the dinner guests. The

Kid realized he was invited just to entertain the revelers with wild tales of derring-do, but doing that would make his life seem unserious, so he chose silence and avoidance. But Paulita kept shyly focused on him and asked, "Are you still in school?"

He shook his head. "I just look young for my age. Are you?"

"Uh-huh. In Trinidad, Colorado. St. Mary's Convent School."

"What's your favorite class?"

She thought for a few seconds and answered, "English or history. I like to read."

She had a squinty right eye that he found fetching. "Me too," he said.

"Have you read *Little Women*?"

"Afraid not."

"I like it ever so much."

They fell silent and just ate for a while, overhearing the other diners trading local gossip in Spanish. Whenever she glanced up from her food she'd smirk as if she found her secret thoughts devilishly funny. Paulita finally asked what she'd been wanting to. "So, do you have a girlfriend?"

"I have lotsa *friends*."

"And the girls—do you kiss?"

The Kid looked up and down the table, but no one else seemed to be listening.

She changed the subject. "Have you seen the actress Sarah Bernhardt?"

"Heard of her."

"What about Fanny Davenport?"

"No."

She passed a requested gravy boat to Sofia and said, "Some women are so ravishingly beautiful."

"I guess that's true."

She forked a cooked carrot but held it poised near her kissable lips. "Why, do you think? What *is* it about them?"

"Well, they have to have those gorgeous coffee brown eyes to begin with."

She was figuring him out, and then giggled.

And her brother, Pete, called from the far end, "We've been leaving you out, Kid. You been to Lincoln of late?"

"No, sir. Texas Panhandle."

"So you don't know Tomcat Catron shut down and sold the House for a mere three thousand dollars. And Jimmy Dolan's buying the Tunstall store instead."

The names nettled him, but the Kid just said, "Nope, that escaped me."

"And Susan McSween is there in Lincoln again. She booted Saturnino Baca and his passel of children out of that house they rented from her so she could selfishly have it." Pete slumped back so Saval could pour more wine into his golden chalice. And then he said as if someone had inquired *What's she like?* "Lewd, profane, vulgar woman. Wholly without principle."

His mother chastised him with "Pedro!"

"Well, it's a fact she's from a house of ill fame in Kansas. And Sheriff Dad Peppin saw her in actual lascivious contact with John Chisum."

Some of the women inhaled in shock.

"I find that hard to believe," the Kid said.

"And *frequent* occurrences where she forced herself on a Mexican boy on the grassy banks of the Rio Bonito."

Billy was fuming. "Where you getting all this?"

"Army scuttlebutt based on Nathan Dudley's investigations," Maxwell said, and he falsely smiled. "You won't shoot the messenger, will you?"

Captain Alexander Chase said, "Such comments seem indelicate, Pete. Especially among ladies and on the birthday of Our Lord."

Pete Maxwell held up both hands as if he'd desist, but then he turned the screw a jot more, asking, "You still horse-thieving, Kid? Or are you just gunning folks helter-skelter?"

Paulita yelled to him, "Have some more wine, Pedro!"

Pete flopped backward as if he'd been punched. "Oh my gosh, my dear little sister's *sweet* on you, Kid!"

She faced her food. "Am not."

"She finds the bad boy fetching!"

"Quit it," she said, her face flushing.

All the dinner guests were fondly looking at the two. The Kid stood up from the table. "This has been lovely," he said. "Scrumptious dinner and there was such"—he sought a high-flown word and found it—"conviviality."

Pete lifted his golden chalice in a false farewell toast and then finished it.

Paulita got up, too, saying, "I'll walk you out." And she touched the Kid's forearm with a soft, consoling hand in their walk as she said, "I'm so sorry for my stupid brother's rudeness. And none of the others sticking up for you. It's indecent."

The Kid smiled and said, "I was about to lose my cherubic demeanor." He put on his gentleman's derby hat and gallantly offered, "But I guess I gave Pete ammunition with all my disorderly doings."

She seemed serious and old beyond her years as she asked, "So, are you changing your ways?"

"If they let me."

"They," she repeated. She seemed to find some wifely satisfaction over his tardy improvement, and then was all formal politeness. "I do hope we'll see you again in spite of this evening's unpleasantness."

"I'd take kindly to that." Then he remembered his gift and reached into a velvet side pocket as he said, "Oh here, for you. I didn't have a bow or paper or anything to wrap it." And he drizzled into her waiting hands the gold lady's watch that Henry Hoyt had given him in exchange for Sheriff Brady's horse.

She held it up to candlelight. "But it's dazzling, Billy! You take my breath away! Oh, I'm so happy! I love it!"

"Well, good."

She hesitated and in a sudden flash kissed his cheek. Embarrassed by that forwardness, she withdrew into the frilly white feminine bedroom as he let himself out, snugging the front door quietly closed.

And then he found himself at the old quartermaster store. "Saval's still butlering," he said. Celsa smiled as she let him in and she invited his carnal enjoyment.

Hard winds and slanting snowdrifts as deep as his horse's stifle slowed his uphill journey from Fort Sumner to a full six days, but the Kid managed to get to Lincoln on the afternoon of February 18, exactly one year since John H. Tunstall was assassinated. He'd heard that Jesse Evans, his former captain with the Boys and in the sheriff's posse that killed Harry, was using Fort Stanton like a free hotel, going and coming as he pleased, so the Kid had written him there, saying,

> *I have been shifting from can to can't and am wanting to shuck our fractiousness. Won't you and Jimmy meet me in Lincoln on Tuesday, the 18th instant?*

The Kid first went to Juan Patrón's house and store, where Tom Folliard was holing up. Juan's wife, Beatriz, served them Arbuckles' Ariosa coffee and told them Jimmy Dolan had effected a truce with Susan McSween so he could buy the Tunstall store. Susan would be holding a piano recital that evening in the home Juan still referred to as Saturnino Baca's. Half the town would be there.

Around five Tom and Billy sloshed through wet snow and mud on Lincoln's only street until they got to Frank McCullum's Oyster House, which overlooked the charred joists and rot of the late Alexander McSween's home. They ate hearty as Tom chattered boastfully about having defiled "a pretty doxy from Socorro just behind the Torreón. Locals got a name for the area but I forget."

"El Chorro," the Kid said.

"Yes! Exactly! What's that mean?"

"The squirt."

Tom Folliard guffawed in a way that caused him to lose some food.

Just before seven they got to Baca's, where children were scrunched up on the floor, genial women were laying their overcoats on a bed, Jimmy Dolan was lurking near the Steinway piano with Jacob B. Mathews, Sheriff Brady's deputy on the morning BB was killed. Jesse Evans was seemingly on parole, for he was sitting there with a ferocious Texas cowhand named Billy Campbell and they looked like they hadn't heard a good joke in years. Jesse noticed the Kid but did nothing since he was dealing with the sour wreckage of drunkenness.

Susan McSween seemed none the worse for wear in a fine gown and an excess of jewelry, and she delightedly greeted the fine-looking "Red Tom" Folliard with a lingering hug and, as an afterthought, Billy—whom she still condemned as "one of those foolhardy boys." She said, "There's someone very important to me that I should like you to meet."

So they were introduced to Huston Ingraham Chapman, a heavy attorney and railroad engineer whom she'd met in Las Vegas and with whom she was cohabiting. Chapman had lost his left arm to a hunting accident in Oregon at the age of thirteen and overcompensated with high dudgeon and irascibility in his practice of law—he was a rule-or-ruin sort that few people liked. And now his right hand kept tenderly petting his red, windburnt face, for he was, he explained, "suffering from neuralgia." Seeing Tom Folliard's frown, he defined it as "sudden intensity of pain in a nerve." Still, he was feisty, and as he talked there seemed to be no lack in him of affidavits, motions, stipulations, and outrage. Enemies aplenty he had, some identical to the Kid's—Judge Warren Bristol, District Attorney Rynerson, and in particular Lieutenant Colonel Nathan Dudley, whom Susan McSween intended to have prosecuted for murder and arson. Huston Chapman's hazel eyes never strayed from the Kid's face as he talked about the miscreants, until he finally asked, as if he'd found a new client, "Aren't there civil warrants out for your arrest?"

But then Susan McSween was sitting at the pianoforte and announcing, "I shall be performing Chopin's *Études* this evening. Opus ten. Composed in eighteen thirty-three. The first is called 'Waterfall.'" When that was over she announced in sequence "Chromatique," "Tristesse," "Torrent," "Black Keys," "Lament," and "Toccata." Each was mercifully short, but little Jimmy Dolan would not leave the Kid alone with his restless eyes, and Chopin's music seemed to hath not the charm to soothe the savage Evans and Campbell. When the opus was finished with "Revolutionary" and Susan McSween stood to more fully absorb the adulation and applause, Evans and Campbell were impatiently standing, too, and giving Jimmy and J. B. Mathews the high sign.

The Kid and Tom shouted some praise to Susan, and she offered a queenly wave as they went outside, following the Dolan faction. Yginio Salazar was healed up from the gun wounds of the Big Killing, and he scrambled up from Susan's fainting couch to follow his cousin.

Hostilities started with Evans urging Dolan to just get rid of Billy, and the Kid saying, "I don't care to open our parley with a gunfight, but even if you jump me four at a time you'll all soon find yourselves toes up."

Tom confided to Yginio, "Billy reads shoot-em-ups."

There seemed to be some silent calculations by the Kid's foes, a few wary looks, and then a pacification of the mood. Jimmy Dolan asked, "So ye be wanting a peace treaty, Billy? What are ye thinking, lad?"

The Kid had in fact given it a good deal of thought and listed some imperatives. "Either side agrees not to kill anyone on the opposing. Anyone we ever called a friend is hereby included."

Jimmy Dolan's deepest friendships were now at Fort Stanton, so he added, "And no soldiers or officers are to be punished for any ting up to this date. We wants to keep the Army outta this."

The Kid shrugged his agreement and continued, "We promise not to give evidence against each other in court. We guarantee to help each other avoid arrests on civil warrants, and if a fellow is jailed we'll try to get him out."

"The penalty for not upholding this treaty?" Jimmy asked.

"Well, it goes without saying," said Jacob Mathews. "Killed on sight."

There was some fretting and stewing, but first Jimmy Dolan shook the Kid's hand and then all seven joined in liking the truce.

"I got no dog in this fight," Billy Campbell said as though he regretted it.

Jimmy Dolan handed around a bottle of George Dickel Original Tennessee sour mash, and all but the Kid drank a jigger's worth. "Quare chilly out here," Jimmy said.

Jesse Evans was hugging himself as he agreed. "Colder than an old witch's tit in a snowbank."

Earlier, Huston Chapman had trudged to Isaac Ellis's store at the east end of Lincoln and woke up Isaac to get a loaf of stale bread for a poultice he thought would act as a cathartic for his neuralgia. Walking back with his medicament after nine, his swollen face bandaged in gauze, he happened upon the seven in parley. J. B. Mathews just glowered, but Billy Campbell thought it hilarious to use his huge size to interfere with Chapman's progress, swaying with intoxication as he demanded, "Who are you and where the hell you think you're goin?"

"My name is Huston Chapman, and I am attending to my own personal affairs."

Looking for any excuse, the infuriated Campbell yanked his gun and jabbed it into Huston Chapman's significant belly. "You'll have to dance for us first."

"Oh, let him go," sighed the Kid.

Huston Chapman took in the seven faces and said, "I do not propose to dance for a drunken, unruly mob."

"Watch your fancy mouth," Campbell said, "or you'll find yourself—"

They all waited for him to finish his threat, but overindulgence in the red disturbance had stolen vocabulary from him.

Susan McSween had informed Chapman of Jimmy's alcoholism, so he tugged his big gauze bandage aside to more clearly see his tormentor. "Am I speaking with Jimmy Dolan?"

Little Jimmy was in fact behind the lawyer, and he smirked. Evans said, "No. Just a darn good friend of his'n."

And suddenly a swozzled Jimmy Dolan fired his pistol vaguely into the man's overcoat. Reacting to the sudden noise, Billy Campbell fired, too, hitting the lawyer just above the navel.

The Kid glanced at Tom and Yginio in disbelief. J. B. Matthews, a half-time deputy, withdrew.

Realizing he was gutshot, Huston Chapman gazed in horror at his blackening waistcoat and exclaimed, "Oh my God, I am killed!" He fell to his knees in the frozen mud as the flash of gunpowder that singed his clothing fed into a flame. He toppled backward, and Jimmy Dolan pitilessly wasted the last of his George Dickel whiskey to fuel a full-blown fire that crept up the dying man.

Looking at Jesse Evans, Billy Campbell smiled and said, "There. We did it."

"Good on ya," Dolan said.

Billy Campbell faced the Kid to explain that he'd promised Lieutenant Colonel Dudley he'd kill that shyster Chapman and he'd gone and done it. His word was his bond.

With his gun still drawn, Jimmy Dolan told the Kid, Tom Folliard, and Yginio Salazar, "Join us in celebration." There was nothing voluntary in the invitation. And the Kid, who forthrightly faced any skirmish and was affronted by every Oh-no-you-don't, for some odd reason complied.

Huston Chapman was groaning in agony as the six went to Frank McCullum's eatery and Jimmy ordered Olympia oysters and full glasses of rye all around. With the slightest of misgivings, he daintily lifted his own gun by the trigger guard and said, "We need someone to put this in Chapman's hand. Like he shot first."

Like you did with Harry, the Kid thought. "I'll do it," he said and took the gun as he got up from oysters and drink he hadn't touched. And Tom Folliard figured it was an excellent occasion to visit the backyard privy. When the Kid was outside in the elements, he ran east at full speed to Isaac Ellis's, where his horse was stabled, and Tom Folliard and Yginio Salazar were right on his heels.

They galloped to Yginio's house in a *placita* near the ranch of Patrick Coghlan, with whom the Kid had friendly acquaintance due to rustling transactions. Hence the Kid was long gone when Army Lieutenant Byron Dawson and twenty cavalrymen arrived in Lincoln at midnight, having heard on the afternoon of the eighteenth that William H. Bonney was afoot.

The soldiers banged on house doors in their search for him and in that way happened upon Huston Chapman's stiff corpse, still on Main Street, his face eaten away by the fire. Worthless Sheriff George Kimbrell, who'd just taken the job, admitted he had seen the body lying there but couldn't find a soul to help him carry it elsewhere.

With disdain, Lieutenant Dawson said *he'd* take care of it, and his cavalrymen deposited Huston Chapman on a courthouse plaintiff's table.

There was no inquest and no meaningful pursuit of a murderer, for, because of his notoriety, the Kid became the only suspect. But the assassination did compel Governor Lew Wallace to write the United States secretary of the interior that "I have further information that certain notorious characters, who have long been under indictment, but by skillful dodging have managed to escape arrests, have formed an alliance which looks like preparation for raids when the spring opens. With that idea I propose a campaign against them."

14

CLEMENCY

The governor would soon meet the Kid, for W. H. Bonney sent this letter to him at the Governor's Palace in Santa Fe:

Dear Sir I have heard that You will give one thousand dollars for my person, which as I can understand means alive as a Witness against those that murdered Mr. Chapman. If it is required that I would appear at Court, I have indictments against me for things that happened in the late Lincoln County War and am afraid to give up because my Enemies would Kill me. If it is in your power to annul those indictments I hope you will do so, so as to give me a chance to explain myself. I have no Wish to fight any more, indeed I have not raised an arm since your November proclamation. Concerning my character, I refer You to any of the Citizens of Lincoln, for the majority of them are my Friends and have been helping me all they could. I am also called Kid Antrim, but Antrim is my stepfather's name. Waiting for an answer, I remain your obedient servant.

The governor invited him to Santa Fe, and a gussied-up Kid got there at night on March 17, 1879, St. Patrick's Day. An Irish festival in the plaza carried the noise of the kettles, pans, and horns of a shivaree as the Kid walked up to a one-story, 350-foot-wide, porticoed Spanish palace of whitewashed adobe that was constructed in the 1600s. He knocked many times on a rough door of sawn wood, and it was finally opened by an annoyed official in a frock suit, who flinched at seeing the Kid's Winchester rifle and holstered six-shooter.

"You must be Kid Bonney."

"Yes sir."

"You're late."

"Had to ride forever to get here."

"Hand over your weapons." With some hesitation, the Kid did as instructed, and as the official carried them away he told the Kid, "The governor is still dining. Wait for him in his office." He nodded his head. "End of the hallway."

The floor of the hallway was earthen but softened by an ill-matched variety of English, Persian, and Navajo rugs. A faint stream of dirt was trickling through a cleft in the ceiling, and fronds of water stain slurred the walls. In the governor's office, four hurricane lamps were lit, and a grand, ambassadorial desk was heaped with books such as *Antiquities of the Jews* by Flavius Josephus, *The Lands of the Saracen* by Bayard Taylor, *Innocents Abroad* by Mark Twain, and a King James Version of the Holy Bible that was bookmarked with many torn scraps of paper. Tacked to a wall was a map called *Terra Sancta sive Palestina*, whatever that was. Billy saw a cardboard stationery box that was labeled *Ben-Hur: A Tale of the Christ*, and a quill pen and jar of India ink were next to a half-filled page of handwriting. The Kid stooped over it to read: "Let the reader try to fancy it; let him first look down upon the arena, and see it glistening in its frame of dull-gray granite walls; let him then, in this perfect field, see the chariots, light of wheel, very graceful, and as ornate as paint and burnishing can make them."

Heel-thumping boot steps caused the Kid to scurry from behind the

desk and stand beside a yellow tapestried armchair. The patrician governor hurried in, wearing a dark broadcloth suit and worrying his mouth
with a toothpick as he glanced at Billy and said, "Sit," then paused as he
sternly added, "And take off your hat in a governor's presence."

The Kid complied.

Lewis Wallace was the son of a former governor of Indiana and had
left Wabash College to practice law with his father. Elected to the state
senate, he was later appointed to the office of Indiana's adjutant general, then joined in the Civil War, where he became the youngest general in the Union Army at the age of thirty-four and was a judge in the
trial of the eight coconspirators in the assassination of Abraham Lincoln. Because lawyering bored him, he wrote a novel about the Aztecs
and twice ran for Congress as a Republican, losing both elections, but
in 1876 he was on the commission to re-count the presidential vote in
Louisiana and Florida, and he reversed the tally in favor of Rutherford
B. Hayes, who, as president, rewarded him with the governorship of
the New Mexico Territory in 1878. Lew Wallace was now fifty-one, a
hawkish, fierce-eyed man with long, graying hair aslant on his skull, a
full beard that seemed almost a bib for his chest, and a wide mustache
that concealed his mouth and forced him now to comb reminders of
his dinner from it.

To be ingratiating, as was his habit, the Kid said, "I lived in Indianapolis for a while. We got Indiana in common."

Lew Wallace seemed unimpressed. "You're younger than I imag-
ined," he said.

"Yet, I'm a full-grown man."

"Aged what?"

"Nineteen."

Wallace looked around his office with dismay. "And are you seeing
for the first time our filthy, falling-down *palace*?"

"Heck, every house I ever lived in could fit inside this."

"Oh yes, I have cavernous chambers, but there are vermin in the kitchen and holes in the roof. A few rooms have cedar rafters that are so overweighted with mud that they sag with the curvature of a pirate's cutlass. Inviting my dear wife to join me here would be the acme of indecency."

The Kid had no idea what to say, and he found himself fidgeting.

Wallace asked, "Have you heard politics called the art of the possible?"

"Nope," the Kid answered, then worried that was rude so he added, "Your Excellency."

"Well, here it's the art of the *impossible*. All calculations based on my earlier military and political experiences absolutely *fail* in New Mexico with so many officeholders on the take from those seeking commercial advantage." The governor squeezed a pair of rimless pince-nez on his nose and lifted his box of manuscript to get W. H. Bonney's letter from underneath it. "And so I welcome problems I feel I can handle, and one is outlawry in Lincoln County. I shall push those Black Knights without rest."

With "Black Knights" Wallace was alluding to an Arthurian romance from the Middle Ages, so the reference went over Billy's head. "Like I say, I'm just hoping for a clean slate and citizenhood. Your note to me gave promise of absolute protection."

"Yes, and I shall be true to that promise." Rereading the Kid's letter, Lew Wallace asked, "You mention indictments. What kind?"

"Territorial for the killing of Sheriff William Brady, but I was just one of a half dozen shooters. And he deserved to die. The federal one was for the killing of Andrew Roberts on the Mescalero reservation, which I definitely did not do." The Kid forgot to mention his killing of Windy Cahill in self-defense, but Arizona seemed to have forgotten that, too.

"You would end up testifying against yourself in all likelihood."

"And that means?"

"Histories and narratives that would include your own activities. But that's neither here nor there, for I am prepared to offer you clemency in return for your full, accurate, and truthful testimony before a grand jury."

"Clemency?"

"Leniency, forbearance. You'll go scot-free with my own official pardon for all your prior misdeeds."

The Kid said he liked the sound of that but confessed the fear that those criminals he named would have him killed.

Wallace told him he'd order a sham arrest and lock him in handcuffs, then jail him with instructions of protective custody. The government would also be arresting those involved in the homicide of Huston Ingraham Chapman. And now, if the terms were agreeable to him, he could begin naming names.

"We ought to have all this in writing," Billy said.

The Kid failed to understand the governor's sneer as he said, "Not until I have your testimony."

Which he guessed was a reasonable hitch to the bargain. The Kid offered the names of those who had joined in the parley on February 18, and then with hesitation he asked, "You *are* staying put as governor, right?"

Lew Wallace seemed defeated and sorrowful as he rocked back in his chair. "Oh, there will soon arrive the time when I have become fed up with this place. Then another governor will be in this hovel of a *palacio* and he'll do just as I did, have the same ideas, undertake the same vain attempts, and with the same heartiness of effort he'll soon cool in his zeal, then finally say, 'All right, let her drift.'"

The Kid was thinking the governor could have depressed the devil, but he stood and smiled as he said in good night, "Well, sir, I guess it's time to pee on the fire and call home the hound dogs."

The governor winced at the vulgarity and shooed the petty criminal off, saying, "I have to get back to my novel."

Acting on further information, the governor sent a sixty-man cavalry detachment to Jimmy Dolan's Carrizozo ranch and overwhelmed William Campbell, Jacob B. Mathews, and Jesse Evans, who were arrested and taken to the Fort Stanton stockade. But Jesse Evans and Billy Campbell convinced an infantry recruit from Texas to help them slink out of their loose imprisonment. Evans seemed to have the Kid's knack for getting out of jails. Billy Campbell "skedaddled for Texas," as Evans put it, and was never heard from again.

Worried that the escapees would be seeking vengeance, the Kid and Tom Folliard volunteered to be handcuffed by Sheriff George Kimbrell and were escorted to a friendly confinement in Juan Patrón's store, where they played Mexican monte with the sheriff and other visitors and the Kid won big as the "house bank." Writing of their jailing to the secretary of the interior, Wallace sarcastically noted, "A precious specimen named 'the Kid' whom the Sheriff is holding in the Plaza, as it is called, is an object of tender regard. Singing and music can be heard in the night as minstrels of the village actually serenade the fellow in his prison."

Lew Wallace was so intrigued by the judicial intelligence of Susan McSween's current lawyer that he chose Ira E. Leonard, a former judge in Missouri, to ensure fulfillment of the governor's interests in the forthcoming spring term of the district court. But Wallace may also have foreseen that his efforts would fail, for he disassociated himself from the process.

Judge Warren Bristol and District Attorney William Logan Rynerson got to Fort Stanton for the grand jury proceedings on Sunday, April 13, and immediately confirmed the habeas corpus petitions—

writs against illegal imprisonment—that were submitted on behalf of fifteen men associated with robberies and murder in the Lincoln County War. The fifteen were released from the fort's stockade after go-and-sin-no-more instructions from Judge Bristol.

The grand jury was constituted with friends of Alexander McSween and handed down some two hundred indictments: against Lieutenant Colonel Dudley and ex-Sheriff Dad Peppin for arson; against Billy Campbell, Jimmy Dolan, and their accessory Jesse Evans for the homicide of Huston Chapman; a hundred against people already dead; and one against Tom Folliard for horse theft.

Tom Folliard and J. B. Mathews were interrogated about their activities and, according to a prior agreement, were then given immunity from further prosecution under the governor's proclamation of amnesty.

But when the Kid offered his full, accurate, and truthful testimony about the night of Huston Chapman's murder and waited for District Attorney Rynerson to do just as he'd done for Tom and J.B., instead the scowling and freakishly tall and Rasputin-like Rynerson objected, "We find in the law no precedence for the governor's presumption of the right to offer a homicidal felon a promise of clemency. The state therefore requests a continuance of prosecution."

Judge Bristol granted it.

Sidney Wilson then took up the defense of Jimmy Dolan, urging a change of venue to Doña Ana County, for the partisan feelings in Lincoln County made a fair trial of his client impossible. Judge Bristol agreed. The Kid's hearing for the murder of Sheriff Brady was shifted there as well.

Soon after the gavel fell on the grand jury proceedings, Fort Stanton also hosted the military court of inquiry that was meant to establish if Lieutenant Colonel Dudley should be court-martialed for the arson of the McSween residence, abetting in Alex's murder, looting the Tunstall mercantile store, and "procuring base and wicked men to make false and slanderous charges against Mrs. McSween in order to ruin her reputation."

The first to testify on the witness stand was His Excellency Governor Lew Wallace, who was humiliated by Henry Waldo, a partner in the firm of Catron & Elkins. The vast majority of Waldo's objections were sustained, and he forced the governor to admit that he'd gotten there from the East months after the incidents in question, his only acquaintance with affairs in Lincoln County being through the hearsay of intermediaries. The presiding judge was condescending in excusing the governor from further attendance at the inquiry.

Susan McSween did even worse, failing to recall things, seeming disinterested and confused, and confessing that she'd not fully read Ira Leonard's affidavit concerning the arson of her home and the murder of her husband. She was soon to marry George Barber in Lincoln and was addled by wedding details.

Then "William Bonney, called the Kid, also Antrim," took the stand and answered Waldo's questions, in general regarding "Where were you on the nineteenth of July last, and what, if anything, did you see of the movements and actions of the troops that day?" After two tiring days of telling and retelling what happened during the Big Killing, Billy was told, "You may retire."

Lieutenant Colonel Nathan A. M. Dudley then enjoyed the affirmations and encomiums of a host of Alexander A. McSween's enemies, including Jimmy Dolan, Dad Peppin, post surgeon Daniel Appel, J. B. Mathews, and Sheriff's Deputy Bob Olinger.

Ira Leonard sent a pessimistic report to the governor, calling Dudley "impetuous, vindictive, overbearing, self-conceited, and meddlesome" and noting, "I am thoroughly and completely disgusted with their proceedings."

The Kid registered his own disgust on June 17, 1879, by wringing the iron cuffs off his hands and dangling the irons to his hospitable jailers in the Juan Patrón store, saying, "Boys, I'm tired of this," and then just walking out the door and heading toward Fort Sumner on his stabled horse.

Foxes have dens and birds have nests, but the Kid had nowhere to lay his head. Either he slept in rooms above the saloons in Puerto de Luna and Anton Chico or he overnighted with Doc Scurlock in Fort Sumner or Charlie Bowdre in his new wrangler's job at the Thomas J. Yerby ranch, or he sang for his dinner in the huts of the ever-welcoming Mexican sheepherders. José Trujillo said of him, "*A todo el mundo le gusta El Chivato. Su mirada penetra hasta el corazón.*" Everybody likes the Kid. His face goes straight to the heart.

Like his older brother, Josie, the Kid earned as a gambler, even affecting the flat-faced gold pinkie ring that card cheats used to mirror whatever they dealt, though such hints were useless in the games of faro and monte that he favored. The house, or bank, had an edge in those games, so he was ever the house, watching pixilated cowhands guess and guess again on cards until their wages were lost. And since he never drank, he never fell ill to a case of the stupids.

The Atchison, Topeka & Santa Fe Railroad was famously having its grand arrival at the Las Vegas depot on July 4, so the Kid headed there to join in the festivities and visit his medical student friend Henry Hoyt, who was then bartending at the Cherokee Hotel on Railroad Avenue. Invited by Henry to the hotel's free lunch, the Kid took a seat in a booth and saw a finely dressed man in his thirties walk in and lean over the oaken bar to make a quiet inquiry of the mixologist. Henry seemed surprised as he answered and lifted his dishclothed hand to indicate the Kid there in the booth, sitting agreeably with a glass of lemonade. The man looked over his right shoulder at Billy and seemed to like what he saw, for he limped over on a bad ankle, a glass of Anheuser-Busch lager beer in his hand. "I hear you're Billy Bonney," he said.

With hesitation, he said he was.

"You been selected."

"For what?"

"Would you be so kind as to let me sit?"

The Kid threw his hand at the bench across from him, and the stranger took off a gentleman's hat. His blinking eyes were blue, his hair was chestnut brown, his beard was trimmed in the fashionable style of a physician. He looked like someone rich and leisured who had the common touch. Offering his hand, he said, "Thomas Howard. Nashville, Tennessee." The Kid shook it. "I have been looking for William H. Bonney. The Kid? I been reading about you in the papers."

"You a reporter or a cattle detective?"

"Well, neither. You might say I'm an entrepreneur."

"I have no idea what that means."

Thomas Howard sipped some beer like he didn't want to and put the half-filled glass on the table. "I run a very profitable commercial enterprise that involves enormous initiative and risk."

It felt like the prelude to some kind of sales pitch. "Would you be hankering for a ham sandwich?" the Kid asked. "They're free."

"Ain't no such thing as free, Kid."

"Still, I'm hungry," Billy said, and he was getting up when Thomas Howard forcibly gripped his wrist with a serious, malevolent, thou-shalt-go-no-further stare.

"Siddown."

"I'm carrying," the Kid warned him.

With gloomy, frightening earnestness, the man gritted out, "Likewise."

The Kid flopped back in the booth like a scolded teenager.

Having got his way, the rage gradually left him, and Mr. Howard seemed to ruminate some before saying, "We had a gang that held up banks and trains, but we had a reversal of fortune. Some pals died, some went to prison. And now we and my family are on the backside of hard times and I'm on a recruiting trip."

The Kid had an inkling. "This reversal of fortune. Where?"

It seemed a sore point, but the man from Tennessee said, "Northfield, Minnesota."

The Kid took it in and then tilted forward to whisper, "You're Jesse James!"

"And like I say, I'm recruiting."

"I hardly do nothing with people involved. Railroads and banks, that's complexicated."

"All's I need is a wizard gunslinger with sand in him. And has to be smarter than the dirt-farmin Reubens I been with. They'd swat at a hornet's nest with their hands."

The Kid said, "I honestly feel flattered that you looked me up. I mean, it's a privilege to meet such a famous person, but I'm riding opposite of the owl-hoot trail now and not interested in your livelihood."

Jesse James seethed like he was chewing rocks, and the Kid's hand inched toward his sidearm in case it came to that. But then Jesse looked around the restaurant and at all the reasonable people there and his hot temper went on ice. "Look at me getting wrathful with a boy just exercising his freedom. Which is all I'm trying to do. I do swear, I'll be the death of myself someday."

Henry Hoyt walked over just to chat, but Jesse was already standing. He shook Hoyt's hand in a genial way but got close to his ear to whisper, "You have met Jesse James. Now you can go ahead and die." And then he was gone outside.

The Kid watched him cross the street and vanish in an alley, and he thought, *If that is an outlaw, you are not an outlaw.*

*   *   *

On July 5, in a scathing, eight-hour peroration to the court of inquiry at Fort Stanton, Henry Waldo sought to exterminate all enemies of Nathan Dudley, calling them ignorant, lying, irresponsible, and shameless. "Especially does Ira E. Leonard loom up above the waste water of the dead sea of selfishness," he said, but he had not yet gotten to the Kid. "Then was brought forward William Bonney, alias 'Antrim,' alias 'the Kid,' a known criminal of the worst type although hardly up to his majority, a murderer by profession, as records of this court connect him with two cowardly and atrocious assassinations. There were warrants enough for him on the nineteenth day of July last to have papered him from his head to his boots. Yet he was engaged to do service here as a witness and his testimony aptly illustrated that he would not hesitate to swear falsely about soldiers firing at him that night as he was escaping. 'A liar once is a liar all the time.'"

Eight weeks after the court of inquiry commenced, the result was this:

In view of the evidence adduced, the Court is of the opinion that Lieut. Col. N. A. M. Dudley, Ninth US Cavalry, has not been guilty of any violation of law or of orders, that the act of proceeding to the town of Lincoln on the 19th day of July, 1878, was prompted by the most humane and worthy motives and of good military judgment under exceptional circumstances. None of the allegations made against him by His Excellency the Governor or by Ira E. Leonard have been sustained and that proceedings before a Court Martial are therefore unnecessary.

PART THREE

WHO IS IT?

(JULY 1879–JULY 1881)

15

SHERIFFS

That summer a smart-aleck journalist asserted that hundreds were in pursuit of the Kid and dearly hoping *not* to find him. But word got to Sheriff George Kimbrell that Billy was hiding out in a shack alongside the Rio Bonito just six miles from Lincoln, and because his deputies were in his office and heard the rumor as well, the sheriff felt obliged to go after the Kid.

There was some dillydallying and a host of invented tasks that he said first needed tending to, so the sheriff and his posse didn't get to the pinewood shack until sundown. They saw no sign of movement from afar, just a wisp of smoke from the chimney. But a forward scout did find a fettered horse near the river. Looked like a hard keeper of an animal indulging in green foliage and watching the timid scout with unblinking disrespect.

Sheriff Kimbrell thought someone ought to crawl up to the only window and have a look-see, but he got no volunteers.

"*You* could do it," a deputy told him.

But a fluttery reluctance befell the sheriff and he confessed, "Nah, it's not just that I like the Kid, it's that I also like living."

Kimbrell changed his strategy to cautious waiting throughout the night in a semicircle sixty yards distant. Soon enough the Kid would open the door and their guns would catch him in a crossfire.

Hunger was overtaking them and skeeters whined at the ears of the posse. They kept slapping themselves in the head and grousing.

Inside the shack, the Kid cooked frijoles in a saucepan, then roasted green coffee beans in the same pan and stirred in water with a fork until he got the coffee to a boil. He let the grounds settle, then filled his tin cup. Hearing an unfamiliar sound, he sidled to a knothole in a plank and peered out into the pitch-black. Humps of infrequent motion lay on the earth and whispering heaps leaned against fir trees.

Wasn't but one way out for a normal person, but the Kid crouched under the window to get to the fireplace, where he doused the wood embers with his coffee and quietly shoveled them, still hissing, into a bucket. Wrapping his firearms, hat, and necessaries into a woolen poncho and tying it to his left ankle with twine, he stooped inside the fireplace and squeezed up inside the hot chimney just as he'd done at age fourteen in the Silver City jail. Alternately reaching up his arms and kicking his feet as in an Australian crawl, the hot bricks scalding and soot-blackening him, he did manage to get out and onto the shingled roof, squatting to haul up the jutting burdens in the poncho and assemble himself in full armory as he looked down at a semicircle of men in front who were either sleeping or swatting at insects. And then there was nothing left to do but jump and jar his legs with the hard hit to the ground and to roll in loam, where he halted on all fours, his finely tuned ears seeking the sounds of notice or stirring. But he heard nothing but an older man mumbling in dream, "Oh dear, oh dear." The Kid stood up and walked toward his horse like just another deputy selecting a night pee in the river, and he left in an easterly direction.

Sheriff Kimbrell and his posse plodded into Lincoln the next morning, slumping with hangdog looks and scratching their itches.

Inquiries were made about what had happened, but the sheriff only stated, "I don't want to talk about it."

Confidence in him was forever lost, and some of the wealthier cattlemen in Lincoln County began seeking a finer and more stalwart candidate for the sheriff's office when next election time came.

Early in July 1879, James Joseph Dolan was examined in a habeas corpus hearing concerning the homicide in the first degree of Huston Ingraham Chapman. Although he'd initially testified that he wasn't there when the murder occurred, then that he was there but without a gun, he now claimed in his own defense that he'd seen nothing because he was so drunk and he *did* fire a shot but at the ground to call off his friends from their hazing of the lawyer. The contradictions and inconsistencies in Jimmy's sworn testimony would have gotten him locked up for perjury anywhere else, but Judge Warren Bristol's affection for him was such that he decided to release Jimmy on $3,000 bail until the next term of court in Socorro.

Upon his leaving the courtroom, a journalist asked him, "Will you be found guilty in Socorro, do you think?"

"Hardly dat."

"So you'll be getting off scot-free?"

Jimmy smirked. "Luck o' the Irish, boyo."

On Sunday, July 13, in a Roman Catholic ceremony held in a friend's parlor, Jimmy married Caroline Franzis "Lina" Fritz, the German-American niece of Jimmy's former business partner and commanding officer at Fort Stanton, the late Emil Fritz. Lina was eighteen and exceptionally pretty, so Jimmy, who was twelve years older, had been forced to overcome many other paramours in his wooing, and he never did earn the approval of Lina's father, who failed to attend the wedding. There was a formal reception afterward, at which Jimmy was reminded that the civil insurrection in Lincoln had commenced exactly one year earlier. "Water under the bridge," Jimmy said. And then the small group waved goodbye as the newlyweds left for a luxurious two-month honeymoon in Texas.

Jimmy could afford it, for he had invested in gold and silver mines in the Jicarilla Mountains northeast of White Oaks and culled enough of a fortune to get into the mercantile business again, the Jas. J. Dolan General Store finding location in John H. Tunstall's building in Lincoln because Thomas Catron held the mortgage on the House. Jimmy even acquired the Englishman's *choza* and ranch on the Rio Feliz, later constructing a solid, handsome home there and joining District Attorney William Rynerson in establishing the Feliz Land & Cattle Company on Harry's former rangeland. Jimmy would be elected Lincoln county treasurer twice, and then, despite his arrogance and contentiousness, he would become a New Mexico state senator.

But Jimmy's family life was filled with tragedy. His first child, a son, was two years old when he died; a daughter died at age five; and his wife, Lina, was just twenty-five when she died after giving birth to another girl. Jimmy soon married his children's nanny, a fretful, unsmiling woman who screamed back at his screaming until she cowered beneath his slaps and Wellington boots. His drunkenness became as regular, reeling, and demented as that of his idol L. G. Murphy, and James Dolan finally died of delirium tremens in 1898, aged fifty. Which was just as well, since he didn't have to deal with the indignity of realizing that his name would have been lost to history were it not for his association with that scoundrel Billy the Kid.

To keep lawmen and cavalry patrols akilter, the indicted Kid rotated among the gambling haunts of Las Vegas, Anton Chico, Puerto de Luna, and Fort Sumner, staying just a few days at each before skedaddling off, and since Manuela Herrera was now residing with Charlie Bowdre on Thomas J. Yerby's ranch twenty miles north of the old fort, the Kid's trunk of finer clothes was stored in the old adobe quartermaster's store with Celsa Gutiérrez.

She'd become the Kid's *querida*, his mistress, and her generally intoxicated husband, Saval, vaguely acknowledged the arrangement before riding to White Oaks to prospect for currency metals, telling the Kid in a glum so-long, "*Billito. Cuida bien de ella.*" Billy. Take good care of her.

But Billito lost too much at cards and he was running out of cash, so in October of 1879, the Kid, Folliard, Bowdre, and Scurlock sought to fortify their scant wages by heading to Uncle John Chisum's rangeland some fifty miles south of Fort Sumner. The cattle there were now officially owned by the St. Louis firm of Hunter, Evans & Company, and the executives had given up the Jinglebob way of branding, in which a hot iron burned a long rail along the cow's flank and an ear was notched so that a large lobe of it dangled like jewelry. The Hunter, Evans brand was far easier to change, enticing the former Regulators led by the Kid to steal a herd of 118 cattle and drive them north to Yerby's ranch, rebrand them, and sell the lot to Colorado beef buyers for about $800.

The Kid divvied up the loot four ways, and then thirty-year-old Josiah Gordon Scurlock stunned the gang by saying his nineteen-year-old wife, Antonia, was pregnant with their first child and he was collecting these earnings, quitting outlawry altogether, and heading off to Texas. His missing front teeth put a whistle in the statement.

"We sure are dwindling," Charlie said. "Won't be but three of us Ironclads left."

Tom said in frustration, "Doc, I'm so mad at ya I'm gonna find an insane asylum and have ya committed."

But the Kid said, "Okay with me if you go, Doc. Could be wisdom is prevailing."

"Well, I just reckon the noose is tightening for us all," Doc said. "We retire now or be retired later."

Doc took his past-due wages from Pete Maxwell in the form of fifty pounds of flour, and then he indeed took Antonia Herrera Scurlock in a buckboard to Potter County, Texas, where he first hired on as a mailman, then shifted to other towns where he became a much-loved schoolteacher, a histrionic reciter of poetry, and a doctor of last resort. Doc and Antonia eventually had ten children, and he died in Eastland, halfway between Abilene and Dallas, in 1929, three years after *The Saga of Billy the Kid* became a bestseller and made his former gang internationally famous. But Doc remained so penitently silent on the topic of his history that only an innuendo about it in one obituary alerted his neighbors to his gaudy and reckless past.

Whenever in Fort Sumner, the Kid earned his income with card dealing, favoring Beaver Smith's saloon for the intimacy of the room and the heat of the coal-burning World & Sterling stove. The floor was tiled, there was a chandelier over the gaming table, and the ornate mahogany bar was hung with four white towels for the wet its customers carried in or slopped in their sottishness. Because of its whores, Bob Hargrove's much larger saloon on the north side of the fort seemed to collect a gunslinger crowd.

With no takers for monte one fall afternoon, the Kid ordered a pint of sarsaparilla at the bar and then recognized the skinny and stoic bartender as the man a near-foot taller than Billy who'd been in livery at Pete Maxwell's Christmas dinner. "You're the one *Los Hispanos* nicknamed Juan Largo!" the Kid said.

"Well, yes. I'll concede that I'm tall." His speech had the slow cadence and syrupy accent of the Deep South.

"We met at the Maxwell house."

The bartender seemed embarrassed—probably because of his but-lering getup then. "That was just for the extra money," he said.

The Kid offered his hand, and the bartender stopped drying a shot glass to shake it.

"William H. Bonney. Kid, my pals call me."

Even in later photographs the future sheriff seemed to have an alien and unsettling habit of widening his eyes as if in shock or as if he were dredging his faulty memory for further information. Whenever captured in a group portrait, he was the lone man who did not fit in. And now his stare seemed to loiter over the Kid's face until his dark thoughts finally became "I heard stories about you, Mr. Bonney. Some of them true most likely."

"Hardly any. And your name?"

"Pat Garrett."

Patrick Floyd Jarvis Garrett was born on June 5, 1850, in Chambers County, Alabama, and grew up on an eighteen-hundred-acre Louisi-ana plantation in Claiborne Parish. Even as a high-strung little boy he imitated the foreman by dragging a bullwhip through the cotton fields while yelling and glaring at the slaves. Although he became expert at hunting, fishing, and horseback riding—really, anything done out-doors—Garrett received little formal schooling, and he followed his father in having no truck with organized religion.

He was fifteen when the Confederacy lost the War of Rebellion and Yankees seized much of the estate. His father drank himself to death within three years, and financial hardship so poisoned family life that at nineteen Garrett left home, condemning his sisters to sudden marriages and his brothers Alfred and Hillary to hardscrabble farming. Garrett was hired as a cattle gunman to fend off rustlers from the huge LS Ranch in West Texas and, after a squabble over a card game, was indicted for "intent to murder" a freed slave in Bowie County. But he managed to shake the sheriff's deputies who were tailing him and they lost interest in the chase.

Rumor later had it that Garrett had married in Sweetwater, Texas, and fathered a child, forsaking both the mother and the baby girl when he walked outside, as he'd told his wife, to smoke his pipe. And then with some partners he became a buffalo hunter in the flat grasslands of northwest Texas on what was called the Staked Plains, slaughtering from fifty to one hundred placid animals per day and collecting twenty-five cents for each three-dollar hide.

Essentially he and a hundred others like him were shooting themselves out of their livelihoods, and soon, with scarce animals to skin, the hunters went sullen and pouty. An Irish kid named Joe Briscoe was one of the skinners and was vexed that he couldn't get the stink of blood and intestines out of his clothes. Watching Briscoe squat by a brook and dunk his shirts in its ice water, Garrett said, "I reckon you have to be as ignorant as an Irishman to think you can wash your camisoles in that mud." The Briscoe kid took it hurtfully and there were oaths and haranguing until he peevishly swung at Garrett with an ax. Without anticipating the certain outcome, Garrett fired his Winchester and killed the kid, watching him topple into the campfire and just lie there feeding the flames until Garrett yanked the body out. After a full day of repentance and self-loathing, Garrett finally turned himself in to officials at Fort Griffin, suicidally wishing to be hanged. But without even an investigation, the officials decided his sounded like an act of self-defense, and so he was off the hook.

Soon he quit his unprofitable hunting job, and, fed up with the emptiness of the Panhandle, he wandered west, drunkenly frittering away his savings with gambling and whoring until he finally found himself, penniless, outside Fort Sumner. Seeing cattle being moved upstream alongside the salty Rio Pecos, he rode his horse up to an overseer in a buckboard and told him he dearly needed work.

Pete Maxwell looked over a dour, wide-mustached, rail-thin man in his late twenties, six and a half feet tall and half of that seeming to be his stovepipe legs. He later recalled that Garrett's nag was so sway-backed his boots nearly dragged on the ground. Maxwell asked, "What can you do for me, Lengthy?"

"Ride anything with a hide and rope better than any cowpoke you got."

Maxwell had faith in the solemn man's integrity and told him to hop aboard.

Garrett's extreme height and Southern formality were fascinating to the far shorter Mexican folks at Fort Sumner, and though he failed in his miserable tries at Spanish, there was a good deal of envy among the señoritas when it was Juanita Gutiérrez who became his wife in 1877. She was pregnant at the time and just a few weeks later died of a miscarriage.

His grief became rage, and when he heard that Comanches had sto-len a herd of twenty-seven horses from a Roswell ranch, Garrett cra-zily took it personally and organized a vigilante group to go after the horse thieves. Relentless in his pursuit and not seeming to need food, water, or rest, he outstripped his pluckless companions, who one by one peeled off for home until it was just Garrett alone heading over a hill at sundown. Six days passed with no word of him, and then he achingly rode into Roswell with half the stolen horses and hefting a gunnysack that he finally spilled out onto the wooden porch of the general store. Ash Upson, who would become his closest friend and ghostwriter, collected the murderous proof that was six pairs of worn moccasins, a few of them still spotted with blood.

Hearing the tale from Upson, John Chisum went up to Fort Sum-ner to interview Garrett about running for sheriff when George Kim-brell's term was up, and then he sent a letter rife with misspellings "To his Exelency Gov Lue Wallis." Uncle John advised the governor on where to station men to "prevent Robers from coming in off the plains on to the Pecos and give protection to this place and the Citizens below." And he noted that "Pat Garrett who resides hear would be a very suitable man to take charge of the squad East of this place if authorized to do so."

Although he stayed on even terms with Pete Maxwell, Garrett sought indoor work with the hard winter coming on, and he found a job in Beaver Smith's saloon. When off his saloonkeeper duties, Garrett persistently lost at five-card draw with the Kid, who generally only played hands that seemed likely to win while Garrett would play even a deuce-seven off-suit, hopefulness his reigning emotion.

Elderly Beaver Smith called them Big Casino and Little Casino. They weren't close friends, they just knew each other, and that was enough for Pat Garrett to fill the silence one rainy afternoon in November by confessing that he intended to marry Apolonaria in January.

"Apolonaria Gutiérrez? Your wife's sister? Celsa's sister-in-law?"

"You drafting a family tree?"

"I'm just happy for you and hope I'll be invited to the wedding."

Garrett tilted forward with a hollowed, nothing-thereness in his eyes, eyes as dead as the buttons on a doll. "I heard all about you and Celsa," he said. "Don't make you a relative."

On November 23, 1879, the Kid celebrated his twentieth birthday by doing the idle things he generally did, but a sidewalk photographer showed up in front of Beaver Smith's saloon with his camera, props, tented booth, and boy assistant, and the Kid decided to indulge himself with a ferrotype portrait that was then called a carte de visite. The cost was twenty-five cents.

With a full measure of snootiness, the photographer considered Billy's rather slovenly, not-put-together look and asked, "Are you wearing *that*?"

"Yep, I am."

"You have nothing more formal?"

"All the ordinaries dress up for picture making. I want to be different."

The Kid's hat that Sunday was a dark fedora, cocked to the right, with a crown that seemed crushed by a whack. A yellow bandanna was loosely knotted at his neck, and under that was a childish blue sailor shirt with an anchor design and a tan unbuttoned vest with lapels overlaid by an overlarge, acorn brown cardigan with a hem that hung as low as his thighs. His trousers were navy blue and tucked inside dirty midcalf cavalry boots constructed with leather so thin the boots rumpled at the ankles. In accordance with the manly style then, Billy posed with his Winchester rifle in his pale left hand, his bulky cartridge belt and Colt revolver slung to the right. His gambler's ring on his left little finger sparked in the sunlight.

Billy said with nervousness, "Some Indians think getting captured by a camera steals your soul."

The photographer was mixing chemicals. "Well, there might be something to that. Look at celebrated, much-pictured people. Such odd behaviors!"

The Anthony four-tube camera was already positioned, so as the photographer painted a collodion emulsion on a lacquered rectangle of thin iron, his assistant guided Billy to his mark, adjusting the U of a vertical brace behind his neck to hold his head stable for the six-second exposure. And then it was done. The wet plate ended up with four fractionally different halftone images, each flipped so that Billy's right hand seemed his left.

The practiced assistant used tin snips to perfectly divide the plate into four separate picture cards, and the Kid carried one to fifteen-year-old Paulita as a gift.

She sank onto her plush white bed to examine his portrait, and she seemed at a loss for words.

"You don't like it."

"I'm just disappointed that you can't tell the color of your eyes. They're such a lovely powder blue. And your hair needs cutting, and it looks dark, not your honey blond. Plus your ears stick out like bat wings."

She kindly did not note what he could see now, that he seemed girlish, with wide hips and narrow shoulders and those ever-unmanly hands. And his squirrely front teeth looked even bigger, like he could eat fruit through a picket fence.

"Oh, please don't misunderstand, Billy. I'm really grateful for this and I'll cherish it forever, but it doesn't do you justice."

"You're saying I look like a slack-jawed oaf."

"So you see it, too? You're a handsome man! You're the kind of cavalier who makes wives fall out of love with their husbands."

The Kid wondered if she knew about Celsa.

"So this is your birthday?" she asked.

"Yep."

"How old?"

"Twenty."

She was chagrined. She scanned her very feminine bedroom and concluded, "But I have nothing to give you."

"A kiss?"

She smiled and softly complied.

"Don't quit," the Kid said. "Kiss me till I'm drunk with you."

She did.

On January 10, 1880, faithful Tom Folliard visited from wherever, and since he'd been alone for weeks he was in the mood for a rollick and soon grew tired of the smallness and innkeeper calm at Beaver Smith's, harassing the Kid to find him some action and sporting ladies in Bob Hargrove's saloon.

Walking across the parade grounds in front of the Maxwell house and in a hunker from the sleeting cold, the Kid was called to by Jim Chisum, Uncle John's younger brother, who'd been in conversation with Pete Maxwell on the front porch. Pete offered a friendly wave and went back inside the former officers' quarters as Jim and one of his hands, a Jack Finan, hurried through the gate of the picket fence to interrogate them.

Jim told the Kid and Tom that he'd been retrieving stolen cattle in Canyon Cueva near the village of Juan de Dios. Would the Kid know anything about that? The Kid said he didn't. Jim and Jack squinnied their eyes at him.

"I'll grant you I have rustled from time to time, but not in this particular instance."

Jack Finan said, "Pete says you prolly did."

"Pete says a lot of things, and he lies like a no-legged dog."

Tom was hugging himself as he asked, "How long we gonna stand out here? I'm frozen!"

The Kid asked, "Would you galoots like to join us in Hargrove's? Just to let bygones be bygones? I'm buying."

Jim Chisum dithered a little, but Jack Finan scoured the Kid with his glower. The Kid chose to take note of Jack's gun, an ivory-handled Colt single-action Army revolver that shone like new chrome. "You got a handsome hog leg in that scabbard."

"Cost me plenty," Jack said, his face hinting at a readiness to smile.

"Could I heft it?"

Jack was tentative as he handed it to him. The Kid felt its weight, tested its balance, spun it on his trigger finger, and looked down the barrel at the front sight as he aimed at a sheet of newspaper flying on the wind.

"Go ahead and try it," Jack said.

The Kid shot, and the sheet of newspaper swatted. "Wow!" he said, just to be charming. He fired again with his left hand, and the first bullet hole got larger. His third shot from hip-high was elsewhere on the page. "Enviable piece," the Kid said. And because they were heading into a public place, he half-turned the cylinder so that the hammer was on the first spent shell and couldn't misfire. Jack took the pistol back with satisfied pride.

Even in midafternoon, there was the noise of someone cranking organ music from a hurdy-gurdy, the hee-haws of drunken laughter at the long bar, and four flirting daughters of joy in frilly, full-length white dresses inveigling fallen men. Red-haired Tom went to one who was no prettier than the others and confided a few sentences. She tugged him by the hand into the stalls in back.

The Kid bought pints of Anheuser-Busch for Chisum and Finan and got a porcelain cup of coffee for himself. And then he heard a drunk yell, "Are you Bunny? I's here alookin for Kid Bunny!"

The Kid leaned toward the mixologist. "You know who that is?"

"Says he's Joe Grant. Says they call him Texas Red."

"Stewed?"

"Half a quart of our rotgut so far."

The Kid waved his hand and called, "Kid Bonney, over here!"

Jim Chisum whispered, "You need help, just say so."

Widening his winter coat to give freedom to his six-shooter, the Kid said, "I'll deal with it."

Joe Grant was zigzagging over to him, skidding off the backs of drinkers and swinging his forearm at the vexation or bumping chairs into screeching changes of position. His hand gripped the bar to hold himself upright. He was fat and hatless, and the fringe of auburn beard at his jaw so matched the fringe on his skull that the Kid thought his chapped, round face would look pretty much the same upside-down.

"So, you Bunny?"

"William H. Bonney."

"We gots a score to shettle."

"Why don't I buy you a shot or two of fire starter and you can tell me all about it?"

"Had enough for now." Weaving and seeming about to fall, Joe Grant's unfocused glances around himself fell on Jack Finan's fancy .45. "Lemme see that gun."

The Kid nodded permission, and Jack handed it over.

Grant admired it for a second, then asked, "Wa was I sayin?"

"Shettling something," the Kid said.

"Here. Here," Grant said to Finan. "My gun while I'm lookin." Exchanging weapons, he shoved his own pistol into Jack's holster, then he lewdly licked the shining barrel and ivory handle of the Colt with his own pitiful impression of rapier wit. "She so perty!"

"So," the Kid patiently said. "What's your plan?"

His face hardened. "Ah'm gonna kill you afore you do."

A reverent, churchlike silence took over as hard-bitten cowhands and gunmen in the saloon edged away from the forecast confrontation, not wanting to get anything on them.

The Kid chose to be pacifying. "Oh, wha'd'ya want to kill anybody for, Joe? Give Jack his pistol and let's solve the world's problems with whiskey."

Joe Grant was shaking his head from side to side. "Nope, mind's made up." But then he tilted a little as he uncertainly focused on Jim Chisum. "You Uncle John? Hafta kill Chisum firs."

His halitosis could frazzle houseplants.

Jim's and Jack's hands were easing down to their holsters as the Kid lifted his hand in the halt sign. "Hold on, Joe. You got the wrong sow by the ear. This is Jim Chisum, Uncle John's brother. And he done nothing to you."

"Well, I gots this shiny gun and she's all *go!*"

"Shall I show you to the door? Walk with me outside." The Kid strolled from Joe Grant's fuddled menace toward the saloon doors, the ever-so-quiet crowd dividing for him as he heard Jim Chisum call out, "Kid!" and then heard the click as the hammer cocked and snapped onto an empty chamber. The Kid hesitated and heard another snap as in frustration Joe Grant tried to kill him again. And then the Kid ducked and twisted around in a crouch and in sudden rage and viciousness fired his own Colt three times, *bang, bang, bang*, each shot hitting Joe Grant in the chin in a gruesome destruction that was the size of a fist. Grant was dead so quick there was no chance for reaction or even for pain. He fell against the foot rail of the bar, and his body sagged gradually to the floor, blood eddying from him.

The Kid considered his victim and said, "Sorry, Joe, but I've been there too often." Recalling Windy Cahill and Arizona, he looked around through the acrid gray haze of gun smoke. The saloon customers were still holding their ears from the noise and cautiously inching away, like this was finally the frightening Kid they'd heard so much about. "You saw what happened, right? It was self-defense."

"He was spoilin for it!" a far-off man yelled out.

Another man agreed, "You had yourself no option in the matter."

Jack Finan bent down to extract his ivory-handled .45 from the corpse's surprisingly firm grip.

"We'll clean all this up," the bartender said. "But you better go, Kid."

Tom Folliard had heard the shots and was running into the main room, his face full of horror as he buttoned up his trousers. "What'd I miss?"

With the jazzy exhilaration he always felt when he found himself still alive, the Kid told him, "Oh nothing. It was a game of two and I got there first."

Because Celsa wanted his company and because Saval was still prospecting northeast of White Oaks, hunting for fortunes that would never be found, she invited the Kid to Pat F. Garrett's Wednesday marriage to her cousin Apolonaria in the white, twin-spired San Jose Catholic Church in Anton Chico. Garrett was nearing thirty, his wife was twenty-two. Joining them in the double wedding ceremony was a Virginian named Barney Mason, who still worked for Pete Maxwell, and Barney's seventeen-year-old bride, Juanita Madril.

Apolonaria's father, José, owned a successful freighting company, and he hosted a fiesta afterward in the Abercrombie general store, founded by a Scottish father and son who'd frequently been hospitable to the Kid. And though Garrett wouldn't himself dance, he howled encouragement and fervently applauded the hilarity of friends making, he thought, fools of themselves. Celsa fed the Kid some wedding cake and got up to see if the quartet would play "Turkey in the Straw." The Kid found the tune irresistible, and he was encircled and cheered as he sang, dancing an Irish jig his mother had taught him. And Celsa noticed that Garrett's face was now solemn, for the Kid of course was famously indicted and Celsa knew that Patrick F. Garrett was considering a run for Sheriff of Lincoln County.

16

THE RUSTLERS

Ever in motion, the Kid recruited into his gang his cousin Yginio Salazar and his pal Pascal Chaves, Garrett's friend Barney Mason, and Billie Wilson, a headlong eighteen-year-old petty thief originally from Ohio with whom the Kid was often confused by the authorities. Wilson had owned a livery stable in the burgeoning tent city of White Oaks, which, since its founding in 1879, was filling up with optimistic miners. But Billie Wilson sold out his faltering business in exchange for a sack full of counterfeit hundred-dollar bills that looked pretty darn good to him. Also in White Oaks, at West & Dedrick Livery & Sales, the Kid recruited the worshipful Dedrick brothers and even thrilled them with the gift of one of his ferrotype portraits. Handed down for generations, it is still the only certifiable photograph of William H. Bonney, age twenty.

Calling themselves the Rustlers, the night-riding gallants reportedly stole forty-eight Indian ponies from the idly guarded Mescalero Apache reservation and roamed up and down the Rio Pecos in the hostile cold of February selling them off to horse traders who could not resist a bargain. In March, it was claimed that the gang went after the livestock of Uncle John's kid brothers, Jim and Pitzer Chisum, riding off with ten steers, ten bullocks, and two pregnant cows. Charlie Bowdre joined them for an eastward foray into Los Portales in May, stealing fifty-four cattle from a Canadian River ranchers' association, steering them cross-country all the way to White Oaks and selling them for ten dollars a head in a deal that the Dedrick brothers had arranged. They thieved from a cattleman at Agua Azul, from a cattleman named Ellis near Stinking Springs, and even supposedly stole seven thoroughbreds from Uncle John Chisum, daring him to try to retrieve them.

But much of that accounting was Ash Upson's and written insincerely in 1882, when he thought exaggeration, outrage, and garish lies would help Pat Garrett's book sales. And Upson could have claimed in 1880 that the Kid was the source of any crime perpetrated in Lincoln County, from burglary to hijacking a train, and a lot of the Anglo citizens would have believed it. The Kid was not yet twenty-one, he still didn't need to shave, and even wary people on meeting him remembered his cordial smile and fun-loving nature. Yet he was increasingly considered a fiend with a lust for blood by those seeking commerce and prosperity for New Mexico, for whom he seemed the impediment, the hitch in the get-along, the enemy of progress. And the Kid was not yet aware that there was a faction that desperately needed to have him done away with.

Heading up the hunt for a new sheriff was Joseph C. Lea, a former Confederate Army officer who'd fought alongside Cole Younger. Lea would later be called the father of Roswell, but in 1880 he was just the owner of its few buildings and a homestead ranch. Hearing praise of Pat Garrett from an excited Uncle John, Lea invited the saloonkeeper to stay in his own Roswell home just long enough to establish residence in Lincoln County. And John Chisum joined them on the homestead one evening for dinner, skirting political topics until Mrs. Lea took the dinner plates and cutlery away and the three men lit Chisum's gifts of La Flor de Sanchez y Haya cigars.

"I guess it's up to me to broach the subject first," Chisum said. "We want to get your mind right on what our intentions are for our new sheriff."

Garrett grayed the air in front to him with smoke before he asked, "Which are?"

"Well, we frankly need you to kill the Kid dead."

Captain Lea used the rim of a saucer to carve the ash from his cigar and took a more lawyerly, brick-by-brick approach. "Uncle John and I have ambitions for Roswell and in fact for all of New Mexico. We foresee a time when most every major town will have a railway depot, a schoolhouse, even a doctor's office. We want land that is platted and fenced. We want roads instead of cattle trails. We want factories and merchants and all the niceties of civilization."

"What we *got* is wildness and anarchy," Chisum said. "We got Kid Bonney on the loose taking whatever he pleases, whenever it suits him. Carefree, headlong, guns in every hand."

Lea said, "The Kid's days are numbered, and I imagine he knows that. We think of him and the frontier he inhabits as doomed, for—"

Interrupting Lea, Chisum spoke around the cigar in his mouth as he said, "Your *job* will be to uproot the Kid and his lackeys like *choke-weeds* in the garden patch!"

Pat Garrett rocked back on his dining room chair and quietly considered his fine cigar. With his Southern formality he said, "Elect me sheriff and I'll be a cold and impersonal legal machine. Without sentiment or malice or resentment, I'll carry out the law to the last letter."

"Exactly what we hoped to hear," said J. C. Lea.

*   *   *

At the Democratic Party's nominating convention, Garrett was vaunted as a strict disciplinarian of impeccable morals who would persevere in an endless manhunt for the Kid and his ilk. Joseph Lea shouted in his convention speech, "Whosoever has encountered Pat Garrett will have noted how coolness, courage, and determination are written on his face! He alone shall bring law and order to the Territory and spell doom to the villains wreaking havoc on our lands!"

Running against him was Sheriff George Kimbrell, a former government scout and justice of the peace and an easygoing Republican who was thought to be too friendly to Billy and too timid in his prosecution of criminals. Even though both he and Garrett had Mexican wives, Kimbrell was far more liked by a native community that despised the wealthy associates of the Santa Fe Ring because of the thefts of their lands.

Louisiana-born George Curry would become governor of New Mexico in 1907, but in 1880 he was just nineteen and working for the firm of Dowlin & DeLaney, when the Kid, whom he didn't know from Adam, rode onto the ranch and was invited to join Curry for dinner. In his twentieth-century autobiography, Curry recalled, "He asked me how I thought the election for sheriff would go in Las Tablas, our voting precinct. I told him our votes would be for Pat Garrett. He asked, bluntly, why I thought Garrett would win, and I replied just as bluntly that Garrett was a brave man who would arrest Billy the Kid or any other outlaw for whom a warrant was outstanding."

The Kid told him, "You're a good cook and a good fellow, George, but if you think Pat Garrett is going to carry this precinct for sheriff, you are a darn poor politician."

The Kid was right about Las Tablas; Garrett got only one vote out of forty. But in Lincoln County's final tally of its 499 votes for sheriff, Pat F. Garrett of Roswell got 320 and was elected.

Paulita Maxwell later recalled, "Nothing ever gave Fort Sumner such a shock of surprise as Garrett's selection by the cattle interests to be sheriff. He was just a saloonkeeper, with no experience as a detective and no reputation as a gunfighter."

The election was on November 2, 1880, and Sheriff Kimbrell would have normally stayed in office until January 1, but with cattlemen providing him a financial incentive, Kimbrell appointed Garrett as his deputy and pretty much vacationed for the next two months.

A journalist interviewing the new deputy sheriff inquired if he thought he could quell New Mexico's outlawry, and Garrett told him, "Yes, I can. Because outlaws all have one thing in common: sooner or later they find themselves wanting to get caught."

Governor Lew Wallace's novel *Ben-Hur: A Tale of the Christ* was published in New York by Harper & Brothers on November 12, and he was in the East, neglecting his government duties and also ignoring the telegraphed entreaties of Billy's lawyer, Judge Ira Leonard, who vowed the Kid would cease his illegal activities if he was just given the clemency that the governor had promised.

Soon everything began turning sour.

About the time that Lew Wallace was getting the first accolades for his bestselling novel, the Kid and his gang were riding into Puerto de Luna, forty miles northwest of Fort Sumner. Arctic cold flooded over the West that November, and they all wore woolen scarves over their heads and ears and hunched under the wind with bandannas over their noses, snarling at the agonies of weather. Wanting food and heat, they hitched their horses and with their spurs jangling walked into the restaurant and general store of Alexander Grzelachowski (Gur-zel-a-hóf-ski). He was a jovial, overweight, fifty-six-year-old former Catholic priest from Gracina, Poland, who'd been invited to New Mexico by the archbishop of Santa Fe, Jean-Baptiste l'Amy. But after some years as pastor of a church in Las Vegas, "my laziness ate all my wits," as Grzela-chowski put it, and he left the priesthood. Billy now thought of Padre Polaco's place as his lair in Puerto de Luna, and he felt like flaunting his friendship with an educated European to his gang. With him were Tom Folliard, Charlie Bowdre, and Billie Wilson. Of late Wilson and the Dedricks were getting away with passing Wilson's counterfeit currency, buying the finest new guns that way and so outraging the stung businessmen Jimmy Dolan and Joseph LaRue that they wrote letters of complaint to officials in the United States Treasury, who thereafter named Wilson, the Dedricks, and, of course, William H. Bonney as "persons of interest."

Wedged into the gang just that morning was twenty-six-year-old Dave Rudabaugh, originally from Illinois. Called Dirty Dave because of his aversion to soap and water, he was an offensive, ruthless, dark-bearded lout filling up the doorway in his slouch hat and rank goat-hair coat. Doc Holliday had gambled with him in Dodge City and was quoted as saying, "Dave Rudabaugh is an ignorant scoundrel! I disapprove of his very existence. I considered ending it myself on several occasions but self-control got the better of me." Wyatt Earp wore out three horses hunting for him following his robbery of a Santa Fe Railroad construction camp, and after Rudabaugh's failed train holdup in Kansas, Bat Masterson finally arrested him. But he was offered immunity if he squealed on his three partners in crime, and he did, avoiding a five-year sentence in Leavenworth prison. Ending up in Las Vegas, Rudabaugh hired on as a policeman just to seem an unlikely stagecoach robber, which he was, but after a friend was arrested for murder, Rudabaugh tried to jailbreak him, succeeding only in killing a much-loved deputy, Antonio Lino Valdez. So Dirty Dave was on the lam, found Billie Wilson in White Oaks, and Wilson in turn convinced the Kid they needed a fifth Rustler. Currying the Kid's favor, Rudabaugh had said, "Real sorry Alex McSween was taken from us. When he was just getting into lawyering, he was a schoolteacher at the Miles farm in Eureka. Taught my little sister Ida. Nice man, she said."

"Small world."

Entering the Grzelachowski establishment, the five were greeted by a genial owner, who flung his arms wide and fondly grinned as he said, "*Halo, Boleslaw! Jak się masz?*" Hello, William! How are you?

"*Świetnie,*" the Kid said. Just fine. "Wanted to introduce you to my pals."

Hands were shaken and names exchanged, and Padre Polaco asked the Kid, "Would you like to take something on the teeth? I have a kettle of borscht on the stove. Red beetroot, onion, garlic, very hearty." Without waiting for a reply, he went to his kitchen cabinet and pulled down six Navajo bowls before calling out, "And some sweet Tokaji Aszú wine for the chilliness? I have."

And Charlie called out, "You still a horse trader?"

Padre Polaco asked, "You need?"

Tom explained, "On the scout so much, we're the ruination of animals."

"I have horses."

The Kid was warming himself in front of the fireplace and saw Billie Wilson dawdling near a display case. The Kid called to him, "You find a naked lady under that glass?"

"I'm shopping. The padre's got some nice things."

The Kid walked over and gazed at the jewelry as he stood beside Wilson. He retrieved a golden crucifix on a golden necklace and held it up to his gang. "Charlie, Tom. Would Paulita like this?"

"Hell if I know," Tom said, and Charlie just shrugged.

The ex-priest asked, "Is she Catholic?"

"Well, she's French and Spanish."

"Then maybe."

The Kid fitted the necklace inside its green velvet pocket and paid Grzelachowski the full price. The owner served the borscht, red wine, and hunks of stale bread to be soaked in the soup. Wrinkling his nose at Rudabaugh's devastating odor, he told him, "I could find you in a room with no light."

Rudabaugh thought it over for a few seconds and then concluded, "You sayin I stink?"

The Kid said, "He's saying you have a strong *personality.*"

"Well, I guess that's accurate."

Charlie interrupted to praise the borscht, saying, "This here is in the nick of time. My belly's been thinking my throat's been cut."

The former pastor asked while laying down cutlery, "And how are you and Manuela faring?"

"She's with child. See, we got this here picture took." Charlie was wearing a gray, caped Civil War sergeant's coat that was called a sur-tout and he found in its inside pocket a ferrotype of himself sitting in his finest dancing clothes and, in the fashion of the time, display-ing his six-gun and Winchester '73, looking again like a gloomy Edgar Allan Poe as his unsmiling common-law wife stood next to him, one hand formally on his left shoulder and the other gently riding the bal-loon of her belly.

"Very laughly," Grzelachowski said. "I am exceeding happiness for you."

Tom craned his neck to see and said she didn't look all that pregnant.

"Old picture. She's as big as a wish now."

"Is nine months the usual?" Tom asked.

"*Oui, mon enfant,*" said Padre Polaco as he sat across from the Kid. They ate in silence until he finally got out, "You have a birthday soon?"

"November twenty-third."

"That's today!"

"Then I have reached my majority."

"Aged twenty-one," Tom needlessly said.

Padre Polaco regarded Tom with pity, then returned to the Kid. "So, no clemency yet?"

"I got Judge Ira Leonard working on it. But the governor's in New York and avoiding me. I'm heading to White Oaks from here to hash out some legalities with Ira."

Wagging his finger but smiling, the ex-priest said, "You are afflicted with the general problem of disregarding the distinction between *meum* and *tuum*."

The Kid frowned.

"Latin for 'mine' and 'yours.' Old seminary joke." The padre lifted up and looked over the Kid's head to Billie Wilson as he yelled, "Ho there! I'll hang dogs on you if you steal from me!"

The Kid hated the fatherly whine in his own voice as he turned and asked Wilson, "Oh, wha'ja *do*?"

Padre Polaco rose from the rough-hewn table and rushed the petty thief.

"Nothin," Wilson explained to the Kid. "I was just holdin it in my pocket. Seein if it fit. I *got* money."

Padre Polaco forced his hand inside Wilson's overcoat pocket and retrieved a Waltham watch in a gold case. "Shame on you!" he scolded.

Anticipating an uproar, Charlie said, "We better eat up, Tom." They both began hurriedly spooning borscht and slurping down wine.

The Kid said, "You were gonna pay him for it, weren't you? You just had more shopping to do?"

Wide-eyed with innocence, Wilson told the ex-priest, "Yes! My family's festive and I have Christmas things to get!"

Padre Polaco examined the price tag. "Thirty-eight dollars. You have it?"

"Here," Wilson said and found a folded hundred-dollar bill in his trousers.

The Kid sighed. "Don't take it, Padre. It's worthless."

Grzelachowski squinted at the note in the lamplight and felt the texture of the paper before holding it over the hurricane lamp and letting the counterfeit bill brown and blacken and flame into ash.

"Hey!" Wilson said, but it was late and halfhearted.

"Enjoyed the dinner," Tom said, getting up.

Rudabaugh was heading outside, but his odor would linger for days.

The Kid saw that no one else was volunteering to pay for their dinner, so with exasperation he said, "Here, let me get this," and generously laid down five authentic two-dollar bills with Thomas Jefferson in the left oval and a vignette of the United States Capitol in the center.

"*Dziękuję*," the owner told the Kid. Thank you.

"I'm really sorry about the fuss."

"Yes, yes." Padre Polaco smiled. "But all my customers bring me happiness. Some by coming, some by leaving." And then he said like the gravest of teachers, "But I have a warning for you about your friends. 'He that lieth down with dogs shall rise up with fleas.'"

Exiting, Billie Wilson yelled, "This is a fine way to treat your dinner guests!"

Padre Polaco yelled back a Polish get-lost expression that in English would be "Oh, go stuff yourself with hay!"

Tying a woolen scarf over his skull and ears again and fixing his sugarloaf sombrero over it, the Kid adjusted his fine sable coat and got up on his latest horse. And then he heard hooting from the night of Grzelachowski's corral as Wilson, Rudabaugh, and a what-the-hell Folliard urged four stallions, four geldings, four mares, and four fillies through the yanked-open gate using spurs to various hindquarters. Charlie Bowdre was overseeing the theft and sheepishly twisted in his saddle. "Won't listen to me, them."

The Kid yelled, "What are you *doing*? Alex is a friend of mine."

"We thought *we* was your friends," Rudabaugh said. "And he disrespected us." His hand was on his six-gun, and the Kid could tell he was wanting to use it. The Kid felt so tired of all this quarreling and menace that he made the mistake of giving in, just riding gloomily toward White Oaks as planned, his skin feeling the itch of fleas.

And that continued as he just watched Billie Wilson sell Padre Polaco's horses to West & Dedrick Livery & Sales and divvy the cash among the thieves. Then Wilson, Folliard, and Rudabaugh felt a hankering for the saloons and sporting ladies of White Oaks, while the father-to-be and the Kid just gambled.

With the dealer shuffling his cards, the Kid asked, "You feel worn-out, Charlie? Not just tonight, but lately?"

"Well, yeah. A-course. We got so much to-ing and fro-ing I don't know whether to scratch my watch or wind my nuts."

The Kid collected his cards and immediately folded. "I'm frazzled, too. We ought've quit the territory when Waite and the Coes did."

Bowdre finished his jigger of whiskey and said, "That locomotive done left the depot."

And then Rudabaugh, Wilson, and Folliard shambled in with a burden of stolen overcoats, woolen blankets, and cardboard boxes of tinned food. Tom Folliard grinned as he said, "Look what we got!"

Wiping his coined winnings into his left hand, the Kid stood. "Where?"

"Will Hudgens's store."

The Kid hissed, "But he's from Lincoln. Will Hudgens knows you and me, Tom."

"So?" Rudabaugh said.

Charlie Bowdre looked at the many rubberneckers in the saloon and whispered, "We best get outta here."

*   *   *

The five hustled out, the Kid forgetting his yellow gloves, got on their horses with their ill-gotten gains, and galloped off to the Greathouse & Kuch ranch and trading post. All that hard, freezing ride the Kid was thinking, *You have lost control.*

Will Hudgens was not just a storekeeper, he was a deputy sheriff in White Oaks. Happening upon the wreckage of his mercantile operation, he shouted a hue and cry for a lynching and collected a posse of fourteen men to chase down the thieves overnight by following their horses' hoofprints in the deepening snow. It was not yet five in the morning when they got to the Greathouse & Kuch roadhouse, so the fourteen reclined on horse blankets in the snow, hating the zero cold as they cradled Winchesters and waited for the sun to rise.

Whiskey Jim Greathouse got his nickname from his moonlighting job of illegally selling liquor to Indians. He employed a short-order cook from Berlin, whose first job that morning was to harness a Clydesdale horse team in the stables. His boots were crunching in the snow and he was hiding his face from the wind with the lifted collar of his buffalo coat when he was tackled and pinned deep into a drift by a few of the White Oaks men.

"Who ya got in that house?" Deputy Jimmy Carlyle asked.

The Kid was first up and heating water for coffee in a fireplace pan when a cook who was floury with snow hurried inside and held out a folded sheet of paper. "Der ist a posse," he said. "Here a message."

Charlie Bowdre and Tom Folliard wandered over as the Kid read aloud, " 'We have you surrounded and there's no escape. We demand you surrender. Deputy Sheriff William H. Hudgens.' "

With the cuff of his overlarge sweater, the Kid wiped a garden of frost from a four-pane window and looked out at rifles bristling in the flare of first light. "We been here before, Tom."

Ever slow on the uptake, Tom Folliard asked, "You mean Alex McSween's house?"

The Kid nodded. "And lived to tell the tale."

Whiskey Jim Greathouse went outside with his cook, feeling it safer to hang with the White Oaks contingent, and to stir up aggravation he told Hudgens, "Kid Bonney says you'll only take him as a corpse."

"We don't just want the Kid. We want Dave Rudabaugh and Billie Wilson, too."

Whiskey Jim shrugged. "Well, if you want them, go and take them."

Because he was famous in White Oaks, Billie Wilson was the first who was asked to surrender. He declined for the time being but asked to talk to Jimmy Carlyle, a young farrier who'd shoed horses for him in his livery stable and was, like Wilson, originally from Trumbull County, Ohio. Whiskey Jim offered himself as a hostage to guarantee the deputy's safety, and Carlyle handed off his rifle and holstered pistol and held his hands in yellow gloves high as he waded forward through knee-high snow to the ranch house.

Young Billie Wilson welcomed him inside with a tin cup that he sloshed full of whiskey. "To take the chill off," he said.

Carlyle drank it all down and held the tin cup out for another ration.

The Kid asked, "You wearing my gloves?"

"I just found them somewheres."

"And I just forgot em. Hand em over."

Carlyle complied.

"You been out all night?" the Kid asked.

"Yep."

"Your men feelin cranky?"

"Well, darn cold and hungry."

The Kid looked to the cook. "Let's get this officer of the law some breakfast."

"Anybody else?" the cook asked.

Hands went up.

Rudabaugh walked into the front room, and Carlyle winced at the overpowering stink of him. "Shall I kill him?" Rudabaugh asked, like he'd just offered the man a fine seat at the table.

"I'll have to see your papers," the Kid told Carlyle. "Your warrants for our arrests."

"How was we s'posed to get papers and chase y'all at the same time?"

Rudabaugh slugged him in the mouth. "Don't sass him."

Carlyle felt his teeth with his tongue, found an incisor floating in blood, and spit it onto the floor. Ever untidy, Rudabaugh didn't seem to mind. Bowdre was watching and told Carlyle, "It'll feel better when it quits hurtin."

"Here's our conditions," the Kid said. "Your posse rides off to White Oaks and we go elsewhere."

"We'd just be giving up!"

"Exactly."

"We got thirteen guns fixed on this ranch house and you're actin like you got the upper hand!"

"Don't you go getting my dander up," Rudabaugh said and held his gun to Carlyle's head. "Seems to me we *do* have the upper hand, far as you're concerned."

Carlyle glumly finished a fresh dose of whiskey, and Rudabaugh holstered his Colt.

The cook served steak and eggs, and Bowdre, Wilson, and Folliard hunkered over their dishware as they chatted about the coldest they'd ever been. Rudabaugh finished one rib eye and tore into another. The Kid cautioned, "Easy on the chow there, Dave. You're swelling up like a tick on a bloodhound."

"I like to be full up," he said and jawed the meat with a wide-open mouth.

The Kid looked out at loitering men fogging the air with each irritated breath and trying to stamp feeling into their feet. A few aimed at his face in the window. They seemed close to storming the house. "Your pals are getting restless," he said.

Rudabaugh told Carlyle, "We'll kill em all. You *know* we will."

"You're outnumbered."

"Don't matter. We're professional killers. They ain't."

"I haf chores to do?" the German cook said. "I haf to go outside now?"

The Kid waved him out.

Soon, though, the cook was back again with a note from Deputy Sheriff Hudgens stating that if Carlyle was not free in five minutes, the posse would execute their hostage, Greathouse.

Rudabaugh grinned at Carlyle. "Where do you want my bullet? Ear? Eye? Lotsa choices."

Wanting to get as far away as possible from Dirty Dave, Carlyle rose from the breakfast table and tilted with intoxication as he sought the Kid. "Would you," he began, and just then a loose and impatient shot was fired from outside. In his drunkenness, James Bermuda Carlyle seemed to think it was from inside, from Rudabaugh, and in a sudden panic he dashed for freedom, crashing through the window glass and wrecking the sash before getting shot by his White Oaks friends, *bang bang bang*! He fell into the snow, crawled just a few yards trailing ribbons and scarves of blood, and then gave himself up to death.

"You idiots!" Hudgens shouted. "That wasn't Kid Bonney! It was Jimmy!"

Still the firing went on for a while, with sixty or seventy bullets pocking the adobe and making that *vwimp* sound as they zipped into the house and at the Kid's command "Don't shoot!" missed the gang that was not yet bothering to fire back. In the chaos and confusion outside, Whiskey Jim Greathouse just stepped backward from the frustrated posse and got on a horse that his partner Fred Kuch trotted forward. They both galloped off without getting shot at.

*　　　*　　　*

Who knows how it went? The Kid claimed the White Oaks shooters were dispirited over having killed Carlyle and slunk off in their despondency. But so much was unexplained. Greathouse and Kuch rode back a full day afterward and found Jimmy Carlyle still dead there on his back, frozen stiff, with snowflakes collecting in his gaping mouth and eye sockets. Their way station had been torched and was nothing but hissing rafters, charred adobe, and defeated furniture. There were no signs of blood anywhere except around Carlyle; no sign at all of the Rustlers. Hoofprints seemed headed west to White Oaks and east toward Fort Sumner.

In Roswell, J. C. Lea got word of the Kid and his gang's depredations in and around White Oaks and on November 27 sent a descriptive letter to Deputy Sheriff Pat Garrett, who'd already collected a posse comitatus that included his gambling buddy Barney Mason, a half dozen neighbors from his four-section homestead outside Roswell, and the Lincoln deputies James W. Bell and Robert Olinger. Riding up the Rio Pecos, they achieved Fort Sumner and found out Tom Folliard and Charlie Bowdre had been seen in the vicinity of Las Cañaditas, twenty miles to the northeast, on rangeland that belonged to the cattleman Thomas J. Yerby. Garrett held a warrant for Charles Bowdre for the homicide of Andrew Roberts at Blazer's Mill, so after a hasty breakfast in Beaver Smith's saloon, the posse of nine men grudgingly took off across a prairie deep with snow, favoring the vales and ravines to stay hidden from the criminals, with Garrett frequently forging up steep hills on his own to scan with field glasses a periwinkle blue horizon.

Eight miles from the Yerby ranch house, the deputy sheriff spied a red-haired horseman a half mile off who could have been Tom Folliard rocking in his saddle on a splendid filly thoroughbred, heading east. The geography was familiar enough to Garrett that he wisely elected to take a shortcut through a gorge that was hard going with its yucca, sagebrush, and tricky shale, but he soon got the posse within three hundred yards of the horseman they sought.

Tom glanced south and saw a sudden gang of nine riders hurtling toward him with guns in their hands. But their mustangs were scuffling through hillocks of snowdrift and seemed overused after a far journey, while his was a racehorse that vaulted forward at the first jab of his spurs, all four hooves flying with thrilling speed as he crouched like a jockey over her withers and crest and fired six rapid shots behind him. They could not overcome gravity and gashed up spits of snow far ahead of the challenging posse.

Even having the advantage of an angle toward the Yerby ranch house, Garrett could see the gap between himself and Folliard widening as the possemen's own horses heaved for air and gradually gave out. He yanked his Winchester out of its saddle scabbard and halted his progress to fire three useless rifle shots at the fleeing thief, then slow-walked to Yerby's before the government horses could keel over dead.

Tom Folliard had raced up to the Yerby barn and called, "Charlie, you in there?"

Wearing a blacksmith's apron, the wrangler hunched outside, shading his eyes from the sun.

"Sheriff's men are after us." Which got his attention. Folliard freed his left boot from the stirrup, and Bowdre inserted his own and swung up behind the saddle cantle and hugged Folliard as the filly racehorse exploded forward again, Bowdre waving back to a concerned Manuela on the bunkhouse porch as she watched her husband vamoose.

After a quarter mile, Folliard veered the horse toward a deep coulee, and a jouncing Bowdre called, "Where the hell you goin?"

"To get outta sight," Folliard called back.

And Bowdre yelled, "But there's a creek!"

Exactly then the racehorse crashed through the snow and ice in the coulee to four feet of ice water below, and Bowdre fell off the filly as she floundered in fear, thoroughly drenching her riders. "This is just awful!" Folliard yelled, but the horse finally found a purchase and scrabbled up onto an earthen bank and shook herself like a dog.

Bowdre wetly crouched in the snow, holding himself and shivering. He said, "I've seen fun times before and this ain't it."

When his posse got to the hitching post in front of an adobe bunkhouse, Garrett found no sign of Folliard, Bowdre, or even Yerby. Garrett furtively sidled inside the bunkhouse, his pistol impatient beside his cheek, and found weeping on cots a pregnant Manuela and Mrs. Herrera, her mother. His Spanish was too poor to fully understand their gibberish and finger wagging, so he went out again. He told Deputy Kip McKinney, "They are hailing our advent with terror-born lamentations."

Reconnoitering Yerby's property, Garrett's posse found four horses they decided were stolen and a pair of mules that the deputy sheriff took as his own because he pretended they could have been those purloined by Mose Dedrick from a Wells Fargo stagecoach depot on the Rio Grande and perhaps later sold to the Kid for his fanciful ranch in Los Portales. Which is where they went next, fifty miles southeast of Fort Sumner, hoping to take possession of the sixty cattle rustled from John Newcomb at Agua Azul. The Kid's hideout near Los Portales was just twenty miles from the Texas border. The Kid having neglected their feeding, a bony yearling and a calf were hungrily tearing dead leaves from whatever manzanita branches were above the snow. But there was at least a fluent freshwater spring that flowed under ice next to a fifteen-foot-high quarry of feldspar, gypsum, and mica that looked like a layer cake dropped from a height on the flatlands, its only welcome being the dark mouth of a cave. The Kid had bragged about his homestead as if it were a magnificent castle, but that was him dreaming again. Garrett scrabbled up to the entrance to find nothing but a damp emptiness, a rolled-up mattress, a pile of foul blankets, and some rusty tin utensils. With no food there other than a shaker of salt and sack of flour infested with weevils, the posse slaughtered the skinny yearling and filled up on steaks and rump roasts before wintering that night in the cave and heading back to Fort Sumner in the morning.

And that afternoon a postman walked into Beaver Smith's saloon to deliver a letter to Pat F. Garrett from Charlie Bowdre, saying he was anxious to parley with the deputy sheriff and wondered if he could make bail should he ever give himself up. With dickering in mind, Charlie offered to meet him one-on-one the next afternoon in the military cemetery.

Looking everywhere around him, Bowdre kept his afternoon appointment and found the deputy sheriff smoking a cheroot in a long gray Civil War overcoat just like his own, Garrett's right thigh resting on a low, whitewashed cemetery wall, his left boot on the ground. He gently lifted his handgun from his side holster and laid it a foot from him on the wall. The outlaw likewise rested his cavalry pistol on the headstone of a private killed in the Indian Wars. Bowdre had a misbegotten, hangdog look.

"You feeling ill, Charlie?"

"Well, I was better, but I got over it."

"You just need your rest."

"You, too, I spect. Hear tell you been runnin ragged."

Garrett flicked ash from his cheroot with a fingernail and with a formality he thought of as Southern gallantry, he said, "I have been told by higher-ups that you'll be needing to forswear your evil life and forsake your disreputable associates. After that, every effort will be made by good citizens such as Joseph Lea in Roswell to procure your release on bail and give you the opportunity to redeem yourself." Hiding his disgust, he thought, Garrett blandly focused on the criminal before him, and Bowdre saw the irrational nullity in his eyes, each as nickel gray as a gun barrel.

Seeking to appease, Bowdre said, "I'd do it if nothing broke or came untwisted, but more'n likely it would. You ain't the onliest lawman after us."

"You'd be safe in jail for a piece and probably get out in time to see your child born. But right now you have to give me something to go on."

"Like?"

"Cease all commerce with the Kid and his gang."

"Cain't hardly not feed em if they's to wander to Yerby's. But I won't harbor em more'n needs be."

Garrett stood from the wall and slapped snow from his overcoat. He took a final drag from his cheroot, dropped it, and squashed it out with his boot. "The upshot is this, Charlie. If you don't quit them and surrender, you'll be pretty sure to get captured or killed. We are in resolute pursuit of the gang and will sleep on the trail until we take you all in, dead or alive."

Charlie Bowdre couldn't help but smirk as he said, "Mr. Garrett, you may be hangin your basket a little higher than you can reach."

And then they parted ways.

17

THE OFF-SCOURING OF SOCIETY

On December 3, 1880, J. W. Koogler—a close friend of the late Huston Chapman—wrote an editorial in the *Las Vegas Gazette* stirring up a campaign against the Kid, Charlie Bowdre, Dave Rudabaugh, and "others of equally unsavory reputation," claiming they were "hard characters, the off-scouring of society, fugitives from justice, and desperadoes by profession."

Koogler was the first journalist ever to call Bonney by his famous nickname as he wrote, "The gang is under the leadership of 'Billy the Kid,' a desperate cuss, who is eligible for the post of captain of any crowd, no matter how mean and lawless." His gang of "forty to fifty men" was "harassing the stockmen of the Pecos and Panhandle country, and terrorizing the people of Fort Sumner and vicinity.

"Are the people of San Miguel County to stand this any longer? Shall we suffer this horde of outcasts and the scum of society to continue their way on the very border of our County?"

Writing Governor Wallace from Fort Sumner on December 12, the Kid sought to justify himself and his actions, maintaining that the Las Vegas journalist "must have drawn very heavily on his imagination." Concerning a claim in the editorial that he was "the captain of a band of outlaws who hold forth in Los Portales" he maintained, "There is no such organization in existence." Of the raid on the Greathouse & Kuch ranch and trading post, the Kid noted that Hudgens had no warrants to arrest or subpoena them, "so I concluded it amounted to nothing more than a mob." After giving his own version of how Carlyle was mistakenly killed by his own vigilantes, "they thinking it was me trying to make my escape," he said the illicit posse then withdrew. And then the Kid took on an aggrieved tone to say that in his absence, Deputy Sheriff Garrett, acting under John Chisum's orders, went to the Kid's cave in Los Portales "and found nothing. And he'd already gone by Mr. Yerby's ranch and took a pair of honestly purchased mules of mine, which I had left with Mr. Bowdre. The sheriff claimed that they were stolen and even if they were not that he had a right to confiscate any outlaw's property." The Kid then petulantly claimed, "J. S. Chisum is the man who got me into trouble and was benefitted thousands by it and is now doing all he can against me. There is no doubt but what there is a great deal of stealing going on in the Territory and a great deal of the property is taken across the Staked Plains as it is a good outlet, but so far as my being at the head of a band of outlaws there is nothing in it. In fact, in several instances I have recovered stolen property when there was no chance to get an officer to do it." He concluded, "If some impartial party were to investigate this matter, they would find it far different from the impression put out by Chisum and his tools. Yours respectfully, William Bonney."

Because the Kid's exculpatory letter needed to travel over a hundred miles by mail wagon from Fort Sumner to Las Vegas and then was sent in a railcar to the derelict Palacio del Gobernador in Santa Fe, Governor Lew Wallace did not receive it until six days later, on December 18. He'd just returned from his eastern book tour and found a canvas mailbag stuffed full with accolades and praise for *Ben-Hur*, but he also found the Kid's letter, handwritten in red ink on ruled paper. Scorning it as he read along, he told his male secretary, "In penitentiaries it's exactly the same. All the prisoners there are innocent, too."

But whatever the Kid said would not have mattered, for five days earlier Wallace had coolly approved a notice sent to every post office and newspaper in the Territory:

BILLY THE KID
$500 REWARD

I will pay $500 reward to any person or persons who will capture William Bonny, alias The Kid, and deliver him to any sheriff of New Mexico. Satisfactory proofs of identity will be required.

LEW. WALLACE,

Governor of New Mexico.

On December 15, Joseph C. Lea in Roswell got a note in red ink signed by "Chas Bowdre," but he was probably helped by the far more literate Billy the Kid. "I have broke up housekeeping," Bowdre claimed,

& am camping around, first one place & then another on the range, so that no one can say that Yerby's ranch is our stopping place. If I don't get my name cleared I intend to leave hereabouts this winter, for I don't intend to have any hand at fighting no more in the territory, for it is a different thing from what the Lincoln County War was, when I was justified. The only difference between my case & my enemies is that I had the misfortune to be indicted before the fighting was over & so did not get the liberty of a pardon. It seems to me that this would occur to the government once & awhile, so they would include us warriors in their clemency & stop their running around causing

havoc. I have no more sentiments to urge in my favor, except that others were pardoned for like offenses. Respectfully, Chas Bowdre.

But on that December 15 the sheriff of Lincoln County and his hand-picked posse of thirteen were seeking the five-hundred-dollar reward and were heading eastward from White Oaks to Fort Sumner, stopping at Grzelachowski's store to stand in the heat of a mesquite fire, fill up on McIntosh apples, and uncork some Jim Beam bourbon whiskey.

They generally averaged a rigorous forty-five miles per day, but on December 17 a fierce blizzard forced them to seek haven at the Gerhardt ranch, twenty-five miles from the fort. Yet Garrett was too restless to overnight there, so he and his men rode out at midnight and just before sunrise finally got to Fort Sumner. There the former rustler Barney Mason heard from Garrett's father-in-law that the fugitive gang had left yesterday, probably for the Wilcox-Brazil roadhouse, twelve miles east. And that was confirmed by Erastus Wilcox's Mexican stepson, a sixteen-year-old named Juan Gallegos, who'd wandered into Sumner to reconnoiter for the Kid. The sheriff threatened jail time in order to convince José Valdéz, an outlaw friend of the Kid's, to write a note in Spanish that claimed the posse had just left for Roswell and the fort would welcome them back. The sheriff then wrote a note to Wilcox and Brazil in English saying,

I am at Fort Sumner and on the trail of the Kid and his gang and I will never let up until I catch them or chase them into Mexico. I request your cooperation.

Barney Mason said, "The Spanish one's for the Kid. The other is for your stepdad."

"Am I stupid?" Juan Gallegos asked.

The Kid was hankering to get back to see Paulita, whom he'd missed the last go-round, so when a sheepish Juan gave him the note from José Valdéz, the Kid read it and told his gang, "The coast is clear. We'll go back to the fort at nightfall on Sunday."

Billie Wilson grinned as he said, "Those poodles heard where we was and trembled to meet up with us. Headed in the opposite direction."

Charlie Bowdre was in the sitting room with Emanuel Brazil when he heard the news, and he wondered aloud if he could still be romantic with Manuela, she having reached the days of her confinement. Emanuel offered, "Well, there's other things she could do for ya."

Charlie cogitated for a moment and then got outraged. "What are you incinerating? Don't you be dementing the mother of my child!"

A larger Tom Folliard got in the way of a fracas to say, "Y'all know where I'll be in Sumner: visiting the scarlets at Hargrove's saloon. I needs me some femaleness."

Rudabaugh had just walked in, and Emanuel grinned as he said, "And you'll be getting a bath, right, Dave?"

Rudabaugh socked him hard in the ear, and Emanuel Brazil fell off his upholstered chair. His hand came away from his ear with wet blood on it. "I'm bleeding! And you got me half deaf, you bastard!"

Bowdre happily clapped his hands. Rudabaugh just shrugged. "Ain't got no sense of humor, me."

Sunday morning the Kid scrubbed his overworn clothes with borax in a copper scullery and then used oven-heated flatirons to press out their wrinkles on a kitchen table.

Rudabaugh idly watched and said, "You're gonna make some fella a nice wife."

Without looking up from his ironing, the Kid said, "Don't get any lewd ideas, Dave."

He then spruced up with a chilly bath, and for the Christmas gift he got Paulita in Puerto de Luna, he found a tag and string fastener, writing on the tag "For My Angel" and bracketing that with hearts. And on the late afternoon of December 19 the Kid, Rudabaugh, Wilson,

Bowdre, and Folliard took the twelve-mile ride to a fort that the Kid still thought of as home.

But he was expected, of course. After hiding their horses in a wing of the Indian hospital on the nineteenth, the sheriff's men tied a wild and spitting Manuela to the iron hospital bed in the triage room, and around six went across the main access road to the old Indian commissary and killed time playing cards.

There was a foot of fresh snow on the ground, and the full moon shone off it so well that the Kid could see the fort entrance and the Indian hospital three hundred yards off. To guard against being overwhelmed in an ambush, the Kid was hanging back to ride drag just as he would when herding livestock. Bowdre and Rudabaugh were twenty yards ahead of him on the left and right wings; Wilson was the flanker, otherwise called the maverick catcher; and Folliard was far ahead, riding point on a cold night salted with stars. The horses' hooves made squeaky, munching sounds in the snow. The Kid could hear Tom singing, "Oh my Sal she is a maiden fair. Sing Polly wolly doodle all the day. With curly eyes and laughing hair. Sing Polly wolly doodle all the day. Fare thee well, fare thee well, fare thee well, my fairy fey. For I'm going to Lou'siana for to see my Susyanna. Sing Polly wolly doodle all the day."

Around eight p.m. in old Fort Sumner, the sticking Indian commissary door was jarred open by Lon Chambers, and Garrett looked up from a five-card-draw poker hand with an ace but junk otherwise. The nighthawk said, "I see five men with rifles coming."

The sheriff and his posse hurried to collect their things, then edged out into a moonlit night of zero degrees, the sheriff hissing instructions that his thirteen men hold still inside the moonless shade of the commissary's high adobe wall. Looking east they heard Folliard singing, "Oh a grasshopper sittin on a railroad track, sing Polly wolly doodle all the day. A-pickin his teeth with a carpet tack, sing Polly wolly doodle all the day."

The Kid could see something far off slinking onto the access road, but it was like a tree walking, and then, when Tom's racehorse was no more than ten yards from the figure, the Kid heard Pat Garrett yell, "It's him!"

Shocked out of his song, Tom reached for his Remington sidearm but never got off a shot as thirteen men were suddenly alongside the deputy sheriff and firing a fusillade that turned the Rustlers into a gallop from whence they'd come. "A big shooting came off," Cal Polk later wrote in a memoir. "They was about forty shots fired."

Tom Folliard had felt the wallop of a slug in his chest but no immediate fierce pain, and he swung his filly thoroughbred around and jabbed at her flanks with his boot heels. And then the hurt was like something excruciating blooming inside him and he folded over to try to submerge it. The racehorse seemed to intuit doom, for she would not run forward but circled and fought Tom's guidance in order to linger a little, as if in deep thought, and then disobediently walk back to the fort with her rider fallen forward across her withers, his hot blood trickling down her heart girth, forearm, and cannon.

Garrett yelled, "Throw up your hands!"

And Tom gasped in the theatrical way of the nickel books, "Don't shoot me again, for I am killed."

The turncoat Barney Mason called, "Well, it's high time you took your medicine, son."

"Is it Billy?" James East asked.

"Unfortunately no," Garrett said. "Wild West tyro is all."

Tom gasped, "Would you help me off my horse and let me die easy?"

The sheriff and his men gently took the six-foot man down from his horse and laid him on the floor of the Indian commissary and ruined a blanket as blood became a pond around him. Tom's eyes were shut, but when Garrett thumbed one open to check his vitals, the outlaw surprised him by rasping out, "Would you have Kip McKinney write my gramma in Texas, informing her of my demise?"

"Will do."

"Well," he said of his dying, "the sooner the better. This is painful." Then other sentences deserted him.

Waiting him out, they got back to their poker game and for about forty minutes were offended by his disgusting sucking and burbling noises as he coughed up blood. Waking from unconsciousness and craving water in "Help me" pleas, Tom swallowed from a tin cup that was held to his mouth, but that seemed too much exertion for Thomas O. Folliard, Jr.'s inner workings, and he wrenched up in agony and expired with a final sigh.

Ever efficient and unemotional, the former buffalo hunter told his men, "Carry him outside in the blanket. We'll chip a hole for him when he's stiff. And one of you clean up his mess. You'll find me with my wife at Celsa's."

Rudabaugh's horse was shot in the posse's ambush and got only a few miles from the fort before it keeled over and just groaned in the snow as Rudabaugh got what weaponry and gear he needed and said, "You was a fine beast of burden and I hate like Hell havin to do this." The horse craned its head up at his voice and he fired a .45 caliber bullet just below its forelock.

Billie Wilson rode back to fetch him and helped Rudabaugh straddle the saddlebags behind his saddle. Wilson looked back at him and asked, "Are you crying?"

The Kid decided there would be no pursuit that night, so he and Bowdre walked their horses back to the Wilcox-Brazil ranch in a slow mope, with Charlie vexed by the sheriff's scurrilous ambush. "There weren't no 'Hands up!' No warning a'tall. Ain't it the rules that you get a chance to give up?" But the Kid was just recalling his good friend's funny quirks and queernesses, his lard-on-toast breakfasts, his honking laugh, his registering of puzzlement with "Wait, what?" And Charlie went along with that, saying, "Always the same with Tom. He not only dint know nothin, he dint even *suspect* nothin, ever. Innocent as an angel."

"Well, he was always fun to be with and ever straight as the string on a kite."

"*Worshipped* you," Charlie said.

Emanuel Brazil was standing outside his stone-walled house in his grizzly bear coat and turban, his left ear whitely bandaged, but smiling insincerely as he watched the outlaws ride up. "Well, Sumner mustn't'a been hospitable to you boys! Whores all get religion there?"

"Tom's dead," the Kid flatly said. "We got ambushed."

"Oh."

They shoved past him into the house.

Worried about his pregnant wife's worry, a crestfallen Charlie Bowdre couldn't sleep that night and stood guard instead, and he was making five o'clock coffee at the old Majestic stove when Emanuel Brazil innocently sashayed into the kitchen in his Navajo bathrobe.

There was an elephantine silence between them that Brazil interrupted with "We sorta got off on the wrong foot, you and me and Dirty Dave. I'd like to patch things by going into Sumner and finding out what the sheriff's up to."

Bowdre coldly stared at him and said, "Shove off then."

Emanuel Brazil was dressed and on his horse before anyone else woke up.

Waking to the aroma of coffee, the Kid went into a kitchen full of the gang's off-putting morning smells. "Where's Emanuel?"

Bowdre tilted a kettle to refill his tin cup. "Off to Fort Sumner to see what's up. Don't matter; he's tits on a bull here anyways."

The Kid frowned at the oddity of the departure, judged it dangerous, and finally said, "*Vámonos*." Let's go.

And he was right about their jeopardy. Brazil rode into Fort Sumner the morning of the twentieth and sought out Pat Garrett in the old military cemetery as the sheriff watched his men swinging pickaxes into caliche earth that was hard as concrete. Tom Folliard was there beside them, as frozen and white as a marble pope on his royal sarcophagus. Garrett regarded the rancher's bloodstained bandage. "What happened to your ear?"

Brazil said, as if that explained it, "They're at our place."

"First things first," Garrett said.

Because he wasn't a believer, he had Apolonaria in her high pile of hair read aloud in Spanish some verses from her Biblia Sacra as shovels of stony earthen clods were flopped onto a corpse now interred.

Wild snows ruled out a further pursuit of the gang until Wednesday the twenty-second, when the sheriff and his posse of thirteen provisioned themselves and took off for the eastern ranch. All were on horseback but for Cal Polk, who was hawing a horse team from the wooden seat of a Wisconsin farm wagon just in case there were bodies to haul back.

The sheriff, his posse, and Emanuel Brazil got to the Wilcox stone roadhouse in the late afternoon and crouched forward in fierce wind and snow, rifles aimed at all three windows, but inside found only Erastus Wilcox there in the kitchen, heating grits on the Majestic. He stirred them with a fork as he told Garrett, "Hightailed it, they did."

Hoofprints heading northeast in the fresh snow simplified their tracking, but the thirteen in the posse were cattle detectives from West Texas or deputies from Lincoln and White Oaks and did not know the Kid's haunts as well as the sheriff-elect, who was in front of them, silent and tireless and seemingly unfazed by a vicious cold that stiffened their leather gear, gnawed at some toes, and hung icicles from the muzzles of their hard-used, slogging horses.

Around midnight James East wearily called up ahead, "How far we going, Pat?"

Without turning the sheriff said, "Stinking Springs."

*   *   *

The Kid and his gang had been there since nightfall, stacking their riding tackle inside a flat-roofed, windowless forage shelter fluffily fringed with snow, constructed with pinkish feldspar rock, and no larger than a jail cell. The Kid said, "Alejandro Perea built this."

"Like that matters to us," Rudabaugh said.

Just thinking out loud, the Kid nominated the cattle town of Tascosa as their next destination, and no one disputed the notion. Bowdre, Rudabaugh, and the Kid tore up a bale of hay and tossed the yellow feed to the famished animals as Billie Wilson found a cauldron inside the house and smashed his boot through the ice of a creek of stinking alkali water that the horses could drink but humans could not. The Kid's stolen horse this time was a fine mare of the reddish brown color called bay, a thoroughbred like Folliard's, and he thought her too high-strung and delicate to tolerate the winter elements, so the Kid pulled her inside the rock house. "She'll be a heater for us," he said as his gang tied their quarter horses to the pole rafters, called vigas, that extended outside.

Rudabaugh removed from his saddlebags two round loaves of sourdough bread that he'd stolen from Wilcox and Brazil, and in a spasm of selflessness shared them with the gang while Charlie Bowdre uncorked an unlabeled bottle of homemade rotgut that seemed to have been flavored with molasses to brown it and had the head of a rattlesnake wobbling in the bottom. Bowdre warned them that he called it strychnine.

Even huddled together near the horse, no one could thaw in that doorless shelter.

"I have to apologize," the Kid said. "I'm really sorry I got us into this fix. We could've fought it out."

Each word fogged in the air.

"We'll be outta here in the morning," Charlie Bowdre said. "And after that I don't wanna be cold anymore. Maybe I'll traipse on back to Biloxi. Work on a shrimp boat or sumpin. Won't ever have to hear Mexican again cept when Manuela damns my hide."

The Kid said, "You could have learnt Spanish."

"Why should I fool with another language? Ain't hardly got English bucked out yet."

Dirty Dave Rudabaugh was not watching or heeding the palaver; he was just sinking deeper into his odorous goat-hair coat and falling asleep. Billie Wilson had his gloves off and was breathing onto his fingers to get some feeling back.

The Kid's racehorse nickered. And then there was quiet except for Rudabaugh's snores, each one seeming louder and like the roar of a strangling lion.

The Kid found the humor to tell the others, "He's doing that on purpose."

The sheriff and his posse of thirteen got near the Kid's hideout around two in the morning. Young Juan Roibal collected all the horse reins as the men dismounted and each took his rolled-up blanket and rain tarp with him as they trudged through deep snow until a hawkeye spotted the gang's hitched-up horses. Half of the men then circled fifty yards behind the rock house as Garrett crept his half of the posse into kennels of snow in an arroyo that looked up a slope to the open doorway. They were no more than twenty yards off. The sheriff wanted to attack while the gang was sleeping, but he was overruled by Frank Stewart, who said his force in back were too cold and tired to shoot with accuracy, plus sunup was only a few hours off. Garrett made a harrumphing noise as he wallowed a sofa into the snow and covered himself with a woolen blanket. His shivering men were grousing in whispers about their frostbitten ears and noses, but he hushed them with a "Shh!"

The Kid woke at the sound and hunched to the doorway. He took off his white sugarloaf sombrero so he couldn't be so easily construed as he looked out into the moonless night, seeing nothing, nothing, nothing. Like it was his future.

Bowdre got up just before dawn and was in his sergeant's surtout and heading outside with a feeble amount of oats in the canvas nose bag that was called a *morat*. When he saw sleet flitting through the doorless entrance, he halted to hat himself with the Kid's sombrero. And he was outside and facing his chestnut gelding as he apologized to him for the lack of feed when he heard Pat Garrett again shout out no warning, just the misidentification, "It's the Kid, boys! Cut him down!"

Bowdre could just glance left with shock, seeing only a few dark, crouching shapes in the snow, and in that fraction of a second half the front posse's rifles fired at him, hitting a kidney, his left thigh, his right scapula, and his liver. Bowdre slammed into the house wall and sagged as the firing stopped, then he gripped the feldspar rock with his hands to drag himself back inside.

The gang was awake with their handguns cocked, and the Kid was holding and soothing his frantic horse in there as Billie Wilson examined Charlie Bowdre's wounds and shook his head no to the Kid, who took his sombrero back and yanked Bowdre's holster to the front of his trousers so Bowdre could get at it. The Kid's eyes were hectic and crazed with anger as he said, "They have murdered you, Charlie, but you go get yourself some revenge. Kill some of the sons of bitches before you die."

Charlie looked down at the gun hanging below his trouser belt buckle as if working to recognize what it was.

Billie Wilson yelled outside, "You have killed Charlie Bowdre and he wants to come out!"

"Let him!" the sheriff yelled back. "But with his hands in the air!"

Bowdre floundered outside, giving vengeance no thought, his hands raised and his legs seeming soft as taffy as he woozily stumbled down to the arroyo, seeking a solemn and very tall Pat Garrett, whose Winchester rifle was held at ease in the crook of his left arm. Bowdre was gurgling and strangling on his own blood as he vaguely lifted his right arm toward the rock house and struggled to tell the sheriff, "I wish . . . I wish . . . I wish." And then he fell forward into Lee Smith, dead. He was thirty-two years old.

With the distraction, Dave Rudabaugh untied his horse and tugged it toward the doorless entrance with the intent of saddling it and charging out of the rock house, his guns full of venom. A few of the posse had read the *Police Gazette* and were on to such criminal high jinks. About four of them lifted their rifles and killed Rudabaugh's horse just as she entered the doorway. She weighed over a thousand pounds and was like a huge boulder of interference.

The Kid looked over the mare at Charlie lying facedown in reddening snow. He yelled, "Are you going to leave him there like that?"

"Cold won't bother him now," the sheriff told him.

"You plan to fight us?"

"We'll just let you stew!"

The Kid slid down against a wall until he was sitting on the ground. With tears in his eyes, he sang for Charlie as he once did for his mother. "I'm just a poor wayfaring stranger. I'm traveling through this world of woe. Yet there's no sickness, toil, nor danger in that bright land to which I go. I'm going home to see my father. I'm going there no more to roam. I'm just a-going over Jordan. I'm just a-going over home."

His racehorse sniffed him, and he petted the soft, downy hair of her nose for a while. He noticed Billie and Dave inquisitively staring at him, and he said, "I have nothing to say."

A half hour later, Garrett patiently called, "How are you fixed in there, Billy?"

The Kid slunk over to the entrance frame and called back, "Pretty well, but we have no wood for a fire! And no food neither!"

Garrett called, "Why not come out and get some from us? Be a little sociable!"

The Kid was hungry enough to give it some thought. "We can't do that, Pat! We find commerce with you too predictable!"

Hours passed, with enough time for Cal Polk to go to and return from the Wilcox-Brazil ranch with firewood and a flank of pink, butchered beef in his Wisconsin wagon. A huge fire was started at sundown, and hacked meat was heaved onto the mesquite branches to roast.

Rudabaugh was near the doorway and asked, "Are you smelling that?"

Wilson said, "How we gonna get them to feed us? Right now I'd take right kindly to gettin greasy round the mouth."

The Kid's own mouth watered at the aroma and his stomach registered need.

"We could surrender," Rudabaugh said.

"And then what?" Wilson asked.

Rudabaugh faced him and in a condescending way said, "You don't always hafta go to prison. There's this here deal called state's evidence. You hand over other outlaws they happen to want more."

"I could do that," Wilson said. "I got lotsa people to get even with."

The Kid noted, "But Billy the Kid is who they want most. And that's dead instead of alive."

Rudabaugh gave him a *So what?* look and said, "Well, I'm doin it," and he found in his foul overcoat pocket a much-used, formerly white handkerchief that he flaunted at the rock house entrance before flinging his guns over his dead horse into the snow and crawling over the immovable mare toward the cookout, still waving his handkerchief in wild sweeps and yelling to Garrett, "Where you gonna carry us?"

"To Las Vegas!" he called back.

"If we hafta go to Las Vegas, we'd just as soon die right here! The Mexicans there want my head on a platter!"

"We'll take you on to Santa Fe, and I guarantee your protection from violence!"

Rudabaugh turned to the gang in the rock house for affirmation and saw the Kid's fine bay thoroughbred hop over the other door-filling horse and run free until she was lassoed by Juan Roibal. Then Billie Wilson was scrambling over the animal and falling forward down the slope, his guns held wide and unshootable.

Garrett fancied the weapons and took them as his own before calling out, "How about you, Kid?"

"Just a sec!" The Kid's rifle and handgun were on the ground inside the building, and he was urinating on them with wide arcs of his hose.

Wilson and Rudabaugh were handcuffed before the Kid got outside, his hands high over his head, his boots plunging so deep in the snow that he tottered, and yet grinning in a way that made Garrett skeptical. The Kid said, "Long time no see, Pat!"

"Been over a year. But not for want of trying."

The Kid looked at each man in the posse, some with their rifles trained on him, some hungrily gnashing rib eye steaks that they held in their gloved fingers. He smiled as he said, "This is a historical occasion. I'd like to shake the hands of you heroes who accomplished it."

With deputies holding guns on the Kid, and the sheriff-elect going up to the rock house to collect the possessions there, many in the posse took turns walking up to the Kid and jerking a firm handshake as they smiled and said their names. "Frank Stewart." "Lon Chambers." "Jim East."

Barney Mason shook the Kid's hand as he sheepishly said, "I changed sides."

"I see that. Good wages?"

"Well, they's regular at least."

Others crowded forward. "Tom Emory." "Lee Hall." "Charlie Rudulph." "*Buenas tardes, me llamo Juan Roibal.*"

"*Hola, Juan,*" the Kid said.

TRIALS

The possemen and their prisoners overnighted at the Wilcox-Brazil roadhouse, filling its rooms, and on Christmas Eve went west to Fort Sumner with Wilson, Rudabaugh, and the Kid shackled on the flat bed of the Wisconsin farm wagon, each of them skirting his legs away from Charlie Bowdre's white, openmouthed corpse, each of them working hard at not noticing his rocking, his jouncing, his seeming to breathe as they hit frozen ruts in the road.

Manuela Herrera was hanging sheets on a clothesline by the Indian hospital when she saw the caravan approach, and when she glimpsed a deputy riding Charlie's horse she ran out into the snow of the entrance road, heavy with child and screaming hatred of Garrett and the justice system in Spanish as she pounded fists against his long thigh.

"You have my sympathy in your loss," he said in a practiced way. And thinking of his five-hundred-dollar reward, he felt some largesse. "Will you buy a suit for Charlie to be buried in and charge it to my account?"

The Kid translated into Spanish for him, and then he softly consoled Manuela as she hugged him and pressed her tear-wet cheek to his own, groaning over and over again the words for husband, *"Mi marido. Mi esposo."*

Cal Polk got down from the wagon, and Barney Mason joined him in hefting Bowdre into the Indian hospital triage room and swinging him up onto a dinner table, knocking salt and pepper shakers onto the floor.

Polk said, "Quite the character, Charlie was."

And Mason said, " 'Quite the character' is what gets you kilt."

The horse thief from Mississippi would be buried next to his pal Tom on Christmas morning.

The three prisoners first were escorted to the old enlisted men's stockade, but when the Maxwells heard that the Kid had been captured, they sent their Navajo servant, Deluvina, with a handwritten note in English from Señora Luz Beaubien Maxwell.

I request that Kid Bonney be brought to our home in the former officers' quarters so my daughter can say goodbye.

Garrett consented and assigned Jim East and Lee Hall as the Kid's police guards. They walked to the house in a narrow furrow that had been haphazardly shoveled between snowbanks.

Sixteen-year-old Paulita greeted the Kid on the front porch in an emerald green formal gown with crinoline petticoats that shaped a bustle. Tears glimmered in her *café* eyes.

The Kid said, "Don't you cry, Sweetheart. I'll be fine."

She hurried a kiss of his cheek and lingered in a hug, her right ear to his hammering heart, and then looked beseechingly at East and Hall. "Would you let Billy join me in my room so we can have some privacy?"

East told the girl that the Kid was too slippery, with an earned reputation for escaping custody. They couldn't risk it.

"Will you all join us then in the Yuletide room?"

The Kid was in leg irons, so she hung on to him with an entwined forearm and slowed her pace in adjustment to the clumsy noise of his shuffle.

A spruce tree flaring with lighted candles filled a corner of the lilac parlor, and Paulita's mother was sitting on the love seat with her forearms crossed in a quarrelsome way as she scowled at the Kid's police guards. Luz said in highly accented English, "You have *caused* what you are now arresting."

"We're just doing our duty, ma'am."

She hmmphed.

Lee Hall took off the Kid's sombrero for him, and his girlfriend groomed his tawny hair.

The Kid told Paulita, "Reach your hand into my overcoat pocket."

She did and removed the green velvet pouch with "For My Angel" on the tag. She was wide-eyed.

"Open it."

She poured out the fine gold necklace and kissed the crucifix in the Mexican way.

Smiling, Señora Maxwell said, "Please to let me see, Paulita." And when she held it up, her mother said to the Kid, "So beautiful. So thoughtful, *Chivato*."

"I saw it in Puerto de Luna and had to buy it. Seemed already hers."

Paulita fastened it around her neck. "You're always giving me such lovely jewelry." She admired it in the reflection of a Victorian pier glass and with a formal pledge of her fidelity to him said, "I'll *always* be wearing this, from now on."

Smiling, Luz said, "And you have a Christmas gift for Billy, no?"

With a sunburst of happiness, Paulita hurried to kneel under the spruce tree and found a small, ribboned box that she opened for her handcuffed boyfriend. It was a tortoiseshell pocketknife and made by

J. S. Holler & Co. cutlery store in New York City. She made a porcupine of it as she pinched out its twelve tools.

"Look at that!" the Kid exclaimed. "Six different blades, an awl, a corkscrew, tiny scissors . . . This will be so *useful*!"

And Jim East took it from the girl, saying, "Maybe *too* useful."

With hopefulness she said, "Well, maybe later."

"For sure later," the Kid said.

Lee Hall intoned, "And now we'll have to say our goodbyes."

"Oh, but no!" Señora Maxwell said. "Won't you have some eggnog at least? Some sugarplums?"

Hall said, "The Kid's a prisoner, madam." She seemed to need the reminder.

Paulita stamped a foot in frustration and pouted as she said, "Billito! You're always just arriving or just about to leave!"

And then, Jim East later remembered, "The lovers embraced and she gave Billy one of those soulful kisses the novelists tell us about. We finally had to pull them apart, much against our wishes, for all the world loves a lover."

Because of the observers, she kissed him with piety at first, but as she seemed to feel the foreignness of his hard-used form, there seemed to become a greater need of belonging, and she kissed him with a passionate *yes* that was as soft as something fluid, that spoke an *Enter me* until she finally pulled a little away and told his ear in a hushed voice, "We are so much in love, Billy. We *have* to be together. I have money. We can marry and I'll ride with you to the ends of the earth in spite of anything you have ever done. I don't *care* what the world thinks of me."

The Kid looked at his watchmen watching him, and excitement and embarrassment warred with each other. And then he kissed her softly and deeply one last time. "*Vamos a ver,*" he said. We'll see.

*   *   *

Hiring only Jim East, Deputy Jim Bell, and his friend Barney Mason to accompany him on horseback, the sheriff-elect sent the other men home for Christmas, and Emanuel Brazil harnessed fresh mules to his farm wagon to haul the three prisoners to Las Vegas.

They got to Puerto de Luna around two o'clock in the afternoon of December 25 and walked into Grzelachowski's store and restaurant to find a fabulous feast being served to some locals. A jolly Padre Polaco welcomed the Kid with an embrace as the Kid said, "Real sorry about your stolen horses."

The ex-priest looked fiercely at Rudabaugh and Wilson as he said, "Oh, but it wasn't you, Boleslaw. It was these fleas. But even them I forgive on this glorious holy day."

After introductions to those he'd never met, Grzelachowski asked, "Would you like to take something on the teeth?"

The Kid told him, "I won't turn anything down but my collar."

Ever the figurer, Sheriff Garrett asked, "Would you have enough for all of us?"

"We have such *plenty* in the kitchen! Please to sit." Then the ex-priest and his cook carried out heaping platters of hot wild turkey, pierogi, cabbage rolls, and the gingerbread called Old Polish piernik. Padre Polaco motheringly sliced the food for the handcuffed Kid and continued refilling his plate until he finally groaned over the excess.

Ever wanting, Rudabaugh viewed the end of their meal with distress.

Headline news of the Kid's capture got to Las Vegas before the captives did on the twenty-sixth, and a huge crowd of rowdy gawkers with their own ideas of penal correction were waiting in the Old Town plaza. The Kid grinned as he shouted out the names of acquaintances he saw, seeking out Henry Hoyt but failing to find him, for he'd gone back to medical school in Chicago. By contrast, Billie Wilson was dour, humiliated, and penitent, his head down to avoid further intimacy with the citizens, and Dave Rudabaugh was in hiding and lying sideways on the flat bed of the wagon, for the hundreds of Mexicans in the plaza sought vengeance for his jailbreak murder of Deputy Lino Valdez. The horsemen rode protectively closer to the wagon and kicked citizens away until they could hustle their prisoners inside the stone jailhouse on Valencia Street.

An Irish mail contractor who was friendly with the Kid shoved his way into the jailhouse with packages of new gabardine suits and other attire for the prisoners because he thought it only right that the notorious ruffians face execution in high style. Their ankle shackles and handcuffs were chiseled off so they could change out of foul clothing that soon would be incinerated.

Because he was about the same age and seemed agreeable, Lute Wilcox, the city editor for the *Las Vegas Gazette*, was granted an interview by a chipper Kid, who found himself in his element as he joked and chatted with somewhat terrified bystanders.

"You appear to take it easy," Wilcox said.

"Well, what's the use of looking on the gloomy side of everything? But I guess you could say this laugh's on me." He glanced around at his surroundings and asked, "Is the jail in Santa Fe any better? This is a terrible place to hold a fellow in."

Sheriff Romero told him in Spanish there was nothing better in store for him there.

And the Kid just shrugged. "I guess I'll put up with what I have to for the time being."

Wilcox wrote, "He was the main attraction of the show, and as he stood there, stamping his boots on the stone floor to keep his feet warm, he was the hero of the 'Ali Baba and the Forty Thieves' romance which this paper has been running in serial form for six weeks or more."

With some surprise and pride, the Kid said, "There was a big crowd gazing at me in the plaza, wasn't there? Well, perhaps some of them will think me half man now instead of some sort of wild animal."

Wilcox wrote, "He did look human, indeed, but there was nothing very mannish about him in appearance, for he looked and acted a mere school boy, with a frank, open countenance and the traditional silky fuzz on his upper lip. Clear blue eyes, with a roguish snap about them; light hair and complexion. He is, in all, quite a handsome looking fellow, and he has agreeable and winning ways."

Sheriff Garrett and his deputies shifted the prisoners to the Atchison, Topeka & Santa Fe railroad depot in East Las Vegas on Tuesday, December 28, and the Kid leaned out an open window of a yellow smoking car to affably continue his interview with Lute Wilcox, hints of self-pity coloring his tone as he said, "I don't blame you for writing of me as your editors have. You had to believe others' stories. But then I don't know as anyone on the outside would ever believe anything good of me anyway." Reckoning what he'd later claim in a courtroom, he lied in telling Wilcox, "I wasn't ever the leader of any gang—I was for Billy all the time. About that Los Portales cave, it was the start of a property I owned with Charlie Bowdre. I heard a stage line would run by there and I wanted it to become a way station. But I have found to my sorrow there are certain men who won't let me live in the Territory, and so I was going to leave for Old Mexico. I haven't stolen any stock. I made my living by gambling. But some forces wouldn't let me settle down. If they had, I wouldn't be here today." He held up his handcuffed wrists in illustration as he said, "Chisum got me into all this trouble and then wouldn't help me out of it."

The Kid seemed willing to go on with his complaints, but he was distracted by hundreds of seething Mexicans crowding around and rocking the railroad car as they shouted for Dirty Dave Rudabaugh to be handed over and hung strangling from the windmill in the plaza.

Rudabaugh sank down in his seat, like a knob of butter melting on a skillet.

Sheriff Garrett sidled down the aisle of the railcar and crouched next to the Kid. "We have a situation here. Could be I'll have to give you a gun. Would you promise me you won't try to escape?"

The Kid sighed, but said, "You have my word. Dang it."

The sheriff then went out to the platform between the railway cars and shouted, "I have promised these men safe passage to Santa Fe! It is my duty as a federal marshal to preserve and protect them!"

Sheriff Romero was below near the knuckle coupler. Looking up at the tall man, he told Garrett, "We have chase the engineer off, so you not goin anywheres. We no care if you take the Billies. Rudabaugh only we wants."

Garrett's right hand rested on the hilt of his Colt .45 Peacemaker as he glared down and dared Sheriff Romero with "Then why don't you try to take him?"

Romero considered both the offer and its consequences for half a minute, and then he and his frightened delegation slunk away. Garrett told Barney Mason, "They look like a covey of hard-backed turtles sliding off the banks of the Pecos."

Seeing the still-furious ruckus outside, a railroad postal inspector hurried through a dining car to get to Garrett, telling him he'd earlier worked as a railroad engineer, "But my lungs couldn't handle the soot and smoke."

Garrett seemed to wonder about the relevance.

"What I'm saying is I could get you out of Las Vegas real fast."

"Good. Go do it."

The Kid watched as the postal inspector snaked his way through the mob to get to the locomotive. "This is exciting!" he told Lute Wilcox. "It's my first train ride!"

And suddenly the locomotive's iron driving wheels screeched as the throttle was pulled fully open, roughly jerking the passenger cars west. The Kid tilted out his window to grandly wave his hat to the *Gazette* reporter and shout back, "*Adíos*, Lute! Call on me in Santa Fe!" And then he held on to his passenger seat between his knees as the train got close to a thrilling fifty miles per hour.

The Kid made the front page of the *Chicago Daily Tribune* on December 29, when it named "Billy the Kid" as the leader of "the notorious gang of outlaws composed of about 25 men who have for the past six months overrun Eastern New Mexico, murdering and committing other deeds of outlawry."

Somehow the *Illustrated Police News* in Boston soon got hold of the 1880 ferrotype of the Kid and engraved the image in its pages in the first national portrait of the "Boy Chief of New Mexico Outlaws and Cattle Thieves."

In Santa Fe, the gloomy adobe jail was at the corner of Water Street and Bridge Street, a quarter mile southwest of the Governor's Palace, and because of his fame as an escape artist, the Kid was confined to a windowless stone basement cell with multiple jailers on watch. Sheriff Garrett was released from his custodial duties as soon as the captives were locked up, and he returned to Lincoln to impatiently await his five-hundred-dollar reward. The governor was in the East again and would not get back until February, but the Kid's jailers gave no hint of that, letting him mail a plaintive one-sentence note to Lew Wallace saying,

I would like to see you for a few moments if you can spare the time.

Because of his celebrity, though, the Kid was seen by a host of others, including Miguel Antonio Otero, Jr., who was just one month older and in 1897 would become the first Hispanic governor of New Mexico. With nothing much to do, the Kid took up smoking for a few days, and Otero brought him gifts of cigarette papers and Old Kentucky tobacco, as well as Wunderlee candy corn, Whitman's chocolates, and Fleer's Chiclets chewing gum.

Years later Governor Otero wrote in a memoir, "I liked the Kid very much, and nothing would have pleased me more than to have witnessed his escape. He was unfortunate in starting out in life, and became a victim of circumstances. I had been told that Billy had an ungovernable temper, however I never saw evidence of it; he was always in a pleasant humor when I saw him—laughing, sprightly, and good-natured."

Judge Ira E. Leonard visited his client in January but just engaged in small talk about his recent move to Lincoln while saying he'd tell the Kid his legal strategy for the forthcoming trial when he returned from the East later that month. The lawyer failed to fulfill his promise.

Still jailed in Santa Fe on March 2, 1881, the Kid wrote to the governor again, claiming,

I have some letters which date back two years, and there are Parties who are very anxious to get them but I shall not dispose of them until I see you, that is, if you will come immediately.

Enticing as those secret letters would seem to have been, they were probably just a fiction.

Hearing nothing from a governor whose office was just three blocks away, the Kid sent another letter on March 4.

Dear Sir, I wrote you a little note the day before yesterday but have received no answer. I expect you have forgotten what you promised me, this month two years ago, but I have not and I think you had

ought to have come and seen me as I requested you to. I have done everything that I promised you I would and you have done nothing that you promised me. It looks to me like I am getting left in the cold. I am not treated right by Sheriff Sherman as he lets any stranger with curiosity see me, but will not let in a single one of my friends, not even an attorney. I guess they mean to send me up without giving me a show but they will have a hard time doing it. I am not entirely without friends in New Mexico. I shall expect to see you some time today. Patiently waiting I am truly yours, respectfully, Wm. H. Bonney.

The Kid could not have known that March 4, the date of the inauguration of the twentieth President of the United States, James Abram Garfield, was also the date that Governor Lew Wallace tendered his official letter of resignation to the president, his fame as a novelist having earned him the grander job of Ambassador to the Ottoman Empire in Constantinople. Handed the Kid's latest letter, Wallace scoffed in his reading and returned it to his secretary, saying, "Would you hurt a man keenest, strike at his self-love."

The first of the gang's trials featured Dave Rudabaugh being convicted for robbing the United States Post Office when he was still a policeman in Las Vegas. Condemned to a ninety-nine-year prison sentence for that offense, he was then sent east to Las Vegas to be prosecuted in another trial for his murder of the jailer Lino Valdez, at which he was found guilty and sentenced to be hanged. While waiting for execution in a decrepit Las Vegas jail, in December 1881 Rudabaugh managed to escape with six other prisoners by hacking a hole through the deteriorating adobe wall of their cell with dinner knives and spoons. He fled west to Arizona, where he hired on with the Clanton gang in their war against Wyatt Earp and his brothers, joining in the killing of Morgan Earp and in the effort to kill Virgil Earp before he skinned out for Old Mexico. Working as a despised vaquero and rustler there, Rudabaugh got into a gunfight over a card game in Chihuahua, killing two men and injuring another before he himself was shot dead in his thirty-first year and had his miserable, psychotic, unclean head sawed off with a machete. It was displayed on a high pole for three weeks before wheeling vultures finally picked it clean.

On January 21, Billie Wilson had been arraigned for robbery and passing counterfeit currency in Santa Fe, but Judge Warren Bristol found that some paperwork was not filed by another judge on time and he declared a mistrial. Wilson, though, was still held for further prosecution, and on March 27 he was sent with the Kid for trial in Mesilla, the shackled pair being escorted by five guards on an Atchison, Topeka & Santa Fe train that had its deadhead in Rincon, about 250 miles to the south.

Just a day earlier the Kid had sent his fourth and final letter to Lew Wallace, who was being replaced as governor by Lionel Allen Sheldon, a three-term congressman from Louisiana.

Dear Sir, for the last time I ask. Will you keep your promise? I start below tomorrow. Send answer by bearer. Yours respectfully. W. Bonney.

Wallace failed to answer, and when a journalist noted that "Billy the Kid appears to be looking to you to save his neck," Wallace smiled as he said, "Yes, but I can't see how a wild fellow like him should expect any clemency from a faithful civil servant."

Sitting beside the Kid in a wooden passenger car on the route to Mesilla was Deputy Marshal Tony Neis of Santa Fe, and just opposite him with a shotgun across his tree-trunk thighs was Deputy Marshal Ameredith R. B. "Bob" Olinger of Lincoln, whose floor-mop hair was as long as Samson's. Born in 1850, he'd grown up, like Billy, in Indiana and Kansas, and followed his older brother, Wallace Olinger, to Seven Rivers, making do as a cattle detective and poker cheat, finding a mentor in Jimmy Dolan, hunting counterfeiters and Regulators, and joining in the siege of Alexander McSween's house before being commissioned, at Jimmy Dolan's urging, as a deputy marshal for Lincoln County. He invented the nickname Pecos Bob, but no one called him that. A Las Vegas editor once praised him as "the tall sycamore of Seven Rivers," but more characteristic was a Texas Ranger's assessment that he was "the meanest man in New Mexico," and there was Pat Garrett's own warning that the cold-blooded Olinger "was born a murderer at heart. I never camped out with him that I was not vigilant lest he harm me. But we had to use for deputies such as we could get."

Along the way to Rincon, Bob Olinger asked Tony Neis, "You notice little Billy won't look me in the eye?"

"I did."

"Hates me is why. A few years ago Apaches swiped his horse and boots and he was famished and afoot for days. Heiskell and Ma'am Jones let him get well over to their Seven Rivers homestead. The Joneses was nine sons! Each of em rustlers. Was John Jones your age?" Olinger asked the Kid. "Heard you'd do chores with him and hunt or whatever."

The Kid said nothing.

Olinger told Neis, "I find it strange that Johnny was on our side during the McSween besiegement, but him and the Kid still stayed friends."

The Kid said, "Johnny was just dirt poor and getting paid for it. He didn't have no dog in the fight."

"Well, a few months after the big killing I was sharing a room at Lewis Paxton's ranch, me with Milo Pierce, a justice of the peace. And here Johnny Jones rides up and confesses to Milo that he got hot under the collar with John Beckwith over some such and he was so very sorry but he ended up killing his friend. Wanted to turn hisself in. 'Likely self-defense, wasn't it?' Milo says, and I know Jones is for sure getting off. So I invoked some frontier justice and fired a ball into Johnny's throat. There he was, stunned and drowning on his own blood, making sounds like coffee percolating, then he fell and lost all sense of hisself on the floor. Was funny to see. Looked like a fish with his flopping and twitching. Took him no more'n half a minute to bleed out."

The Kid filled in, "And I swore to the Joneses that I'd get even."

Olinger grinned at Neis. "You can see how fraid I am."

The Santa Fe deputy marshal said, "And now I hafta forget this conversation ever happened."

The final forty miles along the Rio Grande to Mesilla took nine hours as the felons were locked into a hot, shuttered stagecoach with shotgunned guards bracketing them. Olinger told the Kid, "Your days are gettin short, Billy. Even now I can see that scratchy noose around your neck. You feel it chafing?"

The Kid just squinted out through the shutters.

There was the now-standard crowd waiting for the Kid's arrival in the flatlands of Mesilla (Spanish for "table"), but as Wilson and Bonney squeezed out of the stagecoach a journalist was forced to ask, "Which of you is Billy the Kid?"

The Kid grinned as he aimed the gun of his thumb and finger at a waiting Ira Leonard and said, "That would be him."

The journalist found that amusing enough to be recorded and then asked, "Are you looking forward to your day in court?"

The Kid said, "I'm looking forward to some of those famous green chiles you grow here. I hear they're the best in the world."

"Yes, they are."

Billie Wilson was admiring the spires of the blue and majestic Organ Mountains to the east. "Aren't they pretty," he said. "There's still snow!"

"And us without our sleds," joked the Kid.

The journalist pressed on, asking, "Looking back on your life from this unfortunate vantage point, I wonder if you could tell our readers what you have learned?"

"Well," the Kid said, "I would advise your readers to never engage in killing."

The Kid remained the mixture of contradictions that had made him a heralded criminal, while Billie Wilson became so much an afterthought that there was a continuance of his trial in Mesilla, and another continuance in Santa Fe. Even by September 1882, Wilson had not been tried, and he and two other prisoners managed to overcome a jail guard as he was locking their cell door, then ran up the stairway to the roof, from where they jumped far down to Water Street without grave injury. After Wilson had hitchhiked his way to Texas, he reassumed his original name of David Lawrence Anderson. He became a small-time rancher in Uvalde County, married and fathered two children, and just for old times' sake he sought reacquaintance with Pat Garrett when he, too, moved to Uvalde, in 1891. Eventually Garrett graciously solicited a presidential pardon for Anderson from Grover Cleveland. Which in turn allowed Anderson to become a United States customs inspector and then the sheriff of Terrell County, where in 1918, at age fifty-six, Anderson was killed in the line of duty by a drunken friend.

The Third Territorial District Court's spring meeting in Mesilla, the seat of Doña Ana County, was held in a whitewashed, windowless, fourteen-by-twenty-eight-foot room in a plain, one-story building that later would achieve garish fame as the Elephant Saloon. The judge was fifty-eight-year-old Warren Henry Bristol, who'd been appointed associate justice of the supreme court of New Mexico by President Ulysses S. Grant and since then had become a hanging judge, sentencing more men to the gallows than all his judicial peers combined. Bristol ought to have recused himself from the proceedings, for he was a close friend of L. G. Murphy and Jimmy Dolan and the fierce enemy of John Henry Tunstall and Alexander A. McSween. Yet on Wednesday, March 30, he called for Case number 411, *The United States of America vs. Charles Bowdry, Dock Scurlock, John Middleton, George Coe, Frederick Wait, and Henry Antrim alias Kid*, indicting them for the murder of Andrew L. "Buckshot" Roberts at Blazer's Mill.

Ira Leonard, the Kid's defense attorney, entered a not guilty plea in his contention that the United States government had no jurisdiction in the case, for the homicide had occurred on Dr. Blazer's private island of real estate within the federal lands of the Mescalero Apache Indian Reservation. Judge Bristol considered the facts indicated on a government map and sustained the plea to quash the indictment with a declaration of *nolle prosequi*. But then he swiftly shifted to Cases 531 and 532 and *Territory of New Mexico vs. William Bonney, alias Kid, alias Henry Antrim* for the murders of Sheriff William Brady and his deputy George Hindman, on April Fools' Day, 1878.

A journalist in the courtroom wrote, "Rather pleasant looking was Billy, wavy hair, baby blue eyes, sullen and defiant now, but looking as though they were made for laughter and sunshine and the reflection of the happy smiles of children. There was the mark of a keen intellect in that forehead, but there was also a mark of brutishness in his face, a criminal coarseness stamped across his features."

The prosecuting attorney was Simon Newcomb, the friend of and successor to William Rynerson, who'd repudiated Wallace's promise of clemency in the Kid's first trial, in 1879. Witnesses against the Kid were Lincoln storeowner Isaac Ellis; Bonifacio Baca, whose college education had been funded by Major Lawrence Murphy; and the saloonkeeper who was Sheriff Brady's deputy during the shoot-out, Jacob B. Mathews, the man who wounded Billy in the thigh.

Ira Leonard had subpoenaed Isaac Ellis for the defense and was perturbed to see him huddling with the prosecution. He'd also subpoenaed Robert Adolph Widenmann, who'd been with the gang in the Sheriff Brady killing, but he, of course, saw only jeopardy for himself in an appearance. And even though she probably would not have helped his case, Leonard subpoenaed Susan Ellen Hummer McSween, newly married to a semi-invalid named George B. Barber. She also failed to show.

She would soon buy a ranch she called Tres Rios, and, with a gift of livestock from her former fancier John Chisum, she became the aristocratic Cattle Queen of New Mexico, with fine clothes and a hatbox full of jewelry she carried with her everywhere. She ended a tempestuous marriage to George Barber in 1891, took on no more lovers, lost her wealth in the Crash of 1929, and in old age was shocked to find that the "foolish boy" she'd so disliked was increasingly featured in books and was the title character of the 1930 movie *Billy the Kid*, in which she was further irritated to see that her youthful feistiness in Lincoln was rendered by a lachrymose actress in her fifties. She died impoverished in White Oaks in January 1931, aged eighty-five.

Seeing no possible positive outcome and with no guarantee of payment from his penniless client, Ira Leonard soon left the Kid high and dry, his case being taken over instead by a helpless public defender who was first learning about the history and nature of the crimes as the prosecutor laid them out for the Mexican jury. None of his objections were sustained, and his cross-examinations were a welter of mis-information and stammering confusion.

Jacob Mathews's testimony was the most damning, for, in noting that Sheriff Brady's assailants were hidden behind an adobe wall, he was indicating that the homicide was premeditated, and, in claiming that he'd seen the Kid run out into Main Street with the others, he fitted Billy inside a conspiracy to kill that would have rendered him a killer even if he'd never fired a shot.

Called to the oaken witness chair by Simon Newcomb, the Kid promptly got up but was stalled by his attorney, who voiced the judicial rule that no defendant could be compelled to testify against himself.

The Kid plopped back down but whispered, "Are you sure of this? Looks bad."

The public defender patted the Kid's forearm in a patronizing gesture equivalent to *tut tut*.

Old Isaac Ellis was called forward and was asked if the Kid was a prodigious shot.

"What's *prodigious* mean?" Ellis asked.

"Would he generally hit what he aimed at?"

"Oh, you bet. With either hand!"

"Were you on Main Street in Lincoln that April first?'

"I was."

"Sheriff Brady was in front of you? Walking toward the former convent?"

"Seemed to be."

"And then he was shot down?"

"And don't forget George Hindman, too."

"Could you hazard a guess as to how many shots were fired in the altercation?"

"Oh, twenty or thirty seemed like."

"You saw the shootists?"

"I did."

"Was anyone in this courtroom among them?"

"Yes."

"Would you point him out to us, please?"

Isaac Ellis reluctantly shot his left index finger toward the Kid. The Kid waved back.

"And you knew him to call himself William Bonney?"

"Uh-huh."

"Was there a reason for his act of vengeance?"

"Oh, I reckon."

Newcomb made an inquiry about a conversation Ellis had with the defendant in July 1879, when he was jailed in Lincoln.

Ellis said he'd gone to Juan Patrón's house to play cards with the Kid.

"And he gave you his excuse for the killing?"

"Said they was in a civil war and he was just a soldier in it."

"Kid Bonney hated Bill Brady, didn't he?"

"Well, Bill, he had John Tunstall murdered."

Simon Newcomb faced the jury. "Witness has stated a personal estimation of the facts that is without foundation and is not material to this trial." And then he turned again to Isaac Ellis. "Have you heard of 'malice aforethought'?"

"No. But I can guess at it."

"It has to do with predetermination. You decide something needs to be done, and then you do it. In this case, the act your friend Billy premeditated—cold-blooded murder—was villainous and based on sheer hatred, hence the malice aforethought."

"According to you."

"Oh, I think there's unanimity of opinion on that score," Simon Newcomb said, and then the prosecutor smirked as he told Judge Bristol, "I have no more questions," and executed half a bow before he went back to his table.

The Kid scowled at his attorney and asked, "Weren't you going to object to any of that?"

The public defender explained, "It all happened so fast!"

Only the rites and formalities of the courtroom forced the trial to continue to Saturday, April 9, when Judge Bristol read aloud his nine-page summation of the case, instructing the jury that "if the defendant was present encouraging, inciting, aiding in, abetting, advising, or commanding this killing of Brady, he is as much guilty as though he fired the fatal shot." Within the hour the jury returned a unanimous verdict that William H. Bonney was guilty of murder in the first degree. With sentencing announced for the following Wednesday, the Kid was hauled back to the foul jail cell he shared with Billie Wilson.

And there he found on his cot a perfumed letter from Paulita Maxwell that he read aloud to Wilson. " 'Dear *friend*,' she calls me. But she goes on to say, 'Could I but draw you a picture of my heart it would contain nothing new, just the assurance that the early possession you obtained there, and the absolute power you have obtained over it, leaves not the smallest space unoccupied. I look back on our acquaintance as wondrous days of love and innocence, and with indescribable pleasure I have reviewed our years together and only seen an affection heightened and improved by time. Nor have these months of your absence and cruel imprisonment effaced from my mind the image of the dear man to whom I gave my heart.' "

Although the letter did not seem finished, the Kid let the hand holding it fall to his side. Wilson asked, "Are you crying?"

The Kid lied that he wasn't.

"Well, you should be," Wilson said.

At five fifteen on April 13, the Kid was shackled and squired to his sentencing. In the courtroom Judge Bristol asked, "Have you anything to say before your sentence is pronounced?"

The Kid glared fiercely but shook his head.

Judge Bristol looked down at handwriting in the floral Platt Rogers Spencer style and orated, "The defendant shall be confined in jail in Lincoln County until Friday, May 13th, 1881, when between nine a.m. and three p.m. he, the said William H. Bonney, alias Kid, alias Henry Antrim, shall be taken from his imprisonment to some suitable and convenient place of execution by the Sheriff of Lincoln County." Judge Bristol lifted his scalding eyes to the Kid and with a sneer continued, "And then and there he shall be hanged by the neck until his body be dead dead dead."

The frustrations and injustice got to the Kid then, and he shouted back, "And you can go to Hell Hell Hell!"

THE CONVICT

Authorities widely declared the Kid would be sent to Lincoln County in the next week, but to prevent either rescue or a vigilante lynching, Sheriff Garrett's hirelings instead shifted him eastward at ten on the night of Saturday, April 16, the saloonkeeper Jacob B. Mathews walking into the miserable Mesilla jail and waking up the prisoner. The Kid packed his finer clothing in a haversack as he groused, "Worstest jail I've ever been in. Hot and filthy. Lice jumping off the mattress ticking. Tortillas and beans for all our meals. Water tasted like sewer runoff. And the skeeters whined at my head all night long."

"We'll keep ya comfy cozy in Lincoln," Mathews said. And then he walked with the Kid in front of him, hatless, shuffling in shackles, his hands manacled. Watching the Kid's gait, Matthews inquired with genuine curiosity, "How's your leg where I shot ya?"

"Healed up just fine. Thanks for asking."

Waiting outside for their prisoner with their shotguns upright near their shoulders were Deputy US Marshal Bob Olinger, a half-time deputy sheriff named David Woods, and the newly employed John Kinney, the founder of the gang he called the Boys and many times a murderer even before joining in the gun battle at Alex McSween's.

Smiling when he saw the Kid in chains, Kinney said, "You sumbitch, you shot half my mustache off that night."

"Well, I see it grew back."

"Wanted to kill you daid right then but you was catlike."

The Kid acidly said, "All in good fun, wasn't it?" And then he was guided to a flat-roofed, blue-enameled Dougherty wagon that was on loan from Fort Stanton and was labeled in gold AMBULANCE. Sitting up above them holding the reins of his harnessed mule team was W. A. Lockhart, and next to him was D. M. Reade, cradling a sawed-off shotgun. Tom Williams and David Woods got on fine saddled cavalry horses to ride along outside the ambulance.

The Kid was counting his police guard and said, "Criminy sakes, you got *seven* men watching over me? I must be a dad-blamed monster!"

"Slick as snot is more like it," Olinger said.

Mathews admitted, "We're sorta sponging off Lincoln County. Each of us getting two dollars per diem, a dollar fifty a day for food and room, and ten cents a mile for the hundred forty-five miles to Lincoln. We go back gradual enough, stretch four days to five or six, we'll be sitting pretty for weeks."

Olinger said, "Whereas you'll be the poor have-not getting nothing but grief from me from now on."

Mathews and Olinger wedged themselves and their guns on the bench across from the Kid, and Kinney squeezed in beside him. Kinney was shorter than the Kid but stouter, and Olinger was large, a good seven inches over Billy's height and at least a hundred pounds heavier. The Kid heard his mother saying, *There's a lot of body in those clothes.*

Kinney told the Kid, "We's already reckoned if any your friendly greasers try to free ya, we'll just go ahead and shoot ya daid, get the execution over with sooner."

The Kid flatly said, "Oh my. You fellows are giving me the scares something awful."

The Army ambulance jerked forward.

The Kid asked the deputy marshal, "You jailing me at Fort Stanton?"

"Nope," Olinger said.

"I thought the Lincoln dungeon was filled in."

"So, guess again."

"I got nothing."

"The House. Ever heard of it?"

"The Murphy-Dolan store?"

"Took over by Thomas Catron, then sold to Lincoln County for a courthouse and jail. You'll have the major's old upstairs bedroom."

"Sheer luxury, huh?"

"Well, just for your last month. Sheriff took pity on you."

Kinney asked the Kid, "Ya hear about our friend Jesse Evans?"

"I been outta earshot."

"Him and his gang robbed the Sender and Siebenborn store over there to Fort Davis. Texas Rangers caught him. In the Huntsville penitentiary now."

"Well, it was bound to happen," the Kid said.

Mathews asked, "You know what a rarity you are, Kid? At least two hundred men killed in Lincoln County over the last three years, and you're the onliest one getting hanged. They don't even got other trials on the *docket*."

"I hear they don't try dead people in court," the Kid said. "A lot of my friends are toes-up."

Even before the Kid's trial, the editor of the *Las Cruces Semi-Weekly* wrote, "We expect every day to hear of the Kid's escape. The prisoner is a notoriously dangerous character and has on several occasions fled the bonds of justice where a getaway appeared even more improbable than now, and he has made it his brag that he only wants to get free in order to kill for certain three more men—one of them being Governor Wallace. Should he break from jail now, there is no doubt that he would immediately proceed to execute his threat."

And in fact the Kid was thinking escape when they were more than halfway to Lincoln, in the high elevation of Dowlin's Mill—now Ruidoso—where a restaurant owner wouldn't permit a shackled murderer to dine inside. So Jacob Mathews kept watch on the Kid while the others lunched, but his head kept falling forward in sleep and then jerking up into wakefulness again.

The Kid took off the red bandanna he wore around his neck and wrapped it around the chain between his ankle shackles to hush the clanking, then slid across his bench to ever so quietly open the wagon door.

But then Mathews woke up.

"Oh, sleep, J.B.! You need your rest!"

"You're lucky it's me. Was Olinger you'd be killed right now."

The Kid smiled. "Half a minute more and I'd be history. Riding off into the sunset."

"Well, you couldn't've got away," Mathews said. "You can't mount a horse with chained ankle irons like that."

"I figured I could ride sidesaddle until I found a hammer and chisel."

"Ride like a lady?" Mathews said. "Embarrassing."

Kinney was at the wagon door waitering plates of food. "Meat loaf and mashed potatoes," he said. "But you was hungry for a getaway, weren't ya, Billy?"

"Oh, don't you worry about me," the Kid said. "I generally get what I want."

Sheriff Pat Garrett was scowling and smoking a calabash pipe on the commanding officer's porch at Fort Stanton when the prisoner detail from Mesilla finally arrived. It was Thursday, April 21.

"You're late," he said, but that was all.

Riding his horse alongside the cavalry's ambulance as it followed the Rio Bonito the nine miles to Lincoln, Garrett sought to gladden the condemned man by saying, "You'll be happy with your accommodations with us. And you'll get your meals carried over from Wortley's Hotel."

"Really looking forward to my final dinner. I get to choose the recipe, right?"

"That's customary."

With a grin, the Kid said, "Maine lobster."

Garrett gave it serious thought and offered, "Won't be very special after six days dead in a railroad car."

The Kid smiled. "I'll have to avoid it then. Eating seafood that old could kill me."

The Kid's cell in the House was a high-ceilinged, oak-floored, twelve-by-twelve upstairs room with floral wallpaper on one end, iron jail bars bolted against the east wall, and unscreened, double-hung, north and east windows. Entry to L. G. Murphy's former bedroom was only through his sitting room, now Sheriff Garrett's office. Crucially, the fireplace and chimney were outside the jail bars, so there could be no shinnying to freedom. The hallway above the staircase crossed to a room formerly occupied by Mrs. Lloyd, Murphy's housekeeper, but now was a jail for some petty thieves and public brawlers. A locked storeroom next to that was the armory.

Recognizing that Billy the Kid was ever a flight risk and that it was only a sixteen-foot jump from window to ground, Garrett chained the Kid's ankle irons to the floor with just four feet of leeway and assigned deputies Jim Bell and Bob Olinger to share his watching.

Within the Kid's earshot, the sheriff told his deputies, "You know the desperate character of this culprit. He is daring and unscrupulous and he will sacrifice the lives of any man who stands between him and liberty."

Crossing his eyes and dangling his tongue, the Kid devil-horned his head with his fingers from behind the jail bars. Deputy Jim Bell smiled.

James W. Bell was a kind and likable man of twenty-seven who was raised in Georgia, failed at gold mining in White Oaks, and joined the posse that mistakenly killed Jimmy Carlyle. He took the ever-risky government job just to have a regular income and was one of the deputy marshals who escorted Bonney, Rudabaugh, and Wilson to Las Vegas. Whenever he forced the Kid to do anything, he first apologized by saying, "I'm just doin whatsoever's required." And once Bell said, "Cain't never could work it out in my mind why a fella like you, sharp as a tack, would break bad like you done." Always considerate, he even asked permission of the convict to continue his slow and preoccupied reading of *Ben-Hur*, fearing the governor's name on the novel would be offensive to the Kid. It wasn't.

Whereas Olinger continued his arrogant, sneering, bullying ways. The Kid would be on his cot, peaceably reading Ned Buntline's *The Black Avenger of the Spanish Main*, and Olinger would rock back in his Victorian dining chair and admire his cocked Whitney shotgun as he irritated the Kid with taunts.

Olinger said, "Oh, but I would love it if you tried to escape. I got fat ten-gauge shells with eighteen buckshot waiting in both barrels. Would blow your pretty face to smithereens. You'd look like a spill of spaghetti and sauce on the floor."

Another time he said, "Sometimes when they hang a man, things get catawampus and he strangles for a long, long time, gargling, glugging, his legs dancing an Irish jig. And sometimes, maybe in your case, his neck is so puny his head snaps right off with the weight of the drop.

You hear a *punk* like the pop of a champagne cork. A fountain of blood wetting all the gawkers. Wouldn't I love to see that!"

And he loved talking about the murder of John Tunstall on the Ham Mills trail. Hated it that he was in the larger group that failed to give chase, but his brother Wallace was with the posse that ran down the flummoxed Englishman. "Said after your Harry was hit he wet his trousers like a diapered child. Be sure to empty yourself beforehand so you don't piss yourself on the gallows."

Olinger once took his time loading his Smith & Wesson Schofield .44 pistol, then softly laid it on the floor and kicked it between the iron bars near the Kid's stocking feet. With his shotgun in the crook of his left arm, Olinger grinned and gently said, "Reach for it, Billy."

"I'd still be jailed."

"Well then," Olinger said, and he got up with his big ring of keys and unlocked the jail door, then the Baldur padlock that chained the Kid to the floor. "This is your chance, sweetie pie. Folks say you're so quick you could dive and fan four shots into me before I even got this Whitney cocked."

The Kid looked and looked at the pistol, then sneered at the deputy and kicked the Schofield back to him.

Olinger smirked. "Scared, huh?"

The Kid confided to Sheriff Garrett that "Olinger's needling gets me so hot I can hardly contain myself."

Garrett shrugged. "Well, good thing you're contained, then."

Gottfried Gauss had shifted occupations yet again: from chuck wagon cook for John Tunstall on his Los Feliz ranch to a general handyman in Lincoln and then to a job as a half-blind factotum for the courthouse and jail. His quarters were in the old bunkhouse and shared with Sam Wortley when Wortley felt the need to get away from his hotel. It was Gauss who brought the Kid his three meals a day from Wortley's or Frank McCullum's eatery, and as he sat and watched Billy eat he'd smile as if each scrumptious dish were his own creation. His English was fair, but he'd found less ridicule in silence, so he generally walked around unnoticed, humming Brahms's Lullaby when sweeping up or hoeing his garden patch.

Looking out the north window, the Kid could see the newly leafing branches of a Rocky Mountain maple tree and beyond it the few adobe remains of Alex and Susan McSween's house, now being overgrown with Russian thistle and foxtail grass. He avoided the northern window.

The east window he liked. Underneath it and the Kid's cell was a first-floor post office run by Ben Ellis, Isaac's son, who often slept there. After getting their mail, various Lincoln residents would pause below the east window so the Kid could lean out on the sash and chat. Each afternoon, Juan Patrón pitched him an apple and even once tossed up a small box of Hasheesh Candy, which called itself "enchantment confectionized" and was said to cure "nervousness, weakness, and melancholy."

Saturnino Baca's little girls visited frequently but usually only blushed and giggled.

Isaac Ellis was cradling mail-order packages under each arm when he whistled and the Kid poked his head out. "Don't know if apologies are in order. I was just abiding the law, but that I did you no good is a fact. I'm real sorry you have to get hanged. Course you brung it on your own self, but that don't give me no sort of satisfaction." And then Ellis walked east to his store.

Even the young schoolteacher Susan Gates strolled over to gaze upward and softly talk with him, saying, "I heard folks saying you'd become a nuisance, but I never believed all the evil they associated you with. Excuse my ending with a preposition. Seems to me you're unfairly maligned and misunderstood."

"My, how very sweet and pretty you are, Miss Gates!"

She shyly looked to the ground and may have whispered, "Thank you."

"Why is it I never courted you?"

She seemed to find fascination in her shoes. "I would have liked that," she admitted. Then in embarrassment she hurried off.

Sheriff Pat Garrett shared lunches with the Kid a few afternoons and in an offhand way hoped he could get Billy to admit to his misdeeds, make, as they say, a clean breast of it. The sheriff could have been a reverend as he sat in Murphy's old dining room chair and hunched forward over his lengthy legs and oh so earnestly investigated the Kid's record.

Calmly relighting a churchwarden pipe, he said, "The county justice system needs to clear its books. I'd be grateful if you was to erase some felony cases for me, free me for other things."

"Will that make your pony gallop?"

The sheriff twitched a smile. "Can't hurt."

Like a Roman emperor, the Kid languidly waved a hand. "Proceed."

"Well now, it's been said that you have killed a man for every year of your life."

The Kid frowned and made a *pff* sound.

"How many, then?"

"Just two that I know of. Windy Cahill in Arizona. And Joe Grant at Fort Sumner. And those were both in self-defense."

"Are you forgetting Sheriff Brady and George Hindman?"

The Kid grinned. "Objection: asked and answered."

"All right, what about Buckshot Roberts?"

"My holster was hanging on a peg and I was still a hop-along inside the restaurant on account a my hurting leg. Heard the loudness and saw a glide of smoke under the porch roof and to my startlement Charlie and George and John was lying down in gunshot misery underneath it. Roberts was already lurching off."

Sheriff Garrett rocked back in the walnut chair and sucked on his pipe as he looked down his tilted-up nose in a scornful, assessing way. "You appear to have a plausible excuse for each and every crime charged against you."

"Well, I can't alter what's true. Wouldn't that be so-called perjury?"

"And how about Jimmy Carlyle? Murdering a innocent hostage may have been your most detestable crime."

"Had no hand in it."

"Rudabaugh said you did."

"And liars lie." The Kid lifted his tray of lunch from his thighs and got up from his stool. "I'm tired of this," he said. "I have to go lie down now."

"Are you feeling the prickings of conscience?"

The Kid wrenched off his boots and said, "An old vaquero saying has it that there's a thin line between catching an outlaw and becoming one."

Later, Pat Garrett told Ash Upson, "In our conversations, he would sometimes seem on the point of opening his heart, either in confession or justification. But it always ended in an unspoken intimation that it would all be to no avail, as no one would give him credence, and he scorned begging for sympathy."

The Kid had been incarcerated in the Lincoln jail for just a week when, on April 28, he decided.

Sheriff Garrett was collecting county taxes in White Oaks and the Kid heard Olinger unlock the far jail to walk four Tularosa no-goods down the stairs and across to the Wortley Hotel for their evening dinner. Ben Ellis would have joined them for the free eats and to help with policing. And Gottfried Gauss was generally in his bunkhouse by six. So the Kid was alone with Jim Bell. He went to the jail bars and called downstairs, "Jim? I need to go outside."

Jim called back. "You mean to the latrine?"

"Uh-huh."

The Kid heard the high-pitched scrape of a kitchen chair on the plank floor and then heavy bootfalls as Deputy Sheriff Bell walked to the bottom of the staircase and called up, "But it's not full night yet!"

"Still, I'm feeling an urgency."

The deputy seemed confused in his movements as he called, "I'm fixin to be there directly. I just gotta find that dang ring of keys." A cabinet door was opened and closed, a few drawers were pulled. "Well, finally," Bell shouted upstairs. "Cain't never can figure out Olinger's mentality." His boots rasped on the stairs as he climbed. "Whatsoever oughta be out in plain sight, he hides it."

The Kid was standing meekly in the middle of his cell, his manacled hands held low, a smear of a smile welcoming the hatless jailer, who smiled involuntarily because that was his way, and then Bell hunted the big ring for the jail door key and rattled open the lock. The hinges were freshly oiled but still sang with his shove, and then Bell was gingerly and ever watchfully genuflecting to unfasten the padlock at the floor hitch, freeing the Kid's shackles from their four-foot limitation.

"Like we do," Bell said, nodding sideways. "Me behind you."

The Kid shuffled forward and downstairs. April was chilly at that high elevation. The air was scented with juniper fireplace smoke, and he could almost see his breath. Walking into the jail latrine, he heard Bell complaining, "Look at those saddles and bridles hung up on the fence rail where any passerby could steal em. That just dills my pickle!"

The Kid shook to finish his relieving, buttoned up his trousers, and went out into sweeter air.

Bell trustingly asked, "You want some of my coffee inside? It's already been saucered and blowed."

"I'll pass, thanks. It's late." The Kid walked back to the jail with a quicker pace as Bell again looked to the corral, worrying about the horse tack out for all to see.

And then Bell called, "Why you hurryin, Billy?"

With a two-foot chain between the shackles on his ankles the Kid could still take the sixteen stairs two at a time, and he was fast enough that the deputy was a full flight behind him. The Kid's iron manacles were one-size-fits-all, and he hadn't let on that his often-mocked hands were too peewee for them. He twisted his left hand out, then his right, and dangled the iron cuffs from their chain as he hid upstairs, hugging the hallway wall and hearing Bell pounding upward.

"This ain't funny, Billy!" Bell called out, and then the Kid was in front of him on the landing and he swung his iron manacles hard into the deputy's head, the force of the double blows gashing his scalp and fracturing his skull. "Ow!" he cried, and his hands flew up to his injury. "Why d'ja do that?" The first spurt of blood became red seaweed over his forehead and face until there was nothing but blood. Bell dizzily bent over and braced himself with his hands on his knees. "Oh my!" he said. "I'm beside myself."

"I didn't want to hurt you, Jim. I'm only trying to save my life."

Even watching his lifeblood flood the floor, Bell still upheld that "I'm just doin my duty, Billy." And then he looked up at the Kid, his doleful, frustrated, hazel eyes seeming puzzled by the Kid's wrath and unfairness until he found the fierceness to lunge forward to tackle the Kid, who swiftly fended off the ever-weakening man. The deputy then went to his holster, but the Kid laid his left hand on Bell's feeble right and with just an effortless twist yanked the .44 free.

"Hold up your hands and surrender," the Kid said.

"Won't do that, Billy."

Without lifting the pistol from his hip, the Kid shot him as he turned away.

The bullet pierced under his right arm and skewered his torso. Bell glanced down at his chest and hugged its new pain with his arms as he said in astonishment at the Kid's treachery, "You took my *life!*" And then he fell backward down the staircase until he could right himself and flounder to the first floor.

The gun noise traveled far, and Gottfried Gauss hurried out of his bunkhouse to see James W. Bell stagger outside, fall face-forward into the yard, and there find finality.

Upstairs, the Kid went into Sheriff Garrett's office and got the Whitney shotgun that Olinger often left behind on the oak desk when he went out for dinner. The Kid then hurried into his cell, but with his shackles on it was like he was in a sack race. He fell down to his knees and crouched below the sash as he heard Olinger run out of Wortley's and call to someone on Main Street, "Was that a gunshot?"

"Can't think what else it could be," Bonifacio Baca said.

The Kid cocked both hammers and raised up to rest Olinger's ten-gauge on the windowsill, finding the deputy marshal below him unlatching the fence's gate to the courthouse yard.

"Hello, Bob," the Kid said.

Olinger glanced upward at the worrisome voice and in that half second must have recognized what was next. The Kid then fired both Whitney barrels with their thirty-six heavy shot into the deputy's head and chest. Ameredith R. B. Olinger was dead before he hit the ground, his face torn to pieces.

The Kid rammed his shoulder into the frail closet door to the armory, and it gave way. Choosing twin holstered pistols, a Winchester rifle, and a box of bullets, he clanked out to the hallway again and looked through the north window to Main Street. Half of Lincoln seemed to be there, but no one was venturing to do more than murmur.

Looking down the courthouse staircase, he saw Gauss hesitantly ascending. "I won't hurt you, Gottfried. Just get me that prospector's pickax, won't ya?"

Whether it was in friendship or fear, Gauss obliged and went out.

The Kid sat down to load his stolen weapons, and when he finished Gauss was tossing up the pickax. Widening his legs on the stair step, the Kid slammed down the little pickax over and over again until the chain that connected the ankle irons was chewed apart.

Like the Kid himself was a gun that could go off, Gauss was holding still. And then he was given the instruction to go to Judge Ira Leonard's stable and saddle a horse.

The Kid walked out onto the balcony with his guns. Most of Lincoln's wary citizenry was scattered in front of the Wortley Hotel but exercising restraint in halting Billy. Whether friends or foes of the Kid, no one manifested a disposition to molest him.

He yelled, "I fulfilled Bob Olinger's ambition and sent him to Hell! I liked Jim Bell and did not want to kill him, but it was a case of have to! I haven't considered myself bad heretofore, but I guess I'll have to let people know hereafter what it *is* to be a bad man! And now I just want to ride out of town without interference!"

"We ain't gonna stop ya, Billy!" Sam Wortley called back.

The Kid collected his worldly goods and headed downstairs.

Ira Leonard's horses were elsewhere, but Gauss managed to thieve and saddle a skittish pony belonging to a clerk of the probate court, and he tugged that to the front hitching rail. The Kid got on the frantic, dancing animal after a few failed tries and told Gauss to tell the clerk he'd be sure to send his cayuse back to him. And then the Kid peaceably rode west on Main Street toward Fort Stanton, softly singing the Spanish waltz tune "*La Golondrina*," about a flying swallow, worn-out and tossed by the wind, looking so lost and with nowhere to hide.

- 20 -

THE MANHUNT

Sam Corbet, a former clerk at the Tunstall store, sent an anonymous letter to Silver City's *New Southwest and Grant County Herald* frankly and dispassionately detailing the facts of the jailbreak, and that account was repeated even in New York and London.

The editor of the *Daily New Mexican* seemed exhilarated by the escape, for though he lamented that the swashbuckling outlaw was again on the loose, "one can not help but admire the Kid's coolness and steadiness of nerve." The jailbreak was, the editor commented, "as bold a deed as those versed in the annals of crime can recall. It so far surpasses anything of which the Kid has been guilty until now that his past offenses lose much heinousness in comparison with it, and it effectually settles the question whether the Kid is a cowardly cutthroat or a thoroughly reckless and fearless man."

Another paper reported that the happenings in New Mexico were so sensational that Ned Buntline, the highest-paid writer in America, the author of over four hundred dime novels, "is on the way to our territory to interview various men about the outlaw and thus secure material for blood and thunder literature."

With hard riding Garrett made the forty miles from White Oaks to

Lincoln right after he got the telegram with news of the tragedy. He held a kind of vigil in the dark shed where Olinger's and Bell's bodies were laid out, the red blood on their shirts now dried and stiff and maroon, Olinger's face so mutilated it could have been mistaken for a heaped plate of food.

Gottfried Gauss walked in and told him, "The undertaker is here to undertake them."

And Garrett admitted, "I feel responsible. I knew the desperate character of the man, that he was daring and unscrupulous, and that he would sacrifice the lives of a hundred men if they stood between him and liberty. And now I realize how inadequate my precautions were."

Walking out into the fading light of evening, he found a journalist who was waiting there and who questioned the sheriff concerning people's worries about the Kid being on the loose. The sheriff's mood darkened even more as he caustically responded, "Don't matter what the public feels about it. I'll follow the Kid to the end of time, and there will be a fierce reckoning. There will be a whirlwind he will reap while desperately begging for my forgiveness."

A quarter mile out of Lincoln after the jailbreak on the night of April 28, the Kid turned north to cross the rushing Rio Bonito and headed to the foothills of the Capitán Mountains. In Salazar Canyon, he found the *jacal* of José Cordova, who chiseled off the rivets to his ankle shackles, and near Las Tablas in the wee hours, the Kid woke up Yginio Salazar, who was now eighteen and still idolized his cousin.

Rattling with adrenaline, the Kid told Salazar about his jail escape and his killings, and Yginio took it all in with the solace of approval, telling the Kid that Olinger, for sure, needed killing and with Bell he was given no option. It was kill or be killed in a war that seemed to be never-ending. "Your Spanish friends love you and we'll all hide you," Yginio said. "But wouldn't Old Mexico be safest?"

"There's no job for me there. I need to get some loot first," said the Kid.

Exactly as he'd promised he'd do, the Kid slapped the hindquarters of the Indian pony he'd stolen, and it trotted back to its owner in Lincoln. Then he stole a prized roan stallion and headed south past Agua Azul, weaving through shady forests of ponderosa pine and spruce to overnight at the farm of a John Tunstall ally. There he traded for a fresh horse and headed farther south to the Rio Peñasco, riding in melancholy over the sunny Los Feliz rangelands where he used to cowboy in order to get to the neighboring ranch and *choza* of Harry's friend John Meadows. The Kid told his tales of woe, and then Meadows, too, urged him to continue down to Old Mexico for a fresh start. Ciudad Juárez was on the Rio Grande a little over one hundred miles southwest, and in the opposite direction was Fort Sumner, half again as far. The Kid failed to mention Paulita as he said his old friends there were enough of a draw that he felt the fort ought to be his destination, telling Meadows that he'd just hole up with shepherd pals for the summer or until he'd earned enough cash to head south.

John Meadows scolded the twenty-one-year-old that Pat Garrett had relatives in Sumner. The sheriff would hear he was there and find him and kill him, or the Kid would have to kill Garrett.

But the Kid would not be dissuaded, and rode northeast through sun-bleached grasses as high as his horse's hocks, zephyrs dipping and lifting great swaths of fresh wild barley that seemed to rise and roll like the swells of a storm green ocean he'd never see.

On May 3, 1881, Lew Wallace again published the government's offer of a five-hundred-dollar reward for William H. Bonney. Announced via the newspapers, it did not mention "dead or alive," but those conditions were presumed.

The Kid understood that, yet he still went northeast 150 miles to the locale of his familiars, walking the final 20 miles from Conejo Springs because his stolen bay stallion got spooked one night and galloped away. He was footsore, parched, and exhausted when he got to Fort Sumner and the Indian hospital on May 7. "I feel like I been rode hard and put away wet," he said, and Manuela Herrera, whose new baby boy was sleeping, prepared the Kid a bath.

Watching him lather his hair with soap as she poured in more hot water, the young widow asked in Spanish how long it had been since he'd been with a woman, and he admitted that with jail and being on the run it was too long ago to remember. She said she'd been without for six months, since before Charlie died, and as she toweled him off she saw his interest and they quietly took comfort in each other's bodies.

His hands were still desiring her afterward, but she was nettled with concern as she asked in Spanish, "Why are you here?"

He answered in Spanish, "Here's where my friends are."

"Celsa? Paulita?"

"And you. And others."

"I'm not jealous. We can share. But don't you see you'll be found out? Even getting here you were noticed. Many love you and will keep the secret. Some won't."

He laid his cheek against the scented crook of her neck as his free hand idly floated over her seascape of rise and fall. "I have no roots anywhere else. I have no 'at home' but here. And I feel doomed. Like I'm riding to Hell on a fast horse. I'm not afraid of dying, but I don't want to die alone. I don't want some no one finding me finished off and asking a sheriff, 'Who's that?'"

The baby woke and cooed to himself, but then hunger changed his mind and he cried until his mother got to him.

The Kid found fresh clothes for himself in the trunk he'd left behind, and after a skillet of fajitas, there was nothing for him to do on a Saturday night but steal a fine horse hitched in front of Beaver Smith's saloon and ride it fifteen miles along the Rio Pecos to a Mexican shepherd's camp.

The horse's owner hammered a barracks door to wake up Deputy Sheriff Barney Mason, and he promised the rancher he'd launch an investigation. Because of the Kid's fame, he was no problem to track, just a "*Donde está el Chivato?*" was enough to get children to give Mason a heading, and he and a friend, an oddly unarmed cattleman, got to the shepherd's camp near Buffalo Arroyo that Sunday evening.

The man hunters were still a quarter mile off when the Kid spied them on the open range of sideoats grama grass, and, embittered by Mason's abandonment of their former friendship, he enlisted four Mexican friends to back him up with rifles as the agents of justice ever more gradually rode in.

Some years later, Paulita Maxwell recalled that whenever Billy rode into Fort Sumner, the fearful Deputy Mason would find a reason to ride out, and he lost courage again when from a hundred yards he saw the Kid rise up and shoulder his Winchester. The deputy felt it unlikely he could be hit from that distance, but he wasn't in fact *certain*, so he wheeled his horse fully around and raced off. And he would soon hurriedly collect his wife and child, head to Roswell, and have no other part in this drama.

But the cattleman found the wherewithal to hold up his hands as he ambled his own horse forward, and he was surprised at the Kid's affability as the cattleman told him how much the owner wanted his stolen horse back. It was a gift from his late wife.

With a smile the Kid said, "I'm real upset that I inconvenienced anyone, but you see I'm without transportation otherwise. When circumstances are better with me, I'll either return his horse or give him good money for it."

And with relief the cattleman said, "Well, my business here is done," and he cantered off.

The Kid did return the widower's horse the next noon, doffing his hat to the man in a much-obliged gesture, and then he stole another.

Although the Kid was still on the loose, on May 13, Governor Lew Wallace signed a pro forma warrant of execution as if the hanging were going to happen in Lincoln that day as planned. And then he returned to packing for his long journey east on a Pullman sleeper to Indiana in order to finally join his wife, Susan, and then go onward to the Port of New York and, a few weeks later, to his ministry to the Sultan of the Ottoman Empire. He served four years there, but with Grover Cleveland, a Democrat, taking the presidential oath of office in 1885, Lew Wallace retired from diplomacy and politics in general to focus on his writing, publishing a biography of Benjamin Harrison, the novel *The Prince of India*, and the narrative poem *The Wooing of Malkatoon*. Surpassing even Harriet Beecher Stowe in book sales, he became a hugely wealthy man, and at age seventy-seven he died of gastritis while in the midst of writing a two-volume autobiography in which Billy the Kid was hardly mentioned.

On May 19, the *Las Vegas Gazette* either found out or inferred, "Billy keeps well-posted on matters in the outside world as he is well thought of by many of the Mexicans who take him all the newspapers they can get hold of. He is not far from Fort Sumner and has not left that neighborhood since he rode over from Lincoln after making his break."

Like the town of Lincoln after its civil war, Fort Sumner and its outlying *placitas* were losing hundreds of residents because of the wildness and continuing violence, and that left as its majority Mexicans who were generally sympathetic to the Kid, as well as some hard and dangerous characters who shrugged at the Kid's outlawry, and no more than a dozen Anglos who followed all the potboiled accounts of his wickedness and were terrified of him.

Was it fear that made Garrett reluctant to go there? In late May the sheriff called off his methodical manhunt for William H. Bonney after he or his deputies had interrogated the Kid's enemies and visited all his old haunts—Los Portales, San Patricio, Puerto de Luna, Anton Chico—but found no sign of him. Garrett later claimed he'd failed to investigate Fort Sumner because it seemed like madness for the Kid to go where he was so well known. The sheriff was operating on the presumption of what he himself would do if on the run, which was that the Kid had wisely crossed the Rio Grande into the freedom of Old Mexico.

As May became June, Garrett surprisingly still avoided Fort Sumner, in spite of multiple reports of the Kid's presence there. The sheriff said he just didn't buy it, for there'd been fabrications that the Kid had been killed in El Paso or murdered a trio of Chisum's cowboys outside Roswell or he was in Seven Rivers, Tularosa, Las Vegas, Albuquerque, Denver. Writing Lionel Sheldon, the new territorial governor, the sheriff noted, "I have never taken Bonney for a fool, but have credited him with the possession of extraordinary forethought and cool judgment." So to him none of those rumored locales seemed right. And there was the awkwardness of the Kid's connection to Celsa, his wife's sister, and to the Maxwells, his old friends. He'd rather find Billy far from there, and in Lincoln County. So he handled chores on his ranch outside Roswell, cared for his and Apolonaria's newborn, Ida, and busied himself with official tasks as he became patient as a spider where the Kid was concerned, waiting out a desperado who was too outgoing and free-spirited to stay hidden for long.

And it was true that with heedlessness, overconfidence, and pluck, the Kid larked in and out of Fort Sumner as if he weren't wanted for murder with a reward offer available to anyone doughty enough to lift a gun against him.

The *Santa Fe New Mexican* for June 16 noted, "A man who came to Santa Fe from Lincoln County says that Billy the Kid gets all the money he wants, steals horses when he needs them, and makes no bones of going into and out of various towns. The people regard the sneaks-by with a feeling half of fear and half of admiration, they meekly submit to his depredations, and some of them go so far as to aid him in avoiding capture."

The Maxwell house faced eastward and overlooked the old parade grounds and, farther off, the enlisted men's barracks. South of the house was a garden of wildflowers such as poppies, mariposa lilies, hoary aster, and amaranth. And then there was a dance hall with *bailes* on the weekends where the Kid would carry on in his fine clothes like his old self, flouncing Celsa around in a schottische, formally waltzing with Manuela, and generally agreeing to join on the floor any of the fanning coquettes in mantillas who yearned for him.

Charlie Siringo would later become a Pinkerton detective and gain fame with his cowboy memoirs, but in 1881 he was a Texas range-hand in his late twenties who now and then helped out Pat Garrett in hunting the Kid and his gang. In that way he became familiar with the famous dances at Fort Sumner, and Siringo fell hard for the dark, alluring, high-spirited widow of Charlie Bowdre. Walking Manuela back to the old Indian hospital one night, Siringo confessed that he was smitten and they became affectionate at the hospital door. But though he begged to be invited inside where they could go a little further, she wouldn't let him. She was being virtuous, he thought. And only weeks later, when it no longer mattered, did she tell Siringo that Billy the Kid had been hiding there.

The Kid heard Siringo gallop off that night and he told Manuela on heading out that he needed to find Paulita. She seemed to be avoiding him and he was going to the Maxwell house to see why.

She was not there, but the Navajo maid was. The thirty-five-year-old Deluvina focused on the Kid's holstered Colt .41 Thunderer and feigned ignorance of the youngest Maxwell's whereabouts. But Deluvina had been purchased as a child for fifty dollars by Lucien Maxwell and she felt kin to Billy as a fellow orphan, so she was fond enough to let the murderer wait in the lilac parlor for the girl. She even brought him fresh sun tea and a saucer of apple cobbler as he stewed on the love seat, worriedly thinking of Paulita. *She won't want a wanted man.*

At last he heard the girl on the porch, confiding to someone in Spanish, "*Lo pasé muy bien.*" I had a very nice time. There was a male response the Kid couldn't catch, and he was too cautious to go to the front door. He heard it open and shut, and he stood as he heard her soft footsteps on the floral carpet of the hallway. She may have been heading back to the kitchen, but then she halted in shock at seeing the Kid in the parlor, his face full of tragedy.

"Who let you in?" she asked.

He felt it was the wrong first question. "Deluvina," he said. And he ticked his head toward the front porch. "Who was that?"

"José," she said. She seemed irresolute, even fearful, and she lurked in the hallway as if he were dangerous.

Billy fell back onto the love seat and smiled as in a strained counterfeit of ease he patted a spot next to him. "Enter, my angel! Sit!"

She walked in but took the violet wing chair five feet away from him. She was wearing knee-high boots and the culottes that preceded jodhpurs.

"Moonlight ride?" he asked.

Even in a forced smile her cute dimples showed. "You know how I have always plumed myself on my horsemanship."

"Riding with?"

"My brother's roan mare."

"I meant 'Who's this José?'"

"José Jaramillo. Lorenzo Jaramillo's son." Even in the heat of July her forearms were crossed over her breasts and she seemed to be trembling. She earnestly asked, "You're not going to hurt him, are you?"

"Why would I?"

"Because you *do* that. You do *worse*."

The Kid felt a hot burn of irritation flush his cheeks. "I'm not a ruthless murderer. My hand was forced each time."

She ever so gently said, "Hah." Like she found him delusional.

The night was getting pear-shaped. "And how is St. Mary's Convent School?"

"I graduated."

"Congratulations!"

"Lots of people do it," she said.

"And now what?"

She sighed. "Doubts. Disappointment."

And then Pete Maxwell was at the parlor doorway in a striped nightshirt and slippers. With false bonhomie, he said, "I thought I detected Billy's voice. What a treat to see you again!"

"*Hola, Pedro.*"

With a catch of nervousness in his voice he said, "I hear no officers of the law can find you, yet here you are in plain sight!"

"I hither and yon a bit."

"Well," Pete Maxwell said, and then he seemed at a loss for words. His hands palsied as he stared at the Kid's six-shooter. Then he flung a scowl to his sister as he said, "Don't forget the lamps like you do, Paulita."

She shooed him off with the flick of a hand. When he was gone, she whispered, "Pete disapproves of our . . . friendship. But he won't do anything about it. You fill him with terror."

"Has its advantages, I guess."

"Are you staying in Sumner?"

"Ofttimes."

"With?"

The Kid just said, "With friends."

But she'd heard the rumors of his *queridas*. With sadness, Paulita said, "Oh."

Billy realized he'd let them take another wrong turning, so he grinned and changed the subject. "I got your letter to me in the Mesilla jail! Read it over and over again. Even showed it to Sheriff Southwick there. You know what he said? Said, 'That girl is sure stuck on you.'"

She seemed to consider his oddness before saying, "*Then*. I have outgrown that girl now. She believed you were being unfairly hounded due to misunderstandings and lies and exaggerations." She seemed to want to go on, but simmered. "And you didn't answer that letter."

"My mind was on my hanging."

She tilted her head for a different perspective. "Are you even aware of how hot and cold you are? How you seduce and then withdraw, tantalize and then retreat? Even with men you're like that. You're a mystery to people, you keep us off-balance and guessing. We have to presume what you're thinking or feeling. And instead of being frustrated we find ourselves fascinated, and we make things up about you out of our own hopes and needs and all the dangerous things we're afraid to do."

The Kid felt the outrage that so often sent his hand to his gun. But he governed himself and said, "You seem to have given this a lot of thought."

"What else was there to do before I cried myself to sleep?"

He felt a farewell coming and he hastened it. "So where are we, you and me?"

She hesitated before saying, "José wants to marry me."

The Kid flatly echoed, "José wants to marry you."

"Yes."

"I was hoping . . ."

"I suspected."

"And I don't have a chance?"

Enough of an answer that her coffee-colored eyes glistened with tears.

"Well, it may be July for you but it's near winter for me. All the leaves are falling off the trees." Heartsick, he stood. "I'll be going now."

She was forlorn as she faced the floor.

The Kid paused in the hallway. "I still love you, Paulita."

"And I you," she whispered.

Within a hasty few months Paulita Beaubien Maxwell would marry José Florentino Jaramillo at San José Catholic Church in Anton Chico. She was wealthy and eighteen, the Jaramillos were prosperous, and Pete Maxwell hoped she would no longer be sullied by her relationship with the Kid.

She would give birth to three children: Adelina, Luz, and a son, Telesfor. But in the 1890s the often drunk Jaramillo abandoned her for another woman and she raised the children alone.

In 1884 the New England Cattle Company purchased what remained of Lucien Maxwell's real estate, and then Old Fort Sumner was reclaimed by flooding, its deteriorating buildings were torn apart for scrap lumber, and all its majestic cottonwood trees were felled. Mrs. Jaramillo was forced to spend her last years in a mail-order cottage only four miles north, on the outskirts of a dreary, sun-drenched village that still called itself Fort Sumner. And it was there as she was crocheting a mantilla on the front porch that the journalist Walter Noble Burns interviewed "A Belle of Old Fort Sumner" about the Kid, and Paulita took in the fall's first riotous colors of dying as she denied ever being the Kid's sweetheart. "I liked him very, very much—oh, yes—but I did not love him."

When she was sent *The Saga of Billy the Kid* in 1926, she found she could not finish reading it. Even though avid Kid tourists later found her home and sought to extract intimacies from her, Paulita stayed put in new Fort Sumner and skimped by on an ever-shrinking inheritance until she died of nephritis in 1929, aged sixty-five.

John William Poe was a cattle detective for the Canadian River Stock Association in Tascosa, and because so much rustling seemed to have its origin in Lincoln County, he went there and established headquarters in White Oaks in March 1881. Chancing upon Sheriff Pat Garrett in a saloon, Poe chatted about his job scouring the rangeland for stolen livestock, and Garrett finished a jar of whiskey and asked, "Why don't you become my deputy, haul in evildoers, and get paid twice over?"

Poe did that, and it was he who rode the forty miles from White Oaks to Lincoln to find his boss in the Wortley Hotel, telling him that a White Oaks drunk was sleeping off his hard night in a haymow at West & Dedrick Livery & Sales when he overheard Sam and Dan Dedrick talking about the Kid hiding in and around Fort Sumner.

"Was your informer still squiffed?" Garrett asked.

Poe said, "I just know the Dedricks are old friends of Bonney."

In June the sheriff had written a letter of inquiry to Emanuel Brazil, but it was not until July 11 that he'd gotten a reply, with Brazil admitting, "The Kid's so much in the proximity that I am afraid to go outside." And now this. John Poe was looking at him with the furrowed brow of *Why not?* Garrett felt forced to act and finally decided, "We'll go get Kip McKinney."

Thomas C. McKinney was a deputy US marshal with his office in the still-small town of Roswell. Garrett scared him up there on July 12 and took McKinney and Poe out to his homestead ranch to have Apolonaria's menudo soup and tamales. Garrett had warned his deputies to make no mention of the Kid, but Kip McKinney thanked Garrett's wife for the scrumptious food and just to make conversation said, "Heard you once lived where we're heading!"

With a fierce stare Garrett hushed him, then he turned to his wife. She had a stricken look. "Celsa will be fine," he said.

At sundown on the twelfth, the Lincoln County lawmen headed north for Fort Sumner, achieving about thirty miles of the eighty before finally picketing their horses in the wee hours and sleeping just off the Rio Pecos in their fewest clothes for the cool.

Waking at sunup to the noise of critters thrashing in the weeds in one of nature's kill-or-be-killed dramas, the sheriff found Poe and Kinney awake, too, fully dressed and squatting by the river as they smoked in silence. Lying back with his hands behind his head he told them, "The Kid is a likable fellow. Often quiet. There's no fuss or bluster in him. Wasn't ever quarrelsome, never hunted trouble. But there's something about him even when he's friendliest that makes you feel he could be dangerous to take liberties with. I never saw him mad in my life. Can't remember when he wasn't smiling. But he's the most murderous youth that ever stood in shoe leather, and he's game all the way through."

July 13 the *Nugget* newspaper in Tombstone, Arizona, reported, "Parties now in Las Vegas bring the information that Billy the Kid is on the Red River, near the Texas line, at the head of twenty men." And on that Wednesday, the sheriff and his deputies instead journeyed another fifty miles on the Goodnight-Loving cattle trail in a hundred-degree oven, hearing the sizzling noise of locusts in the sagebrush and snakeweed, feeling their sweat soak their shirts and vests and scallop their hatbands, riding in silence into each heat shimmer ahead before finally halting to camp in sandhills near Taiban Creek. Emanuel Brazil was to meet them there, but fear of the Kid's vengeance made him a no-show.

Still fruitlessly waiting for him at midnight, Garrett finally ended his silence to confide to his men, "I know now that I will have to kill the Kid. We both know that it must be one or the other of us if we ever meet."

- 21 -

"QUIÉN ES?"

After a breakfast of hardtack and coffee on Thursday, July 14, Sheriff Garrett and his deputies walked up a high hill and Garrett used his field glasses to scan the prairie between them and the fort, finding nothing but far-off sheep and boy herders with sticks long as fishing poles. The sheriff determined that he and Deputy McKinney were too familiar in Sumner, and that Deputy Poe, who'd never been there, should ride in and reconnoiter.

Hitching his horse in front of Beaver Smith's Saloon at ten, Poe saw the old owner tilting back in a front porch chair. Smith frankly asked, "Who are you and why are you here?"

John Poe offered his name, told him he'd scavenged too little ore from Lone Mountain near White Oaks, and now, "With my tail between my legs, I'm wandering back to my homestead on the Red River, in Mobeetie, Texas."

"Hidetown?"

"Yep, we used to call it that. When there was still buffalo."

Smith stood up. "Are you thirsty?"

Soon there were ill-humored and questioning men crowding around him in the saloon. Poe ponied up for house whiskeys and introduced various topics of conversation until he could innocently worm in a few tourist questions about this Billy the Kid. Wasn't he a resident once? Any of you see him kill Joe Grant? Who's this sweetheart I been hearing about?

Each time the Kid was mentioned, silence chilled the room and glances were exchanged so that he was forced to return to homely saloon talk, like him getting to watch the Albuquerque Browns play semiprofessional baseball on the fairgrounds. Couldn't make head nor tail of the game.

At noon Poe lunched alone on tacos and then loitered in the shade, making affable comments about the hot weather to passersby and finding some willing to get into conversations. But whenever he would undertake even a casual inquiry about the Kid, his companions would just walk off. He later told Garrett, "The fort's residents were secretive and suspicious of me, and it was plain that many of them were on the alert, expecting something to happen."

With the heat again at a hundred degrees on July 14, Celsa Gutiérrez doubled up on the Kid's stolen palomino and they rode out to the salty alkali lake of the failed Apache and Navajo reservation at Bosque Redondo. Billy took off Celsa's clothes and she took off his. They admired each other's bodies and kissed and fooled around, then they swam and floated and splashed like children. Then the couple lay naked on the salt-limed shore, letting the fury of the sun dry them and then induce crooked trickles of perspiration.

The Kid woke to find Celsa up on an elbow, a full breast pillowing against him as she softly glided a finger over the gunshot wound in his thigh. She said in Spanish, "I forget how you got this."

"Jacob Mathews shot me in Lincoln."

"But why?"

"Well, fair's fair, I guess. I was trying to kill him."

She smiled. "You have not been shot often, have you?"

"Just that once."

"You're like the cat with the nine lives."

"I hope I haven't used them all up."

Celsa kissed him. "There. I am a fairy princess. And now you live forever."

The Kid grinned. "And will you be with me all that time?"

Weeks later Celsa would be frustrated that she could not recall anything more of what they talked about. She was certain though that there were no confidences, no worries or guilt, no plans for the future except for the still-vague idea of finding a new life in Old Mexico. She told people, in Spanish, they frolicked, and that was all.

Because Saval was returning at six from his failures at silver mining in White Oaks, they hurriedly dressed and rode back to the fort in midafternoon, happening to pass Deputy John Poe as he exited Sumner. Each of them ignorant of the other.

Poe later recalled seeing a lithe, hatless man in his late teens riding a palomino with a beautiful Mexican woman hugging him, her face fondly nestled against his white, collarless, long-sleeved shirt as she rocked with the horse's slow pace. Poe was heading north seven miles to the post office in Sunnyside. Garrett had torn a page from his vest pocket notebook and written a note of introduction to the postmaster, Milnor Rudulph:

My dear friend. This is my deputy, John Poe. I hope you will welcome him with your usual hospitality. P. F. Garrett.

Rudulph was originally from Maryland and was fifty-six but looked far older—he would die within six years—a bald, officious man with a wide white sickle of a mustache and a hard-bitten schoolteacher's glare of scrutiny. Upon reading Garrett's note, he stuffily claimed, "I have a friendship of three years standing with Pat and have nothing but admiration for him. I would be very glad to accommodate any friend of his for the night."

The formality made Poe suspicious.

Rudulph's Mexican wife served them a dinner of red potatoes and fresh-caught cutthroat trout, and as she handled the dishwashing Deputy Poe invited conversations from her husband about general things like the mail service and gardening problems and his own viewing of the Albuquerque Browns, and once Rudulph had lit a clay pipe and seemed fully relaxed Poe asked, "You had a friendship with Billy the Kid when he was here?"

Rudulph's wife turned from the sink in distress, but Rudulph himself just fidgeted as he said, "Well, he sent mail like people do."

Deputy Poe introduced the topic of the Kid's jailbreak and the report from Emanuel Brazil that the Kid was in their neighborhood.

"Excuse me," Rudulph said as he got up from the dinner table and fiddled with things in the kitchen so his back would be shut to Poe. "I have heard that such a report was about," Rudulph said. "But I do not believe it, as the Kid is, in my opinion, too shrewd to be caught lingering in this part of the country."

John Poe could see the quaver in the postmaster's hands as he put dried saucers away in the cupboard, and he told the postmaster he was convinced he was well intentioned but like so many others he was afraid of the Kid and would not hazard to say anything whatever about him. Rudulph's wife seemed to give her husband a silencing look.

Deputy Poe continued, "I have come to you with the express purpose of learning where the Kid could be found. We believe he is hiding in Fort Sumner. Is that so?"

With a hint of embarrassment in his vehemence, Rudulph defended himself by saying, "My son Charlie, and just eighteen for gosh sakes, took it upon himself to serve on that posse that captured the Kid and his gang at Stinking Springs. We can be depended on to tell you if that murderer was around."

John Poe stood and thanked the wife in English, saying the good feed was all he needed and instead of staying overnight he would ride back to his friends in the fresh cool of the evening.

Milnor Rudulph failed to hide his relief.

The deputy rejoined the sheriff and McKinney north of the fort at Punta de la Glorieta, where the irrigation ditch called Acequia Madre crossed the northwest road to Las Vegas and Fort Union. Poe recounted the secrecy and uneasiness in Fort Sumner and Milnor Rudulph's odd agitation, which seemed to confirm the many reports of the Kid's whereabouts. So they mounted up and the sheriff and his deputies rode south to Fort Sumner, with Garrett saying in his formal, Southern way, "I have but little confidence in accomplishing the object of our trip." Without giving the name of Celsa Gutiérrez, he told them there was a rented apartment in the old quartermaster's store that the Kid had formerly frequented. Maybe they'd see him going in or out that night. Garrett failed to acknowledge the gossip his wife had passed along, that Celsa was pregnant with Billy's child. There were so many stories.

To avoid detection in Fort Sumner, the trio stayed on what was called the Texas Road behind the old Indian hospital, then went around Bob Hargrove's saloon to the green and fragrant expanse of the peach orchard on the northern boundary of the fort. They staked their horses with their muzzles within reach of the fruit, but the horses lowered their heads to tear up the high grass between their hooves. Garrett left the 1873 model Winchester rifle he'd taken from Billie Wilson in his saddle scabbard, but he wore in his holster Wilson's fine new Colt .44 pistol.

The sheriff and his deputies went forward on foot to wait near the fence around the orchard, hanging out in the night of the trees with views east to the front of the old Indian hospital in case the Kid visited Manuela, and south across the parade grounds to the old quartermaster's store and the quarters of Saval and Celsa Gutiérrez, just left of Beaver Smith's saloon. With the full moon overhead they could see from a hundred yards away a pretty woman in her twenties pass in front of Beaver Smith's, hugging sheets she'd just pulled down from a clothesline. She walked farther east and inside the adobe building, disappearing.

John Poe asked, "Who was that?"

Garrett quietly said, "My sister-in-law."

The deputies gave him a look. Kip McKinney asked, "Why not ask her if she seen the Kid?"

Wordlessly, Garrett pinched some Blackberry Long Cut tobacco from its pouch and tamped it into his calabash pipe with his thumb. His deputies waited for his rationale but finally realized he was going to say nothing more, so they went back to their lookout. Chirring insects and nickering horses were the only sounds. It was nine p.m.

The Kid intended to hide away that night in an old Navajo hogan with a Mexican sheepherder who worked for Pete Maxwell. But the sheepherder kept putting off their dinner with games of cards until he finally confessed around eight that he actually had no food. "Well, that's no good," the Kid said, and the shepherd told him he'd slaughtered a steer for Don Pedro that morning and hung it on the porch for aging.

The Kid was hungry enough to trot his horse back to the fort.

Jesús Silva said he found the Kid strolling in darkness behind Bob Hargrove's saloon that night. The Kid told him he was hungry, but Silva said in Spanish, "Have a cold beer with me first."

"Cold?"

"I hung the bottles in the Pecos with fishing lines."

The Kid was coaxed, and Silva took him to the far end of the peach orchard, where there was a tin pail with green bottles in it from the Cervecería Toluca y México. They sat under the peach trees in high grass and talked very quietly with it so late. Jesús Silva later recalled that the Kid was in his usual high spirits, though he did allude to the trouble he was in and cautioned, "Holding on to hatred is like drinking poison and expecting the other person to die."

Spanish was being spoken quietly and indistinctly far behind Garrett, but there'd been a fiesta and many Mexicans were still up. Hearing an "Adíos," he turned in the peach orchard to see a lithe man in a slouch hat and waistcoat gracefully and easily jump the orchard fence and head east. Even with the full moon, Garrett couldn't tell if he was Anglo or Mexican, couldn't even make out where he ended up going. Watching like this seemed such a waste of time. He told his deputies, "We seem to be on a cold trail, fellows. We come to the end of the alley."

Even much later in life, Candido Gutiérrez remembered being up late and shyly hiding behind his mother's skirt as she handed the Kid a butcher knife at the back door and told him she would cook the steaks if he got one for Saval, too. Candido's father drunkenly called out from the front room that he wanted one as big as a Bible.

And then Candido heard his mother confide that she'd been told a stranger was in the fort that afternoon questioning people about Billy the Kid.

In Spanish, the Kid said, "A lot of people do that. I'm a curiosity. I ought to be in the freak show with the Siamese twins."

"Still, you'll be careful?"

"I'll be fine." With it still so hot, he took off his hat and waist-coat, then his holster so he wouldn't attract attention, and finally he wrenched off his boots. In English he said, "Hold these for me, will ya? I'll be walking on cat's paws." And then he tucked his smallish Colt .41 Thunderer into his right trouser pocket.

"Ready to go?" a frustrated sheriff asked his men.

But John Poe insisted, "Don't you think we ought to talk to Pedro Maxwell first? We haven't questioned him yet."

Kip McKinney said, "It's after eleven. He'll be sleeping."

His wariness was overcome by his methodical nature, and Pat Garrett decided, "We're old friends. Pete won't mind me waking him."

The sheriff and his deputies left the peach orchard for the former officers' quarters but went there in a wandering, unpredictable way just in case a gun was trained on them, McKinney even backpedaling to watch the area to their rear.

Poe saw a very large house with porches on three sides and a picket fence that was flush against the street. At the front gate Garrett nodded toward the first-floor room to the left and told them in a hushed voice, "That's Maxwell's room in the southeast corner. You fellows wait here while I go in and talk to him."

It was still so hot that Maxwell's unscreened windows were fully raised and the front door was wide open for the sultry breeze. The sheriff walked up the porch steps, and Poe followed just far enough to sit on the stoop, while McKinney squatted outside the fence with his rifle in both hands.

The Kid lofted himself over the fence dividing officers from enlisted men and walked toward the Maxwell house, cockleburs catching his stocking feet. He saw there'd been a fiesta in the dance hall, and with the near-full moon he could see some people still strolling on the parade grounds though it was probably half past eleven. The Kid found more night so he could relieve himself in the high grass that Pete's sheep hadn't got to yet. He could see the curing carcass of the steer hanging under the eave of the north porch and could have butchered the porterhouse steaks from the short loin right then, but his loyalty to his old friends caused him to seek permission, so he shook himself and walked around to the front of the house, fastening his trousers.

Waiting in the hallway for a moment, Garrett listened for sounds of wakefulness in the house and heard nothing but the song of insects outside. The shade of the front porch roof made the interior moonless. Walking inside the twenty-by-twenty south bedroom, he could make out Pete Maxwell sleeping flat on his back in a nightshirt, his white top sheet flung off in the heat. Garrett went to the head of the double bed, felt the sag of the mattress as he gently eased down onto it, and sitting there he softly laid a hand on Maxwell's forearm as he whispered, "Pete."

Maxwell inhaled in a shocked "Huh?"

"It's Pat," he whispered. "We're looking for the Kid. Seen him here?"

Maxwell was still waking and wiped his left eye as he said, "Week ago."

And then they heard a voice outside asking, "*Quién es?*" Who is it?

The Kid was about ten feet away and fastening his trousers when he attracted John Poe's attention. The deputy thought it could have been Maxwell himself or a houseguest walking back from the privy, so he just watched. There was no sign of a gun.

Because Poe was partially hidden on the stoop, the Kid failed to see him until he could have reached out and felt the figure's rifle. Electrified as always by danger, the Kid hopped up the steps, whispering, "*Quién es?*"

McKinney and Poe did not understand Spanish.

The Kid was backing away from the deputy as he headed toward Pete Maxwell's bedroom and said again, "*Quién es?*"

John Poe still presumed the Kid was a houseguest, and he stood up with a calming hand and said in reassurance, "Don't be afraid of us. We're visiting just like you."

The Kid recalled Paulita saying, *You're not going to hurt him, are you?* And he felt off-kilter.

John Poe was just a few feet from him when the Kid ducked into Maxwell's room, calling out, "*Pedro, quiénes son esos hombres afuera?*" Pete, who are those men outside?

Sheriff Garrett heard the voice outside but failed to recognize it at first as he worried that it could be Maxwell's brother-in-law and frequent houseguest, Manuel Abreu. But the form of the man was like that of the Kid, and as he asked Pete his frantic question, he was walking close enough to reach a hand out to the foot of the bed.

Garrett yanked out the newish Colt .44 he'd taken from Billie Wilson, and the Kid heard the scratch of leather and the four clicks of a hammer getting to full cock in the hand of a just-recognized upright shape on the bed, and, in his precaution to not injure a friend, he left his Colt in his trouser pocket but held out the butcher knife in his left hand as he skewed farther away, asking again, "*Quién es? Quién es?*"

Without warning, Garrett fired at the Kid, and the flash of the gun faintly illuminated him as a .44 caliber bullet hit the Kid's chest and the left atrium of the heart so hard it turned him around and he fell faceforward onto the floorboards. And Garrett did nearly the same as he fell to all fours from the bed and fired again with a wild aim that drilled through a wooden washstand and hit the headboard next to Pete in a loud ricochet so that outside John Poe thought he heard three shots. The room was filled with the haze and pungent smell of gunpowder, and the sheriff and Maxwell were so deafened by the noise that neither one heard the Kid's few gasps and then a final groan.

They fled the room, Maxwell falling to his knees on the south porch as he yelled to the deputies, "Don't shoot! Don't shoot!"

Sheriff Garrett told Deputy Poe, "That was the Kid, and I think I got him."

John Poe said, "Are you sure? You may have shot the wrong man."

Kip McKinney joined them on the east porch, and with caution the three lawmen stooped to peer through the open windows to see if the Kid was dead or just waiting for retribution. But with the roof shading them, it was too dark to have any certainty, so Pete went to the far end of the house for a candle as alone Garrett cautiously walked back inside the room with Billie Wilson's Colt in both trembling hands.

The Kid's blood was a widening pond on the floor, and Garrett worried as he saw that the Kid had no gun, just the butcher knife. There would be scandal. Garrett looked out to the front porch and saw that McKinney and Poe were facing east in caution as native people ran to find out what the gunshots were about. Ever so quietly Garrett squatted to frisk the Kid and felt relieved when he found the smallish Colt .41 in his trousers. Garrett gently laid it beside the Kid just as Pete arrived on the front porch with a lighted tallow candle and stood it in its own wax on a windowsill.

With the help of the fluttering flame, Maxwell was pretty sure it was the Kid, and he said he seemed dead as a doornail, and by then Deluvina and Jesús Silva were running in. She and Jesús rolled the Kid over onto his back. His face was white as paper, his mouth was loose, and his flashing eyes were finally dulled. With two fingers Deluvina tenderly closed his eyelids, and when she noticed the tall sheriff lingering beside her in silence she hurled a full load of curses at him. "You pisspot!" she screamed. "You traitor! You snake in the grass! You have murdered our little boy!"

Pete Maxwell walked back into his room, and he and the sheriff exchanged glances. He who'd been afraid of the Kid was now afraid of Garrett. And then Paulita was there in a nightgown. With a face that lacked emotion, she looked at a nothing-there Kid and flatly said, "And now he'll never be old."

The gun was raised and then it flashed. The shock of it was like a punch that spun the Kid and swatted him to the floor. Then there was a fiery, searing pain that overcame all other feeling, but it waned as the Kid's body acquired its education in dying. The Kid felt himself floating upward, felt a surprising happiness. With each quitting of an organ or process there came a greater liberation, an aliveness, an awareness of never having been so real. Seeing himself on the floor and the chaotic concern around him, he felt affection for all of them, felt pity for who he used to be, but he was overwhelmed by his new fluidity and increase, his ever-greater sense of wonderful love and limitlessness, of having now what he'd always wanted but couldn't ever name.

There was a ruckus outside as the Kid's Mexican friends crowded around the Maxwell house, seething. Had there been anyone to urge them on, they would have rioted against the Kid's murderer, but the one who could have induced them to do that was now dead. Still, the sheriff and his deputies stayed wakeful inside Pete's bedroom that night, barricading themselves to forbid access, their guns ever in their hands in case the locals sought retaliation. Garrett looked at the dead body still on the floor and told his deputies, "Kid Bonney was as cool under trying circumstances as any man I ever saw. I guess he was so surprised for an instant he could not collect himself."

At one in the morning of Friday the fifteenth, Celsa and Saval, Deluvina and Jesús, and a boy named Paco Anaya carried the Kid eastward across the old parade grounds to a carpenter's shop on the southern limits of the fort, where they laid him on a workbench. With lumber scarce, some of Maxwell's shepherds tore apart the roof of the falling-down stable next to the Indian commissary and used its ceiling planks for the Kid's interment. Jesús Silva then sawed and nailed the boards to construct a basic coffin as Manuela and Celsa and other weeping señoras washed the Kid's nakedness, brushed his hair, dammed the Colt .44's large exit wound with a rag, and dressed him in a fine linen shirt and trousers donated by Pete Maxwell. They left the Kid's white feet bare and arrayed yellow beeswax candles all around him, and off and on his friends visited him for a night wake of rosaries and Spanish funeral hymns.

Sheriff Garrett and his deputies left the fort around noon that Friday, and soon after that his friends tenderly laid the Kid's corpse into the coffin and shoved it onto Vicente Otero's hauling wagon. Then the entire population of Fort Sumner, even saloonkeepers who never closed up, followed the funeral cortege to the old soldiers' cemetery. Young Paco Anaya had worked all morning with Vicente digging out a grave next to those of the Kid's pals Tom Folliard and Charlie Bowdre.

There was no priest or minister to handle the rites, so Hugh Leeper, a Christian nicknamed the Sanctified Texan, read from the fourteenth chapter of the Book of Job: "'Man that is born of a woman is of few days, and full of trouble. He cometh forth like a flower, and is cut down; he fleeth also as a shadow, and continueth not.'" And: "'Thou shalt call, and I will answer thee; thou wilt have a desire to the work of thine hands. For now thou numberest my steps; dost thou not watch over my sin? My transgression is sealed up in a bag, and thou sewest up my iniquity.'"

In Leeper's funeral sermon he continually referred to the Kid as "our beloved young lad" and closed by telling the congregation, "Billy cannot come back to us, but we can go to him and will see him again up yonder. Amen."

Then Paco hammered into the ground a simple cross made from a stave from the Maxwells' picket fence. Crudely painted on it was BILLY THE KID, but nothing more.

With a sheriff's annual salary of only two hundred dollars, Garrett had campaigned hard to finally collect the five hundred dollars from the government for the Kid's capture at Stinking Springs, the reward getting to him only some months later after much public pressure. So in Fort Sumner he left nothing to chance and invited Alejandro Segura, the justice of the peace, to form a jury of six, including Saval Gutiérrez and José Jaramillo's father, Lorenzo, with Garrett's friend Milnor Rudulph acting as foreman of the inquest. It was the jury's judgment that William H. Bonney died due to a fatal wound inflicted by a gun in the hand of Pat F. Garrett, but in an odd conclusion to such a report, Rudulph wrote in his friendship to the sheriff, "Our decision is that the action of said Garrett was justifiable homicide; and we are united in the opinion that the gratitude of all the community is owed to said Garrett for his deed, and that he deserves to be rewarded."

In July 1881 no fewer than eight New York City newspapers hurrahed the killing of "the scourge of the Southwest," and there were notices about it in all the major cities in the United States and Great Britain.

In the Kid's former hometown of Silver City, an editorial noted: "The vulgar murderer and desperado known as 'Billy the Kid' has met his just desserts at last."

The *New York Daily Graphic* looked backward to the December 1880 capture of the Kid, when "with fangs snarling and firing a revolver like a maniac, W. H. Bonney fought his way out of his ambushed robber castle at Stinking Springs where he lived in luxury on his ill-gotten gains with his Mexican beauties." And it vouchsafed that the Kid "had built up a criminal organization worthy of the underworld of any of the European capitals. He defied the law to stop him and he stole, robbed, raped, and pillaged the countryside until his name became synonymous with that of the grim reaper himself. A Robin Hood with no mercy, a Richard the Lion-Hearted who feasted on blood, he became, in the short span of his twenty-one years, the master criminal of the American southwest. His passing marks the end of wild west lawlessness."

And the *Santa Fe Weekly Democrat* took on a scoffing tone as it jested: "No sooner had the floor caught his descending form which had a pistol in one hand and a knife in the other, than there was a strong odor of brimstone in the air, and a dark figure with wings of a dragon, claws like a tiger, eyes like balls of fire, and horns like a bison, hovered over the corpse for a moment and with a fiendish laugh said, 'Ha, ha! This is my meat!' and then sailed off through the window."

With the passing years the Kid's life became just a collection of fabrications that lost American interest to such an extent that in 1925 a journalist opened an article with the question "Who remembers Billy the Kid?" But by then the Chicago journalist Walter Noble Burns was in New Mexico interviewing hundreds of those still alive who were friends of the Kid. Published in 1926, *The Saga of Billy the Kid* became a huge bestseller that got many things wrong and fictionally duplicated some hoary legends, but depicted a jaunty yet tragic Kid defying death to carry out his oath of vengeance against those who murdered John Tunstall and a majority of the Regulators. "The boy who never grew old," Burns wrote, "has become a sort of symbol of frontier knight-errantry, a figure of eternal youth riding forever through a purple glamour of romance."

Pat Garrett did get his five hundred dollars for the Kid's homicide, but half a year later he declined to run for reelection as sheriff of Lincoln County—John Poe won that job—and instead, with his Roswell postmaster friend Ash Upson, Garrett wrote *The Authentic Life of Billy, the Kid, the Noted Desperado of the Southwest, Whose Deeds of Daring and Blood Made His Name a Terror in New Mexico, Arizona & Northern Mexico.*

The first fictionalized version of the Kid's life had been published within weeks of his fatality by the Five Cent Wide Awake Library, which the Kid himself used to dwell on as a boy, and there were four other so-called biographies in 1881, including *Billy the "Kid" and His Girl*, which appeared in Morrison's Sensational Series and sold 100,000 copies. The Kid's assassin was not often extolled, as there was a whiff of cowardice in his actions. Although Garrett's own book contained some wild inventions up front, its latter half was far more factual: a frank, methodical, self-vindicating account of how the Kid was hunted down. Yet it did not sell well, and it was only because Jimmy Dolan, John Chisum, and generous readers of the *Las Vegas Daily Optic* donated a fortune to him for slaying the Kid that Garrett could retire to his ranch outside Roswell and found the Pecos Valley Irrigation and Investment Company.

It was just one of many commercial partnerships that failed for him as he shiftlessly moved his family from place to place in pursuit of other luckless schemes. In 1896 he became sheriff of Doña Ana

County and lasted five successful but miserable years before President Theodore Roosevelt rescued the famous Pat Garrett by naming him collector of customs in El Paso. Hundreds of written complaints about his incompetence were sent to Washington, however, and he so over-spent his time in the Coney Island Saloon downtown that after five years an insulted Roosevelt replaced him.

Garrett's financial problems continued as he moved Apolonaria and his eight children back to New Mexico, saw his clothing and pos-sessions auctioned to pay off liens, signed a five-year lease on his land in Bear Canyon, and was distressed to see his cattle ranch taken over by a renter with a drove of twelve hundred goats. Garrett became increasingly aware that he'd squandered all his opportunities, and that they'd been available to him only because of his fame as the killer of Billy the Kid. In his fifties he said, "I sometimes wish that I had mis-fired and that the Kid had done his work of iniquity on me. He was the end of an age and I belong there, too."

His final end came on an afternoon when Garrett was haggling with his business partners on a road outside Las Cruces. He sought to prevail by telling the thirty-year-old hothead riding a bay horse along-side his buggy, "You forget I've dealt with your kind before. I'm the man who killed Billy the Kid." Seeking an intermission from the argu-ments, he got his Burgess folding shotgun for defense and climbed down from the buggy to urinate. And he was just unbuttoning his trousers when Jesse Wayne Brazel fired a bullet into the former sher-iff's skull, killing him instantly. It was February 29 in the leap year of 1908. He was fifty-seven years old.

Because Garrett was a nonbeliever, he'd wanted no religious rites at his funeral, so the owner of his favorite El Paso saloon read aloud a graveside eulogy by the English atheist Robert G. Ingersoll: "Life is a narrow vale between the cold and barren peaks of two eternities. We strive in vain to look beyond the heights. We cry aloud and the only answer is the echo of our wailing cry. From the voiceless lips of the unreplying dead there comes no word; but in the night of death hope sees a star and listening love can hear the rustle of a wing."

Even as his celebrity continued, there would be no monuments honoring Pat Garrett, no museums dedicated to his life's work, no highways named after him. Yet, like so many others, he stayed heard-about and famous because of books and movies that featured a Kid who'd become, to a great degree, each person's wild invention.

ACKNOWLEDGMENTS

This is a work of fiction based on fact. I have streamlined the history and eliminated some characters to spare the reader, but as often as possible I have stayed faithful to the Kid's biography and the period. To get it right I mainly relied on the following books:

Bob Boze Bell, *The Illustrated Life and Times of Billy the Kid*
Walter Noble Burns, *The Saga of Billy the Kid*
Mark Lee Gardner, *To Hell on a Fast Horse*
Pat F. Garrett, *The Authentic Life of Billy, the Kid, the Noted Desperado*
Joel Jacobsen, *Such Men as Billy the Kid*
Leon C. Metz, *Pat Garrett: The Story of a Western Lawman*
Frederick Nolan, *The Life and Death of John Henry Tunstall*
———, *The Lincoln County War*
———, *The Billy the Kid Reader*
Miguel Antonio Otero, Jr., *The Real Billy the Kid: With New Light on the Lincoln County War*
Stephen Tatum, *Inventing Billy the Kid: Visions of the Outlaw in America, 1881–1981*
Robert M. Utley, *Billy the Kid: A Short and Violent Life*
Michael Wallis, *Billy the Kid: The Endless Ride*

ACKNOWLEDGMENTS

My thanks to my editor, Colin Harrison, for his discerning suggestions about the manuscript; to my agent, Peter Matson, for his advocacy and care; to Juan Velasco, for help with the Spanish; to Drew Gomber, for an informative private tour of Lincoln; and to my sister Gini, who accompanied me on visits to all the Billy the Kid sites. I'm particularly indebted to my helpful correspondence with the ever-responsive historians Frederick Nolan and Mark Lee Gardner.

The first readers of these pages were my friend Jim Shepard and my lovely wife, Bo Caldwell—their insights and enthusiasm were invaluable to the making of this book and I owe them.

ABOUT THE AUTHOR

Ron Hansen is the author of nine novels, two collections of stories, and a book of essays. He graduated from Creighton University in Omaha and went on to the University of Iowa Writers' Workshop and Stanford University. His novel *Atticus* was a finalist for both the National Book Award and the PEN/Faulkner Award. His novel *The Assassination of Jesse James by the Coward Robert Ford* was also a finalist for the PEN/Faulkner Award and was made into a movie starring Brad Pitt and Casey Affleck. Hansen's writing has won awards from the National Endowment for the Arts, the Guggenheim Foundation, and the American Academy of Arts and Letters. He is currently the Gerard Manley Hopkins, S.J., Professor in the Arts and the Humanities at Santa Clara University in Northern California. He is married to the novelist Bo Caldwell.